I0831169

JEWELER TO THE BLESSED

JILLIAN WITT

Cover Artwork by JV Arts

Map by @fantasy.cartography

Development Edit by Rebecca Faith Editorial

Line Editing by Paper Poppy Editorial

Proofread by Isla Elrick

Published by Myth & Magic Book Club

Copyright © 2025 by Jillian Witt

All rights reserved.

No part of this book may be reproduced in any form or by any electronic or mechanical means, including information storage and retrieval systems, without written permission from the author, except for the use of brief quotations in a book review.

KAVIOS
OLDWOOD MINES
OLDWOOD
FOREST'S EDGE
GLANMORE CASTLE
CROSS STREET
EASTERN GATE
1. ALARIC'S WORKSHOP
2. FOREST'S EDGE TAVERN
LOWER HILL
CENTRE STREET
WOODSIDE
J·E·W·E·L·E·R
CENTRE GATE
4. JEWELER
3. EMBERLINE'S FAMILY APARTMENT

For those the world taught that emotions are weakness.
There is strength in feeling.

1

Whether it's a blessing or a curse, she must decide.

— ALARIC SARE'S LETTERS TO ISABELLE ARKOVA

Being Alaric Sare's niece was a blessing and a curse.

Many would consider the before-sunrise study sessions as falling firmly in the curse column, but an uncle willing to invest in my education felt like a blessing.

"Are you still making your horrid coffee?" Alaric called from the shop front.

A curse—Alaric hated coffee. He was always raving about the soothing properties of his tea. It smelled like mint, but he mixed more than a few herbs into the tiny sachets. I boiled enough water for both drinks, no matter my distaste.

"It's almost done," I said.

A thick, gold curtain that had seen better days hung between his workspace and the front counter. It separated Alaric's workshop the way I imagined he compartmentalized his mind. The front, where he met with his exclusively Blessed customers, was pristine. Fine gold rings, broaches, and even necklaces with pendant settings were in glass display cases, each waiting for an adamas gem to make them whole.

This space—behind the curtain—felt like the true version of my uncle. Bookcases lined one wall, filled top to bottom with leather-bound tomes. Some he double-stacked, and others, he shoved in horizontally and vertically to maximize space. One of the shelves opened to reveal a small, tightly packed storage room where he kept his more interesting books.

We'd been looking at some of those this morning.

The other side of the workshop looked like it belonged to a frenetic alchemist convinced he was about to crack the secret of a philosopher's stone. Glass beakers, precious metals, and all manner of tools were scattered across an L-shaped table. Additional books, logs for the fire, and other objects that made me scratch my head were tucked away beneath. I was sure Alaric had precise applications in mind for each one.

My fingers tingled as I reached for a piece of adamas, anticipating the comforting warmth of its weight in my palm. The gem felt *right* in my hand, which was odd because all it seemed to do was ruin my life.

It was why I was leaving the city—why this would be one of my last study sessions with Alaric for the foreseeable future. The Library of Linia would have the answers I sought. Few left Kavios, but I had to know why the Blessed's magic didn't affect me. It was proving too dangerous not to.

I bounced the stone lightly in my hand while I waited. Due to the nature of Alaric's clientele, he worked primarily in adamas. Officially, I apprenticed at Father's jewelry shop, though it felt more like I ran the place these days. We worked in Woodside, a district devoid of Blessed, and dealt exclusively in quartz.

The two gems looked remarkably similar to the untrained eye—well, to nearly every eye except mine and Alaric's.

Both were hard stones, clear when cut and polished, but one could store stolen emotion, transforming it into magic. The other could not.

The gurgle of boiling water drew my attention. I set the adamas down and searched the room for a towel to pull the pot from the fire.

Alaric parted the curtain and joined me as I filled a cup with his herb mixture. I slid a second cup under my makeshift filter and grounds, pouring over the water and leaving it to drip.

He had an uncut gemstone from the Oldwood Mine outside the city.

"Quartz or adamas?" He dropped the stone into my left hand as I passed him his mug with my right.

This was definitely a curse of being Alaric's niece.

I must have given him a look because he offered a tentative smile. "Admit it: You'll miss our game."

Swallowing thickly around the swell of emotion, I tried to speak. Of course I'd miss my uncle and my parents, but as Mother pointed out in her more lucid moments, this was my life, and I needed to take control of it.

Avoiding the topic, I focused on the cold stone in my hand. I was never sure how Alaric knew the answer. He refused to tell me. We'd started playing this game when I was five. I was now twenty-one and no closer to understanding.

I rolled it between my pointer finger and thumb, lifting the stone to the light. It had a glassy luster, but that, too, was common in both stones, as was the crystalline structure. This was all for show. The answer was quartz. I knew it when he dropped it into my hand, absent the familiar heat of adamas. But as I enjoyed learning history and how things came to be, I desperately wanted facts, reason, and requirements for *how* I knew this was quartz.

I'd never been comfortable with gut instinct—especially my own.

Even with all I'd learned about cutting, shaping, shining, and caring for the stones, I was no closer to a concrete method of distinguishment. I could answer Alaric correctly, but I couldn't teach someone else how to do so, which was maddening.

I hid my frustration with practiced ease. Letting the gem roll back into my palm, I answered as I had for the last sixteen years—with intuition.

"Quartz." I handed it back to him.

The smile he returned was big and bright, warming the room the same way the fire did. "Very good."

"How can you tell I'm right?"

"Quartz doesn't hold and wield magic."

A curse: his wholly unsatisfying responses.

I shook my head, turned, and headed toward the front. "I need to water the plants."

Potted plants covered almost every surface by the windows. My fingers sank into the still-damp soil of the first pot. The dirt came from the Oldwood, the forest surrounding the city, just like the plants. Though moist, a lingering warmth dwelled below the surface. The Oldwood was all contrast like that: hot and cold, dead and alive, terrifying and captivating. As I pressed my fingers deeper into the dirt, I felt the woods call. Darkness overtook my vision as I strained to hold myself apart.

"Alright, Emberline?" Alaric placed a hand on my shoulder.

Flinching, I shook my head in direct contradiction to my words. "I'm fine."

I'd have to pass through the forest to leave the city and begin my journey. My experiences in the Oldwood had been abnormal at best. This practice was supposed to help keep my mind clear when I ventured through tomorrow night.

I glared at the dirt like it had personally offended me. My tests had been going so well. Whatever just happened was disconcerting.

Alaric didn't speak as he followed me behind the curtain.

I gestured to the books strewn across the two highbacked chairs and footstools. "I'll get this cleaned up. The sun is rising."

Being in this part of town when the rest of the city woke up was dangerous.

Alaric's shop was in Lower Hill, a city district in the shadow of the looming spires of Glanmore Castle. This part of Kavios would soon be overrun with the Blessed, and the risk was too high for me to be in their proximity.

I had one rule: Never let the Blessed touch my skin.

They were so-called because they'd received the king's blessing, as evidenced by the adamas jewelry he permitted them. When wearing adamas, the Blessed's touch stole emotion, granting them magic.

My secret, and the reason I was leaving, was that they couldn't steal from me.

I had no explanation for why their magic didn't work on me. Emotion was stolen from citizens on the streets every day. Alaric told me Eris, Goddess of Chaos, protected me. That answer was no longer good enough. The texts in Alaric's collection cataloged information about the Sibling Goddesses, magic, and history. I'd spent years sifting through it all but had found no satisfying answer for my condition.

The books referenced a library in a neighboring kingdom. It claimed to have answers to the most unique forms of magic. Anywhere had to be better than Kavios, where the only information freely given was that which supported the king's narrative for the city.

In the meantime, I didn't want to discover the consequences if a Blessed learned of my immunity. It threatened the validity of King Rodric's blessing if someone could be unaffected. I might miss my family, but they would be in danger if I remained.

It was a true curse that Alaric worked for the Blessed. He was responsible for sourcing the precious adamas stones and making them into jewelry. No one else in the city could do it. Well, I could, but he refused to let me. Everything he did was to keep my unique abilities hidden from the Glanmores. I was done with him risking everything on my behalf.

My one rule, to never let the Blessed touch me, had come from him and Mother. It was a hard lesson to learn, and the familiar roil of guilt churned in my stomach as I thought of the price Mother paid for my education.

I sipped my coffee and flipped through the first open book on the chair.

"Sneaking another glimpse at *Champions of Kavios*?" Alaric bent to close and stack another book.

"No," I said with little conviction.

He chuckled. "You don't have to be embarrassed. Everyone wants to root for the handsome ruler raging against a goddess-given fate."

He was right. I was embarrassed, but not for the reason he thought.

Champions of Kavios was part history and part musings. My interest lay in the supplemental material. The less cynical considered them prophecy. They made little sense to me, but Mother loved trying to decipher the passages. On her good nights, she asked about specific sections, and I refused to disappoint.

The book was banned literature under the current king. He'd outlawed any writing that told of the Goddess of Chaos.

King Rodric Glanmore's city worshiped the Goddess of Order.

Though dangerous, I included Alaric's book collection in the blessing column. My uncle was brave enough to realize the detriment of such thinking. He hoarded banned books like a dragon hoarded gems.

He could be imprisoned for his collection, possibly worse. Generally, I appreciated rules, but Alaric had instilled in me the importance of questioning what didn't make sense. These books were banned because they spoke of a goddess who held no sway in this city. Deciding for the citizens which goddess they were allowed to worship didn't make sense to me.

I took a stack to the hidden room and returned to the chair for more.

"Some of these are so clear." I read a sentence from *Champions of Kavios* aloud. "*Hide your fear, lest the Cursed King bring his nightmares.* Others make no sense."

Alaric chuckled, but it was forced. It was the same laugh he used when he dismissed my concern for him—when he told me working for the Blessed wasn't too bad.

He arched his brow. "Prophecies are never clear. Lines that seem straightforward may not mean what we think."

Maybe that response went in the curse column. He was baiting me. Whether I believed them to be prophecy or not, I was positive he would teach me something about this passage.

"This one isn't hiding anything." I leaned into his trap. It was one of my favorite ways to learn. "The Cursed King is the only Blessed who can wield fear. When he steals fear, he brings forth nightmare magic."

Different emotions were tied to different magics. Wielding nightmares was something only one Blessed had ever done.

"Scholars would contest several points in your analysis. Do we know that he's Blessed?" Alaric asked.

I'd been through this book a hundred times, and it hadn't occurred to me to question whether the Cursed King was Blessed. He was Order's Champion, the presumptive ruler; of course he was Blessed. Leafing through the pages, I searched carefully for any mention of the adamas gem that would mark him as such. The gem I was now sure the Cursed King didn't wear.

"Take a guess, Ember. It's getting late."

I swallowed. Alaric was intent on teaching me to trust my instincts. "Adamas is never mentioned. He doesn't wear it to wield magic."

Alaric nodded, giving me a look I couldn't decipher. "That is the mark of a champion. They don't require adamas to use their power."

I put another stack of books in the storage room. "What do they use?" I hadn't heard this before, but Alaric knew more about the Sibling Goddesses and their champions than anyone in the city.

"I believe that answer depends on the champion."

We were back to wholly unsatisfying answers. At least answering one of Alaric's queries made the world make sense for a moment, even if it raised new questions.

There were so few things in Kavios that I could control. That was one part of *Champions of Kavios* I identified with. Themis, the Goddess of Order, summoned the Cursed King as her champion. Many considered it an honor, but the choice was not his. I understood the lengths he went to fight against a fate he didn't choose.

As citizens of Kavios, we couldn't control the Blessed's magic or when they preyed upon us. We couldn't control the earthshakes that continued to make work in the mines more dangerous. We couldn't control who King Rodric selected in his upcoming ceremony.

At least I could control the risk my immunity presented to myself and my family by leaving, no matter the obstacles to my journey.

A knock sounded on the shop door before I could question Alaric further.

We both froze. In all the mornings I'd spent here, no one ever arrived before I left. Alaric's eyes widened momentarily, but he was faster than me to find his footing. He rolled his shoulders back and ran his fingers through his golden blond hair, an exact match in color to mine.

"Put the rest away." He gestured to the remaining books, then tucked his white dress shirt in his dark trousers. The motion highlighted how loose his clothes hung on his thin frame. Alaric worked too hard, my lessons included, making me wonder when he cared for himself.

"Stay back here. I'll tell whoever it is to return later." He spoke with a cool swiftness, a contrast to the encouragement I usually found in his patient tone. This intrusion disturbed him more than he wanted to let on. He spun the gold ring on his middle finger with his thumb, proving his nerves were much more than they appeared and snapping me to attention.

I hurried to complete the task. "Sure, Uncle."

Another forceful knock sounded before Alaric parted the curtain. This time, the clink of a gem against the glass window front was evident to my jeweler-trained ears. It was almost certainly a Blessed at the door. Alaric's shoulders raised slightly as he hesitated, undoubtedly drawing the same conclusion.

He turned to face me. "If I can't stop them, lock yourself in the storage room."

With no pause for my acknowledgment, he swiftly parted the curtain, a smile plastered to his face for his early customer.

2

Like calls to like.

— FROM CHAMPIONS OF KAVIOS

With unsteady hands, I did as Alaric asked, stacking the remaining books in the hidden storage and giving a cursory nod to the dragon statue Alaric kept there. The dragon represented Chaos. I hoped the goddess was looking out for him now.

My head tilted slightly as I listened for signs of the unexpected customer. Unable to hear anything, I left the storage room door slightly ajar and crept to the thick curtain. Overhearing the conversation was the only way to determine if I needed to hide—at least, that's what I told myself. I wiped my sweaty palms on my skirt as the jostle of the turning lock reached my ears.

The door creaked open. "What are you doing here?" Alaric said.

I'd only ever heard him use that tone with Father when they argued about me. When Alaric told Father he put too much pressure on me, or when he reminded him that Mother's accident wasn't my fault.

With all the practice of one who strived to go unnoticed, I took another silent step toward the curtain. Shapes were not visible through the dense gold fabric, so I couldn't tell if Alaric and the stranger weren't speaking, or if I simply couldn't hear. I guessed I should be thankful for the curtain. The visitor was hidden, but it hid me from them too.

"You didn't come by last night." The man's voice was rich and smoky. A heat, like that of an adamas stone in my hand, filled my body with the sound.

Alaric didn't respond.

"Ava was worried." As the man spoke again, I couldn't help but think his voice felt how a sip of whisky in Woodside tasted. My insides may warm when the cheap drink slid down my throat, but the final bite of the liquor was unavoidable.

"I didn't have time," Alaric finally said.

"Don't you need more youngleaf?" The man phrased this as a question, but something in the confidence of the words told me he already knew the answer.

Alaric sighed. "Yes, but she has a few more days of—"

"You never miss a pickup." This was a statement, but even I heard the question beneath.

My hands balled into fists at my sides as I realized what they were discussing. I had sparse details of the shape of Alaric's evenings. He worked for the royals, but their commissions were infrequent outside the Selection. To my knowledge, he spent his time on his experiments. I didn't care for the man's tone, but I, too, wondered why Alaric wouldn't have time to pick up the herb we used for Mother's tonic.

Alaric sounded defeated, almost apologetic in his reply. "I had work to do."

"Ahhh." The man drew out the syllable like he was drawing out the endgame of a chess match he already knew he'd won. "But the Selection starts tomorrow. You haven't received the commissions yet. Nothing else could be more important than the youngleaf for your sister."

Alaric sighed, and I could imagine his left fingers twisting the gold band on his right hand again. He didn't want to own up to whatever he was doing last night, when he was meant to meet with this man. I snuck a little closer, drawn to the voice in a way that should probably have made me uncomfortable.

"Are you in trouble? I've made it clear that an attack on your person is an attack on me." The man was urging Alaric to speak—to give him some indication of what was going on.

My hand started to shake. Why would Alaric be in trouble? Who was this man to command such authority in Kavios? I'd think the prince was at the door if Alaric hadn't answered so rudely.

A million other questions surfaced. This conversation had me wondering what I knew about my uncle. I knew he liked tea instead of coffee. I knew where he kept the tools to cut the adamas. I even knew his favorite passages in the histories of Kavios. I spent more time with him than anyone in the city, but I had no idea what his day looked like outside of our mornings together.

This man knew things about Alaric that I didn't.

A mirror hung on the other side of the shop, angled to let Alaric see entering customers during the day while he worked behind the curtain. I'd need to cross the workshop to use it, all but removing my escape route to the storage room.

"I can start the work for the Selection without knowing the full commission details." Alaric ignored the man's question about his safety.

A low chuckle sent tingles across my skin. The man was laughing, though the sound rang hollow. My body moved before my mind decided. I crossed the room like a moth drawn to a flame, desperate to glimpse the stranger at the door.

"If you were doing that, why did Soren see you at the Eastern Gate?"

"Eris, curse him," Alaric hissed.

My mouth hung open. To the wrong ears, the chaos goddess's name was treason. He spoke of her to me often, but I never considered that he might have spoken to others about such a dangerous topic.

I reached the workbench and looked up. Alaric was thin but tall, and like he'd known what I would do, his body was strategically angled to block the man's face. Whoever the stranger was, his frame was broad. His shoulders stretched past Alaric's. He wore a black tunic that looked rumpled even as it hugged honed arm muscles. The Blessed were always beautiful, but the messy folds of this man's shirtsleeves made it look like he worked for his physique instead of stealing joy from the others to pay for his vanity. His hair was a rich chocolate brown. It might be knotted at his neck, but I couldn't see that or any other distinguishing features through Alaric.

"Why were you in the Oldwood?" The man pressed. "You weren't going to the mines, were you?"

I envied Alaric's ability to pass through the Oldwood with relative ease. Some said the gnarled branches sheltered more than dangerous creatures. I got lost in them once, and as this morning had proved, whatever lurked in the woods still threatened to overtake me when I entered, no matter my attempt to numb myself to its impacts.

The Oldwood Mine was deep in the forest, near the mountain foothills. Alaric visited regularly, to direct the miners to the adamas deposits within. Usually, he journeyed during the morning shift. The dark cover of the Oldwood's trees was a little less threatening in the light of day.

"If you know so much about my whereabouts last night, why don't you tell me?" Alaric said.

That wasn't a denial. I was fascinated by this man's understanding of Alaric. He jabbed at him, even as he showed concern. It sounded like they were ... friends.

The pattern of Alaric's work, both the demands of the Blessed's schedule and his inquisitive nature, made him independent. He could be lost for days when inspiration struck for an experiment or project. It was another reason why I met him here in the mornings. I never knew when he needed to be brought back to reality. He frequently reminded me that he was an adult and could care for himself in my absence. I hoped that was true.

"I think you went to the mines. I think you know something you're not sharing." The man's voice grew hard at the last statement.

I couldn't comprehend what Alaric might be doing at the mines at night. Would he even be granted entry without a visit scheduled by the king?

The man's pale white hand reached for Alaric's shoulder, and I flinched back, thinking the hand was reaching for me. It was a familiar gesture, one I couldn't comprehend why Alaric would allow. This man was Blessed. We'd heard the ring knock against the window. Even though Alaric wasn't like me, it was still dangerous to let his hand so close to Alaric's skin.

Many Blessed were known to take first and claim an accident later.

The stranger's ensuing words were so soft that I almost

missed them. "You know what this means to me. I'm running out of time."

It was unusual because the Blessed had nothing but time. Between stealing lust and joy, they had healing magic and eternal youth. Time was not in short supply.

The adamas ring on the man's finger drew my gaze, now visible where he gripped Alaric's shoulder. Was Alaric going to let him *take*? Stealing emotion could drain energy, but it wasn't necessarily deadly. Some girls in my building said the pleasure from the touch made it worthwhile. It seemed fitting that a predator would have a means to lure its prey.

I held my breath to see what the adamas would signal—a different color for each emotion. This was another secret I kept. Only the Blessed could see the color in the gems. I wasn't Blessed, but I could see the magic on display. Not even Alaric could do that.

"You know I'd tell you if I could." Alaric sounded sincere, if not a little sad. The ring on the man's finger was still clear.

The gem flashed color when emotion was taken and it glowed a solid color when the stored emotion's magic was used. One emotion fueled one magic, each connected by a color. Red for anger, granting physical strength. Orange for lust, granting physical healing. Yellow for happiness, its magic granting eternal youth, the ageless physical appearance of the Blessed. It was common to see these collected and wielded.

The second set of powers manipulated the mind instead of the body. The emotions required for these magics were deeper—more complex.

Green for envy, fueling the power of persuasion. It was a dangerous thing to have the ability to convince people to do something they wouldn't otherwise.

Blue for sadness, fueling the power to calm. It may seem harmless on the surface, but I'd witnessed King Rodric wield a calm so intense it was an opiate to the masses, those soothed unable to remember the horrors they'd been ready to protest.

I'd never seen the last color firsthand. As the passage from *Champions of Kavios* indicated, only one could wield it: violet for fear, fueling the power of nightmares. The wielder made those impacted see images of their greatest nightmares played out. The power alone made me hope *Champions of Kavios* was more fiction than Alaric claimed.

The stranger stared at Alaric for a long time, locked in a wordless battle I didn't understand. Alaric's body still blocked my view of the man. With no sign of change in his ring, I tilted my head to see if the mirror would grant a glimpse of him from any angle.

A silent gasp slipped from my lips as his gaze lifted. Forest green eyes met mine in the mirror. This wasn't a sip of whisky —it was a full glass—downed all at once. Warmth flooded my senses, and I clenched, waiting for the bite that was sure to come.

It lasted less than a second. I didn't think Alaric realized what the man had done. He'd known precisely where to look to check the mirror—further evidence of his familiarity with the workshop. There was no doubt in my mind that he'd seen me. I held my breath as my heart galloped. What would the man do with the information that someone was behind the curtain?

The man dropped his hand. "Fine."

Alaric's head dipped in a nod.

"Should Ava expect you tonight for the youngleaf?"

The ground shook beneath my feet. An earthshake. I glanced at the mirror to see Alaric holding the door frame for support.

The movement stopped as quickly as it started.

A brief rattle, not even enough to break one of the glass beakers on the workbench. Still, I knew what it had to be.

"The mines," Alaric said.

The man growled something unintelligible under his breath, then turned on his heel and stormed off down the street. Alaric's forehead rested on the doorframe with the stranger's departure as if that conversation had cost him more than I could understand.

The earthshake should have worried me more, but their growing frequency left me numb to their impacts, and Alaric's behavior was too unusual. Hoping no one was injured, I padded to the storage room with soft steps. I didn't want Uncle to know how closely I'd been watching.

Alaric brushed the curtain aside, his gaze sweeping first to the workbench, like he suspected where I'd be. His brow pinched slightly, finding I wasn't there.

"You need to go."

I'd be offended if he wasn't correct. That interlude had put me behind schedule. The streets would be filling. I wasn't guaranteed to get out of Lower Hill unscathed. But I had so many unanswered questions. Why hadn't he picked up the herb for Mother's tonic? Who was that Blessed, and how did Alaric know him? None of what I'd heard between Alaric and the visitor made sense.

"Who was that?" I asked. I knew Alaric's work put him in contact with the Blessed regularly, and I couldn't understand why this apparent friendship with a Blessed bothered me. One conversation had opened up a whole new side of Alaric, one I'd selfishly never considered. Something ugly twisted in my gut as I wondered what else the stranger knew about my uncle that I didn't.

"I'm sure you heard more than enough."

"Is he a client?"

Alaric pinched the bridge of his nose. "No."

"Well, who is he?"

He mumbled something under his breath. I was confident he was cursing my curiosity, but he shouldn't have instilled it in me if he didn't want to deal with it.

"Do you need me to collect the youngleaf?" I asked. "It's for Mother's medicine, isn't it?"

Alaric made a tonic for Mother that energized her and prevented her condition from worsening. He gave me a new vial twice a week. This made me exceedingly nervous because he would be solely responsible for delivering it to her after I left.

"Absolutely not. Forest's Edge is no place for you."

My eyes must have widened in surprise, and Alaric realized what he'd said. Forest's Edge Tavern was east of Uncle's shop on Cross Street. As the name implied, it abutted the Eastern Gate, leading to the Oldwood. The name had always given me pause. The Oldwood was as much a forest as a cave cat was a pet, ready to rip off the arm that reached to stroke its head. To call it such, the tavern's owner must be fearsome or foolish.

It was one of the busiest establishments in the entertainment district. They served drinks in spades, but the tavern held much more than that. I'd never been, but the girls in Woodside talked about it regularly. Private rooms, rented by the hour upstairs, were one of the places magicless citizens could experience the pleasure of the Blessed's touch. Gambling tables filled the back hall with stakes few could afford, although maybe Uncle could, given the amount the Glanmores paid him.

It still didn't make sense.

"Are you in trouble?" I focused on the heart of the matter. Yes, I was intensely curious about who the man was and why the herbs for Mother's medicine would be collected from Forest's Edge, but at the root of this constricting feeling in my chest was worry, bordering on fear. Alaric was never late with Mother's medicine. The knot of concerns slowly untangled as I reminded myself Alaric had a day before we needed another dose. I could almost convince myself Alaric knew what he was doing.

"I'm fine, Ember." His eyes didn't meet mine. They had veered back to the workshop where, in my haste to return to the storage room, I'd slightly moved one of the glass beakers on the bench. "Ha! I knew you were snooping."

I knew he was changing the subject, but I'd learned my stubbornness from him. I certainly wasn't going to win against him in a battle of wills.

"It wasn't snooping when you told me to listen for him entering the shop."

"And you had to see his face to hear him?" Alaric said.

He'd already caught me, and now he was baiting me again. "You know I didn't see him. You were standing directly in the mirror's line of reflection."

A self-satisfied smile crossed his face, like a child who found his gifts hidden under his parent's bed. Just as quickly, though, his smile turned sour. "You need to get going."

I nodded, picking up my brown leather gloves from the table. My white blouse had a high neck and long sleeves, so my hands were the only exposed skin. My heavy gray skirt and thick brown boots covered my waist to the floor. Pulling on the gloves, I was as ready as I would be to brave the Lower Hill at this hour.

He gave a final nod, and I turned toward the front door. Alaric was behind me as I parted the curtain to slip through.

"I'll see you tomorrow morning; one more session before you leave?" he asked.

"Of course."

Alaric nodded. Resigned to my decision. "You know I won't stand in your way."

I knew how he would finish. “I won’t be gone forever, Uncle.”

He attempted a smile, but the flare of his nostrils showed the emotion he restrained.

“You, Mother, Father...” I started. “You’re all in as much danger as I am until I figure this out.”

His mouth opened and closed twice, as if searching for words he couldn’t find. “I should go with you through the Oldwood, just in case.”

“You’ll be needed at the Selection Festival, Uncle. We discussed this.”

He nodded, his gaze distant, like he was deep in thought. “What if I could get someone else to escort you?”

“Someone you trust?” My mind immediately strayed to his visitor.

“Yes. Ember, it would make me feel better about this whole thing. Please.”

The trek through the Oldwood was the scariest part of my journey—more terrifying than leaving the only home I’d ever known. I had no reason to turn down the help. “Sure, Uncle. If you trust them, they can escort me through the Oldwood.”

We held each other’s gaze a beat longer than necessary. I hoped he understood everything I wasn’t saying: *You’ve given me everything, and I am thankful. I’m not leaving you. I’m trying to protect us all.*

Would I have said more if I’d known that was the last time I’d speak freely with Alaric—that our planned goodbye would never occur? The question would haunt my nightmares, even as nightmare and reality interwove, turning my world upside down.

3

Their magic is a bastardization. It wasn't theirs to begin with, so they must take to sustain it.

— ALARIC SARE'S LETTERS TO ISABELLE ARKOVA

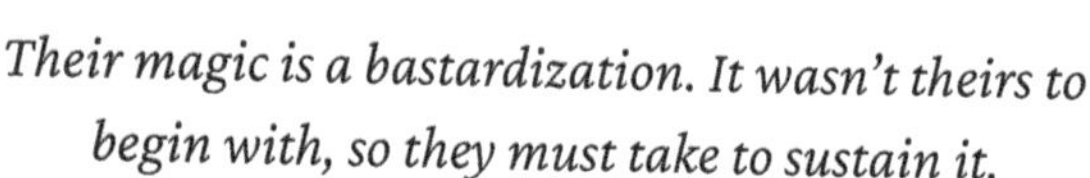

Lower Hill was more alive than I cared for, but this morning's earthshake provided a distraction. Many had stopped to talk about the movement. As I quickly scanned the street, my gaze lingered on Forest's Edge to the east. It was a bit distant but didn't look like much from the outside. Dingy windows prevented passersby from seeing in. The large wooden door looked like it might prove heavy to open. Everything about the building seemed intent on turning away visitors, but I guessed that was its appeal.

Few wanted their vices paraded for all to see.

I took a deep breath, and the sweet scent of doknots hit my

nose. The only part of the Selection Festival I enjoyed was fried dough covered with sugar and cinnamon. White banners were being hung from all the buildings in preparation for tomorrow.

With a final glance at the tavern, I slipped into the flow of people walking. I wouldn't learn more about Alaric's visitor by staring, and standing still only made me an easy target for the Blessed.

"Emberline! Wait up." Jasmine, a friend from my apartment building, hurried down the street. Our friend Serena followed behind, looking tired and dazed. My pulse spiked as Jasmine's long black hair swung with her enthusiasm to catch me. Having any emotions on display made me anxious on her behalf.

The Blessed out this early appeared occupied with festival preparations, but one was never sure when they would take.

Of course, the law required consent from the fed-upon party. It just rarely happened that way in Lower Hill. This area was so much the domain of the Blessed, it seemed any guards here looked the other way when *accidents* happened.

The Blessed didn't have a foolproof way to know when someone was experiencing an emotion. Facial cues were often used. The tilt of Jasmine's lips as she caught up told me she was excited, but the Blessed would see a smile and think happiness. They'd see tears and assume sadness. It was always best to keep your emotions from your face. Years of practice helped me mask mine. Sometimes, not even that mattered. Sometimes, they simply sampled—with a glide of their hand against exposed skin—hoping to collect the needed power. To a passerby, it could look as innocent as bumping into someone on the street, but we all knew better.

"What are you two doing here?" I asked as the girls fell into step with me.

Jasmine gestured to Serena. "I had to collect this one from Forest's Edge."

Serena's smile was devious, but the dark circles beneath her eyes gave away her exhaustion.

Jasmine's brown eyes danced with mischief. "I think you should give me a going away present."

I wanted to laugh but held it in. "I'm the one leaving. Traditionally, you would gift me something for my journey."

She waved me off. "I'm still not convinced you'll do it. No one ever leaves Kavios. It's not done."

Her tone was playful, but it hinted at a truth I'd only suspected. Miners and traders were the only ones who left the city regularly. I didn't know anyone else who had. It was partially why I planned to leave during tomorrow's festival, when those selected were announced. I'd use the city-wide distraction to slip away unnoticed.

"Anyway,"—Jasmine innocently twisted a strand of hair around her finger—"I wanted to ask you if Matthew has been by the shop?"

A snort nearly escaped my lips. "You know I can't tell you that." I paused, tilting my head in thought. "Besides, would you really want to know if he had?"

Serena rolled her eyes. "Oh, she wants to know."

Jasmine bounced again enthusiastically. The action accidentally disturbed the cream-colored sleeves of her dress, exposing her dark brown skin. Quickly, she pushed them back down. I wasn't the only one who took precautions.

"Please." The hint of a whine entered her voice.

"I would never tell you if Matthew purchased jewelry for you. Particularly not a specific piece, like, say ... an engagement ring."

"Is that you telling me he's been to the shop?" She squinted at me as we walked, as if trying to make out a secret language scribbled on a page.

I shook my head, repressing another smile for my friend. "It's not a code. This is jeweler basics. Never talk about who commissioned what pieces. You never know who they're for."

She started to laugh but covered her mouth with her hand when Serena gripped her arm in silent warning.

"I bet that's a juicy story." Serena's words were calm as she slowly surveyed the street.

Confirming her near-outburst went unnoticed, Jasmine returned to the conversation. "Matthew doesn't have a mistress. He can barely handle me."

She wasn't wrong. Matthew worshiped the ground she walked on. He'd been waiting for Jasmine to give him a chance for years, and she finally had. I wondered what had made her give in. She used to frequent Forest's Edge with Serena and spoke highly of how the Blessed could make her feel. Matthew wasn't Blessed. Maybe she realized the high was only temporary. Anything permanent between a Blessed and one without magic was a joke.

I struggled to bury the envy that tightened my chest as I thought about having a permanent attachment to anyone. The weight of my secret made a true partnership impossible.

"I wish you'd allow for some flexibility in this relationship. It would make my trips to Forest's Edge more fun again," Serena said.

Jasmine flipped her hair. "You told me you finally took a shot at that guard last night! You're doing fine without me."

It was considered an honor to repay the King's Blessing by protecting the royal family or the city. Guards were the only positions of service Blessed took. They needed to wield magic to defend against the worst scenario. Only Blessed could stop Blessed.

Serena pursed her lips. "Saying hello and bedding him are not the same."

"Well, at least it's not just you. I heard he turns everyone down," Jasmine said.

"I'm running out of time," Serena whined.

"Yeah, where are you going on your date with Jacob tonight?" Jasmine elbowed Serena with a smile.

"We're not exclusive yet." Serena sounded defensive. "But I don't know how long I can avoid the conversation. Jacob keeps trying to bring it up." They both stifled giggles.

The group in front of us laughed loudly, and it seemed like one of them had dropped something on the street. I wouldn't judge them for finding joy wherever they could, just like I wouldn't judge Jasmine and Serena's inability to suppress their feelings—even if it was ill-advised. The man who laughed stopped to pick up the item, and another man bumped into him.

It was no accident.

The man who ran into him wore an adamas gem, and yellow flashed as the Blessed's hand slid against exposed skin, taking the displayed emotion.

Recognizing his prize, the Blessed, a dark-haired man who appeared to be supervising the street vendors for the festival, wrapped his hand more tightly around the first man's wrist. I didn't think gripping harder helped steal the emotion any faster. It was just another example of a Blessed exerting power.

It only lasted seconds, the Blessed taking what he could before the flash of yellow in his ring cleared—the first man's joy spent. The Blessed mumbled something that sounded like 'excuse me' under his breath before walking away.

Stumbling to catch up with his companions, the first man took a few steps to collect himself. As the girls said, taking could be ... intoxicating. Eventually, he was back on track, moving like nothing had happened.

The normality of it disgusted me.

The violation. The disregard. The ability to be used and then thrown back into whatever you'd been doing. Maybe that man returned to his friends with a little less life than he had before.

That's what no one liked to think about.

Our emotion—the way we felt—was the essence of who we were. I'd studied this with Alaric. What we experienced and how we reacted to the world around us made us ... uniquely us. Every time a little of that was taken, a little of our life went with it. It was impossible to know how much was gone. I'm sure every emotion was even a little different.

As a child, I once naively entered a Blessed's house, where Mother worked as a cook. The Blessed homeowner tried to take from me. When she couldn't, she tried again. She didn't touch me the second time. Mother intervened. The Blessed woman must have pulled harder with her magic, thinking she'd made a mistake. That deeper pull was what Mother intercepted, placing herself between me and the Blessed. Its intensity took years of her life, her hair graying and skin wrinkling before my eyes. Maybe it took a little of her mind too.

Mother gave everything to protect me from discovery. This, too, was part of why I must leave. I couldn't let anyone else pay the price to protect my secret.

While my condition had made it dangerous for me and my family in Kavios, I was thankful never to have lost these little parts of myself. Part of me wished I could do more to protect everyone else too.

Our trio was sobered by what we'd witnessed and kept our heads down as we continued walking. Farther down the road, as we finally exited Lower Hill, a Blessed woman pulled a man onto one of the side streets. The orange blinking of her ring signaled lust. The goofy grin on the man's face said he was well aware of what he was giving and what she was getting. I wished the value exchange of emotion to the Blessed was always so clear.

When we arrived in Woodside at our building, I waved to Jasmine and Serena as they dipped into their first-floor apartments. Since Mother couldn't work and Father spent much of his time caring for her, we all lived together. While it made sense financially, I counted having my own space as a fringe benefit of leaving the city.

The building held twenty units, most of which were filled with families like mine. I sighed in relief as I leaned against the cool stone wall and looked up the empty staircase. Scaling the three floors to my family's apartment was much preferable to the streets of Lower Hill.

Though I doubted many shared my assessment, I found our hallway welcoming. Sure, the walls were gray stone, covered in a dinge that never entirely scrubbed clean, but each doorway had its own attempt at comfort. Some doors boasted white banners that matched those in the streets, representing the Blessed and the Selection celebration. Our door had vines arranged into a circle. These were from the Oldwood too. A further attempt to surround myself with the enigmatic forest, to soothe my reaction to it.

The door was unlocked.

"Father, what have I said about the lock?" I walked down the entryway into the open room encompassing the kitchen, dining room, and living space. He still hadn't turned from where he stood by the hearth, a fire crackling and a skillet set up to make breakfast.

"Father." I tried again. He looked so disheveled. His hair was uncombed, and his tunic untucked, the buttons off by one all the way down.

"What work do we have today, Emberline?" He finally glanced up as I silently took his place and ushered him to a seat in the living space.

"We have two rings to finish today." I was most excited to finish the one Matthew had commissioned for Jasmine.

He waved away my accomplishment as he sat on the chair. "Anything after that?"

I shook my head. "All eyes will be on the Selection and the ceremonies starting tomorrow. I'm sure commissions will return when it's over."

I frowned. At least, I hoped business would return. Alaric would take care of Mother and Father. I couldn't worry too much about my decision to leave, though, as with Jasmine's teasing that I wouldn't *really* do it, I wasn't sure Father truly accepted my imminent departure either.

Father cleared his throat, pulling me from my thoughts. "I hate this time of year too."

The Blessed who took too much from Mother did so the night of Selection Festival. While Mother's condition was never far from my thoughts, it hadn't been the focus of my current melancholy. I empathized with Father anyway. "I know."

"She asked about you—after the earthshake."

"I was at Alaric's. We were fine."

Father's face hardened. Whether from the mention of Alaric or the earthshake at the mines, I couldn't be sure. I was confident Father would have cut off contact with Alaric years ago if he wasn't essential to Mother's treatment. They never quite saw eye to eye—especially about me.

I returned my attention to breakfast. "A Blessed man came by Alaric's shop today, while I was there. It seemed like they were ... friends."

No matter how much they disagreed, Father knew more about Alaric than I did, and I was desperate to see if he knew anything about the stranger.

"Alaric doesn't have friends. He has projects."

I couldn't help but hear the implication that I, too, was only a project to Alaric.

"Do you know where Uncle gets the herbs for Mother's medicine?"

Father stood from the chair, heading for the desk in the corner of the room. "Why do you ask?"

Was that worry etching his voice? He rifled through the desk drawers. It didn't surprise me since it concerned Mother's health.

"The man said Alaric was late picking it up."

Father's back was to me, but his shoulders visibly tensed, and I could hear his following words through clenched teeth. "How late?"

Immediately, I knew this line of inquiry had been a mistake. It would only anger Father and further distance him and Alaric. I really should have seen that coming, but I'd been driven by my desire to know whatever Father did about Alaric.

"Just a day. It sounded like he would pick it up tonight," I said.

"What exactly did they say?"

I considered this. The man had been very clear that he expected Alaric this evening. Had Alaric responded? The earth-shake had cut off the conversation. "I'm not sure, but Alaric has never been late with Mother's medicine."

"He's also never been late picking up the youngleaf," Father grumbled.

The stranger had said that too.

"Ember, is that you?" Mother called from the bedroom. No matter how hard I tried not to, I flinched at the lack of inflection in her voice. She had been such a vibrant woman. Mother had once confronted the Blessed daily as a cook in one of their households and still brought a radiant happiness home with her every evening. We'd prepare the evening meal as a family and sit around the hearth telling stories from the day. Her rich laughter had been my favorite part of our evenings together as a child. Sometimes, I'd make up adventures of stealing away from the shop, braving the Oldwood, and running deep into the mines. I'd tell Mother that something called to me there. That there were more than snakes slithering down pathways, chasing after mice. There was an animal out there that was meant to be my friend. A glint would shine in Mother's eye, one I was always excited to bring forth. Then she'd reach for me and say she hoped that was true, but I better not let a bigger, scaled creature get me first. The tale would devolve into a frenzy of giggling as she tickled me where the fabled creature would bite.

Thinking back on it now, it didn't seem like a typical story for a child. But what is typical? It was ours, and I missed it—desperately.

"Ember," she called softly again from her room.

Whatever it was, it was gone now.

"Coming, Mother."

Father crossed the room again, meeting me before the fire. His voice was low. I almost thought I imagined it. "If Alaric misses tonight's pickup, you must go to Forest's Edge to retrieve it before you leave."

My breath caught. It was the first time he'd acknowledged

my plan. If Alaric missed the pickup tonight, we'd have bigger problems than me collecting the youngleaf. I held Father's stern gaze. Something balled in his fist drew my attention: a piece of paper with Alaric's familiar scrawl visible.

"Your mother is waiting."

I knew a dismissal when I heard it. I shook my head and walked down the hall to her room. At least she wasn't still in bed. She sat in the wooden chair by the window with a book in her lap.

She gestured to the bed. "I thought I heard your voice. Come sit with me."

I perched on the corner of my parents' old mattress. Mother's bright blue eyes looked a cool gray today. It was one of the signs indicating she needed more medicine. I knew how to use the youngleaf to make the tonic, but before today, I'd not had cause to wonder where it came from. If it came from Forest's Edge, it couldn't be legal.

"How was your morning?" Mother pulled me from my thoughts.

I folded my hands in my lap, always a little unsure how much she'd engage. "It was fine. I was with Alaric."

"How is he holding up?"

Something stung behind my eyes at the question. Mother was especially alert to notice.

She held out her hand. "I didn't mean to make you feel bad, baby. We've talked about this. You have to do what's right for you. It's all any of us want."

My head turned toward the living room and Father. It wasn't necessarily true of him.

Mother reached for my hand, and I knelt beside her so she could pat it. "You know it's not entirely his fault. He's not protected like we are."

"Why not?"

"Sweetie, that's his choice. It's easier for him to let the magic overtake him on my bad days."

That was news to me. I wasn't even sure I knew what that meant. She wasn't immune to the Blessed taking from her. It was hard to tell given her overall lack of energy, but I thought she was implying the mind magics like calm and persuasion didn't affect her. Her gaze went distant before I could ask follow-up questions, and a faint smile curled her lip. "Did Alaric give you a passage?"

He'd had one ready for her the moment I arrived this morning. "Let me grab it."

I jogged down the hallway to retrieve the copied words from *Champions of Kavios*. Whether she talked about the passage he wrote was hit or miss, but her lips usually twitched toward a smile when I read them. Her gaze locked on mine as I returned to my seat on the bed, pulling off the ribbon and unrolling the paper.

> *Chaos may have cursed him, but she had bigger plans.*

This was a little ... useless. The Cursed King was Order's Champion, her favored. The text said something drove him to reject his fate, to confront Chaos instead of waiting to fight her champion—I imagined hubris. Chaos didn't take kindly to anyone making demands of her, especially her sister's pet, so she cursed him.

I'm not sure anyone knew how.

The Siblings weren't known for their care for humans, those with magic or those without. Their champions were often described as little more than playing pieces on a game-board. Maybe Chaos had bigger plans when she cursed her sister's champion, but I didn't think she cared too much.

This wasn't about my analysis. It was an exercise for Mother's mind. I glanced at her as I finished reading the line. Her eye glistened, the rim overflowing as a tear fell to her cheek. I set the paper on the mattress and knelt before her. "Are you alright, Mother? What is it?"

She took my hand and squeezed it in her lap. Her grip was light, as if she lacked the strength to do more.

"Be careful, Ember." She wiped at the droplet with one hand.

"What's wrong?"

She shook her head. The hand that still held mine squeezed again.

"The meal is ready," Father called from the living space.

I wanted to push Mother further, but she shook her head again as if responding to my unspoken prod.

"Do you want to come out for breakfast? Or should I bring you a plate?"

She let me go, her hands bracing on the arms of the chair as she strove to rise from her seat. My heart broke anew as she tried, but her body wasn't lifting. Her strength must be at an all-time low.

I swallowed thickly, working to clear the emotion from my voice before I spoke. "I'll bring you some."

After delivering the food and fleeing her room, I quickly ate my own. It was time to open the shop, and though unease about Alaric sat heavy in my stomach, the youngleaf, thc

Oldwood, and leaving my home, I was ready to complete my last day of work as a jeweler in Kavios. It would be a bittersweet accomplishment to finish the final rings. As with the one for Jasmine, I knew they'd get used at tomorrow's festival. I just wouldn't be there to see it.

4

Are we really going to let her leave? They need her to choose.

— ALARIC SARE'S LETTERS TO ISABELLE ARKOVA

Rising early had become second nature. My last day in Father's shop had been a blur, but we'd completed everything. We'd returned home and I'd gone over my maps and plans again, before falling into bed, exhausted. Today was the day I would leave Kavios, but not without a final visit with Alaric.

The apartment building still slept as I pulled on my gloves, grabbed my cross-body bag, and slipped out the door. I'd wait on coffee until I was at Uncle's workshop. It gave me more time with him and more to bicker about.

Walking from the apartment toward Lower Hill before the

sun rose, I couldn't help but think how different it was from yesterday. The streets were fully decorated for tonight's Selection Festival. White banners of the Blessed lined Centre Street, and wooden stalls filled every inch of Cross Street.

Tonight, this street would be packed with festival goers, all citizens of Kavios, attempting to fit into too little space. I'd relax once I'd made it out of the city.

The key to Alaric's workshop was heavy in my pocket. I jingled it in the lock when I opened the door. The noise aimed to alert him of my arrival and pull him from whatever project occupied the earliest morning hours.

Alaric doesn't have friends. He has projects.

Father's words repeated in my head. They rang true to my understanding of what Alaric did with his free time. I desperately wanted to believe I wasn't a project. To allow that hope, I had to keep my mind open to the possibility that Alaric had friends—Blessed friends, even. This led me back to Alaric's customer yesterday.

Anything to occupy my mind from the silence of the workshop.

"Uncle," I called softly. The front section was unlit. It wasn't unusual. We spent our morning sessions in the workspace. There was no need to make the shop windows look inviting.

No rustling of curtains or clinking of glass filled my ears. I froze, realizing the silence was too deafening.

"Uncle," I called again.

Where was he? Alaric knew I would come today. It would be our last session before I left. He wouldn't miss it.

"Uncle," I said with less hope this time as I pushed back the curtain, revealing the workspace I knew would be empty. Nausea threatened as I considered my options.

Alaric was Jeweler to the Blessed. They liked to keep him

close, so he had rooms in Glanmore Castle. Maybe he was still there.

But he'd never not been here when I arrived.

I took a deep breath. Searching for him at the castle was out of the question. Not only would I never be admitted, but it was also the last place Alaric would want me to go. It was crawling with Blessed. I would be searched—touched—before I was allowed to enter.

Tears swelled with my frustration. I closed my eyes, fighting them back. It didn't look like the place had been searched or contraband found. No matter how much everything inside me said something was wrong, I couldn't overreact.

I pinched the bridge of my nose and assessed the room more closely. The secret storage room door was safely closed. I opened it quickly, confirming the books were all in place. *Champions of Kavios* was crooked on the stack. I would never leave it like that, but Alaric would. All that mattered was that it was there—that they all were.

A glass of dark brown liquid sat on the workbench with only a single sip remaining. It drew my gaze, and my footsteps followed. Alaric left much out, but usually, it had to do with his work or experiments. He was tidy with household necessities. Looking more closely at the tabletop, I recognized the other items. Wild mint from the Oldwood, lemon, and water ready to be boiled—these were the other ingredients that went into Mother's tonic.

Only the youngleaf was missing.

A different reason to panic overtook me. I put myself in Alaric's shoes. Had he gone to Forest's Edge? The drink suggested he expected to return shortly, or he would have cleaned it up. Had he been working on the tonic and was interrupted? If so, where was the herb?

Only questions filled my mind, and the only person who could answer them was missing.

That wasn't exactly true. If my question was whether Alaric had disappeared while making the tonic or if he'd never returned from collecting the herb, surely, someone at the tavern could tell me. I replayed the stranger's conversation with Alaric. Ava—that's who he said was waiting for Alaric yesterday. She could tell me if he ever arrived.

I pushed back the heavy gold curtain, checking the sun's rise. Could I visit Forest's Edge at this hour?

Thinking of the time of day triggered thoughts on which I'd rather not dwell. What if I didn't find him before the festival? I couldn't leave on my journey without finding Alaric. Mother would need her tonic.

This could not be happening.

Soft purples and pinks painted the horizon with the rising sun. I briefly remembered an adage about red skies in the morning meaning to take warning. I'd barely finished the rhyme in my head when the jingling of the doorknob had my heartbeat skyrocketing again. I hadn't locked it behind me—too distracted by the lack of response from Alaric as I walked in.

Maybe it was fine. Maybe Alaric was returning from an errand, and this was one big overreaction on my part.

The man who let himself in was the last person I wanted to see.

I sucked in a breath, belatedly realizing the situation I'd put myself in. This man was Blessed. We were alone in Alaric's workshop. I slid behind the counter to put it between myself and the king's advisor.

He was about my height, but I didn't believe I could get past him for a second. The adamas ring on his finger was large. It was twice the size of the stranger's yesterday.

The size of the adamas gem was an indicator of the king's favor. Larger gems could store more power, so they were granted to those in close service to the royal family. And Vaddon Camm had the king's favor. His position was the most powerful outside of the royal family.

My gaze rose to his face. His sharp features pinched as his blue eyes darted from the swinging curtain to me. Vaddon ran his hand through close-cropped black hair like he wasn't sure how to proceed.

He could join the club.

"Who are you?"

I immediately hated his voice. It was nasally and entitled and spoke of everything I despised about the Blessed. Unfortunately, his position empowered it. I had to tread carefully. I'd defend myself if necessary. Thanks to Alaric's training and precaution, I always had a dagger hidden beneath my skirt. But using it on the king's chief advisor meant I'd be a fugitive. My mind was spinning into worst-case scenarios. With another deep breath, I tried to devise a more reasonable plan.

"Emberline Arkova."

He wasn't impressed by my lack of explanation following my name. Silence hung between us as he waited, likely for me to provide more context. I didn't. He appeared to be testing the name, determining if he knew it.

"Alaric's niece? Why are you here?" The way he glanced around the room, his lip curling, showed his distaste, as if he couldn't imagine why anyone would choose such a space on purpose.

I couldn't exactly admit he taught me banned history. "I'm a jeweler too. He teaches me new techniques."

Vaddon waved his hand in a motion that demanded I continue my explanation, even as his gaze searched the shop, clearly uninterested in my response. At least the way his eyes roamed the shop, the unfamiliarity, gave me hope he hadn't been here to arrest Uncle for his banned books.

That only meant something else was wrong.

"That's it," I said.

"Is he here?" Heavy footfalls took Vaddon across the shop to the curtain.

"What do you need?"

His fingers wrapped around the curtain, readying to pull it back. He paused and glanced at me again like I was an inconvenience in his morning. "I'm Vaddon Camm, advisor to King Rodric." The curl of his lip said he knew he needed no introduction. "Alaric missed an appointment."

I tried to swallow but found my throat suspiciously dry. This might be worse. Alaric would never miss a meeting with the king. It was one of the only reasons he gave for why he couldn't meet some mornings. The king required only infrequent visits, but when called upon, Alaric said it was unwise to be late. It was one of the only times he seemed ... fearful.

Alaric hadn't said anything about a meeting with the king yesterday.

"Is he here?" Vaddon asked again. He'd pulled back the curtain, revealing the empty workspace.

I shook my head.

"Where did he go?" Vaddon clenched his teeth, and his nostrils flared like this entire experience of chasing down the jeweler was beneath him.

I didn't know what else to say. "He wasn't here when I arrived."

Vaddon's brow furrowed in frustration with my unhelpful answers. "Were you supposed to meet him?"

He stretched his fingers and glanced at his ring, allowing me to do the same without his notice. The edges glowed green, and the slightest pressure graced the back of my neck. He wielded persuasion. Vaddon intended to make me answer his questions under the influence of magic. He thought I was lying.

This presented a problem of a different kind. The feeling on the back of my neck intensified slightly as Vaddon repeated his question.

Like taking emotion with adamas, the gem's wielded magic also didn't work on me. Whatever pressure the magic applied, it never sank beneath my skin. But if Vaddon didn't think me compliant—if he thought the magic didn't persuade me—it would be as bad as a Blessed trying and failing to take from me. I had no choice but to provide more information, so he didn't question the gem's power.

"Yes, I was supposed to meet him this morning."

His sneer was unpleasant at best. "How much has Alaric Sare taught you?"

"Everything he can." It was a dangerous choice, but truthful, as the ring's magic would demand. I hoped Vaddon would understand it to mean he taught me how to work the gem, not how to source it.

There were two key parts to prepare the adamas to hold magic. First was finding it. Sourcing adamas in the mine was a skill that couldn't be learned. Alaric had convinced the royal family years ago no one else in the city was capable. They'd searched, of course, but could find no one else with his talent.

Second was cutting the stones. The same essence that allowed Alaric to find the stones ensured his ability to determine the right shape and density of the magic within the gem. Again, this was unteachable to any who couldn't identify the stones to begin with.

While I'd never worked the adamas myself, I knew all of Alaric's techniques, and I knew the difference between quartz and adamas. I was confident I could navigate working the gem to store magic as well.

Not that I wanted the royal family to know that. Alaric had done everything in his power to make certain I avoided their notice.

Now, he was gone.

Vaddon appeared to calculate things I hoped he wouldn't. He surveyed my features as if wanting to test the theory that none of Alaric's relations could source the gem. Even though my dark brown eyes, upturned nose, and bow-shaped lips looked nothing like Alaric, I was sure Vaddon saw me as the same tool to the royal family.

He had no proof.

The curve of a smile on Vaddon's lips told me any hope I had of getting out of this, of searching for Alaric myself, or of visiting Forest's Edge to ask about the youngleaf, was misplaced. "Well, Emberline. You need to come with me."

"Where?" I asked.

Already, he strode toward the door, expecting me to follow. "We're going to the castle. Prince Elias will want to speak with you."

5

They worshiped Order with or without her champion.

— FROM CHAMPIONS OF KAVIOS

To say my morning wasn't going well was an understatement. My world seemed to be crashing down around me.

Alaric was missing, and my only reassurance was that I could scratch *arrested for blasphemy* from the list of potential whereabouts. Everything else was on the table. My plans to leave that night felt like they had already slipped through my fingers. I couldn't tell if my anxiety was due to my uncle being missing, my plans falling apart, or the fact I was on my way to Glanmore Castle.

Vaddon's urgency made everything worse. He swiftly marched me out of the shop and down Cross Street.

"Doesn't your father own the shop in Woodside?"

I had no idea what kind of answer would be less damning. "Yes. I work with him there."

"He doesn't teach you?"

I wasn't sure what he was getting at. Everyone knew Alaric was the better jeweler. Father was fine, but Alaric's talent was matched only by my own. "They both do."

"How long have you worked there?" He sounded like every question he asked was a breath he couldn't get back.

At least, following the king's advisor as I did, I wasn't worried about any Blessed taking from me. Few people were on the street this early, and Vaddon glared at everyone we passed.

"A few years," I said.

Now, Vaddon turned to glare at me.

With the Selection starting tonight, he was probably on edge about Alaric's absence. In a few hours, the streets would fill with merchants selling food, drink, and trinkets. Alaric should receive four commissions from the royal family tonight —one for each Selected to become Blessed at the end of the festivities. While Alaric prepared what he could ahead of time, he would have less than eight days from the Selection Celebrations to complete the finished pieces.

I wasn't sure they had a backup plan without Alaric.

Vaddon's quick strides told this story. He moved purposefully like he'd found the prize he was looking for, even though he sneered every time he glanced at me.

"Have you ever worked with adamas?" he asked.

My palms started sweating. I couldn't be the backup plan.

"No." I had no problem answering honestly. Alaric and I always played our little game, but I'd never cut, shaped, or polished the adamas stone. We'd only ever worked on quartz.

Vaddon continued our march down the street regardless of my answer.

I didn't wish to go anywhere near the castle. Wandering alone at night in the Oldwood sounded preferable. Craning my neck, I stared up the hill as we approached the steps. The castle loomed, imposing with its spired towers and backdrop of mountain peaks.

The grand staircase almost seemed another defense for the royal family. The steps were wide but unpredictably spaced. I spent the entire hike up the hill staring down at my feet so as not to trip. As Vaddon unbelievably increased our pace up the sham of a staircase, I couldn't even appreciate the intimidating beauty of the Pinnacle Range peaks circling the castle.

I paused to catch my breath and chanced another glance up. The mountain range all but surrounded the castle—a second line of defense to the wall encircling the city. I knew from Alaric's history books that Kavios grew up around the Oldwood Mine. When the quartz was discovered, people flocked to its offered work.

It seemed Vaddon was out of questions. Was I allowed any? I was terrified for myself, but I needed to use this situation for what I could—information about Alaric. "How long have you been looking for Alaric?"

"Long enough," he said.

I'd been with Alaric only yesterday. How quickly after that could he have gone missing? I continued up the steps.

"Do you have any idea where he is?"

Vaddon made a noise I could only call a dignified snort. "If I did, I wouldn't be talking to you."

I was mildly insulted, but at least he, too, considered this a bad outcome. Maybe they would decide I couldn't handle the work in Alaric's absence, and they'd send me home. It still left a lot of questions about how I'd search for him, what I'd do next, and how the shape of my plans would change, but at least it would remove me from the Blessed's crosshairs.

We were at the top of the stairs, high enough to see over the city wall. Kavios was hard to get to, but I suspected King Rodric liked it that way. Imported and exported goods entered the city, so traders made the trek. Some legally, like our quartz leaving or grain and vegetables arriving. Others illegally—like I now suspected of the youngleaf for Mother's tonic.

"Hurry up. We don't want to keep the prince waiting," Vaddon said.

The castle's giant double doors opened as Vaddon strode in. My mouth hung open at the size of the doorway. What could even require such space? I had no time to contemplate it as I rushed to keep up with the king's advisor. As we entered the castle, I found solace in the fact that I wasn't meeting with the king. While I was immune to his power—like any other Blessed's—its strength genuinely terrified me. He kept the city in a state of constant calm when the citizens should feel anything but.

I wasn't sure I could look him in the eye and hide my true feelings about him.

Prince Elias was the face of the royal family. The king may conduct the Blessing Ceremony, but the prince was the master of events and festivities for the city's celebrations. He would host the festival tonight, announcing those selected. He hosted almost all the events in the eight days of celebration: the Cornucopia, the Presentation, and the Masquerade.

Prince Elias was all smiles for his people, and the city loved him for it. Maybe I should have warned myself that weaponized charm was just as dangerous as what his father wielded.

The prince's head tilted ever so slightly as Vaddon ushered me into his study. He stood from his seat at a large wooden desk, clearly assessing me.

My utterly random thread of thought said his first question must be who taught me to curtsy. The problem was that I didn't know either. I thought I made it up. His lips pursed like he didn't know what to make of it as I rose from my attempt.

His hand scratched his clean-shaven chin in thought. "Who is this, Vaddon?"

Vaddon glowered at me as if he expected me to speak. I didn't—the prince had asked him a question, not me. Instead, I used this opportunity to study the room. Two large chairs sat in the corner, a table between them filled with bottles of dark brown liquid. The walls were almost barren, which seemed disappointing. I don't know what I expected. Maybe more books? More things should be needed to run a city-state like Kavios.

A single tapestry depicting Themis, Goddess of Order, hung behind him. Elias circled the desk, the fall of his light brown hair interrupting my appraisal of the room's decor. Now that I'd seen him, his face was too perfectly symmetrical to look away. Green eyes stared back at me, less striking than the deep forest green ones that had, only yesterday, held mine captive in the mirror's reflection.

"Alaric's niece," Vaddon finally answered when he realized I wouldn't.

The prince looked like he'd say something, but Vaddon continued. "She was in his workshop when I arrived."

Elias turned to me. His hand stroked his chin again as he appraised me. "What's your name?"

"Emberline," I said.

"Emberline." My name on his lips sounded lush and full of promise. "Why were you in Alaric's workshop?"

"We meet for training some mornings."

"She also works in her father's shop. The one in Woodside." Vaddon's voice was so slick, it seemed the words might be used to hold his hairstyle in place. It made the hair on my neck stand on end, but I kept my features neutral. I was in the castle—the heart of the Blessed. Currently, I was under Vaddon's protection, but that could change at any moment. One wrong move, one touch, and someone could learn my secret—that I was immune to their magic.

This was everything I'd been trying to prevent with my plan to leave.

Vaddon's lead had brought me past numerous guards unchecked. If the prince found me helpful, he'd probably use me as a replacement jeweler. It would put me at risk of being exposed for my ability to detect adamas, but maybe he'd aid in a search for Alaric. I might not escape the castle without a Blessed attempting to take from me if he didn't.

It was unclear which option to hope for.

Neither were ideal. Both gave the royal family information about me that Alaric had done everything to prevent them from learning. I'd be furious with Alaric for putting me in this position if I wasn't also terrified for his safety.

The prince peered at me like I was one of Uncle's experiments to be closely observed. "I see. And how long have you been studying under Alaric?"

The phrase sent a chill up my spine. The prince couldn't know about Alaric's forbidden tomes. I'd checked this morning, and they were undisturbed in the storage room.

"How long have you been training?" Vaddon asked. He seemed impatient for me to respond as he wandered the edge of the room.

I couldn't understand why *he* was agitated. He was the one who dragged me here, but I clung to the rephrasing he offered.

I shrugged, repeating the answer I'd given Vaddon. "A few years."

The green of Vaddon's adamas was glowing before he next opened his mouth. Unsatisfied with my answer, he would force one from me through persuasion. But before he could speak, Prince Elias held up his hand, silencing him.

"You must be as confused as we are." The prince's voice was soothing, like a groomsman coaxing a spooked horse. "We think Alaric is missing, and we're looking for any information about his whereabouts. Do you know where he is?"

This must be why the city loved him. He had more power than Vaddon, but he didn't wield it as such. He used honeyed words to pull answers from my lips.

I shook my head, still not having the ones he sought. "He wasn't at the workshop when I arrived."

"When did you last see him?"

I hesitated, but I'd already admitted to being there regularly. "Yesterday morning."

Prince Elias nodded as he shared a look with Vaddon. The prince pushed himself off the edge he'd leaned against and walked back around the desk. He spoke as he opened and closed a drawer just out of view.

"With the Selection starting this evening, we'll need to plan in case he doesn't turn up." He said it so casually. I'd assumed as much on the walk up the steps, but his words ruffled me. They effectively wrote off Alaric and moved on with running the city.

Was this what it was to rule under Order? It was almost cruel in its efficiency.

"Maybe he's in his room," I said.

"He's not," Vaddon replied, as if my idea were something he'd stepped in on the street.

"Vaddon checked there before going to Alaric's workshop," Elias said more gently.

I'd clung to hope that Alaric was simply somewhere I couldn't go. He wasn't in his shop or his rooms in the castle. The fact that Vaddon had already searched them indicated Alaric had missed a meeting a while ago. It was still early. This couldn't all have been accomplished this morning. Where else had they searched? The Oldwood? The mine? Forest's Edge? Given what I'd overheard with Alaric's visitor yesterday, I couldn't ask about those places. If Alaric was visiting the mines without the king's permission, now would not be the time to bring it up. I'd need a way to search myself. A nervous energy overtook me as I cataloged Alaric's potential whereabouts and what I'd need to do to find him.

Meanwhile, I stood in the prince's office, unsure what he and Vaddon would do. They needed a jeweler. A green glow crept over the large stone on the prince's pendant before I could consider what they'd ask.

I exhaled as the skin at the back of my neck prickled, but magic never overtook my mind. The prince wasn't as nonplussed as he acted. He wielded persuasion, and I'd need to act affected.

The prince had said something to me. I knew from the green on his necklace that I should agree even though the words hadn't registered. Being pliable was my only defense if he was trying to persuade me of something.

"Are you—" he started, and I was sure he would ask if I had Alaric's talent sourcing adamas.

"Pardon me, but when did you last see Alaric, Your Highness?"

It was clear the prince needed me. At a minimum, he needed a jeweler. He'd be even happier if he realized I could directly replace Alaric. I felt reasonably confident I could afford a few questions without earning his wrath.

Vaddon's glare from across the room said he thought I was deserving of no such thing.

"I can't say for sure. He missed a meeting last night with my father. We have guards searching the city—and the mines," the prince said.

I schooled my features even as my heart beat faster at his words. They checked the mines. Had Alaric planned to go yesterday? Did they know of the unauthorized trip his visitor accused him of?

The prince continued. "Alaric ..." He held my gaze. "Well, Alaric knew the risks."

I couldn't tell if the prince actually cared or if he was the city's greatest actor.

"I've been requesting Alaric allow a personal guard for years, but he refused. I've honored his decision as he'd proved he could defend himself. But that didn't erase the risk."

Proved he could defend himself. An image flashed in my mind. Alaric, wearing adamas glowing red as he overpowered the Blessed who'd touched me—the one who'd taken from Mother. He had smothered her face with a pillow—suffocating her. Alaric proved the lengths he'd go to protect my secret from exposure. That day, He'd also proved that magic wasn't only for the Blessed. It was for those with adamas—no matter how it was acquired.

A fact very few in the city seemed to realize.

I shook myself free of the scene I worked hard to repress. "Alaric was in danger?"

I feared the prince saw too much. He spoke gently again, as if consoling me. "Some in the city don't appreciate his service to the royal family."

The pieces the prince's words danced around fell into

place. Alaric was the only one capable of sourcing adamas. A Blessed without adamas couldn't wield magic. I guessed it was a simple enough calculation to decide if you removed the source of the gem, then you removed the Blessed's ability to make new wielders.

The Feared—a rebel group who believed such things—were whispered about in Woodside. I didn't realize the prince knew of their existence.

Their plan seemed shortsighted since it did nothing about the city's current wielders. But with the Selection Festival about to start, attacking the Jeweler to the Blessed would send a powerful message.

Unbidden, a voice I couldn't entirely forget slid into my mind. *"Are you in trouble? I've made it clear that an attack on your person is an attack on me."* Something rancid coated my throat. Was Alaric's visitor yesterday one of the Feared?

I swallowed thickly. "You think the Feared ... what? Killed him?"

Even breathing the idea felt like a betrayal. Alaric was fine. He had to be. He was just ... somewhere, not here.

But Alaric would never willingly put me in this position.

Being in the prince's study, in the castle, wondering if the prince and king's advisor knew I had a talent for sourcing adamas was a situation Alaric had done everything to prevent.

If I was here ... he might well be dead.

Prince Elias slid his hands into his pockets and returned to the front of his desk. "We don't know, Emberline. Of course, we'll continue searching for him. But you also must see our predicament. The city would revolt if the Selection didn't proceed as planned. We can still announce the Selected, but the Presentation requires a jeweler, and they need time to prepare. Vaddon's next stop is... your family home to collect your father."

My heart stopped.

First, Father couldn't source the adamas. Second, I couldn't imagine the trouble he'd get into with the royal family. He was beyond forgetful when his mind was on Mother. The prince may seem kind, but I had no illusion that any disappointment would be met with the same soft words he currently used on me.

"If you take his place, we'll take care of you. You'll receive Alaric's salary until he's found. And you'll have full access to the continued search for him."

The prince took a step forward as if to reach for my hand. Though they were gloved, my flinch was automatic. The prince smiled as he must have realized he found another lever. "No Blessed will touch you, if you're my jeweler."

No wonder the city loved him. He had power and knew how to use it to get what he wanted.

Distracted by the veiled threat to Father and the boons he'd just granted, Prince Elias pulled a gem out of his pocket and tossed it to me.

This must have been what he pulled from his desk drawer. Every instinct told me Elias knew the answer to what type of gem this was. It must be a raw scrap Alaric had already sorted. I caught the stone without hesitation, the warmth in my palm, even through my glove, brought an automatic smile to my face.

"Quartz or adamas?" Elias asked.

It was such a familiar game but with wholly different stakes.

I could lie. I could answer incorrectly and say it was quartz, but the prince had to know what this gem was if he pulled it from his desk. Alaric had to have identified it for him at some point.

The prince was staring at me like I was a pool of water, and he'd been stranded in the desert for weeks. I didn't think he'd believe me if I lied. He looked at me like he knew my secret.

But he couldn't.

Before responding, I allowed my mind to run through everything he'd told me. I made a show of pulling off my glove, rolling the gem between my fingers, and pretending to evaluate it as I did when playing a simpler version of the game with my uncle.

Alaric was missing—presumed dead by the prince. The Blessed needed someone to source their adamas.

Answering incorrectly was a risk. My gut told me the prince would know the lie.

Answering correctly was also the only way I would have information on the royal family's efforts to find Uncle. I didn't need more reasons, but Alaric's salary paid for Mother's medicine. Now that I knew the herb was contraband, I couldn't imagine how much he paid for it.

All of this meant my own plans were shot. I couldn't leave Kavios without truly knowing Alaric's fate. Not even the prince's stark words could convince me to give up on him so easily. Plus, I only felt confident leaving Mother because I knew Alaric would care for her. I'd need more time to establish other means for her tonic.

I took a deep breath and eyed the gem. Its gentle warmth was my only comfort as I made a decision that could cost me everything.

In the end, my choice was no choice at all. The word slipped from my lips. "Adamas."

6

Unfortunately, I like him, but it's not my secret to tell.

— ALARIC SARE'S LETTERS TO ISABELLE ARKOVA

With one answer, I became Jeweler to the Blessed.

The prince may have already given Alaric up as lost, but I wouldn't. I would take the granted boon—full access to the details of their search. My position would be temporary. Alaric would return. He would explain and make the scattered puzzle pieces fit together as he did with the city's histories and literature.

I could still leave eventually. Just not now.

Now, I'd need to be more careful than ever. The prince promised no one would take from me. I believed he had that power, but it probably came down to who was enforcing the requirement when he wasn't there.

"She'll need a guard," Prince Elias said.

Vaddon nodded. "I'll take care of it this afternoon."

"Now."

Alaric's visitor yesterday also indicated that the threat the prince alluded to regarding my new position was real. I wasn't ready to consider that something had happened to Alaric, though. He knew how to defend himself. I had hope he was alive.

Hope was a dangerous thing, however. It may not have been an emotion the Blessed fed on, but they leveraged it to maintain the status quo.

There was no better example than tonight's Selection. A little thread of hope dangled over our heads—that we could become one of the Blessed. Even if it was a one-in-a-million chance.

The prince won his discussion. Vaddon crossed the room to open the door where one of the helmeted guards stood at attention. "Send for Carver. Tell him to bring his best men."

The metal shield covered the guard's eyes and nose, but his exposed chin dipped as he bowed slightly and left to fulfill the request.

"Do we have to assign one now?" I asked.

After the prince's explanation, I had no objection to a guard, but I had another task to complete before submitting to one. Mother's tonic hadn't been completed. I'd need to attend to it today. Especially now that I knew where the youngleaf came from, it seemed like it would be much easier to investigate illegal goods from sellers I didn't know without a guard in tow.

"Your safety is of the utmost importance," Prince Elias said.

Vaddon rolled his eyes.

"It seems..." I hesitated, not sure how far I could push them.

The prince noticed my hesitation and gestured for me to continue.

"It seems only you and the guards know about Alaric's disappearance. I should be safe until tonight's festival. That's when Alaric's absence will be noticed, right?"

It wasn't ideal, but at least this would give me the day to move freely through Kavios. After that, well, I'd plan for that later. Unlike Alaric's, I knew my defense skills weren't enough to dismiss a guard.

I had to take care of the family. Alaric may not have wanted me in this position, but he wasn't here. This move protected Father from the royal family and ensured I had funds for Mother's tonic. The royal family knowing I could source the gems was different from knowing I was immune to their magic. Alaric could source gems but had no such immunity. Knowing one wouldn't necessarily lead to knowing the other.

This had been my best option in a bad situation.

Today, I'd investigate the youngleaf and ask around the tavern for Alaric. Maybe I could get an ongoing delivery set up, so I wouldn't have to worry about trouble with my guard when Mother needed the next one.

The prince hesitated. "I'm not sure ..."

Vaddon folded his arms over his chest. "That should give us time to choose the right person."

The prince held Vaddon's gaze, a silent conversation I wasn't privy to. Finally, he nodded. "Alright. After the Selected are announced, come to the castle steps. Your guard will meet you there."

I attempted another awkward curtsey, not wanting to risk my luck with any more words. This gave me time to sort things out with my parents. Mother needed her tonic.

Father's instruction from last night repeated in my mind. *If Alaric missed the pickup, I needed to retrieve the youngleaf from Forest's Edge.* All signs in the workshop indicated he hadn't collected the herb. Maybe that was only my mind assuming the worst. I would go to Forest's Edge and ask for myself.

I needed to be careful, even though Alaric had left me few options. While I didn't begrudge Alaric for doing anything and everything for Mother's tonic, the fact that it was an illegal good made my line of inquiry more … complicated. At least I had the name spoken between Alaric and the stranger yesterday: Ava.

I'd see if I could find Ava at Forest's Edge and get some answers.

"You're dismissed then," Vaddon said.

The prince shot him a glare at his tone, but I didn't care. On some level, I appreciated that Vaddon was transparent in what he thought of me.

"We'll see you tonight," the prince added. His gaze held mine a moment longer than necessary. "Vaddon will walk you back to Cross Street."

Vaddon's nostrils flared, but he didn't object.

I left the room before anyone changed their mind. Vaddon followed, and though I knew he hated this, I was thankful for it. I wasn't sure I could find my way out of the castle. And wandering through the halls filled with Blessed, while no one knew of my new position was unadvisable at best.

"Seems like you left some information out on our walk." Vaddon gestured me down the hallway.

I didn't respond. Had he thought I'd spill all my secrets to him as he dragged me to the castle?

Vaddon seemed like he would press the matter, but three men in guard uniforms strode toward us. The one in front nodded toward Vaddon.

"You and His Highness called for me?"

This must be Carver. That meant the two beside him were his best men. One of them could be my future guard. I let my gaze roam over them without being too obvious. The formal dress meant I couldn't see beneath the metal visors anyway.

Vaddon waved his hand in my direction. "The prince waits in his study. I have less glorious tasks to attend to."

Carver removed his helmet. He had light brown hair that framed his face. "His guard said it was urgent."

"It is," Vaddon replied. "Go ahead; you don't need me."

Carver stared at him. Like the strategist he likely was, he tried to understand what he was walking into, but Vaddon was unwilling to provide more information.

A prickle along my cheek returned my gaze to the men behind Carver. This wasn't the feeling of magic attempting to penetrate my mind. It felt like I was being watched. A glare so heavy it had a physical presence against my skin. But I couldn't see either guard's face to determine which one it was.

"We should get to it then," the guard on the left said. His voice was all I needed to hear. The familiar low rumble sent warmth flooding through my insides. I didn't need to see his eyes to know they were forest green.

Alaric's visitor was a ... guard? One up for the position of my personal defender.

I swallowed. The stranger didn't know anything about me. The prince had more dangerous information than this guard did. But the guard was the one who mentioned the youngleaf to Alaric yesterday. Was he the one Alaric bought from?

Vaddon strode to the towering double doors, and I rushed to catch up. Maybe Alaric had accepted a guard, and the prince hadn't known it? Alaric's visitor potentially becoming my guard was a complication I couldn't begin to unpack.

Yesterday, any information about this man who knew

Alaric better than I did would have been my top priority to investigate. Today, with only hours to take care of Mother's medicine before my life would be turned upside down, it would have to wait.

It was barely midday, but that was irrelevant given the Selection Festival. Cross Street was abuzz with excitement. Shops and businesses in the rest of the city rushed to close early. All eyes were on the castle steps, wanting to know who would join the ranks of the Blessed, even hours before the Selection.

Vaddon shooed me away at the base of the hill. His sneer was becoming too familiar. "We'll see you back here tonight."

I hadn't turned completely when his lip curled into an appalling smirk. The king's advisor was low on my list of worries today. I pulled my gloves up again to confirm I was fully covered and slipped undetected into the flow of people on Cross Street. My instincts were on high alert as I walked east. There were too many people and no reasonable way to distinguish Blessed as they all passed so quickly. My best chance was to be invisible. Thankfully, I'd had years of practice.

The mines must have closed this morning for tonight's celebration. Workers gathered on Cross Street, packed tightly like a school of fish attempting to appear larger than they were to the surrounding predators.

"Emberline." The voice had the hairs on the back of my neck standing on end. "Emberline, what are you doing here?" Macen called from the group. I may have escaped the Blessed this morning, but not everyone without magic was good news either.

At one point in our youth, Macen would have been considered gangly, but unfortunately, he'd filled out. Most now would describe him as handsome. His light brown hair was expertly tousled. Looking at him made me cringe. It wasn't entirely his fault. He reminded me of traits I wasn't particularly proud of. Like when I was young and stupid and found him charming.

His attention had been an escape from the fear of discovery, from Mother's condition, and from the responsibility Father piled upon me after. I may have thought I was in love then, but sleeping with him also conveniently distracted me from my growing list of responsibilities.

He repeated his question as I tried to pass without acknowledgment. "What are you doing here?" Rather than drawing more attention to where I was going, I paused to speak to the group.

"It's a little late to meet with the jeweler, isn't it?" He sounded annoyed. "You've been running your father's shop for years, Emberline. Do you still need his pointers?"

I didn't rise to the bait of his backhanded compliment. It wasn't playful like when Alaric did it. This was just one of the long list of red flags that made me realize Macen wasn't for me.

Father's devastation after Mother's accident had been eye-opening. He wasn't the same man. It made me wary of love like theirs. A love so consuming that his world made little sense to him without her present.

So, I might have been fine with Macen. I found him attractive, and we both had a quiet, seething anger about being exploited by the Blessed. If only the rest of him wasn't so ... terrible.

"Emberline?" he prodded, growing impatient.

"I've got errands."

"Did you hear about the mine cave-in yesterday?" Macen asked. It bothered me how easily he switched from annoyed to engaging—trying to draw me into the conversation. Were either real?

I shook my head, remembering the earthshake yesterday morning. "I'm sorry to hear. I do have to get going."

"I can't be worse than the Blessed leech." His voice was low, but a few others in the group must have heard him. An older man beside him narrowed his gaze, evaluating whether to interfere, if I had to guess.

My every instinct wanted to ball my hands into fists and slug one into his face, but expressing anger in public was as stupid as expressing joy.

This was new, though. The angle of Macen's irritation appeared to have changed. Once, he was easily jealous of anyone and anything I spent time with. Now, it seemed he looked down on those who worked with the Blessed.

"So, you despise anyone trying to make a living in the city?" I hated myself for engaging. I'd heard the term "Blessed leech" before. Usually, it was directed at those who sought the Blessed's touch—those who wanted to get lost in the delirium of taking.

"Not all those who work for the Blessed grant them the power your uncle does."

Macen's comment had gooseflesh dancing across my covered skin. This was too close to the warning I'd just received from the prince. Even worse, his words seemed to claim the gem granted power instead of the king—another conversation I did not want to have.

"You sound like one of the Feared," I whispered.

It didn't entirely surprise me that he ended up here. He wasn't only angry with his position in society. He resented the Blesseds' prosperity.

While *Champions of Kavios* was the only copy of its kind, it wasn't the only text that told the Cursed King's story. It was a whispered fable for children. So much so that the rebel group had named itself for his unique power to take fear. They found power in the idea of the Cursed King's defiance.

Citizens, sick of Blessed taking, were far too easy to relate to, but my practical mind was too quick to play out the possibilities. What came from the group—rebellion? What chance did they have, without magic, against the magic of the Blessed?

Macen smiled a boyish grin. He opened his mouth to speak again.

A boy standing beside him beat him to it, nudging Macen's shoulder. "Who do you think it will be?"

Macen clenched his teeth, a muscle in his jaw ticking as the boy rambled on, oblivious to Macen's annoyance.

"Excuse me?" Macen replied, unable to make the connection.

"Jasper, you can't just assume everyone else is thinking about the Selection like you are," the older man, who'd been watching my exchange with Macen, said. He winked at me, and I was beyond grateful for the interference.

Jasper flushed, and his brow furrowed slightly as if unsure how anyone thought about anything else. He addressed the older man. "Fine, Farrow. Who do you think will be selected?"

Tonight's Selection was Kavios's largest celebration. Now that I was staying, I would have to deal with it—more than deal with it. Now that I was Jeweler to the Blessed, I'd be central to the celebration.

Every year, eight days of festivities marked the Selection of four new Blessed. The event concluded with the King's Blessing and bestowing of adamas. While only the fates of the four were changed, the entire city came alive with anticipation.

Anyone could be Selected.

"I'm sure there are four children of the Blessed who will steal up the spaces," Farrow said. "Don't get your hopes up."

It was true. A child of two Blessed wasn't granted the King's Blessing at birth. The child had to wait for Selection, just like the rest of us. Although, they tended to be waiting in the luxury of a Blessed household instead of the too-packed apartments in Woodside. At eighteen, they became eligible for Selection and were prioritized.

Usually, the Selection of a Blessed child was a formality. Though, I'd read a story in one of Alaric's banned books about a Blessed daughter leaving Kavios rather than being Selected.

I hoped it was true—hoped people really did leave this city—even if my chance to do so had slipped through my fingers.

Jasper scratched his neck. "Stephen said there were only three Blessed children eligible. At least one of the Selected must be from a magicless family."

He smiled at Farrow with unchecked enthusiasm. The older man nudged him closer to the center of the group of miners. He appeared to be protecting the boy from his wildly expressive face.

"Aye, you may be right," Farrow replied. "But that doesn't mean it will be you. Keep your head."

The scent of spiced meats flooded my nose. I glanced farther down Cross Street. Food stalls, market vendors, and game stands were ready for tonight. The festival kicked off the celebratory events. A city-wide Cornucopia followed the festival to foster community. Shortly after that was the Presentation. When those Selected went to the Oldwood Mine and were shown the adamas they would receive. If the Selection Festival and Cornucopia were for the city, the Presentation and Masquerade Ball were for the Blessed. These were events to welcome the soon-to-be Blessed into their ranks.

The King's Blessing concluded the celebrations. This was

done behind closed doors in the castle throne room. Few were privy to it—as Jeweler to the Blessed—I would be.

"Were you talking to the king's advisor?" Macen asked as the conversation with the other miners fell into a lull. I was genuinely caught off guard.

"He just wanted me to get away from the steps. They were setting up for the stupid festival." I wasn't sure what Macen had seen, but my response was plausible enough.

"Stupid?" Jasper turned again, inserting himself into our conversation. Farrow glanced at me, likely gauging my reaction. Whatever he saw on his face had him nodding his approval to Jasper's continued interruption. "Do you not like the festival? It's the Selection!"

I wasn't sure how to answer that. Farrow came to my aid. "Not everyone enjoys packed streets and mingling with the Blessed, kid."

"But that's the fun of it!" Jasper said. "We mix and mingle like we're the same."

"It's not all mingling with the Blessed," Macen replied. "Sometimes it's good to outnumber them. Show them they won't be able to take forever."

Farrow guffawed, echoing my earlier words, his tone just as hushed. "You do sound like one of the Feared."

"Maybe they have the right idea. Maybe the Blessed can no longer hide behind their magic gems." His words were finally hushed as he spoke proudly of something only rumored.

Farrow turned, his mouth opened and closed in momentary speechlessness. He licked his lips as if finally deciding on a response. It sounded like an elder scolding a child. "Don't let others hear you talk like that."

I tended to agree with Farrow's assessment but wasn't willing to engage in this conversation with Macen. His mind seemed made up. If he were one of them, did that mean the rumors were true? His speech made it sound like the Feared had gotten their hands on adamas gems.

"I'll say what I believe," Macen said.

I ignored them as I considered the implications. Adamas was rare. Even if the Feared had one gem, what could they do with it? What was one magic wielder against a ruling class of hundreds? I didn't have time to consider it now, reminding myself I had too much to do before tonight's festival.

Farrow started to respond. I jumped in quickly. "I'll see you all later."

I left before anyone could object. Farrow engaged Macen deeper in their argument. I wouldn't waste more thoughts on whether Macen had joined the Feared. His dangerous choices weren't my problem. At least, that's what I told myself as I took the escape.

7

They say he chose his fate, but that rings false. He only chose not to be her champion.

— FROM CHAMPIONS OF KAVIOS

I approached the door to Forest's Edge, my gaze drawn east to the twisted, gnarled branches of the Oldwood visible just outside the Eastern Gate. The sun may be at its peak, but the darkness the trees granted seeped over the unassuming tavern. A stone wall stood between them, but I swore the building looked like the forest itself. Hesitation slowed my progress. I couldn't help but think Alaric kept me away from this place for a reason—maybe it would be just as dangerous for me as the Oldwood. That no longer mattered, I guessed. Mother needed the tonic, and Father had explicitly asked me to collect the youngleaf if Alaric hadn't delivered.

Before my guard was assigned, I'd take care of the tonic.

Then, I'd start searching for Alaric myself. He had a lot to answer for.

I shook myself free of whatever hold the Oldwood had on me and returned my focus to the tavern. There was little else to do but go inside. The youngleaf was my priority, even as something gnawing in my gut said this was my only lead to finding Alaric.

The heavy door swung open as I grabbed for the handle. A large, burly man stumbled out as though shoved. I sidestepped, giving him space as I glimpsed the adamas ring on his finger.

I was surprised to hear a woman's voice inside the door. "No sampling. This is strike one. Don't come back until you learn to behave yourself."

"But Ava ..."

Finally, something was going my way. Alaric's visitor said Ava was worried about Alaric. He'd mentioned her more than once. She was the one I needed to speak to at Forest's Edge.

Ava must not have been impressed with the man's excuse. The next thing I knew, he grumbled something unintelligible and stomped away. I stepped forward, eager to see who had easily thrown such a large man out of the building. She wore no adamas. I wasn't sure if she hid it or if that was natural strength that had tossed the patron out. Her sleeveless tunic showed medium brown skin and toned biceps, so I decided it was natural strength. With arms crossed over her chest and a knot of dark hair messily styled atop her head, she raised an eyebrow as my gaze met hers.

"We don't do virgin sales," she said.

I wanted to look over my shoulder, wondering who she was speaking to, but she was staring straight at me.

Her voice gentled. "You'll have to go elsewhere if you need money. We can't help you."

I froze as her words registered.

Virgin sales. Did she think I was ... trying to auction my virginity to the highest bidder? My cheeks heated. I wasn't even a virgin! The last thought was slightly irrelevant as I had no intention of offering myself for service, but it flitted through my mind anyway, along with too many other tangents to count.

I opened and closed my mouth, trying to find a reply.

"I'm not ..." I tried. "That's not why I'm ..." I couldn't even get the words out. My inability to refute her assumption only helped her case. I cleared my throat and straightened my spine for a final attempt. "You're Ava?"

Something changed in her face, though I couldn't name it. It didn't soften precisely, but a new curiosity crept across it.

"Who's asking?"

"I'm Alaric Sare's niece."

For a split second, she froze. One hundred emotions flitted across her features, but she quickly masked them.

I dropped my voice. "Do you ... Do you sell youngleaf?"

She glared at me. "I don't, and if the seller were here, he'd say he doesn't do virgins either." Her head tilted to appraise me better. A smirk raised her lip as she toyed with me. "Though he might make an exception for you."

My cheeks flushed again. I gritted my teeth. "I'm not here to have sex with him. I'm here to talk to him."

She shook her head. "You should leave. You don't belong here."

I looked over her shoulder. I definitely couldn't get into the tavern without her agreement. If the seller was the guard, he wouldn't be here anyway. I needed information, though—information I was sure she had.

Given that I still had hours before a guard would protect me, I didn't want too many people to know of my new position or that Alaric was missing. But something about the way Ava had frozen at his name—about the way Alaric's visitor had weaponized her to change Alaric's behavior—I hoped she could be trusted.

I couldn't leave without the youngleaf, so I didn't have much of a choice.

"Do you know where Alaric is?" I asked.

The smile playing on her lips from our prior exchange faded. Any evidence of laugh lines at her eyes disappeared at the implication of my words.

She sidestepped, gesturing me into the building and pointing to an empty seat at the bar. "You'd better sit down."

I'd heard consent for taking was enforced in Forest's Edge, but I kept my guard up as I entered. Serena claimed the owner's line was, "Why take when most will freely give?" They must be serious, as I'd seen with the man tossed out. How Ava, who didn't appear Blessed, could control them was another question, but my logical side said it was good for them too. If this place was somewhere Blessed could reliably go to take from willing citizens, none would risk it by breaking their rules. And if someone did break the rules, like the man Ava had thrown out, surely no one else would risk their taking ground to defend him.

I sat as instructed while Ava tended to those waiting for drinks. The center of the room was open with wooden tables and chairs. It looked unimpressively like any other dining establishment. I scanned the corners, where curtains hung over more plush seating. One of the alcoves had the curtain pushed back, exposing the leather chairs and long couches. I could only imagine their uses.

Another alcove had sheer curtains. Though the pair within the space were unidentifiable, the act they performed was clear. One partner lay sprawled back on a seat long enough to hold their body. The other partner was on their knees, face bent between the former's legs. One of the two must be Blessed because even from where I sat, the rapidly flashing orange light of the adamas stone was evident. One of the partners collected lust. It might be widely available here, but lust's power to heal almost any wound was one Blessed liked to have stored.

I shifted in my seat as my mind roved to the other stories Jasmine and Serena had shared about this place. What would it feel like to have a Blessed take my lust? The memory of forest green eyes boring into mine through the mirror yesterday sent an inferno rushing through my body.

Sliding off the stool, I stood, if for no other reason than to stop my apparent squirming. I needed to collect the youngleaf for Mother's tonic, learn what I could about Alaric, and get out of here—quickly.

Ava interrupted my spiral, sliding me a cup of coffee. I was momentarily stunned by the gesture. My regular cup at Alaric's had been forgotten. Drinking coffee wasn't uncommon in Kavios, but she passed it with a confidence I couldn't help but question.

"It's rude to stare," she said, noting my perusal of the room.

"I doubt they would have picked the sheer curtain if they didn't want someone to watch."

"Touché." Her lip twitched, fighting a smile.

I held up the mug. "Thank you."

She nodded and turned to help the next customer. Every patron was served in moments, and there were no complaints or questions about what they received, though I didn't hear any of them order. I couldn't tell if Ava was that good or if the patrons feared her so much that they didn't question what she delivered.

Finally, the line quelled, and she disappeared through a

curtained doorway behind the bar. Anticipation prickled my skin.

Ava returned with a frown on her face. Her lips pressed together in thought.

"Everything alright?" I asked.

"He's not at his workshop?" I didn't need her to clarify whom she meant.

"No."

She glanced up and down the length of the bar, determining who could overhear us. "Who knows?"

I wasn't sure how to respond to that. "Everyone will know tonight. You haven't seen him?"

She shook her head. "The seller isn't here either."

"But my uncle didn't come last night?" I needed to confirm this.

Her head shook again. "I should have known ..." She glanced at the ceiling. If I had to guess, I'd say she blinked back tears.

I bit the inside of my lip, waiting to see what she'd say next.

Snippets of Alaric's conversation with the visitor flashed through my mind. He'd made it sound like the herb was waiting for Alaric. Ava was waiting for him. I could try that angle. All that mattered was that I left with the youngleaf.

"Do you have what I need? My mother can't wait."

Her hand moved to the pocket of her apron. I had a feeling the vial with the herb was there. I laced my fingers on the counter, trying again to find an outlet for my nervous energy. Ava may not wear adamas, but she held a different power. She knew I needed something she had.

"Do you have any idea where he is?" she asked.

I shook my head.

Her eyebrow raised again as when she'd first evaluated me

at the door. "You just came to collect this for him, though he's told me not to let you into this establishment?"

I shouldn't be surprised by that revelation. She'd only let me in when she realized he was missing.

"He'd want me to take care of Mother first."

A brief flash of concern crossed her face, leaving me to wonder what mine gave away. Before she could press, someone else emerged from behind the curtain.

"Just give it to her," he said. The man was tall and lean, with blond hair that fell over his eyes and partially covered a scar running down the side of his pale face.

"Soren." Ava turned to the man, hissing his name through gritted teeth.

Soren leaned on the counter in front of me. I stepped back, not liking the way he pushed into my space. He was unbothered, tapping his fingers on the bar top.

He glared at me. "Well, isn't this a surprise? Alaric's niece. Are you like your uncle?"

Hairs raised on the back of my neck. That could mean a thousand things, but somehow, I knew he referred to Alaric's ability to detect adamas.

"Here then." Ava handed me the vial. "Take this and go." She kept glancing at Soren like he was a rainstorm rolling in over the mountains, ready to unleash a downpour on the unsuspecting populace.

"She just got here." Soren's smile made me want to step back farther. I held my ground with Ava and the bar between us. "She hasn't answered my question yet."

"She doesn't have to." Ava's expression spoke volumes. I was suddenly sure she knew Alaric better than I realized—that she was protecting me now—another friendship he'd kept hidden.

"Someone has to. It seems Alaric left key information out."

Soren sounded angry.

"What do I owe you?" I asked, directing my question to Ava. I agreed with her. I needed to leave, though I didn't understand why.

Soren's laugh was hollow. "What do you owe us? How about some fucking honest answers."

Ava put her hand on his chest, pushing him behind her as she stepped back into my line of vision. I sucked in a breath. Something about the way his anger radiated made him seem volatile. The visitor and Ava may be friends of Alaric's, but it was clear Soren was not a fan.

"Alaric is settled for this one," Ava said.

Soren laughed again, though he didn't interrupt.

I needed to get out of here—but I also needed to plan for the rest of Mother's pickups. "What about his regular deliveries? I need them. It will be hard for me to get away."

I'd said the wrong thing.

Soren's rage flashed across his face in a display that would have had Blessed reaching for him to take. "And we deserve the truth. Not to hear our suspicions proven by a girl who has no idea what she's stepped into."

The city would soon know I was replacing Alaric as Jeweler to the Blessed, but my pulse beat faster as I considered Soren's anger. Was I in danger? I took a deep breath, reminding myself I'd have a guard shortly. This man couldn't intimidate me. It wasn't my fault Alaric had left me in the dark.

Ava's brow raised again. Something in her face looked less welcoming than before. Like she, too, was disappointed with the revelation that I might be like Alaric. "We can't settle that now. You'll have to come back."

My gaze focused on Soren pacing behind her. Whatever he thought he knew from our encounter, I didn't like it. He turned quickly, giving me a final glare, and tore behind the curtain without another word.

“What if I can’t?” I asked.

“I’ll tell the seller you were here.” She glanced over her shoulder as Soren disappeared. The worry in her face gave me pause, but her words gave me even more. “I’m sure he’ll find you.”

8

I know he searches for her. I'm just not sure what he'll do when he finds her.

— ALARIC SARE'S LETTERS TO ISABELLE ARKOVA

With no leverage to speak of, I had to accept that the seller would find me.

I entered Alaric's workshop and focused on concocting a dose of the tonic with the current youngleaf supply. Once Mother had this, then I could worry about another batch. Even I realized the foolishness of trying to plan when it felt like the world was still shifting under my feet.

Alaric could return before then.

I shook my head at my own naivete. Parting the curtain, I strode to the workstation. Again, Alaric's visitor crossed my mind. He had been fixated on Alaric's pickup yesterday. Based on words alone, the man seemed no stranger to violence. Would he have done something if Alaric hadn't come? I dismissed the thought just as quickly. If Alaric was his customer, he wouldn't have a reason to hurt him. Then, Soren's anger flashed through my thoughts, confusing me further. Could Alaric's visitor have been just as angry?

None of this made any sense.

The shop was the same as it had been this morning. I was unsure what I expected. It seemed Alaric's dangerous friends and foes were at Forest's Edge, and if I were to trust my gut, I'd say Soren and Ava learned of Alaric's absence from me. They would have had no reason to search the shop previously. Maybe they would have a reason to search it now that they knew he was missing.

I mixed the ingredients for the tonic and left it to steep. It was like tea that way and even had the faint scent of mint, like Alaric's favorite brew.

While I waited, I considered where to search for Alaric. Prince Elias's words knotted my chest. He thought Alaric was gone. I squeezed my hand into a fist, unwilling to accept that. Still, I had no idea where to look. Forest's Edge had been my only lead, and they hadn't known he was missing.

I needed help. Maybe Mother and Father would know something.

Once the tonic was ready, I slipped out the door onto Cross Street to deliver it. I kept my head down and my face hidden. If no one could see any emotion, they wouldn't be interested in trying to take from me. Not more than a few blocks from Alaric's workshop, the red glow of an adamas gem caught my eye.

"Incoming!" a man shouted.

Someone flew through the air across the packed street. People darted and jostled to get out of the body's trajectory. The ring on the Blessed's middle finger glowed a furious red—

fitting, since anger was the emotion used to harness the increased strength he flaunted.

I hoped throwing the man would settle the Blessed, but with the way the ring still shone, I doubted it. There was nothing I could do but get out of the way as the Blessed stalked across the street to his prey.

The man thrown—or, more aptly, the crumpled body—was already in bad shape. It looked like the Blessed had gotten a few punches in before the initial toss. The crowd shifted again, and I tucked myself in the nearest alley to avoid the fray. I pulled at my gloves, feeling helpless as the crumpled man tried to crawl away from the Blessed.

This wasn't a taking gone wrong—it was worse. I searched the street for anyone who might intervene. Many stopped on the side of the road to watch as it became clear this was an altercation. A few scurried by, hoping to avoid whatever was about to happen.

No help for this man then.

The Blessed grabbed the crumpled man's tunic, lifting him and pulling his fist back for another hit.

"This will teach you to try and take from us."

Another ugly crunching sound filled the street. I winced. His nose was definitely broken after that. The man didn't even attempt to defend himself. The Blessed's words didn't make sense. How could one of us take from one of them? Did he mean steal? If so, what an uncommonly foolish thing to do.

"Father, please," a woman yelled from the doorway of one of the establishments. Her long blond hair was more than mussed. It may be the middle of the day, but the robe hastily tied around her waist and the exposed skin at the shoulder and neck cleared up all my questions about what the man had stolen. The door behind her boasted another of the city's less reputable taverns with rooms for rent by the hour.

She was old enough to know better but young enough to risk it. It wouldn't be her paying the price for the indiscretion after all. The poor man being bludgeoned hadn't stolen coin but had the audacity to bed the Blessed's daughter.

Her eyes were red, and tears streamed down her cheeks. I couldn't empathize, though, not when she would face no consequences, and the man on the street might not survive.

"Lucinda, get your things and wait for me inside," the man who must be her father called.

A pathetic whine came from the limp body. "Luce ... tell him ..."

The words were feeble, even from where I stood, but it was clear from the horror on Lucinda's face that she heard them. What little color her skin had was gone, and her father turned to face her.

"Tell me what, Lucinda?"

"Nothing, Father. Let's go home. Please, leave him alone." To her credit, she begged, but it wouldn't help her lover.

"Get inside!" her father yelled again.

I shook my head as the woman disappeared. Her father turned back to unleash more wrath on the man hanging from his clutched fist.

"The Feared will have your gem for this," someone called from the crowd.

It was an empty threat. If the rebels were here and could do something to stop this, they would have by now.

The Blessed laughed, dropping the man and giving him a solid kick to the ribs. He didn't seem worried. Something in me snapped as he bent to reach for the man again.

Maybe it was the helplessness of trying to find Alaric. Maybe it was how little I knew about my uncle. Maybe it was fear of what I'd have to do for the royal family in his absence. Maybe it was seeing my own plans destroyed by circumstance.

Or maybe it was the Selection Festival and its stupid hold on this city. Whatever it was, I found myself unable to do *nothing*.

Another magically fueled punch might be this man's end. His only crime was to think a Blessed would treat him with decency.

My defensive training wouldn't allow me to stop the violence. The red glow on the Blessed's adamas ring reflected eerily on the man's already broken face. I couldn't tell if it made his injuries seem worse or if they were truly that bad.

I shuffled nervously, considering what to do. My foot kicked a rock as it jumped and retreated with indecision. The noise drew my attention. Small stones and pebbles littered the dirt-packed streets.

That could work.

With this crowd and the shouted threat of the Feared, it wouldn't take much to tip the scales—for the street to erupt in a brawl.

The people were already volatile. They only needed a reason to loose the shackles of societal restraint. I could give them one.

Causing a riot to give the man time to escape seemed extreme, but at least it was a plan. I wasn't sure he'd be able to get away with his body as it was, but I had to try.

I bent to grab a handful of rocks and pulled my arm back.

"I think he's had just about enough."

I knew that voice.

Maybe I wasn't the only one so affected by it. Hitting all the right notes of authority and severity, it brought the previously lively street to a standstill. I clutched the handful of stones in my grip, hesitating.

I searched the street for the man. He was easy to spot. I couldn't believe I hadn't recognized him immediately in the castle. His broad shoulders parted the crowd as he moved. His hand rested on the sword at his hip. The guard's uniform fit him like a glove, leaving little to the imagination. He was a wall of solid muscle, his breadth tapering to a trim waist. I just needed to see ...

His forest-green glare met mine. He was no longer wearing a helmet. To the crowd, he appeared to rub the scruff on his face casually as he assessed the scene.

Panic flooded me. Did he recognize me? Did it matter? I was not at all sure.

I quickly pulled my gaze from his, deciding how to proceed. The guard didn't have to stop this fight. He could look the other way. His interruption indicated he was here to help. Indecision held my hand.

Chancing another look at the guard's face, I tried to determine his motives. Those brutally green eyes pinched as they found mine again, his gaze flicking to my fist, primed to launch chaos into the street. His glare demanded to know what I thought I was about to do.

"He needs to learn not to pursue those above his station." The Blessed raised his arm again for another punch.

My fist tightened again around the rocks.

The guard pressed his lips into a thin line, and there was no mistaking the brief, sharp shake of his head. His instruction was explicit, but that didn't mean I had to take it.

"I'd hate for word to get back to the king that you were making trouble before the Selection Festival," the guard said.

The Blessed's arm froze before releasing another punch. He turned to face the intruding guard, appraising his large frame.

The command in the guard's tone was the same he'd used on Alaric. His pose was casual, but his body looked primed to deliver violence should he choose to. I couldn't see a glow from an adamas gem on the guard. In fact, I didn't see a ring or pendant at all. That he'd interrupted the fight without its glow was its own signal of strength.

The Blessed must have made the same calculation I did as the red of his ring faded. He dropped the man. "Fine. He's not worth my time anyway."

A group of men quickly swooped in to take the crumpled man away before the Blessed changed his mind.

I sighed in relief and closed my eyes. My heart was still beating rapidly, so I leaned against the brick of the alley wall, waiting for it to calm. Finally, my clenched fist opened, and I spilled the handful of stones back to the street. It was a testament to the stress of the situation that I shut my eyes in the alley long enough for someone to approach.

"What were you going to do?"

That voice.

The words themselves didn't register so much as the disdain. I opened my eyes to find the guard standing a little too close—staring a little too directly. That anger, I had thought reserved for the abusive Blessed, was now directed at me.

I stood quickly and tried to step back, but realized I was already against the alley's wall. I sidestepped to give myself more space.

"Fucking Chaos." He ran his fingers along his jaw again.

I searched the alley over his shoulder to see if anyone was close enough to hear. Alaric had cursed the goddess's name with him yesterday, but this was the middle of the city's busiest district, and even alluding to the second goddess was treason.

"No answer to my question?" His voice pulled my focus.

What question? I was still trying to determine if he recognized me from Alaric's workshop. Or from our run-in at the castle. Or maybe I'd imagined it all, and our gazes locking had not seared into his mind the way it had mine.

I didn't speak, maybe couldn't speak, and he continued.

"Starting a brawl wouldn't have helped." The anger in his voice was still present, but it wasn't the petulant display I'd just witnessed from the Blessed on the street. This was something simmering, something with an unleashed potential I never wanted to experience.

I shook my head, gathering my bearings. "I didn't see anyone with better ideas."

The guard crossed his arms over his chest, the action accentuating the size of his biceps. Every part of me wished I hadn't noticed.

He was trying to intimidate me. I really should be scared. Was he aware of who I was? He might take from me in this alley if he didn't know I was the Glanmore's new jeweler.

Fear should've been prickling down my spine. I was alone and cornered by a Blessed. My immunity still needed to remain a secret, but something about this guard emboldened me. Maybe it was his imposing stature, or the sharp lines of his face, or the fact that Alaric trusted him—that he knew information about my uncle I didn't. Whatever it was, I didn't even consider the knife at my hip. Instead, I pushed my shoulders back with a confidence I didn't truly have.

"Your kind can't be relied upon to help," I said.

His spine straightened. "I did what I could."

That fire that burned through me at the sound of his voice returned as he held my gaze. It was to blame for how I continued to push my luck. "So, he's just going to walk away? No repercussions for his actions?"

The guard's eyebrow arched. "I found saving the man's life the top priority."

It wasn't worth arguing about. The guard had done the bare minimum, which was, unfortunately, more than could be expected of most. Still, I wouldn't thank him for it. He could look elsewhere if he needed his ego stroked.

"I have to go." Having wasted enough time here, I turned to step past him. Mother needed the vial in my bag. My emotions were too volatile to be on the street. He said nothing about seeing me in Alaric's shop or the castle. Maybe he didn't recognize me. That was fine by me. I needed the few more hours of anonymity.

The guard's eyes held mine as I stepped forward. He opened his mouth as if to say something. Sweat coated my palms as fear of being alone with a Blessed caught up to me. The alley wasn't wide enough to pass outside his reach. Finally, my hand twitched near my hip, considering my dagger. I guessed I could defend myself if he tried to take from me. It wasn't a great plan, but other options evaded me.

The guard flinched. My head swung around, thinking something was behind me, but only the wall was there. When I turned again to face him, he'd stepped back, giving me more than an arm's length of distance between us.

I rushed past him, not wasting time wondering why. The street had cleared from the fight, but plenty of people were starting to celebrate. I didn't intend to look back down the alley. The guard let me pass, and I hadn't heard him move to follow. Something turned my head, but I don't think it was my self-preservation instinct.

It might have been the opposite.

The guard's gaze was fixed on his hand. It was balled into a fist at his side, stretching and flexing like he was considering whether to do something with it. The unchecked anger present at the beginning of our interaction was back.

I needed to leave, but something was urging me to stay. I lifted my foot—to what? Take another step toward him? I shook my head at my stupidity, turned quickly on my heel, and fled.

9

She didn't cause chaos. She inspired it.

— FROM CHAMPIONS OF KAVIOS

"Absolutely not," Father said when I told him I started work for the Glanmores tomorrow.

After encountering the guard, I came home to give Mother the tonic. Father arrived shortly after, confirming all the orders we completed yesterday had been collected. Like many other shops in our neighborhood, he closed early for the festival. Initially, we both focused our attention on Mother. She hadn't gotten out of bed today. The tonic's effect was immediate, though. Color sprang to her cheeks as she downed the vial. She sat up before it was drained. We couldn't wait this long again.

Father and I had returned to the family room to make a meal, where I told him about Alaric.

His voice grew quiet. "There is no way you're going to Glanmore Castle. It's the one place she doesn't want you."

I glanced down the hallway to Mother's bedroom. I had been about to question Father's concern, but this made sense. There was no question who the *she* was in that sentence. Even I knew that everything Alaric did to teach me history, to teach me about the world outside Kavios, and to defend myself, was because Mother requested it. Were any of us living our own lives, or were we each doing what we thought she wanted of us?

I paced in front of the fire. Feeling caged wasn't unusual for me, but my day had left me on edge. Alaric always said not to make decisions from a position of weakness, but that was all I'd been doing today.

"We don't have a lot of options, Father. Do you know where Uncle is?"

"He's finally gotten himself killed." Father turned again to look down the hallway to Mother's room.

I sucked in a breath. "You don't know that."

He rubbed his hand through his hair, considering. "You know better than anyone the kinds of contraband he had in the workshop. If someone found them ..."

"No one found the storage room. The workshop was just how Alaric would have left it. No one but myself and Vaddon had been in there."

Father sighed. "If not the books, then chasing down the information within them. He didn't know when to let something go."

I tilted my head, not sure I understood this line of thinking. What from the books was Alaric tracking down? It was just another reminder of how little I knew about him. What did it say about me that even Father, who didn't like the man, had ideas I didn't about his whereabouts?

"What was he researching?" I wasn't too proud to pursue any lead that might come my way.

Father's lip flattened into a thin line as if realizing he'd said too much. His brow furrowed in thought, and then he waved dismissively. "Oh, it could be anything."

"That's not what it sounded like."

He shook his head again. "We can't count on Alaric's return." He ran his fingers through his hair in frustration. "Neither can we have you in the castle."

My hands balled into fists at my side. The weight of the day hung heavy like a millstone around my neck. Alaric was missing. I was dragged to the castle. My journey to Forest's Edge was only a stopgap to the problem of Mother's tonic. The plans I'd so painstakingly made for myself were now out of reach. The near street brawl impressed how volatile the city was. I must have stopped paying attention when I decided to leave.

That all changed now.

"We can't talk about this like it's a choice, Father. I have two options. One, I do what the prince requires. They will assign me a bodyguard. The prince guaranteed the Blessed wouldn't take from me. Or two, I run. I leave Kavios and leave you and Mother to fend for yourselves. You'll have to procure the youngleaf with money we don't have."

He sighed deeply. I didn't dare hope he finally understood the responsibility I carried for this family.

"Let me guess. The prince will also pay you Alaric's salary so we can afford the youngleaf?"

I nodded. "It's the only choice, Father. You have to see that."

"I could go." This was unexpected. Even as Father made the offer, his gaze darted toward Mother's room, and I knew it was an empty one. He couldn't be separated from her. I said the one thing that would free him of guilt for not taking my place. He couldn't do what Alaric and I could.

"They know I can source the adamas."

Father's head hung heavy with my words. "Fine."

When he finally lifted his head, and his eyes met mine, they were resigned. "Go see your Mother. I'm sure she's more alert now."

I held in a sigh. Father and I would never truly understand each other in this. We'd both lost Mother the day the Blessed stole from her. What he didn't seem to realize was that I'd lost not only my mother but also my father. His whole world became caring for her, even at the expense of caring for me. Turning, I strode down the barren hallway to Mother's room.

She was sitting up in bed. "Ember, I'm so glad you're here. Father and I want to go to the festival as a family."

I leaned against the doorframe, wondering how to respond.

"You want to go to the Selection Festival?" I repeated. "Are you sure you're feeling well enough?"

Of course, I had to go, but I didn't think Mother was up for it. She'd been in bad shape only minutes ago.

"It will be good for us. With the wheeled chair Alaric made me, I'll be fine." She folded her hands in her lap, looking down at them. "He's gone, isn't he?" Her voice returned to the dreamier tone I was familiar with. It was hard to converse when she was like this. Part of her mind was elsewhere, and the thoughts between this conversation and wherever else she resided never seemed to connect.

"He's missing," I said.

Her fingers turned white as their grip on each other strengthened.

"Do you know where he is?" I asked. "Where I should look for him?"

Father wasn't sharing what he knew with me, but that didn't mean Mother would take the same stance.

She shook her head. "If anyone can help, it's you."

With Mother's encouragement, we readied the custom chair and walked toward Cross Street. People were everywhere. Groups like ours walked to the festivities, showing more emotion than I was comfortable with. They laughed loudly, and some whispered excitedly of the attack I'd witnessed on the walk home. There were also many theories discussed about who the Selected would be.

Maybe it was my experience with the crowd this afternoon, but the energy of those around us seemed to teeter between frenetic and excited—like the balance between order and chaos in Uncle's books.

The citizens of Kavios felt too much—joy over the idea of the Selection and some anger at their place in this city. And that wasn't to mention lust, which was all too easy to get lost in with places like Forest's Edge. Emotions were high. The city was a powder keg. It might only need a match to explode.

A Blessed bumped into a man in front of us. It was the same act I witnessed daily. Mother must have seen, too, because she reached for my hand as Father pushed her chair. She was unbothered by my automatic flinch in reaction, holding tight to the hand she took. I squeezed back, unsure if she was trying to tell me something or keep me from being bumped into in the crowd.

The march to Cross Street was like that to my own funeral. Each step we took increased the beat of my racing heart. With

Father, I claimed I'd be fine at the castle. The prince said I'd be protected. Nonetheless, this role meant I was in as much danger from the Feared as from the Blessed.

The sun was about to set as we neared the corner of Cross and Centre. Pushing away the weight of the day, I knew exactly where to look. With the castle as a backdrop, Matthew held Jasmine's hand as he took a knee, holding out the ring I'd carefully crafted as he asked her to share her life with him.

It was risky to propose in such an open space, but for whatever reason, the tradition dictated that this corner on the evening of the Selection Festival was lucky. Those who could afford the risk took it.

No matter how much Jasmine claimed to expect the proposal, the look on her face radiated joy. I hated myself a little as I wished she could hide her feelings quickly—before a Blessed chose to interrupt.

Mother's gaze followed mine to Jasmine and Matthew. She gave my hand another squeeze. "Friends of yours?"

I nodded as we turned right onto Cross Street.

"Emberline," Serena called, jostling through the crowd. I let Mother's hand fall, allowing Father to push her chair as Serena fell into step beside me.

Her smile was huge. "You kept your secrets well. Jasmine wasn't sure until the very last minute. Not even as Matthew walked us over to the intersection."

"I'm glad it was a surprise."

"My work here is done." Her slightly slurred words led me to believe she'd started celebrating early. "I'm off to Forest's Edge. You should come! Oh, wait, maybe not."

I tilted my head in question. I hadn't exactly wanted to go, but it was unlike Serena to revoke an invitation so quickly.

Answering my unasked question, she continued. "I was

there this afternoon. The employees were talking about you behind the bar."

The flow of people in the festival area was even trickier to manage than the regular sections of the city. I waved Mother and Father ahead, slowing to talk to Serena as we navigated the packed street.

"What did they say?" I asked. Soren's anger still bothered me. While Ava genuinely seemed ready to help, having an enemy like Soren at Forest's Edge would be a problem since I needed to collect Mother's herbs regularly.

"I only tell you to be careful. They seemed upset with you. Or maybe it was with your uncle? I couldn't tell." Words slipped from her mouth with little care for their impact. "It doesn't matter. Anger was the prevailing emotion. I wouldn't return there too quickly if I were you."

"Thanks, Serena."

She smiled. "Now, I'm off to try my hand at that guard again."

I hoped she knew what she was doing as she bounced toward the Eastern Gate.

The Blessed's white banners waved in the evening's soft wind. Mother and Father were just ahead of me, but I didn't want to push through the crowd to return to their side. I took my time inhaling the scent of the doknots and deciding which stall to purchase one from.

I scanned the packed street. The chatter and excitement of the other festivalgoers were a low roar around me. My life was changing beneath my feet. Serena's news about Forest's Edge had me tense. And on top of everything, I hated being around this many people. It made it impossible to predict the actions of the Blessed.

Colors flashed around me.

I expected the yellow of joy being taken and even the

orange of lust. The festival celebrated hope, possibility, and all manner of dreams. It was easy to imagine how Serena could convince herself tonight was the night—not to be Selected but to finally catch the eye of the Blessed she hoped would take from her. Just as easily, I could imagine a Blessed taking the evening's joy from happy families or couples like Matthew and Jasmine.

Red flashed in my periphery as much as yellow. The red of anger surprised me. It only further impressed what I'd been thinking on the walk over. Kavios was a city on the brink of ... something.

I thought of the shout from the crowd this afternoon. *The Feared will have your gem for this.* They were whispered about in Woodside, but I'd never heard them spoken about so brazenly before the Blessed. Maybe the manic energy in the crowd tonight was their doing.

Passing the alley where I'd encountered the guard earlier, a Blessed woman took from a man. She wore her adamas in a necklace pendant, marking her as important to the king. My brows raised in surprise as the red flash lit up the face of the man she pressed against the wall—it was Macen.

Unsure how it happened, our gazes locked across the crowded street. I tried to look away, but he quickly pushed her back and stumbled toward me. "Emberline!" he shouted as I tried to escape farther into the crowd. The Blessed woman he was with let him go, unbothered by the interruption, and I was not fast enough to slip out of sight.

"Emberline!" he called again. I hoped this wasn't some misplaced guilt. Truly, I didn't care what Macen did with his time. But neither did I want my name shouted down the street, drawing attention. Macen elbowed his way to me. I kept my parents in sight as he slowed with his approach. "I'd hoped to find you tonight."

Not interested in spending time with Macen, I gestured ahead, where Mother's chair was still visible. "I need to catch up with my parents."

He nodded. "I'm glad she's feeling up to it. Let me help you."

The red glow I'd seen on the woman's gem earlier should have warned me that the smile on his face was false. Before I could respond, he began pushing forward with an aggression that matched the harsh light of the Blessed woman's gem.

The crowd split where he shoved through. It took me a moment to realize he wasn't precisely aiming toward my parents.

As he pushed, the crowd pushed back. That wild energy spilled across the mass of people in the street. I wanted to hide in an alley until emotions returned to simple joy, but there was no path out of the fray.

Someone grabbed my wrist.

Fear, pure and raw, shot through my limbs. My gloves were on, but whoever this was had found the slip of skin where my tunic pushed back with the jostling. My vision tunneled in panic, but I couldn't focus on the threat—too many people were around. I didn't feel the pressure of the Blessed's magic attempting to pull what it could not take.

Whether they were Blessed or not, I didn't care. Breaking the hold was my goal, and I twisted and kicked with everything I had.

I just needed to get free.

"Oomph," sounded behind me as the clasp around my wrist was loosened.

Shooting forward, I followed a cleared path down a side street, needing space to breathe. The street opened to another path south of Cross. I told myself I wasn't trapped. No one had me. My head craned, trying to keep an eye on my parents as the crowd in the street continued with an animation that no longer seemed capable of containment.

Macen appeared before me.

I didn't know what he was doing, but I didn't want to be anywhere near him. "I need to go." I turned to walk past him. My parents had slowed, purchasing the snack I wanted from a vendor. Mother tilted her head to look through the crowd for me. Now was the time to get back to them.

Macen blocked my path. "Not so fast. I have some friends who want to speak with you."

I cursed myself for not getting away from Macen faster. The side street may not have been a dead end, but a wall of people filled it as I looked behind me. One of whom I unfortunately recognized: The scar on Soren's face was evident beneath his dark hood.

I stepped toward Macen. "What are you doing?"

He might have set me up, but I didn't think he would physically restrain me. Unfortunately, the group didn't seem to think he would either. More men and women filled in any gaps I could have slipped through to return to Cross Street.

Awareness of the knife at my hip flashed through my thoughts. But at least a dozen people were surrounding me here. I was, once again, outnumbered.

"What do you want?" I asked, my voice shaking more than I cared for.

Soren stepped forward, his voice harsh. "It's nothing personal. We need to cut off the Blessed's adamas supply."

10

The Feared have become a problem. He leashes them, but for how long?

— ALARIC SARE'S LETTERS TO ISABELLE ARKOVA

I knew a threat when I heard one.

The side street felt too small. I was surrounded by those who meant me harm. From what the prince had said that afternoon, these had to be the Feared.

Another thought struck me just as quickly: Soren had known Alaric, or at least, he appeared to. Soren didn't seem to like him, but he'd had dealings with him from my brief interaction at Forest's Edge. Which could only mean one thing: Alaric knew the Feared.

Anger flashed through my growing dread as I found another thing Alaric had kept from me.

I rolled my shoulders back. Right now, it didn't matter why. It only mattered that my life was in real danger. Soren must be one of the Feared, and I had fallen into the one thing the prince had warned me about this morning. Silently issuing my own curse toward Macen for whatever part he played in this, I reached for the dagger beneath my skirt.

Macen leaned forward to stop me, but I elbowed him—hard. He doubled over, breathing heavily as I started to back away from the group. They moved together toward me, but slowly, with a confidence that said there was no way I'd escape.

Keeping my eyes on my opponents, I took careful steps back toward the bustle of Cross Street. I ran into something solid, like a wall behind me.

I flinched. Turning sideways quickly to face this new threat, my head tilted back, and my gaze locked with one of forest green. The dim glow of torchlight made clear that the imposing figure was one I was growing increasingly familiar with. The guard from this afternoon stalked past me. His sword was still sheathed, and his adamas still wasn't visible, but authority radiated from him, even as his movement was stilted. The faces of those on the side street changed with each step, their conviction faltering. As I caught a glimpse of his face, I knew why: his scowl wasn't one I'd forget.

"What are you doing?" he hissed.

Unsure who the question was for, I waited silently. My back faced the stone wall of the side street buildings, and I was unsure who the more significant threat was—the guard or the group that'd learned my identity so quickly and wanted me gone.

The guard glared at the gathered individuals with a ferocity I wouldn't wish on many—but as Soren had threatened me, I'd decided they deserved it. Even though the guard was severely outnumbered, those gathered glanced carefully toward Soren, as if asking for direction.

"You know this is the only way," Soren said.

The guard's hands balled into fists at his side. "I told you she's mine."

Heat rushed through my body even as the breath stole from my lungs at the declaration. When had he said that? How did he know the Feared? I swallowed as I realized any hope I had that the guard didn't recognize me from Alaric's shop or the castle hallway was long gone.

Soren spared a dismissive glance at me. Then, a look of resolute determination crossed his face. "And maybe I don't think you can be entirely trusted with this."

The growl that ripped from the guard would have been enough to terrify anyone else. Soren stood his ground, though I did notice a few of those gathered quickly exited the side street.

"I'll give you one chance." The guard's anger seemed focused on those remaining in the group, but it hadn't been all for them when he'd stepped onto the side street. He prowled forward, the stiff movement of his right leg catching my attention.

Nothing about this situation should be funny. The Feared wanted me dead—worse, they'd found me with annoying ease. This guard knew them, but also seemed the only one intent on me leaving this street unscathed. I was at a mental breaking point for the day, unable to stop the smirk threatening to take over my face at the guard's slow steps. Realization struck. He must have been the one to grab me on the street. My kick had landed. Lifting my hand to smother the tilt of my lips proved insufficient. A giggle loosed, and the intense green glare was once again squarely focused on me.

He stopped an arm's length away from me, like the

distance he'd given me in the alley that afternoon. "This is not funny."

With another step toward the Feared, he put his body slightly in front of mine, placing himself between me and Soren's group. I didn't know why, but my gut said he protected me. It infuriated me even though it was exactly what I needed.

I had so many unanswered questions. But decided they didn't matter at this precise moment. No matter what I did or didn't know about my uncle, I knew he trusted this man on some level. This man helped him with the herbs for Mother's tonic. They cursed openly about forbidden goddesses together. I'd figure out how they knew each other and why Alaric trusted him if he got us off this side street alive. His knack for showing up when I needed him was almost enough for me to regret how hard I'd kicked him—almost.

"I didn't know it was you," I whispered.

It was another mark of his strength that he took a moment to glance at me. This wasn't so much a glare as an assessment. "And if you'd known?" His voice was more wry than angry as he arched his eyebrow, ignoring the group of Feared staring at us.

He may have been pretending they weren't a threat, but I was confident he tracked every movement they made while we spoke.

The mob had lost whatever steam they'd been building when the guard stormed in. Rage still filled Soren's face, but he waited for something.

"I still would have done it," I replied without hesitation.

The guard's face was working overtime to stop his lips from curving into a smile. I thought he liked my answer.

He nodded to the men and women before us, the gruff tone again taking over. "I was trying to help you."

I looked around. We were very much outnumbered. He

seemed to be implying he had known they would be here. My mind flashed to our hallway encounter at Glanmore Castle. This guard must be my guard. He must have been appointed to protect me. It wouldn't surprise me to know Prince Elias had sent him after me sooner than we'd agreed.

Clearly, I needed it.

"It's too late to help her. This is the only way." Soren drew the guard's attention back to him.

He was the only real threat left.

The guard pressed his lips into an even firmer line. "You have no idea what you're doing."

"Do you?" Soren challenged.

His words felt personal. I didn't know the relationship, but like the conversation I'd overheard between the guard and Alaric, it was clear these two knew each other.

"Get out of here while you still can," my guard said.

"He lied to us!" Soren hissed under his breath.

Another voice shouted, entering the side street behind the guard. "Protect the jeweler!"

My guard straightened at the new voice. He pinched the bridge of his nose as he cursed. "Fucking Chaos."

This was all happening fast. My guard's glare snapped between his incoming colleagues and the group of the Feared. I'd say he didn't want to fight the Feared. His threats felt real. I believed he would fight them, but something in the clench of his jaw told me he had been trying to avoid whatever confrontation was unfolding.

My questions stuck in my throat. His relationship with the group, his relationship with Alaric, and confirming his position to protect me would all remain a mystery for now. A half-dozen royal guards moved to flank us.

"Surround her." One of them pointed at me.

My guard's shoulders tensed. He heard the words, but he

didn't turn to look at his colleagues. Instead, he glared at Soren as if waiting to see what he'd do.

Soren made the exact wrong decision. "Grab her!"

Another low growl tore from my guard. "Stupid son of a bitch."

His words were angry, but he looked worried.

My guard turned to me in the seconds before Soren and his group collided with the newly arrived guards. Our gazes held. He seemed to be doing a calculation as the guards neared and the rebels raged forward. He was attempting to communicate something—a message I did not understand.

Then he lunged at me, and my flinch was irrelevant as he pressed me against the stone wall. Heat flooded my body at his proximity. I didn't have time to assess if he touched my skin. My guard shielded me, his body turned to face the clash of wills on the side street, and chaos surrounded us.

11

When his nightmares wake, you'll know he's found her.

— FROM CHAMPIONS OF KAVIOS

Screams erupted around me.

Fear spiked as the firm hand on me, forcing me from harm, dropped. My guard fell to his knees. I turned my head. No one had touched him.

Something pressed against my neck. It was the feeling of a mind magic unable to infiltrate. But no adamas glowed around me.

The rest of the combatants on the street, both Blessed and Feared, were crumpled heaps on the ground. I glanced back toward Cross Street and saw the same there. Some screamed, some twitched, all expressions I could see were drawn in ...

terror. I knew then that all were experiencing their worst nightmares in a way only they could perceive.

Nothing else could cause this display. It was magic I'd previously considered no more than legend, but the bodies on the street proved how incredibly wrong I was.

My stomach should be plummeting at the discovery that stealing fear to wield nightmares was real. Instead, my entire body was alight with it.

This was ... different. It felt good. What was happening? I'd been so scared when my guard lunged for me, believing he touched my skin. I knew it wasn't his intent, but our bodies shuffled as he moved to defend me. For the first time in my life, the guard touching my skin was not the worst thing to happen.

I looked down at him. His knee was bent, his hands were at his temples, and his face pinched like he was in pain. He didn't scream like the others. It was a testament to my guard's mental strength that even as his nightmares caged him, he didn't break.

Nightmare was wielded by collecting fear, a power history claimed could only be used by the Cursed King, a figure, up until this moment, I thought was as much fiction as fact.

The Cursed King was real.

He was here.

He was in Kavios? If Themis's Champion was here, shouldn't he be on the throne?

Finally, I came to my senses and dropped to my knees in case anyone else was unaffected. Standing out was the worst thing I could do. Assessing the scene before me, I didn't see a purple glow anywhere in the darkness. The timing was too perfect to be a coincidence. This attack supported the Feared.

They named themselves after the Cursed King's ability to take fear. I guess I shouldn't be surprised if he were real, he'd help them. But I was still adjusting to the fact that the magic was real instead of being hypothetical text on a page.

The Feared's plan seemed simple enough: take me.

I swallowed. Kill me.

No more adamas for the Blessed.

I hated that it was a good plan.

Scanning the scene on the street again, no one else appeared unaffected. The wielder had to be close. I needed to get out of here before the Cursed King showed his face and finished what his followers had been unable to do.

My guard still knelt next to where I crouched. I couldn't do anything for him. He came after me, even after I'd kicked him. Even when the fight was erupting, he'd tried to shield me. I shook my head. He also told me to get out of there. Well, that might have been a warning for the Feared too. Either way, this must be his job, assigned by Vaddon and the prince. He'd want me to get to safety.

I kept low, crawling on hands and knees off the side street and onto Cross Street.

My mouth hung open. From my previous vantage point, I could tell some on the main street had been impacted. Now, I could see it was the entire festival. Pulse racing, I crawled through the bodies, still not wanting to give myself away. Most were fully curled up on the ground. Few were on their knees. Screams turned into sobs as their minds trapped them, replaying their worst nightmares.

I glanced at the castle balcony, where, sometimes, a blue glow emanated over the city, calming the masses. It was dark. With a power display like this, proving incontrovertibly that the Cursed King was real and not a figure of legend, King Rodric needed to watch his back.

Limbs shaking, I crawled closer to my parents. Mentally, I

began cataloging everything I knew about the hero of Mother's favorite book.

The Cursed King was ... cursed by a goddess. *Champions of Kavios* claimed he was Themis's—Order's—Champion, cursed by Chaos. History didn't detail what curse he carried.

He stole fear, turning it into nightmares. I looked around and had to cover a laugh as I crawled. It was wholly inappropriate, but that piece of information was now uncontested. There was no other explanation for the curled up and screaming masses on the street. No one else at the festival was standing or moving. This attack's reach would be impressive if it weren't so terrifying.

I searched for Mother's chair. It should have been visible now that most people were below its height.

My eyes locked on it, and I crept forward. I was almost there when the twitching body next to Mother's chair stopped moving. Another woman's eyes opened next to her.

The magic was releasing.

They were awakening, and I needed to blend in. I slowed my crawl—almost there.

As the festivalgoers woke, the terror spread. The fear present in their minds permeated this reality. The careful balance between frenzy and excitement had slammed down on the scales, tipping toward panic. Citizens got to their feet and no longer wanted to be anywhere near this place. Some started racing to leave the festival. Some were still crying. The Selection hadn't occurred yet, but the party was over.

As more found their bearings, more raced toward paths that took them away from Cross Street. The wide street wasn't big enough to facilitate a mass exit soaked in nightmare-fueled hysteria. People turned on each other in their newly ignited fear, in their desire to get away from whatever they had confronted in their minds.

I was at Mother's side. Father was getting to his feet. "Emberline." He squeezed my shoulder as the sea of people around us rose and shifted. A mass of alarm turned to a mob of anger as they realized they couldn't get away fast enough.

"We have to go," I said.

Father was still shaky on his feet. I moved to his position behind Mother's chair, gripping the handles to push her. He was almost steady when jostled by another festival goer, dropping one knee on the ground again for support.

I reached to help him back up. "I've got Mother. Can you stand?"

Father didn't answer, only glaring at me as he rested a hand on Mother's chair. I didn't question him further—just started pushing. Elbows knocked, screams and shouts still filled the streets, but we found a path toward one of the side streets connecting Cross with the lower parts of the city.

We were almost to it.

Father's shoulder banged into me—hard—stealing the breath from my lungs. I stumbled, catching myself before I hit the ground, but Father continued to fall.

I had to get him up. People were already tripping over him as they stormed forward. They were past caring who or what was in their way. It was like trying to swim upstream as I reached for him. People surged on all sides, everyone equally affected by the fear, now desperate to escape its reach.

I stooped to lift Father. He was thin, like Uncle, but so much taller than I. His height alone made his mass more than I could lift. My thoughts spiraled as someone else tripped over his ankle. He groaned in pain. I winced, thankful I hadn't heard a crack. All I could do was hope it wasn't broken.

My worry turned quickly to a rage I failed to suppress. I hated everyone around me. Father was injured, possibly unable to walk. Mother was swaying listlessly in her chair, requiring my attention to get her to safety.

Anger was too easy to reach for. My rage at today—at the plan I'd been forced to give up, at the situation I'd been required to accept—bubbled inside me like a kettle about to boil. I resented every person in my way. Hiding my feelings didn't seem so important at this moment. There was too much chaos, too much confusion. Even the Blessed were running scared from the nightmares they'd just experienced.

I had plenty of anger to go around. Anger at this city—at the Blessed—at how citizens were treated. Maybe the Feared wouldn't exist if those without magic were treated with an ounce of dignity. I let it all bubble until the erupting scream was from me as I lifted Father's weight and set him onto Mother's lap.

She grunted, but her arms wrapped around him, keeping him in place.

My pulse was still pounding from the adrenaline, so I pushed the chair forward with both of my parents in it. I ushered us through the side street and back into the safer streets of Woodside.

I shouldn't have been able to do it. Logically, I knew that.

We were in no place for me to question it. So I pushed. The farther we got from Cross Street, the more exhaustion replaced the throbbing anger. The crowd thinned significantly with each block. As my rage depleted, so did my strength. Unable to move the chair another inch, I crumpled to the ground as I should have when fear struck the festival.

"Emberline." Father turned when the chair stopped its forward progress. He pushed himself off Mother, hopping on his good foot as he tried to see where I was.

My breaths came rapidly. I chased each one with another, hoping the next breath would slow my heart's rapid beat. I swallowed, giving myself a moment. This was no different than my calming exercises when my emotions spiked.

Except—I'd lifted my father, a man a foot taller than myself. I'd pushed him and Mother through multiple streets. Things I really shouldn't have been able to accomplish—a strength I didn't know I had.

"At least you listened this time," a familiar gruff voice came from above me. It sent ice down my spine, but it was a balm to the hot wrath flooding me moments before.

My guard had found us.

I didn't know this man—I didn't know his name, didn't know what he wanted, but I couldn't deny the relief flooding through my body at the sound of that voice. Maybe it was just the adrenaline. I hoped that was it as my guard assessed Father's ability to walk.

"I'm fine. Let me see my daughter." Father waved him off and peered around my guard's bulky frame.

My breathing had returned to normal as the guard stepped aside. Father helped me stand, seeming to accept that I was uninjured. He looked like he'd say something—ask questions, but then he turned and shot an angry glance over his shoulder at my guard.

Father's glare went unacknowledged. My guard had already taken a position behind Mother's chair. His hands gripped the handles tightly, the knuckles turning white. He was pushing it forward before I could protest.

My guard gestured with a nod to Father. "Don't argue with me. Help him."

Father still limped heavily from whatever had happened to his ankle. My guard's stiff movement from earlier appeared to be gone.

It was indisputable that Father needed support, and whatever unknown strength had rushed me to get us away from the festival was gone. I didn't think I could push Mother and help Father if our lives depended on it. As much as I didn't want help from a Blessed—we weren't in any position to turn him down.

This was becoming an unwelcome pattern.

"Fine," I said.

Father turned to me in surprise. "You're letting him push your mother?"

"We don't have a lot of options," I said.

Father glared at my guard. "Who is he?"

My guard opened his mouth to ... what? Introduce himself? It didn't matter right now. We had to get off the street. "He's a friend of Alaric's."

Father glared at me this time, unimpressed with the information.

"His hands are on the handles." I nodded toward them. "Keep them where we can see them, and we won't have a problem."

It was an empty threat. Neither Father nor I could stop my guard if he wanted to take from Mother. But my guard kept pushing, only pausing to ask me for directions.

We eventually made it to our apartment building in Woodside. Father and I lifted Mother to the foot of the stairs. She shook nearly as much as Father did. With his hand on the rail, Father looked as if he'd try to hobble up the stairs with her. I didn't know if they could make it.

"I have to put the chair away. I'll be right back."

My guard followed me to the storage space around the corner.

"How did you get out of there so quickly?" he asked.

"I thought you were impressed with my ability to follow directions?" I said, deflecting. "Guess that didn't last long."

I was banking on the night's chaos to explain my quick escape. He still had a haunted look that made me think he bought it.

He closed his eyes, and his nostrils flared. It was a familiar move—one I used to calm myself regularly. I almost sympathized, but I knew we were still in dangerous territory no matter how much he'd helped me today.

I may have acknowledged his friendship with Alaric to appease Father, but I still didn't know how much my guard knew. It was likely he was the guard Prince Elias and Vaddon had chosen. He'd shown up when I needed him. I had to assume he had a reason.

A small part of me didn't want to ask.

It would have been nice to think someone was looking out for me in this city, but that was not my reality. And Alaric taught me never to shy away from questions.

"Did you know who I was before the other guards arrived?" I asked before I could think better of it.

I was unsure if I imagined it or if a wince crossed his face. It was gone as quickly as it had come. "Yes."

The reaction made sense, given that Prince Elias had my guard follow me before the agreed-upon time.

"I was unsure you knew who I was," he said.

Really, I still didn't, but I was too tired to clarify. When I turned from parking the chair in the storage space, my guard was closer than he should be. The prince said I'd be protected from taking. Did my guard know that?

I should step back—should put more distance between us. He hadn't moved his hands from the handles on Mother's chair the entire walk back, but both hands were free now.

For some reason, I wasn't as worried as I should be.

"Are you ..." I didn't know what to ask. Was he my guard? "Are you mine?"

Immediately, I was thankful for the dim lighting of Woodside. My cheeks flamed as I heard the words come out of my mouth.

I cleared my throat, stammering to correct my point. "I mean—"

"It looks that way."

I could barely hold his gaze. There was ... a revulsion there. It was gone before I could question it.

"I was assigned as your personal guard," he said.

"The prince saw fit to have me followed? Even though we agreed I could have until after the Selection?"

My guard folded his arms across his chest. "Not to split hairs, but you should be thankful he did."

I couldn't help my glare. He might be correct, but I didn't have to like it. I felt myself growing in confidence with each sentence we exchanged. The arm's length he kept between us helped.

"What do we do now?" I asked. "The festival didn't exactly go as planned. Do you have to take me to Glanmore Castle?"

I didn't want to go but wondered what he'd say. He had little reason to lie about being assigned as my guard, but I still only had his word that was why he was here. I'd rather hear it from the prince or Vaddon.

He shook his head. "No. The streets are still a mess. You're safer here tonight." He pinched the bridge of his nose again. "We'll go in the morning. I'm sure Elias will want to expedite the festivities. He won't risk the Blessed looking weak in light of ... everything."

"In light of the Cursed King's little tantrum?" I filled in the blanks for him.

His laugh was rich but sharp, like I'd caught him off guard.

In another situation, I might seek to draw forth the sound as often as possible.

"Exactly."

"I didn't think he was real." I wasn't sure why I admitted it. Maybe because of the way he laughed at the statement.

"I'm sure you're not the only one. King Rodric honors Themis a little too well, making everyone forget he's not her champion."

"Everyone will remember now." As soon as the words were out of my mouth, a blue light in the distance caught my attention. Fear raced down my spine. We were far from the castle, but I knew what this was. In the darkness, the blue glow was visible even from here. It was what I'd searched for on the castle balcony amid the Cursed King's attack.

My guard arched an eyebrow as the glow strengthened. I didn't like the warmth spreading through my limbs at my guard's proximity. The rapport was too familiar. I didn't know him. He knew Alaric, but Alaric hadn't seen fit to trust me with any information about him. My emotions flowed too freely in front of him.

And he was still Blessed—no matter how much help he'd been.

Now, the way he glared between me and where my gaze locked on King Rodric's balcony made me wonder if he was aware of how the king calmed this city. Most under the influence didn't seem to realize they were.

The blue light identified the calming magic King Rodric wielded. Though the opposite of the nightmare magic used tonight, its impacts could be just as harmful. Those affected only paused momentarily before continuing their lives in a slight stupor. It made those it touched forget their fears and worries, along with their hopes and dreams.

I couldn't prove it, but I was convinced this magic held the citizens complacent in this city so stacked against them. It made the life they led here not seem so bad.

Not having felt the magic at the base of my neck, I knew it hadn't reached us yet. I realized too late that I shouldn't stare so openly at the blue glow. As a magicless human, I shouldn't be able to see it. I still had so many questions for my guard. Questions about Alaric, the youngleaf, the Feared—but this night had been too long, and I didn't want him to question me, and I had absolutely no desire to fake the calming magic's impact. If my guard wasn't lying, I'd see him in the morning anyway.

"I have to go. My parents need me."

He kept his arms folded into his chest, giving a final glare between me and the direction of the blue glow as I jogged back to the staircase to help them.

12

I have to save him. He grows weak down there.

— ALARIC SARE'S LETTERS TO ISABELLE ARKOVA

I didn't want to face the day. Getting up and going to the castle meant Alaric was still missing. It meant everything that happened yesterday was real. My plans to leave the city were indefinitely on hold. I was now Jeweler to the Blessed. Sourcing the adamas and crafting the gems that would granted the Blessed power were my responsibility, and because of that, my life was in danger from the Feared.

I could lay here a bit longer.

Staring at the ceiling, I thought about the history of the Cursed King.

The heart of his story was defiance. He railed against the fate he didn't choose. Those summoned by Themis were required to be her champion. In books forbidden in this city, one could learn that Themis's sister, Eris, also chose a champion.

Her champions were granted choice.

It was said Eris's Champion came first. She wanted someone to challenge the order Themis had imposed.

From there, it had become a game of thrones across the continent. Which kingdom worshiped which goddess? Kavios was one of three. There was a time when Themis was the only goddess worshiped in all of them. Eris had changed that.

In Linia, the kingdom I'd planned to escape to, a descendant of Chaos's original Champion still held the throne. Hence, information on both goddesses was more freely accessible. I believed Aven, the third kingdom, worshipped Order like Kavios.

All I knew of the Cursed King from Alaric's texts was that he fought his fate. I wasn't sure if he didn't want to be Themis's Champion or didn't want to be told what to do, but whatever he did—attempting to make demands of a goddess ensured his curse.

I wondered how much the rest of the city would fear the Cursed King's presence and the power that came with it. King Rodric's calming magic had overtaken my parents on the staircase last night. Afterward, they had seemed almost unbothered by the evening's trauma. Father's ankle was still in bad shape, of course.

The Cursed King's magic had been used in service of the Feared at the festival—to get them away from a fight they might not have won. The more I considered it, the more I decided the power could challenge the Glanmores and the Blessed if the Cursed King chose.

I swallowed thickly as my thoughts found the necessary conclusion. If the Cursed King supported the Feared—would his considerable power aim to remove me? He hadn't made himself known last night, or tried to end me while I should have been incapacitated. I didn't know what to think. With no purple glow in sight and no one else that seemed unaffected by the magic, I had no idea who he was.

I pulled the blankets back over my head. Maybe if I hid, none of it would be real.

Yesterday had been a disaster.

The only good thing to come out of it was that I'd have access to the Glanmores search for Alaric. I needed to find out what they were doing—where they had already searched. My position afforded me information, and I would use it to find my uncle.

I also needed to understand where my guard stood. Alaric trusted him, but I wished I knew why. We'd need to discuss the youngleaf for Mother's tonic as well. Hopefully, our conversation wouldn't backfire like mine with Soren had at Forest's Edge.

The Feared had known my guard. I'd even say they'd been afraid of him. What was his place with them? If he was the youngleaf seller, as I suspected, he must cross paths with them regularly. Why would a Blessed work with the Feared, though?

I needed to know if he was a danger to me or if he'd protect me as his new duty demanded.

This was no longer a productive distraction. I guessed that meant it was time to get out of bed. Besides reporting for duty at the castle, my priority today was to search Uncle's workshop for clues to his whereabouts.

What had Father said ... *Lost on a quest from one of his books.*

At least I knew where to look.

With that, I threw back the covers. I might as well get started.

There was no argument that morning as I left. Father's ankle was swollen, and he was using a walking stick we had for Mother to help keep pressure off it. I stopped by Jasmine's apartment before I departed. Her mother was a healer, and she'd been known to care for those in the building when required.

"You kept me in the dark." Jasmine's teasing smile as she opened the door told me I wasn't truly in trouble.

"You wouldn't have wanted it any other way."

"I know." She wrapped her arms around herself, still smiling, floating on the high of her engagement. At least she didn't appear to have lingering effects from any nightmares at the festival.

Not wanting to bring her down, but knowing I had to depart, I pulled her back to reality. "Do you think your mom can check on my father today?"

"Sure. What's wrong?" Her question must have reminded her of everything she—or the king's calm—buried from last night. "Was he hurt in the ..." She didn't know how to finish the sentence.

Neither did I. I nodded, though. "I think he sprained his ankle when we tried to leave."

Her eyes widened. "I'm so sorry. Yes, of course, Mother will stop by. I didn't realize. Matthew and I snuck away after the proposal. We felt the ..." She stared into the distance. "Well, we felt the magic but avoided the mobs trying to escape Cross Street."

"I figured." I caught her eye to reinforce the truth in my words. "I'm glad you weren't there. No one could have helped."

Her face looked haunted. I didn't think it was over Father's condition. Whatever nightmare she'd seen last night must be resurfacing. I wondered how well King Rodric's calming magic had worked on the rest of the populace.

"Thank you. I have to get going."

She nodded.

I forced a smile. "Congratulations again."

Turning from the door, I left to start my new position. I may have escaped last night's nightmare, but I was living a different one.

Given the chaos unleashed during the festival, I couldn't imagine the prince would be in good spirits. I wasn't sure it was wise to try to enter the castle—at least not without my guard. Last night had been so eventful, I'd not bothered to ask where we should meet or how this would work.

My best bet was Uncle's workshop. I could start my work for the Glanmores and spend more time searching Alaric's things.

The closer my footsteps brought me to Cross Street, the more utter disarray surrounded me. Booths were tipped over, some destroyed, and garbage was scattered everywhere. I shouldn't be surprised. It was still early. No one would have had time to clean up. I was sure the guards had spent most of the night searching for the Cursed King.

The stage where the future Blessed were to be presented was still erected at the foot of the castle steps. As I walked by, I let out a breath and wondered what the Glanmores would think of all this. In all the chaos, I doubted they had apprehended any of the Feared.

I unlocked Uncle's workshop and walked inside. As I entered, I bit my lip—it was how I'd left it yesterday. It might seem silly, but my first order of business was watering the plants. I'd skipped it yesterday. When I pressed my fingers into the semi-damp soil of the Oldwood, the dirt's heat was as familiar as it was unsettling.

How long before they sent me through the Oldwood to the mines?

Unsure how long I'd have before someone came searching for me, I didn't dare open the storage room. The drawer under Alaric's workbench held his current projects. He had started the ring bands for the Selected, but without their identities, he hadn't sized them. At least I could confirm my assumption about our adamas reserves.

Uncle wasn't one for inventory. When I couldn't find an adamas stone, I dug through the papers up front. I swore there had been one here two days ago. This only meant I'd have to go to the Oldwood Mine sooner rather than later. I was a little ashamed of the thrill that thought sent through me. Secretly, I'd always wanted to know what the sourcing part of the process was like. I swallowed, thinking about what I'd signed up for with the Glanmores. I knew I could find adamas in the mines, shaping it to wield magic would be a different test. We'd have to cross the bridge at some point.

I tapped the end of a quill against my cheek as I made my list, trying to remember when Alaric last spoke of traveling to the mines. His visitor—my guard—said he'd been seen leaving the Eastern Gate two nights ago. Why go that way if not for the mines? I shook my head. Alaric had whole swaths of his time that I didn't understand. I couldn't make any assumptions.

"What are you doing here?" a guard called from the doorway, interrupting my thoughts.

I glanced up, noting the uniform, but knew it wasn't my guard by voice alone. That should probably have been more concerning, but I let it slide.

"I'm trying to organize Alaric's things. Prince Elias wants me to take up his work until he returns."

Another guard filed in behind the first, and they gave each other a suspicious glance. "How did you get in here?"

The second guard's gaze raked over me from head to toe. It wasn't lingering, but it was certainly uncomfortable.

"As I said, I'm the new jeweler until Alaric returns. I have a key." I reached for the key from my satchel, which I'd set down on the counter.

The guard halted me. "Don't move!"

I might be in trouble. As quickly as news had spread to the Feared that I was the new jeweler—these guards seemed in the dark. And I bet they were on edge from last night's chaos.

I raised my hands in a gesture of peace. "I was just going to show you the key." I pointed to my bag. "I'm here on Prince Elias's orders."

"Sure you are," one of them replied.

I didn't need his mocking tone to know he didn't believe me.

"Ask my guard." The words flew out of my mouth before I could think them through. I winced at how dumb it sounded. Opening my mouth to try again, I silently cursed myself for not asking my guard's name last night.

It hadn't seemed important in light of...everything else.

One of them laughed. "Your guard?"

I held my hand above me to estimate his height. "He's tall. And broad." I was rambling. "He has dark hair and a strong jawline, not clean-shaven like the rest of you."

I was happy my brain had finally latched onto a distinguishing feature. Regrettably, I was less happy when my guard strode through the door next, looking precisely as I'd described him.

He did nothing to hide the smirk on his face.

I silently cursed myself again, wondering how much he'd heard.

Any amount was too much.

"This description is getting good." His voice filled the room. "Please continue to wax poetic about my jawline."

His hand moved to his now clean-shaven chin, his finger and thumb tilting it slightly to highlight the angle. "I'm sorry to disappoint. I do have to be presentable with my new assignment." He held my gaze, my cheeks heating in embarrassment. "But, personally, I like the sound of *my guard*."

So, he'd heard all of it then.

I wanted to crawl into the secret storage room to die of embarrassment.

He finally acknowledged the two other guards as he said in a conspiratorial tone, "The possessiveness works for me."

The two guards looked at him, puzzled. "Who are you?" the one on the left asked.

His eyes locked on mine again before responding. "I'm her guard."

"She doesn't have a guard. She's breaking into this workshop," the other said.

My guard took another step toward the duo. I hadn't exaggerated the size of his frame. He towered over the two men. "You're the ones Carver sent to start organizing cleanup on the street, right? Let's assume this"—he gestured to me—"outranks you. I need to escort her to an audience with Prince Elias."

The guards looked chastened at his words. My guard realized that, too, and pressed on it.

"Carver said he'd be out to check on you within an hour. I think he'd want to see more progress than has been made."

My guard glanced out the window at the street through the hanging plants. Some efforts had started in earnest while I was in the shop. But it didn't look like it was progressing very quickly.

"Fine," one said. "But don't let us catch you breaking in anywhere again."

I opened my mouth to defend myself. I wasn't even angry. It was just pure stupidity that needed to be addressed. My guard caught my eye and shook his head.

I sighed, knowing he was probably right. I shouldn't waste my breath. The two idiots left Alaric's workshop, and my guard's gaze roamed the room.

"You look like you belong here," he said.

Was that his way of starting a conversation about Alaric? Should we talk about what he knew? I still hadn't decided if he might pose a threat to me like Soren apparently did.

My guard had defended me yesterday, but why?

Hesitation cost me the moment. My guard's words pulled me from my analysis. "I wasn't lying, Chaos. We need to get you up to the castle. Elias wants to talk to you."

My heart rate sped up at the name. Not the prince wanting to speak with me, but my guard calling me *Chaos*. It was beyond dangerous, but something in my chest thrummed in what I could only describe as anticipation.

"My name is Emberline," I clarified, deciding not to address the heresy of the nickname.

"So it is." His green gaze hit me hard. "Emberline Arkova, niece of Alaric, who he claimed was a talented jeweler and nothing more."

I wasn't sure why, but the words stung. Of course, that's what Alaric would have said about me. He didn't want the royal family or the Blessed to take notice. Maybe since this man was his friend, a part of me had wondered if Alaric had told him more about me. I guess the answer was no.

"And your name is..." I let the sentence hang, unfinished, hoping he would fill in the blank.

He laughed. "You don't know? One would assume Alaric spoke of me."

I shook my head, and I swear he looked ... relieved.

"We've run into each other quite a few times, Chaos. You're only asking now?"

Still, he used the name. Still, my pulse raced at the comparison to the forbidden goddess. "I don't make a habit of learning the names of the Blessed."

He frowned briefly, like maybe he didn't understand the connection. "I think I prefer *My Guard*." The smirk curled his lip again. As much as I wanted to wipe it off, I couldn't deny it suited him. "Don't tell me you didn't ask Alaric who I was after I visited the shop the other day," he said.

I put my hands on my hips. "He didn't think I needed the information. Now it seems like I do, if we're going to keep meeting like this."

His chuckle was warm. "That sounds about right. Call me Hart. Now, we have to go."

The name wasn't what I expected. It suited him as much as it didn't. It was powerful and held no airs of formality. I wasn't sure why I pondered it so intently as I followed him out of the workshop and toward the castle.

13

The Glanmores embodied Order, so why did the firstborn fight the summons?

— FROM CHAMPIONS OF KAVIOS

Hart didn't say a word as we scaled the grand steps of the castle entrance. That was fine with me. I still didn't know what to ask him. Just beyond the doors, Hart stopped to retrieve a helmet. As he pulled it over his head, I found myself loving and loathing the shield from his piercing green gaze. He led with purpose through the cavernous hallways. Yesterday was my first time in the building, and the twists and turns left little possibility for me to find my way unescorted.

We stopped before the large wooden door Vaddon had dragged me through previously. Two guards stood on either side of it.

Hart nodded to them. "The jeweler to meet with the prince."

The guard on the right stepped forward. "We'll take it from here." The adamas glowed green before the guard's following words. "Do you intend to harm the prince?"

The tingle of magic danced across my neck, but the guard's power was faint. I hadn't found a persuasion, calm, or now nightmare I couldn't avoid. This was no different. What little I could see of Hart beneath the visor showed his lips pressed into a thin line in the other guard's direction.

I answered the guard. "No."

The green glow of his ring deepened as he urged a response. "It's alright, you can tell us."

The magic at least pressed against my skin this time. It didn't make a difference. Not that it mattered, but harming the prince wasn't on my priority list. He was maybe the only person I knew who didn't want me dead and claimed interest in finding Alaric.

In the end, the truth was irrelevant. I could speak the answer they needed with a straight face. "I don't mean him any harm."

My gaze met the shadow of Hart's beneath his helmet as the guard ushered me forward. He looked at me with a curiosity I wasn't sure I wanted.

"I'll be here when you're done," he said.

I swallowed and stepped into the room.

"Ah, Emberline." The prince closed a book on his desk and stood from his seat. "Please come in. I'm so glad you're here."

His mood was more chipper than I expected. I reminded myself that Prince Elias was the mouthpiece of the royal family. He finessed messages many would dislike every day. Nothing would get done if he silently stewed about yesterday's events. I shouldn't expect to see his emotions written plainly across his face. Similarly to how I masked my feelings before the Blessed, I'm sure he masked his before ... everyone.

"I'm sorry I didn't meet at the appointed time yesterday." There was no way he expected me, but something about him made me want to explain myself.

He waved me off. "Your guard reported in. I'm glad you made it out of that mess."

I guessed that served as notice that Hart wasn't lying about his guard duties.

"Did you find the one responsible?" I asked.

The Glanmore's position on the Cursed King was unclear. On the one hand, he was a champion of their goddess, which made him the rightful ruler of Kavios, according to Themis. On the other, he appeared to reject that fate and, given his actions yesterday, aligned himself with those who sought to overthrow the Blessed.

"It's nothing you need to worry about, Emberline." He spoke gently, and I heard the exhaustion in his voice.

"I think the Feared already identified me." Hart and I hadn't discussed how much of yesterday he'd reported. I had to believe this was relevant information.

"I'm aware. It's sooner than expected, but it's why we agreed you'd have a guard." Elias gestured toward the door. "Was he to your liking?"

I didn't know how to respond to that. Hart defended me from the Feared. Alaric trusted him, though I still didn't know why. In all likelihood, he was the seller of the youngleaf I needed for Mother's tonic. But I couldn't be blamed for not loving his familiarity with the group that tried to kill me yesterday. Hart had saved me from them, but the connection was ... concerning.

I had no idea if he was to my liking. His piercing glare and stupid smirk crossed my mind, and I stretched and flexed my fingers at my side as if to exorcise the image. I cleared my throat. "Yes, thank you."

"He will be with you at all times during the day. You'll move into your uncle's rooms in the castle. And we'll have other guards stationed outside the door at night."

I swallowed. This was a logical step for my protection, but it did hamper my ability to search for Alaric and sort out Mother's tonics. Neither could be done if I died, though. It was a grim thought, but it grounded me. I'd deal with the inconvenience later.

Expecting no objection, the prince continued. "I wanted to give you the list of orders we have for the Selection."

"Of course. I went to Alaric's shop this morning to look for it without disturbing you, Highness, but I'm afraid I couldn't find it."

He toyed with the gold chain around his neck, holding his adamas pendant, before pulling another paper from his desk. "We need four new pieces and one enhancement." Handing it to me, he continued. "These are the designs for the new pieces. I think Alaric had the design for the enhancement in his book."

I'd have to check it more thoroughly that afternoon. "And ... has there been any sign of Alaric?"

The prince looked at me with pity. "I'm afraid not. The guards have been a little occupied since our last conversation."

I cleared my throat again, a blush touching my cheeks. "Of course."

"We'll continue the search as soon as the Selection is back on track."

He paused as if waiting for me to ask another question. I wasn't sure what. We stared at each other in silence.

Before I knew what was happening, I felt a prickle at the back of my neck. Lost in my own thoughts, I hadn't seen the green glow creep over his pendant. The prince repeated himself, as I'd missed his initial question. "It's alright, you can tell me. Do you know who was responsible for last night's events?"

I tilted my head. "The Cursed King."

No matter the royal family's opinion of him, I didn't think it was dangerous to say what everyone already knew. The magic displayed yesterday made his existence indisputable. I wasn't sure if his question was meant to unearth more, but I was confident my answer would be the same even if I were subject to his persuasion.

His nose twitched at my response like he smelled something foul. "That doesn't help me."

I couldn't blame him exactly. Part figure of legend, now real threat—my answer didn't provide much to go on, but I didn't have anything else.

Unsure how to respond to his comment, I waited for him to continue. He toyed with his adamas again. I guessed I could use this opportunity to see if he had any better luck getting information from the Feared.

"Were any of the Feared captured last night?" None would have been if my suspicions were true, that the Cursed King's attack was intended to create a distraction for them to get away.

The prince's jaw flexed, his teeth clenching as he shook his head. "They escaped."

I may not understand why the Cursed King worked with the Feared, but that seemed evidence enough that he did. Which meant I had even more to worry about. If his goals were aligned with the Feared, it was only a matter of time before he came after me directly.

Hart had almost stopped the Feared in that side street. I couldn't claim he'd hold the same power against the Cursed King.

"The Cursed King is your only answer for me, Emberline?" The prince posed it as a question, but the green glow of persuasion meant he coaxed another answer.

Truthfully, I had nothing else to say. "This is the only answer I know."

Anger crossed his face, there and gone before I could be sure of myself. I stepped back inadvertently.

As if he noticed my hesitation, the hard lines of his face softened. His voice was calm, without a hint of persuasion, as the green light left the room.

He folded his hands together. "I apologize. I'm sure you had a trying evening, and here you are today, starting a whole new set of crucial responsibilities. We are thankful for your willingness to step in. You'll be well taken care of for your service."

His words felt like something slimy and slippery, coating my skin. Years of practice hiding my emotions helped me school my features. "I'm sorry I don't have better answers for you."

I didn't believe the prince's words when he felt the need to guide the conversation with persuasion.

He spread out his hands, palms up. "Let's talk about your work. We will proceed on schedule, announcing the Selected at the Cornucopia tomorrow. You must see them before then to get their ring sizings."

I nodded. I wasn't surprised to hear the prince wasn't changing the scheduled events. Fitting the announcement into the Cornucopia was the smoothest way to keep the celebration on track. The path of least disruption was the obvious path to help the city move past last night.

The look on Jasmine's face this morning, as she remembered her nightmare, was proof the city needed the distraction. Others, with less to celebrate, must be in worse shape. Prince

Elias had his work cut out for him, rebuilding the city's morale —and could only do so as long as the Cursed King didn't unleash his power again.

"I can have them stop by tomorrow. That should give you enough time to settle in. Remember, it's not only the four Blessed but also the one receiving additional favor from the king."

I dipped my head, preparing to leave.

"You'll need to go to the mines."

He'd waited until the end to drop this seemingly offhanded comment. I knew he'd done that intentionally. This would be the first real test of my use to the Glanmores.

I couldn't help but suck in a deep breath. "Today?"

Alaric had refused to speak of his work in the mines themselves. I didn't know what it truly meant for a jeweler to source the adamas. And to get there, I'd have to go through the Oldwood.

He nodded. "I believe Alaric was out of materials."

I couldn't argue. As much as I wanted to go to the mines to learn this part of Alaric's job he'd kept from me, it was also intimidating. I'd passed the prince's test to determine adamas yesterday, but what test awaited me in the mines? And could I even get there, given my latest reaction to the Oldwood?

The prince interrupted my thoughts. "That's not a problem, is it?"

I knew it for the rhetorical question it was and shook my head.

He clapped his hands together. "Good. We need the talent only you and your uncle seem to possess to select the correct pieces from the mine. Then we'll see if you're as good of a jeweler with the adamas as you seem to be with quartz."

Excitement filled me as quickly as anxiety. I knew these tests would come. I'd had little choice but to accept this role and take them as they did. Still, each step was a new challenge. The Oldwood had to be my first focus.

Only days ago, I'd convinced myself I could traverse the Oldwood to escape Kavios. Now that my plans to leave were on hold, I could admit I was unsure of my ability to pass through it without losing myself to its hold.

At least it was early enough that we could return before dark if we left now. I'd have Hart with me, too, though I was unwilling to concede that was a good thing. It would only give him more information about me I wasn't sure I wanted to share.

I swallowed, but my throat was dry. I would have to take this one test at a time.

14

He is pure chaos. He calls to her through the Oldwood.

— ALARIC SARE'S LETTERS TO ISABELLE ARKOVA

I followed Hart through the complicated hallways once more. As eager as I was to learn about where the adamas was mined, I wasn't sure what to do about the Oldwood. To keep to Prince Elias's schedule, I needed more adamas quickly. Delay would not be an option.

Attempting to glare daggers into Hart's shoulders wasn't helping. I needed him to answer some questions before we ventured into the Oldwood together.

"Let's go, Chaos," he grumbled beneath his helmet.

I wouldn't deign to respond to that. We were still in Glanmore Castle—literally the worst possible place to use the goddess's name. He might think it funny, but it could get him killed if the wrong person heard it.

He shook his head free when he removed his helmet at the castle entrance. His chocolate brown hair was knotted at the nape of his neck. He raised a thick brow at me. I must have been staring.

"Does everyone not have their own helmet?"

"Are you picking topics to avoid discussing where we're headed?"

I sighed. "How do you know we're going anywhere?"

He arched his brow impossibly higher, like it was insulting that he wouldn't know our next stop, even if I hadn't realized how quickly it would need to happen.

I'd get nowhere trying to decipher everything in my head. It would only serve to drive me mad. I opened my mouth to ask one of the many questions brewing as we started down the steps.

"Not here," he whispered. Louder, he said, "We do have our own helmets for formal occasions. Mine is in my quarters. So, a few loaners are available when guards unexpectedly have duties in the castle."

"I see."

My heart raced the rest of the way to Alaric's workshop.

Hart stood back as I twisted the key. I drank in the space again as we entered—a space I hadn't had time to continue searching. Hart disappeared behind the gold curtain. I needed time to review Alaric's books in the storage room. Today was out of the question. Getting to the mines and back would take the rest of the daylight. I refused to be caught in the Oldwood after dark—even with a personal guard.

A personal guard who might find the Oldwood's influence on me ... odd. Maybe, more importantly, a personal guard I needed to ensure wasn't planning to kill me.

"How do you know Soren?" I called.

I could have started with Alaric, but that felt *personal*. This question was about knowing whether I was in danger with Hart.

He popped his head out from behind the curtain. "What?"

"The man in the street yesterday. You knew him." I admit there were times when I couldn't tell if he was talking to me or the group, but there was a point at which he spoke directly to Soren. There was no mistaking a familiarity between them.

"I thought I did," Hart said.

"What does that mean?"

"That not everyone is who you think they are. Soren proved that yesterday. I won't let him get that close to you again."

It wasn't exactly an answer to my question, but the determination was, unfortunately, reassuring. I knew I shouldn't let it cloud my judgment.

"It's odd, isn't it? Alaric asked me only a day ago to escort you through the Oldwood." He raised his brow. "I don't think this is what he had in mind."

Of course he did. In mere seconds, he'd overcome both of my objections. Alaric had pleaded with me to accept an escort through the Oldwood with my plans to leave. I didn't think Hart was lying about it. He couldn't have known about the request unless Alaric had discussed it with him.

I shook my head. "He asked ... you? Who are you?"

His lip tilted into a smirk I was becoming too familiar with. "We've been through this." He pointed to his chest. "Hart. *My Guard* if you prefer."

No one could blame me for rolling my eyes. "How do you know Alaric?"

"We're friends."

I clenched my teeth. "I gathered that. How did you happen to become friends?"

"You already know the answer to that, don't you? It'd be why you were at Forest's Edge already yesterday."

This man was infuriating. I assume he meant they became friends through Alaric's need for youngleaf, but I'd be damned if I continued to press for information Hart already thought I had. I wished Alaric hadn't left me so in the dark about ... everything.

"Do you know where he is?"

Finally, Hart seemed to sober. He shook his head.

"Then I'll thank you for not judging my attempts to find him."

He dipped his chin, conceding. "Come on, Chaos. We need to get going to make the return trip before nightfall. Do you need anything before we go?"

He sent my mind scattering with a simple question. My excitement to learn about the process in the mines had overshadowed thoughts of what tools I would need. I may not know precisely what was expected of me, but I could make a few educated guesses.

The miners did the physical work, but they needed my talents to pick the location they mined. I had no idea how potential new spots were identified.

My stomach knotted as I realized I wouldn't require tools. I'd have to do what I hated: trust my gut. No matter how unhappy it made me, my gut instinct was how I'd determined adamas from quartz every other time Alaric tested me. I might as well admit that was how I'd proceed in the mines.

Getting to the mines was another issue.

"Let me grab my tool kit from the back." It didn't hurt to look prepared.

Hart raised his left hand, coming fully into view in the front of the shop. He carried the mentioned kit. "I figured you'd need this."

He continued forward, not stopping to hand me the bag as he headed toward the door.

"I can carry it."

I took the handle from him as he passed. My gloved hand slid against his fingers wrapped tight around the handle. I flinched back, and he released the handle immediately. Moving the bag to my other hand, I stretched my gloved fingers. My breathing was uneven. It was a mark of how careless I'd been in the last few days that I hadn't considered the movement more carefully.

Rationally, I knew he couldn't steal my emotions through the gloves. I even knew the prince had mandated no one take from me. Nothing about this situation was ... safe, but I was protected from my usual fears.

That wasn't the problem. The more important problem was that something about Hart had me disregarding my proximity considerations. They'd been non-existent yesterday when the fight broke out with the Feared. And that didn't contemplate what his voice did to me.

He hadn't moved since I'd snatched the bag. His stillness bothered me. Knowing I was fine, I swallowed but silently reprimanded myself for the judgment lapse.

It wouldn't happen again.

"Shall we go?" I said as cooly as I could, turning on my foot to leave the shop.

"Do you know what to expect?"

My gaze snapped to his. The question surprised me as much as that voice unnerved me. I hoped he never learned how it made me feel.

"I can handle it." I turned again to leave.

"That's not what I asked." He stood in my path. "I have no doubt you could handle anything you put your mind to, Chaos. What I asked was, do you know what to expect?"

Anger flared along with my nostrils. If he knew what to expect, it could only be because Alaric told him—another piece of information Alaric had shared with him and not me.

"We don't have time to waste. I don't want to be in the Oldwood after dark," I said.

We stared at each other for a long moment. In no world was I going to admit to him that I had no idea what I was doing. He had too much information already.

He let out a heavy sigh and stepped out of my way.

I wasn't exactly afraid of the Oldwood—I respected it. Before Mother's accident, we would meet Alaric when he returned from the mines. We would wait outside the Eastern Gate, on the outskirts. Playing hide and seek in the trees and bushes had been one of my favorite ways to pass the time. I was young, but I know I scared Mother the last time we played.

"I'll find you, Emberline," she'd called around a tree.

I was tucked into a hollowed-out log fallen just off the path. She'd never find me here. I was sure of it.

Nestling into the dirt and brush felt ... comfortable. I could stay here all day. Mother searched, and time passed. I burrowed in deeper. The fallen leaves and hard-packed soil were warm. I wanted to sink into them. I pressed the side of my face down, letting the feeling—the heat—surround me.

"Emberline."

Someone whispered my name. The tone was opposite Mother's screech as she continued her search.

"Emberline. Wake up."

It was so comfortable here. The Oldwood was more freeing than Kavios. I wanted to climb onto it and let it fly me away from the trappings of the city. Maybe I had. A distant part of my mind registered that Mother's search became more frantic, that another familiar voice was added to it. That the sun's light was quickly dwindling.

I didn't want to leave yet. The Oldwood was important. It meant something to me.

"Emberline!" The voice was a roar in my head—fierce and fiery. The warmth of the ground now scorched my skin.

My eyes shot open. My head popped up from inside the hollowed-out tree in which I hid.

"Emberline."

"Emberline."

Mother's voice blended with the ferocious tenor. I wasn't sure that both had ever existed.

Something in the present pulled me from the memory: another time, another blending of two voices.

"Emberline."

"Emberline." Hart's voice demanded my attention. The side of my face was pressed against a tree on the edge of the path to the Oldwood Mine. My glove removed, I'd knelt, rustling the leaves and soil to sink my fingers into it.

What was I doing? Had I heard the voice again?

"I guess this is why Alaric thought you required an escort." Hart stood on the forest path. His fingers twitched around the handle of his sword—more than ready to pull the blade from its sheath once he identified the danger. "Everything alright?"

The danger might be only in my head.

That day, I remembered, was the last time Mother had brought me into the Oldwood. When Alaric found me that day, he said I'd been hiding in the woods for hours. Mother had been frantic. Father had been called. No one could find me. They almost went to the guards. That told you how desperate they were—asking the Blessed for help.

As I prepared for my trip, I tried to surround myself with

dirt and plants from the forest, working to desensitize myself to the strength of its call. The Oldwood didn't seem to affect anyone else this way. I glanced at my position, leaning against the tree off the path. It seemed that part of my plan was a failure.

I wiped my hand on my skirt and slipped it back into my glove. "I'm fine."

Hart appeared unconvinced.

That made two of us.

Wandering back to the trail, I needed to focus. While I doubted Hart would let me out of his sight long enough for me to disappear for hours, I didn't honestly know what these woods held. Or why I reacted so strongly to them. Wild animals roamed, and it wasn't unheard of for workers to disappear on the walk to and from the mines. Dangerous predators and fabled creatures crept from the mine tunnels in search of easier prey.

I glanced up, attempting to peer through the thick tree cover. The forest was so dense, I could hardly tell the time. "We should keep moving."

Hart, for his part, didn't press. "It's best to stay on the path."

Like I was unaware. It had never been my intention to leave the path in the first place. I didn't even know what had drawn me into the trees. Still, I couldn't believe he didn't question my behavior. He simply gestured for me to lead, following to the right so he had a clear view of any incoming threats.

"It's a bit of a hike to the Oldwood Mine. Have you been?" he asked.

I was sure he knew the answer, but I played along. "I haven't."

"We'll follow this trail until the fork. Then, we'll head left, where the path curves into the Pinnacle Mountains. The mine entrance is at the base."

How many occasions had he had to trek to the Oldwood Mine? Guards weren't usually required out here. The only Blessed was the mine foreman. None of the other workers had magic.

"Keep the trip short," he continued. "We can't be in the mines for more than an hour or risk returning in the dark."

I didn't like the sound of that. "Should we come tomorrow morning when we have more time?"

He shook his head. "I don't suggest ignoring a direct … *request* from Elias."

The pause told me all I needed to know. Hart didn't believe the charming front the prince put on for the masses, although his perspective may be biased, since I was confident he sold illegal goods.

"We should talk about your trip to Forest's Edge." His voice was louder than I'd grown used to. He was closer than I expected, his mouth beside my ear.

I turned, striking out in surprise.

He caught my gloved wrist before I made contact.

"Chaos, I'm not trying to touch you. I want to talk."

I pushed hard against his grip, and he let me go.

Inadvertently, I took a step back. All the fears I thought I'd quelled in Alaric's workshop came rushing back. We were alone in the Oldwood. I'd already proved I needed him to pull me back from whatever hold the Oldwood had.

"Ava said you tried to set up a regular pickup for the youngleaf."

Gooseflesh pebbled my skin. I tried to relax. This was the conversation I needed to have. My trip to Forest's Edge had left me a little scarred, especially knowing that I'd interacted so casually with the Feared, and that their plans for me were … unacceptable.

I took another step back and felt the knife at my hip. No matter how much I reminded myself that Alaric trusted Hart. I couldn't get past Hart's familiarity with the Feared.

Hadn't Alaric been familiar with the Feared as well?

Hart held his hands up in a gesture of peace. "You heard me speak to your uncle." His teeth gritted as he referenced Alaric. He sounded … annoyed about something.

My breathing steadied. Alaric had known Soren too. Hart and Alaric had spoken of him in the conversation I'd overheard. Knowing a person wasn't an indication of sharing their beliefs.

"What are you getting at?"

He pointed a finger at me. "You came looking for me, Chaos."

He might have a point.

"Don't call me that," I replied. I chanced a glance around. We were in the middle of the gnarled wood, and no one was around for miles.

"Why not?" His lip curled. "You certainly inspire it."

Eris was mentioned little in *Champions of Kavios*, but Alaric loved the words about her. Uninvited, they ran through my mind: *She didn't cause chaos; she inspired it.*

I shook my head, unwilling to engage with such a dangerous comment. "What arrangement did you and Alaric have for the youngleaf?"

His gaze turned to the thick trees as if to confirm he only shared his secrets with them. "I'm sure you've realized it's not an herb readily available in Kavios. I helped him get the youngleaf. And I don't think I have to tell you that Alaric is one of the foremost experts on the Sibling Goddesses. He used his knowledge to help me search for something in return."

"What do you search for?"

Maybe this was what Alaric went after. Maybe it was Hart's fault that Alaric was missing.

When his gaze returned to mine, it hardened, and the thoughts left my mind as quickly as they'd entered. "Something, I learned, he had no intention of helping me find."

That wasn't an answer. But that rage from yesterday was back in his features—a barely leashed wrath fighting for control.

He shook his head. "It doesn't matter." Then his half-smile was back. "You still need the youngleaf, I take it?"

"Yes."

It was a terrible bargaining strategy, but Hart already knew about my mother. He had to know I had no other options.

"But if you don't tell me what he helped you search for, I can't continue his bargain," I said.

He laughed. It was mirthless. "I have a different need of you."

Absolutely not, I thought. Even as my stomach fluttered in anticipation. He would never take from me.

"I see that intrigues you more than you'd like."

He couldn't possibly know that. The half-smile widening on his face said he was awfully sure of himself. No matter his appearance or what Jasmine and Serena swore by, I couldn't let a Blessed touch me.

It was my one rule to hold on to.

The one secret I had left.

Alaric may be gone, but me and my parents were still in danger if anyone found out.

"Calm down, Chaos. I'm not going to … touch you." He spoke with his usual confidence, but I didn't miss the hint of hesitation as he said it.

"I need you to trust me."

“What?” I couldn’t help my surprise. “That’s not exactly a demand you can make.”

He was grinning now. “You’re the one who needs something from me. Youngleaf is the main ingredient in a tonic for your Mother, is it not?”

What a bastard. “This isn’t a great first step to gaining my trust.”

Heat danced in his eyes again. It was tough to say whether it was anger or amusement.

“You need to trust that I won’t take your life. You can’t flinch every time I approach.”

I clenched my fist at my side. “That’s impossible. My physical reaction is out of your control.”

“Is it out of yours?”

I folded my arms over my chest.

He looked pensive. “Alright, then. We’re going to build trust. You’re going to owe me a favor.”

That was too broad. I knew it. He knew it—but he didn’t seem to care.

Damn Alaric. Hart knew I wouldn’t let Mother’s condition worsen just because I couldn’t stomach how he leveraged his position. Whatever he asked, I had to agree.

When I replied, he was already striding past me, sure of my acceptance. “Fine.”

He called over his shoulder. “Knew I could count on you, Chaos.”

15

The firstborn's grand plans crumbled with the discovery of chaos

— FROM CHAMPIONS OF KAVIOS

The towering entrance to the Oldwood Mine was even more impressive than I imagined. Alaric had described it to me—I'd read about it in his history books—the real thing was better.

With doors so tall I had to crane my neck, the width was as massive as that of the castle entrance. It seemed excessive. Even today, with wagons of quartz coming out, only one side of the doorway was open, and it was more than enough space.

I hadn't thought the mines would be so grand, but with a copse of trees surrounding the entrance, it had an air of mystery, of majesty. I wished Alaric were here, so I could experience it with him.

Satisfied there was no one around to attack me, Hart left me to my gawking while he alerted someone to our presence. Tamara and Gregory, the Blessed foreman and her right-hand man, returned with him.

"We've been waiting for you," Tamara said. "You've missed the break. Now we'll have to take you down past active sites."

Her tone didn't imply that she cared for my safety, more that she was disgusted by the inefficiency of it all.

"Follow me and stay close. We go to the deepest part of the mine." Immediately, she turned on her heel and led us through the door.

Hart took his place at my back as we began the descent. We had a long walk, giving me time to stew on our recent transaction. I couldn't believe he demanded a *future favor* for the youngleaf. How Alaric trusted him when he'd been so quick to take advantage of the situation was beyond me. Had he leveraged my sick mother against me? I would need to talk to Alaric about his friend choices when he returned.

The thought sent a pang through my chest, like some part of me knew I wished for things I had no hope of getting. I buried my churning emotions and focused on the walk.

Keeping steady as I followed Tamara's quick pace was more challenging than anticipated. The main path was wide, with room for carts and miners to walk side-by-side. She took us past multiple dig sites, and each path had two more offshoots to explore.

The mine was massive, which shouldn't have surprised me. So many of the citizens were employed here. I knew the operation was extensive. The scale of the sprawl had my mind spinning. Our descent appeared to head west, and paths veered south. Did the path eventually return to Kavios? I hadn't seen any maps of the mine layout in Alaric's books. They must stretch beneath the Oldwood at least.

Lanterns hung in regular intervals on the path. This journey would be far more treacherous without what little light they offered. Too many people on these paths had worn them down. Combined with the dampness of the caves, I slipped twice as we journeyed deeper. As we continued to descend, I let my hand drag against the wall. My fingers grazed the cold dirt. When had I taken off my glove?

"Emberline."

The voice. The one from the Oldwood.

I sucked in a breath as my foot slid again on the packed surface.

Hart's presence at my back threatened to invade my space. His arm was outstretched, as if to toss me toward the wall instead of allowing me to fall into the open expanse. My breathing was heavy—it matched his.

I met his gaze over my shoulder. The fierceness there made me want to flee. He opened his mouth.

Gregory turned, hearing the disturbance. "Careful."

"Don't slow us down," Tamara said.

I slid my glove on and rolled my neck carefully, collecting myself. Hart pulled back his arm and shook his head.

"Fucking Chaos." His words were so low, only I could hear him.

My mind was elsewhere. I needed to focus. These mines were dangerous, even without the increase in earthshakes. I swallowed my fear and kept walking. Living long enough to discover how the Jeweler to the Blessed sourced the adamas kept me focused.

We turned farther west as the path split again. Now, it felt like we were walking into an enclosed tunnel instead of having the expanse on the right side in which to fall. This didn't ease my worries as I considered a cave-in like the one only days ago.

The path finally ended at another large door. It was not quite as massive as the entrance.

Tamara gestured to a pile of gems and a cart beside the door. “These stones need separating.”

“I just put the quartz into the cart?” The cart had a clear label. “What do I do with the adamas?”

She gestured to my bag. “You will report the adamas you find but take it with you.”

My mouth turned down, and my gaze narrowed on the door. Sorting already cut gems wasn’t what I wanted to do. Somehow, I knew that whatever was behind that door was what I wanted to learn about. That had to be where they found the adamas.

“I was under the impression I had to select the site to be mined. If I had to separate something already prepared, why not bring it to me in the city?” I used my best researcher’s voice. One I had used on Alaric when he started an argument about history with few facts. It begged the question, why are you wasting my time with this?

Tamara was unimpressed. “Prince Elias sent you. I suggest you take any questions up with him.” Her dismissive tone had a bite I had yet to perfect.

My gaze moved again to the pile of gems. Did they expect so little adamas from this stack? I knew adamas was rare, but my bag wouldn’t hold much, and the pile was as big as I was.

“Will this be all she’s doing?” Hart asked. “Elias mentioned she’d need to come back. If this is all you require, we might not need to.”

Tamara leveled a glare at Hart that, even in the lamplight, needed no clarification. It wondered whose side he was on in this debate.

Tamara spoke of me as if I weren’t even there. “If she proves successful at this task, others will be given to her.

We'll give you an hour here. Any longer, and you won't make it back before dark." She glanced at Hart like this was his problem. "We'll discuss anything further after the Cornucopia."

With no further instruction, Tamara and Gregory disappeared into the paths. I couldn't imagine it was worth their time to return to the surface before collecting us again, but presumably, they had other duties within the mines.

What other tasks would she deign to assign me if I proved myself worthy with this one? The discussion rankled me. I almost didn't want to sort the stones out of spite. The rational part of me knew that would be counterproductive to my goals.

If I didn't do it, they would make Father try, and they would stop searching for Alaric.

I wasn't that naive. If I didn't respond to the prince's honeyed words, I was sure Vaddon would threaten violence next. I picked up the first stone—it was hot, not simply warm. I quickly set it aside as adamas.

"How did you know that?" Hart picked up a stone and rolled it in his palm before dropping it back into the pile.

I shrugged and tossed him one piece of quartz and the adamas. "Do they feel the same to you?"

He tilted his head. "Do they not to you?"

Alaric had told me no one else could sense the stones like we could, but I'd never tested anyone else. Hart seemed to stare at the stones before mumbling something and shaking his head.

I took that for my answer. "I just know I guess."

He returned the stones and stepped toward the large door. A brief glance over his shoulder told me he knew this was ill-advised. He did it anyway, tugging at the large handle.

The door didn't budge. It was locked.

"Eris curse him."

It was unclear who Hart cursed or why. I wished he'd keep his voice down when being blasphemous.

"You should be careful with your curses." I picked up another stone.

He bowed gallantly. "I wouldn't want to offend your delicate sensibilities."

I shrugged. "It's your funeral."

He was behind me again before I realized he'd moved. "Does that bother you? That I'd no longer be here to keep you safe?"

I stepped away under the guise of picking up another stone. It was the warmth I was familiar with. "I'm bothered that anyone could be killed for their beliefs."

"Even a Blessed?" He picked up another stone and tossed it into the air. Catching it, he threw it again. His action relayed a casual air, as if it was an offhanded question and my answer was unimportant, but there was a tension in his stance that had been missing only moments ago.

I hadn't realized what I'd implied. The fact that, for even one moment, I hadn't thought of him first and foremost as a Blessed was concerning. Then, I considered his question. Every Blessed accepted power in exchange for King Rodric's rules. They knew what they were signing up for, and they did so willingly.

My mind strayed to the story of the Blessed child fleeing the city before accepting her Selection. I liked to think it was true—that there were means for escape, even for those who grew up only knowing the trappings of the Blessed. I didn't know Hart's history. Maybe his entire family was Blessed, and he didn't know how to leave. Perhaps he liked the power. Maybe he had no one and was simply looking out for himself. The real question was whether any of that mattered. Should I condemn him for that one decision? Were the Blessed capable of change?

I liked to think change was possible.

Images of Blessed stealing citizens from the streets, taking, filled my mind.

Hart grunted. "I'll take that to mean you've reconsidered. And I'm allowed to curse using whichever goddesses I please."

I didn't respond as I bent to sort another gem. I hated that he had me considering my position. It was something usually only Alaric invited. Sorting another stone—quartz—my stomach bottomed out at the thought of how much I wished Alaric were here.

I'd be moving into his room tonight. It was more overwhelming than I'd taken time to consider. I felt so lost without him. In the mine. In this role. With the Blessed. At every turn, I was presented with a new ... choice ... but none of them felt like choices at all.

Alaric always seemed to know precisely what to do.

We continued silently until I dropped the last stone into the quartz cart. I only had a handful of adamas pieces, as Tamara had indicated.

Gregory returned and led us back to the surface. The worksites we passed were now inactive, but every one of them had carts filled with quartz. These were the production levels I was familiar with. This mine was responsible for quartz distributed across the other two kingdoms on the continent. It was in high demand in both Linia and Aven. I'd read Linia's throne was made entirely of quartz. I swallowed as we neared the entrance. Would I ever see Linia as I'd originally planned?

The shift must have finished. Miners trudged up the paths ahead of us.

"Is that enough for your commissions?" Gregory nodded toward my bag, now filled with adamas.

"I can get started with it. I'll need more to finish."

"Good. We'll expect you back after the Cornucopia."

I guess I'd passed this test.

My nerves grated to hear Macen's voice in the group before us. We'd joined the miners leaving for the day on the return walk through the Oldwood. There was safety in numbers.

I tucked my chin, making myself small, like I would in any group. Instead of avoiding the Blessed, I was avoiding Macen's notice. I didn't know what I'd say to him.

Why had he set me up? Did he want me dead? We may not be anything to each other anymore, but I'd never considered murdering him—unless we were counting now.

"Is that the little prick you knew from the side street?" Hart asked under his breath.

He hadn't said much to me since we'd left the mines. I didn't know if he was upset with my response to his question about the Blessed. It was best if I didn't know—didn't care.

Hart had made his choice the minute he accepted the adamas.

"Emberline!" Macen waved.

He waved?

My eyes must have doubled in size. Was he saying hello like he didn't try to have me killed last night? I couldn't find an appropriate response as he slowed his steps, walking beside me.

"What are you doing here?" he asked.

Hart and I were already trailing the others. We were far enough behind the group of miners that I didn't contain my response. "Are you serious right now?"

I rarely let my emotions flare in public like this. I was

reasonably confident in Hart's declaration that he wouldn't take from me. There was no question in my mind that he would stop anyone else who tried. Not that there was anyone around besides my idiotic, magic-less ex.

Hart's hand twitched like he would take action.

"I've got this," I said under my breath.

"What are you upset about?" Macen genuinely looked befuddled.

I gently tugged off my glove. Had I found this easygoing charm endearing at some point? Before answering my mental rhetorical question, I turned and slapped his face. The crack of my palm connecting with his skin was one of the most satisfying sounds I'd heard today. "You tried to have me killed!"

I didn't need to dance around it. Hart had reported the Feared had found me. It was a miracle Macen hadn't been arrested.

"You weren't in real danger," Macen said, rubbing his cheek.

My mouth hung open. "Are you joking? Macen. That man wanted me gone."

"Gone, not dead."

Replacing my glove, I shook my head. I couldn't comprehend what he thought the difference was. "Don't come near me again."

Macen reached out like he'd grab my arm.

Truly, I considered stabbing him with my dagger. This seemed like a lesson he needed to learn. Hart was there before I could react.

Macen's arm was twisted behind his back, and he had fallen to his knees. "I wasn't—"

A quiet rage seeped from Hart's every word. "Her instructions were clear. Come near her again, and I'll kill you."

Macen swallowed. Hart leaned impossibly closer, twisting

Macen's arm even higher around his back. Hart whispered something I couldn't hear.

"Yes, sssir," Macen stammered.

"Get out of here," Hart said, releasing his hold.

Macen shot forward, inserting himself back into the group.

"I said I had it." I glared at Hart.

He shrugged. "What can I say? You inspired me, Chaos."

16

She'll never be found—until she chooses. I've taken care of everything.

— ALARIC SARE'S LETTERS TO ISABELLE ARKOVA

I'd designed my life around staying away from the Blessed. As we scaled the hill to Glanmore Castle, I considered all the ways that had gone wrong. Not only was I entering the castle, but I'd also be living there—with a Blessed guard leading the way.

There were so many ways this could end poorly. I reminded myself I had little choice at the moment. Until I had more information about Alaric or a more reliable plan for youngleaf, my hands were tied.

I glared daggers into Hart's back at that.

We'd stopped by the workshop so I could collect Alaric's

design book. It would at least give me something to work on when locked in my rooms tonight. While it was comforting to think the Feared couldn't get in, I also couldn't get out. It was its own kind of prison.

I wanted to fall apart. A little self-pity could do a girl wonders. I just had to take a few more steps.

My focus returned to the large and brooding guard walking ahead of me. His words from this afternoon still bothered me. He'd seemed mad at Alaric when we spoke of their agreement for the youngleaf. I was desperate to know what Alaric claimed to help him with that he didn't intend to follow through on. That didn't sound like my uncle.

Then again, until a few days ago, I didn't know my uncle was buying contraband herbs. I hated acknowledging that maybe I didn't know Alaric as well as I thought.

Hart hadn't seemed very fond of Macen in the woods but also hadn't arrested him. His connection with the Feared was no clearer after that interaction.

Spiraling, I ran face-first into Hart's back when he stopped. "Umph."

He was so solid—his body so unforgiving. I bounced back, more aware than I'd like to be of all the places our bodies had just collided. He turned, arching an eyebrow, his face giving me nothing. This was one of the few times I wished I had an adamas stone. I could slide my hand along the sharp planes of his face and see what color the stone flashed—could see what emotions lingered close to the surface.

I shook my head. I needed to get some rest.

"We're here," he said.

To my left, two guards stood outside a small wooden door. Torches on either side of the hallway lit the space. I nodded, moving away from Hart.

"I should check the room." He stepped in front of me to open the door.

"We already did," the guard on the left said.

Hart ignored this as he stalked into Alaric's room—my room. I followed. I'd never been to Uncle's rooms at the castle. They were richly appointed, as I'm sure any room there would be, but they were also on the main floor, toward the kitchens, indicating his place of servitude. Looking around the room, I couldn't see anything that reminded me of Alaric.

The bed was neatly made with white linens. The desk was tidy, with only a few pieces of paper out of place. It was a different sight from the state of his workshop bench. The bureau was large and made of intricately carved dark wood, but I did not imagine Alaric picking it out for himself. I wanted to go to the desk and see what might be hidden in the drawers. I'd wait until Hart was gone to do so.

He scoured the room, even crouching to check beneath the bed.

"Looking for monsters?" I asked.

He stood as he finished his assessment, stopping beside the fireplace. "You don't seem to realize how many are out there, Chaos."

I held in an eye roll. The monsters I feared were in this castle, draped in fine clothes and smiling to my face while they stole life from the citizens of Kavios. "I'll be fine."

His curt nod was dismissive. "I'll be back first thing in the morning. The guards outside won't let you go to Alaric's workshop without me."

An ornately furnished cage indeed.

Hart studied me like he would pry the thoughts from my head. The fire in the grate cast a deep glow on his features, highlighting those forest-green eyes that pierced so deeply.

Before he could say anything else, a knock sounded at the door, drawing his attention.

"Oh!" A faint voice echoed as Hart opened it.

"Who are you?" he asked.

"Prince Elias assigned me to see to the jeweler's needs."

I tried to glance around Hart's broad frame, but he filled the doorway. I waved a hand over his shoulder, trying to draw her attention. "Hi, I'm Emberline, the jeweler."

Hart sighed and sidestepped, allowing me access to the woman. She was petite, with light brown hair and large, expressive eyes. Upon seeing me, her smile lit the hall, and she dipped into a curtsey. I reached for her, desperate to pull her into the room, but I was too slow.

The guard on the right let his hand slide up her arm—the adamas ring on his finger flashed yellow. Her smile faded as the guard stole the slip of joy she'd shown.

"Careful there." The guard let her go as quickly as he'd touched her, but she hadn't stumbled or asked for his aid. There was no mistaking what the guard had done.

Hart stepped between the woman and the guard, guiding her into the room. She stumbled, and her gaze darted toward Hart over her shoulder as he closed the door.

"He won't touch you," I said.

Hart held my gaze. I couldn't decipher what lingered there. I didn't know why I said it. I was confident enough that Hart wouldn't attempt to take from me, but I had no such guarantee he wouldn't take from a servant in the castle. They, especially, were paid well, with the expectation of such occurrences.

After collecting herself, the woman appeared to accept my assurances. "Have you eaten? Would you like a bath?"

I hadn't considered what seeing to my needs might entail. I shook off the connection with Hart, focusing on the woman. "Are you alright? Do you need anything?"

She waved me off. "I'm here to serve you."

I nodded, accepting that she wanted to move on. "You can make a meal and a bath happen?"

Yes, I was in the castle, where luxury I'd never experienced was available, but I hadn't expected it to be offered to me.

She curtsied. "Of course. I can have hot water and food brought in."

"What is your name?" I asked.

"Penelope."

Not having to leave this room for these necessities was wholly satisfying. I was dirty and exhausted from the mines. Sadness and worry clung to me like bad habits. Washing and eating wouldn't magically cure it, but they would be solid steps to catching my breath and collecting my thoughts.

"Nice to meet you, Penelope. Food and a bath sounds wonderful."

Hart opened the door to leave. "Goodnight."

He let a pause linger in the space between us before exiting. It left little doubt that he added the nickname, Chaos, in his mind, even if he knew better than to say it with an audience.

I was right. Eating and washing helped clear my head. Nothing had been solved. I still worried for Alaric and myself. The trip through the Oldwood today and into the mines was still unnerving. I couldn't believe how quickly I'd failed to stay focused. The Oldwood's pull was as strong as ever, no matter how much I'd attempted to numb myself to it.

Alaric had been right; I'd need an escort if I ever had the opportunity to leave Kavios as originally planned. I begrudgingly admitted that Hart proved a decent choice.

Still, the necessity was disappointing and utterly confusing. Why was I so affected by the woods? Hart didn't appear to have any issues, nor did any of the miners.

I shook my head, having no answers, and focused instead on something I understood: jewelry making. If nothing else, I was a competent jeweler. I would craft the rings for the soon-to-be Blessed, and Prince Elias would continue his search for my uncle.

It felt like such a feeble promise from a man who held such power. The prince held all the cards. I wasn't sure how to change that—wasn't sure that I could—but I would certainly use everything Alaric taught me to try.

I'd laid out the other option for Father yesterday, but as I'd told him, it wasn't a real one. I could run away. If I left, the Feared wouldn't need to try to kill me. I'd no longer be granting the Blessed power.

They could try to recruit Father, but he couldn't source the adamas. If he tried and failed, there was no telling what the royal's wrath would entail. Not only that, if he was eventually returned to Mother in one piece, they'd have no funds for the youngleaf. While Hart hadn't indicated he'd charge me coin, I couldn't assume that's how he operated with all his customers. Mother needed the tonic.

Leaving was a nice dream, a goal I'd believed attainable before Alaric went missing, but it was now out of reach due to the realities of my new family responsibilities. I sat on the bed and flipped through Alaric's notebook.

The notebook held every design he'd ever created. He was meticulous about that, as he was when recording any experiments he did in his workshop. Things around him might seem in disarray, but he knew precisely what needed to be done and what he'd learned from a prior attempt.

Designing rings and the adamas gems to fit them was no different.

Prince Elias was right in his assumption. Alaric had designed the new pieces already. I tilted my head in thought. This seemed like too much forethought for Alaric. He never missed a deadline, but he wasn't exactly a planner. Alaric tended to procrastinate on his work for the Blessed. Why were these designs ready? With his disappearance, they must've been prepared days before the Selection.

I nestled deeper into the blankets as I flipped through the pages. The designs were lovely, but I wouldn't say they were complicated or unique for Alaric's skills. Instead, they highlighted what the Blessed cared about: the size of the adamas stone.

The four settings and gems for the Selected were straightforward. My brow furrowed as I studied the enhancement. This ring was thick with ornate carvings, and it looked familiar. The designs on the gold band stretched like licking flames over the knuckle, teasing the memory I needed. I recognized this ring. Hart had been wearing it the morning he'd visited Alaric's workshop.

This design had been turned in to the prince for approval on the same day as the meeting with Hart. There was no way Hart could have been wearing it unless this design was a duplicate of a ring already in existence.

Why would Alaric be making a duplicate?

The name beside the commission was R. Lourd. I read Alaric's scribbled notes in the corner next to the name. Usually, it was details about size, fit, or style. Here, it referenced another page in the sketchbook. I flipped to the referenced page.

It was a much earlier design, but it matched this one exactly. The commission name was the same: R. Lourd. This was the second commission of the same design for the same Blessed. I wasn't familiar with enhancements, so maybe this made sense. Usually, they served to give the Blessed a larger adamas stone. This one didn't.

That wasn't what bothered me, though. R. Lourd wasn't even close to Hart's name. The image of the ring on Hart's finger wouldn't be dismissed. Why did Hart have it? Why hadn't he worn it since that morning?

It was odd that he didn't display his adamas like the rest of the Blessed.

A simple answer swirled in my mind, but I didn't want to think it. It added another layer of complexity to all the current spinning thoughts I had about Hart. But Alaric never did let me shy away from a difficult question. Holding his sketchbook, I couldn't shy away from this new thought. What if the ring wasn't Hart's?

The Feared will have your gem for this. A reckless shout from a man in the street as we watched a Blessed beat a man for no reason. The conversation with Macen replayed in my head. *Maybe the Blessed can no longer hide behind their magic gems.*

What if R. Lourd didn't have the original? What if it was missing—stolen?

I'd been searching for a link between Hart and the Feared. He'd reassured me about his intentions toward me but hadn't addressed his relationship with them. Their conversation had been fraught in the alley. Hart had seemed ... disappointed in Soren's behavior. Some part of my mind had decided it had to do with the fact that Soren worked at Forest's Edge, and Hart used it as a location to sell his contraband items.

What if it was more than that?

The Feared were rumored to be stealing adamas from the Blessed. With Blessed never taking the gems off, it seemed impossible for someone without magic to overpower and steal a gem.

What if a Blessed stole from the Blessed?

I was putting puzzle pieces together in my mind. While the edges made sense, the middle was still a jumble of shapes with the same colors and patterns.

A Blessed stealing from a Blessed was the only way I imagined this working, but it left out a gaping question that I didn't think could be answered so quickly.

Why would Hart help them? Why would a Blessed help the Feared?

17

His curse was that he needed her. What he'd do when he found her was far from certain.

— FROM CHAMPIONS OF KAVIOS

Sleep was elusive as my mind turned over reasons why Hart—a Blessed—would help the Feared. Each hypothesis I considered was more unlikely than the last.

Maybe Hart still had family without magic. It happened occasionally, though I was convinced King Rodric focused his Blessing on those who would be most grateful—those with no one else.

I didn't know how to confront Hart about any of this or if I even should. The fact that he had an original, of a ring needing to be duplicated, was damning. It put him even more in bed with the Feared than I thought.

Macen might know of his role in all of this. It would explain why Hart didn't arrest him.

Hart may be duty-bound by the prince to protect me, but he was also duty-bound not to commit treason. With these sins uncovered, I questioned my safety.

Mornings spent in Alaric's workshop usually calmed me. I knew a big part of that was the man himself, but the urge to be in his space was overwhelming. As I started this new day with so many unknowns, I needed to get to Alaric's workshop—without Hart.

I wanted time to search Alaric's things. Maybe something in them could help me make sense of...anything.

The last few days had been a lot, and each new piece of information seemed like it would be the last straw.

Mother needed her tonic. Alaric needed to be found. I wanted to leave on my planned journey, hiking through the Oldwood undeterred.

The Feared wanted me gone. I didn't want to die, but I also didn't disagree with their logic. If I were gone, the flow of adamas would end.

These thoughts cycled as I readied for the day. Hart said to wait for him, but I wouldn't—couldn't. I had too much to sort through, and though I was pretty confident Hart either knew of Alaric's banned books or wouldn't care, I didn't want him with me. I wanted to clear my head.

When I opened the door to my room, both guards stood at attention outside. They turned toward me, helmets in place, blocking my ability to read their expressions.

"You can't leave," the one on the right said.

I gave him my best glare. "Hart is going to meet me at Alaric's workshop."

They glanced at each other. "That's not—"

"Emberline, with me." Vaddon's cloak billowed around him as he rounded the corner, storming down the hallway.

The guards slowly glanced at each other. The one who'd just spoken shrugged. Telling me no was one thing, saying the same to the king's advisor was another.

Vaddon was steps beyond my door now. He hadn't slowed. "Emberline."

I shook my head, getting what I wanted even as I was called like a dog to come. *Focus on the win*, I told myself. I was getting out of my room without Hart.

"How were the mines?" Vaddon asked.

"Fine. But I don't have enough adamas for the pieces Prince Elias approved. They said I'll need to return after the Cornucopia."

"Very good." Vaddon wasn't a particularly tall man, but his steps were brisk. He had a cold efficiency that, in another life, I might have respected.

We were at the massive castle doors before I got my bearings.

"I'll leave you to it." Vaddon stormed off as quickly as he'd arrived.

This seemed too easy. I stared down the steps, wondering if I should worry. I glanced from side to side. Nothing had gone my way for the last two days, so maybe—just maybe—Alaric's goddess was finally sending some luck my way. With a final check over my shoulder, I descended the staircase.

The streets were easy enough to navigate so early. I arrived at Alaric's workshop quickly. My fingers flexed, thinking about touching the familiar books in his storage room. I wasn't focused on my surroundings as I pulled the key from my pocket.

Unfamiliar hands grabbed me, pulling me toward the alley. I panicked. My leg kicked back, and my hand reached for the dagger at my hip without thought. As my foot met my attacker's groin, I turned and slammed the blade into their shoulder.

They grunted in pain, and the hood fell back, revealing his face, as I pulled the dagger out and pushed myself away. My hands shook. I didn't recognize him as he fell to his knees. Before I could look up, another pair of boots appeared beside the man I'd just dispatched. My breaths came faster as I realized there were others.

I couldn't release a scream before another attacker lunged.

Swiping again with my blade, I ran.

Screaming wouldn't help. No one would stop to help. This city didn't take care of its own. If I survived this encounter, I'd remind myself how stupid it was to leave the castle without a guard, even if I currently doubted mine.

I sprinted down a side street, cutting south. Maybe I could lose them. But just like the night of the festival, my access off the side street was blocked. Another group of men and women stood there, arms crossed, waiting.

"It'll be easier if you come with us." A woman held a knife in her hand and leaned against the wall. She seemed unconcerned that I was armed and even less concerned I would do any damage with my single weapon.

I turned to run back the way I'd come, but the Cross Street entrance was filled with those who pursued me.

This was it. My heart thudded in my chest. They were going to take me. My knuckles turned white as I regripped the dagger with determination. The least I could do was take a few of them with me. I angled myself to see both sets of attackers and stepped back. The stone wall of the building greeted me. I had nowhere to go.

"Put down the dagger, and we'll make this painless," a man with dark hair and a beard said.

I shook my head, unable to find words to respond. Scanning the group, I didn't recognize anyone from the last encounter at the festival. Were there really so many of the Feared?

As much as I sympathized with their rationale, it was my life they were targeting. I wouldn't let it go so easily. My jaw clenched, and I lifted my blade as I readied for whoever came at me next.

"Fucking Chaos."

The voice should be the last one I wanted to hear, but I couldn't remember why. My shoulders almost sagged in relief as Hart came into view.

His sword was out, and anger radiated from every inch of his body. Something dripping from the sword caught my eye ... Blood?

"Anyone else?" Hart asked. A body lay at his feet, unmoving.

Efficient, I thought, as my heart still raced.

My attackers appeared unconvinced. The ones who blocked my path took slow steps toward me, and those closest to Hart readied for a fight.

"So be it," Hart grumbled.

Our gazes held across the attackers. He nodded in reassurance even as he looked like he would strangle me himself. The next swing of his sword dropped another attacker. The man screamed in pain, but Hart was already stabbing another.

I dragged my attention from Hart's brutal progress. The woman against the wall lunged. I slashed with my dagger, but she dodged. My pulse raced again as she grabbed my arm. I hadn't even checked if they were Blessed. No magic prickled my neck. I felt no pull, no attempt to take, as she wrapped her arms around me, jostling my protective layer of clothing. I kicked and flailed my head back, striking her face. My arm broke free, and I sliced through the air again with my dagger.

Someone else grabbed me. The man's hand wrapped around my exposed wrist. Still unsure if they were Blessed, the direct contact drove me to panic. They were going to take me—going to kill me. I couldn't look up, couldn't see where Hart was. The idea that he could fight off a dozen people alone was laughable. Why hadn't I doubted it earlier?

I didn't want to die. Fear shook my body.

The man's hand released. A scream broke from his lips. He fell to the ground, clutching the sides of his head in agony. The pose was familiar, but I didn't have time to consider it much as Hart's blade slid into his chest.

Then, Hart's eyes met mine, searching. "Alright, Emberline?"

I didn't think he'd ever used my real name. He spoke it hesitantly now. Which made no sense as I pulled my gaze from his and scanned the side street.

What happened to the last man who'd attacked me? The question in Hart's gaze was the same as mine.

Six bodies lay between where he stood and where I was now. The seventh was the man he'd stabbed at my feet. I glanced south. Those who had stood there, ran. I couldn't blame them. Turning, Hart still appraised me. His left hand lifted like he'd reach for me. Maybe in reassurance? Either way, I flinched on instinct, my body pressing against the stone wall. He tilted his head and looked to the sky, his eyes closing.

He looked longingly after those fleeing down the side street like they were a treat he couldn't wait to consume. "Let's get you back to the castle."

"No." Finally, I found my voice.

I stopped shaking as I realized the danger was gone. Hart had stopped them. Something had happened to the last man who'd touched me—I still didn't know what—but the overwhelming fear that had overtaken me dissolved. I wouldn't go back to the castle and cower. There was too much I had to do today, and I had wasted too much time already.

"No?" Hart asked.

If anything, this attack proved how unprepared I was for my position. Apparently, I needed a guard, one that I trusted. I had to determine whether that was Hart.

"No."

I couldn't sit and stew on this. Those had to have been the Feared. Hart had saved me—again. I didn't know what more I could expect from him. He may be in league with them to take down the Blessed, but as I surveyed the bodies on the ground again, he was clearly opposed to letting them take me. I needed to know why. We needed to talk about the ring, and I needed to go through Alaric's things.

"Take me back to Alaric's workshop. Please."

His nostrils flared like he'd prefer any other request. He knelt and wiped his blade on the body before us—the body that had fallen before Hart had even touched it. The one he still looked at with suspicion, or maybe that was how he looked at me.

The sound of metal sliding into his hip sheath drew my gaze. "As you wish, Chaos."

18

I don't want her to go, but I worry he knows she's here.

— ALARIC SARE'S LETTERS TO ISABELLE ARKOVA

As we entered the workshop, I ignored Hart to the best of my ability. Coffee would help. I slipped behind the curtain to start the fire and fill a pot with water. My awareness of him, while he paced back and forth in the front, made me uncomfortable. He was like a caged animal deciding whether to remind his captors of what made him wild.

Whatever internal struggle Hart was fighting, he lost it.

He pushed the gold curtain back, entering the workshop space. "I gave you one instruction."

That couldn't have been true. He had given me plenty of instructions. I crossed my arms over my chest, then paused, remembering the stolen ring. I needed easy access to my dagger. My hand hung at my side, and I grazed where my blade rested beneath my skirt.

Hart's gaze tracked the movement. He crossed his muscled arms over his chest as if to prove he had no interest in reaching for me. "Back to thinking I'm going to take from you, then?"

"I don't know what to think of you."

His brow pinched. "What does that mean?"

I pulled Alaric's design book from my bag and opened it to the page detailing the enhancement design. "Why did you have this on your hand only days ago?"

For a moment, I thought he wouldn't look. Our gazes locked.

He pulled his hand down his face and looked at the page I pointed to. "I can explain."

"Can you?"

I wasn't sure where my confidence came from. If he tried to attack me, he would most certainly win.

"I stole it for the Feared."

My hand dropped behind me, hoping the stool was where I thought it was before I fell onto it. He'd admitted it. I should be happy. Mostly, I was scared.

"What do you want?" I said with as much strength as I could muster. I'd only get one swing with my dagger. I had to make it count if he approached.

"Fucking Chaos." He let his hands fall to his side. "I just saved your life. Again. I'm not trying to kill you."

I knew that was correct, but it didn't make sense. I wouldn't be satisfied until he answered it all. "Why? Why not let them have me? Why not kill me yourself?"

He pointed to the street, indicating my attackers. "First of all, those were no Feared I've ever seen." He ran his hand through the strands that fell from the knot at the back of his head. “Second, I’m not going to kill you. I don’t know what else to do to prove that.”

“Why are you helping the Feared?”

He arched a brow. “I’m not sure it matters.”

His anger stoked my own, though I worked to keep my features even. “You’re giving me no reason to trust you!”

He threw his head back and laughed. Still staring at the ceiling, he spoke. “Maybe it’s better if you don’t.”

When his gaze finally returned to mine, his shoulders lowered, and disappointment coated his slow movements. He shook his head, breaking our standoff. “I’ll be outside.”

He exited the building and stood sentry beside the front door.

What was that?

My head spun as the water finally started to boil. I calmed my shaking hands with the familiar ritual of pouring the hot water over the grounds. Hart had told me nothing. He’d admitted my fear but had given no information to help me understand.

He had saved me again, though.

Goddess, I was so sick of him. In no world would I let him weaponize my guilt. Should I ask for another guard? A gnawing in my gut said I didn’t want to, and it stoked my anger all over again.

As soon as the coffee was ready, I took a scalding sip. I was unsurprised when it did not grant its usual calm. Discussing Hart’s motives was exactly the kind of discussion I would usually have with Alaric, but he wasn’t here.

I sighed. My original plan had been to use the time without Hart to search Alaric’s storage room. The morning had taken a very different shape, but at least Hart stood outside. He would alert me if anyone tried to enter. I pulled the curtain closed and set a scene at Alaric’s worktable. A stack of books, a coffee cup, the stones, and the tools for cutting and shaping. All evidence I'd been hard at work should I need to let someone in quickly.

I granted myself another sip of coffee before letting myself into the storage room.

The organizational structure likely only made sense to the two of us. It was first by genre and second by topic. *Champions of Kavios* was stacked atop the pile of histories. Alaric must have put it in his preferred location. I picked it up and flipped through its pages as I considered what to look for first.

Alaric answered the question for me: a note fell from between the book's pages, his familiar script evident even in the dim light of the closet-like room.

When I stooped to collect the paper from the floor, the bell rang in the front of the workshop.

Quickly, I slipped the paper back into the book. I would have to come back later. I shut the door and secured the shelf entrance. It looked like nothing was there. Parting the curtain, a group filed into the shop with another guard in the lead. Hart nodded to him as they entered.

I grabbed Alaric's sketchbook from the workbench and readied for my first customers.

The new guard announced the group. "These are the Selected. They are here to be fitted for the rings."

Hart slid in the door behind them. No matter how angry he was, he seemed unwilling to leave me in the shop with so many unknowns. I mumbled his favorite curse under my breath as I tried to figure out what to do with him. He stood quietly in the corner, avoiding my gaze.

"Welcome. I'll be happy to take care of each of you."

I was unsurprised that three of the four Selected were relatively young. It was just as the miner had guessed—the children of Blessed families would take most of the slots.

The final Selected was a woman in her mid-forties. She

looked vaguely familiar, but I didn't know her name. She had medium brown skin and black hair tied back at her nape. Even through her apparent nerves, her smile lit up the room.

She appeared more than happy to be the king's rags to riches story, giving the rest of us hope that someday we could be Blessed too.

Nausea roiled in my stomach. How complacent were the citizens in Woodside because of this one opportunity?

I pulled the tray of sizing rings from beneath the counter. "We'll test these on each of you to see what fits best."

Alaric's sketchbook lay open to the pages of the new designs, and I called the first Selected. "Caitlyn."

The younger woman stepped forward. Her shiny, long blond hair and aquiline nose gave an appearance of wealth. She held her hand over the counter as I slid various-sized rings on to find a fit.

We found one that slid comfortably down her finger. "How does that feel?"

"It doesn't have a gem."

I swear I heard Hart's eye roll from the corner. I wanted to hold his gaze and laugh silently together. Then I remembered his unsatisfactory answers earlier. I wouldn't let the tension between us break so easily.

I responded to Caitlyn. "This isn't the final piece. It's just to get your ring size. You'll see the final pieces at the Presentation and get to keep them after the King's Blessing."

She glared at me as if it were my fault she didn't know this.

"So, does this feel alright? Is it too tight? Too loose?"

"It's fine." She slid the ring off and stepped back into line with the others.

I jotted down her measurements and flipped the page to the next commission. "Deidre."

The woman from Woodside stepped forward. "I still can't believe it was me."

I slid a ring on her finger, testing the fit.

Deidre glanced around the shop. "Although, you must feel the same, taking over this position."

My smile was polite. I never wanted it to be me, but she couldn't know that.

She leaned forward as I tried another size. "I'm sorry. I didn't mean to offend. I'm still in shock."

I tried for a warmer smile. It wasn't my goal to ruin what little joy this woman had. Even if her choices meant she would be stealing emotions soon enough.

"When did you find out?" I asked, trying to sound interested. "With everything ..."

I hadn't meant to bring up the mass explosion of nightmares either. My small talk could use some work.

She smiled in a way that said she knew I was trying, while I slid another ring on her finger.

"The king's advisor came to my apartment the following morning. I almost passed out from excitement. I had to go tell the neighbors—tell the whole building!"

The words were out of my mouth before I thought better of it. "What about your family?"

Her smile thinned as she responded to the ring I slid on her finger. "This one fits."

I noted the size in Alaric's book.

"My partner died in the mines a few days ago," she said.

I dipped my chin and remembered the morning earthshake. "I'm so sorry."

"It makes this even more of a dream come true. I would never have left my Linette. But now that she's gone?" Deidre shrugged. "What do I have to lose?"

I couldn't be the only one to realize that the king seemed to pick those most likely to give thanks for the Blessing. More likely, no one cared enough to notice. It was the dream we were sold—the dream that would keep us complacent.

Deidre returned to the others as I called the next name. "Wil."

The final two sizings were quick. "All set." I wrote Arthur's size. "I have everything I need. You all enjoy the Cornucopia tonight, and I'll get to work."

The group filed out the same way they'd entered. The bell chimed again as the door closed behind them.

Hart stepped forward. I folded my arms over my chest at his approach. His smile was maybe the first genuine one I'd seen as he took another step toward the counter.

"I'm sorry," he said.

My mouth hung open. His apology made even less sense than his actions.

"You've been through a lot the last few days, and I'm not making it any easier. I've helped the Feared before, but as you saw, not all of them are who I thought they were."

I gave him an assessing stare. "That doesn't explain why you helped them."

"And Alaric never explained why he worshiped Eris. We don't always get to know why. I need it to be enough for now that I'm more interested in your safety than I am in their goals."

If I wasn't willing to go to the prince about switching guards, I gave myself no choice but to accept his apology. "Fine."

He didn't wear the stolen ring anymore. He must have given it to the Feared. It still bothered me that I didn't know where *his* adamas was. It was unusual not to show it. "Where is your adamas?"

He laughed. "I'd rather leave it to your imagination."

I hated myself as my gaze roamed his uniform. Even beneath the tight fit, I didn't see the outline of a stone against his chest.

"See something you like, Chaos?"

My gaze snapped to his face. A smirk curved his lip, and his brow was raised in challenge.

"You shouldn't call me that."

He canted his head. Slow steps brought him across the storefront to the counter. He pressed his palms to it and leaned across, his eyebrow still raised. "I find the more I'm around you, the more you inspire it. It suits you."

I raised both arms and gestured around the room. "It's still not wise to grant me the credit of a goddess. Better not to tempt fate."

He laughed again. This one richer and smokier than the hollow ring from our earlier argument. The low rumble did something to me that I was unwilling to examine. "I don't think she'd mind."

His words were confident. A truth cementing in place between us that I didn't understand.

19

Maybe Chaos knew what she was doing after all.

— FROM CHAMPIONS OF KAVIOS

My palms were sweaty, and my fingers shook nervously as I readied Alaric's workshop to work the adamas. Each piece from the mines was small, but they still needed to be cut down before I could start preforming. This was the start of my next test. Could I shape the adamas to hold magic?

Alaric had determined that only adamas, as such a hard material, could be used to shape adamas. Any excess stone was returned to the tools used to cut, shape, and polish. He'd made saw blades of adamas for such a purpose.

Hesitation would only give me more time to worry. As much as I hated it, I knew my instincts would guide me with the stone. I pulled the blade from its wrap in the drawer and set up the first piece. Father liked to use a vice to hold the gem in place for the more significant cuts, but Alaric insisted one needed to hold the adamas to feel its true shape. His method included someone holding the adamas in place while he cut.

I'd never cut the adamas myself.

My experience was with quartz, and the materials were identical to everyone but me and Alaric. Hopefully, that was good enough. I swallowed, and Alaric's absence hit me again like a punch in the gut. There was no getting around the fact that this part was a two-person job.

I heated the wax to hold the gem securely. There was no time to wish Alaric were here. Whatever led to this situation—it was now mine to deal with.

The professional challenge of the work overtook me. I wanted to prove that I could do this. A new task was exactly what I needed to focus on amid everything else.

In the back of my mind, I knew I'd have to decide at some point what to do with the adamas. Part of me still wondered if there was any chance I could swap it with quartz—do something to limit the power I granted. I'd been avoiding the question. If I truly believed the Blessed made a decision the moment they took the adamas, I knew I would be making my own decision the moment I turned adamas rings over to the Glanmores for use.

The gem may not be for me, but I'd judge myself just as harshly for enabling them.

Tonight was the Cornucopia, which meant I had six days to make a choice I could live with.

"Do you need help?" Hart's low rumble preceded him as he parted the heavy gold curtain, joining me in the workshop area.

I searched his face a bit more boldly than I usually would. "Have you ever done this?"

A smile curled his lip. "Have you?"

He had me there.

Still, his help would put him … in very close proximity. I sighed. His apology wasn't an explanation, but it was enough for now. I needed his help, and I had a feeling he knew it.

I waved him over. "Fine. Come hold this."

His steps were slow as he approached. Almost as if giving me time to change my mind.

I wouldn't.

"Where do you need me?"

I pointed to the edge of the workbench. "Stand there. Hold this." I handed him the small metal rod.

I'd melted wax, setting the edge of the stone in it. This gave him at least a few inches of handle instead of holding the stone directly. "Don't let it slip."

He nodded.

I pointed to the space beside him, picking up the saw again. "I'm going to stand here."

"And you'll be armed," he said dryly.

I waved the blade before setting to work. "I am. So don't get any ideas."

He smirked. "You can't outlaw ideas. A man can dream."

I shook my head, attempting to focus on the work and not exactly *what* the Blessed beside me was dreaming about. My gloves felt bulky as I let the blade touch the stone. I usually worked with them off. Part of me knew I'd need to remove them. If the warmth told me when a stone was adamas, I'd have to follow the heat to shape the stone. It was the difference between the two gems. Inherently, I knew the more heat, the more magic the stone could contain. But my hands would need to be uncovered beside Hart to find said heat. I held Hart's gaze as I set down the saw and pulled off the gloves, setting them on the workbench beside us.

He paused. "I won't touch you unless expressly asked."

No chance of that.

"Ready?" I asked when I'd caught my breath.

"Ready."

I turned slightly, giving him my back as I angled myself to cut the stone. It felt like every instinct I had should be screaming against this. I shouldn't leave him unchallenged, inches from my side, but my usual panic wasn't present.

I may not like Hart's non-answers, but my body believed I wasn't in danger. My gut trusted him, the same gut that wouldn't let me request another guard. Steadying breaths slipped from my lips. Hot air on my neck told me he did the same. Was he uncomfortable? I wanted so badly to look at him, to assess what was hiding behind the forest green of his gaze. I leaned forward instead, pressing my fingers to the stone, feeling the temperature change across its surface. There was a warmer section towards the center. That was what I'd need to preserve.

The first cut demanded my complete attention. Any slips would mark more of the stone than I wanted, leaving me less to work with when shaping. I drew the blade across the stone multiple times, creating a groove.

Once I had the line, I started in earnest. Hart's exhales matched each stroke of the blade. It was a pattern, a connection I didn't understand until interrupted.

The fracture of breaking glass assaulted my ears. I'd cracked the gem.

Reacting automatically, I reached for the side of the stone connected to the pipe Hart held. My hand touched the gem, steadying it from my error, and before I realized my other mistake, my palm brushed his finger.

Fear flooded me as I became aware of the connection. Heat

rushed through me. Purple flashed in my periphery as I lifted my hand and stepped back.

Hart hadn't moved. His words were calm. He stared at the stone, still holding it in place. "That was all you, Chaos. You better come back and finish this."

Finally, he turned to look at me. His gaze held a hundred questions, but his words expressed none of them. "It's a small crack. You can cut it out after shaping."

I let out a shaky breath and looked at the stone. He was right. Alaric would never have panicked after making such a small mistake. I nodded. "I'll go again."

"Good girl," he said, and I was glad my back was to him. Heat flooded me again, this time curling low in my stomach.

I slid the blade back into the groove and returned to work. His imposing presence at my back had me on edge, but he was right. He'd kept his word. *I* was the one who'd touched him. I could convince myself I'd imagined a flash of ... *purple* in the gem.

I'd only ever seen a gem flash the color being collected.

I tried to shake off the feeling that I was missing something as the final cut slid through, and the piece of gem broke off.

Hart set down the pipe and stepped back. "All set?"

I nodded. "Thank you." The two pieces of stone now felt different. One held the warmth of adamas. The second piece now felt like quartz to me. It was a small thing, but I couldn't deny the satisfaction that this had worked. I guess I didn't know that it had; there was still room for error as I shaped the stone, but my gut was sure I was on the right path.

Maybe I should be concerned that I was capable of everything the royal family needed, and that this was one more step to granting them more power, but part of me was vindicated. Alaric had never let me do this step, but I'd been so sure that I could.

Hart stared at the gem before raising his gaze to meet mine. "Anytime."

His face held just as many questions as when he'd approached me on the side street after the attack this morning.

I opened my mouth to ask him something. What? I still wasn't sure. "Can you power the shaping?"

He tilted his head, unsure what I was asking. I pointed to another circular blade on the workbench. A rod ran straight through it and the workbench, connecting via an arm to a foot pedal beneath the table. "You have to step on the pedal continuously. It spins the blade that I use to shape."

I pulled out the stool for him instead of looking at his face when I asked. This wasn't a task I strictly needed him for. I could power the blade and shape by myself, but with my nerves all over the place, I didn't think it wise to do both. He'd be standing somewhere in the building whether I used him or not. If I wasn't worried he would touch me—what was I afraid of?

He raised a brow. "You can't do both simultaneously?"

I sighed and turned away from him to do the work. "I can."

He chuckled. "I'm happy to do it, Chaos. I'm just curious."

The devious slant of his lip when I turned to face him was intoxicating and infuriating in equal measure.

Maybe this was a bad idea. "I can—"

"No, no," he said. "I accept. I'm now head stepper in charge of the foot pedal."

"Are you now?" I was unable to restrain the smile curling on my own lips.

"You'll see. I have fantastic stamina."

I cleared my throat, turning away from him so he didn't see what was surely a flush touching my cheeks. "Just start stepping."

His low chuckle danced across my skin even as I picked up

the piece of adamas still attached to the small metal pipe to start working. The blade spun with each press of Hart's foot. I waited for it to gain a steady speed before angling the rod and pressing it against the blade.

This was my favorite part of working with quartz. I loved finding the shape of the stone as the rest fell away. I'd heard artists say that when they looked at a block of material waiting to be made into a statue, they could already see the figure beneath. Their job was cutting away the pieces that weren't required. This was smaller in scale, but the description felt right.

I wondered what shape it would take. This process was different, as every few minutes, I'd pull the stone back to feel for the heat. It was harder to tell now where the warmth congregated in the stone. The process of shaping caused its own heat. But the difference was still there.

Hart's steady steps were like a beating drum. I used his rhythm to guide my hand, shaping away the pieces that weren't quite as warm as the rest. Each step was a new stroke. Each stroke revealed a new facet. I leaned in close as the layers carved away unearthed an imperfection in the stone.

It wasn't a crack. I pulled the rod away and turned toward the windows to get more light.

Hart's stepping slowed, but he didn't stand. "What is it?"

"There's something ... almost like ..." I couldn't believe I was going to say this. "It's almost like it's melted ... inside the stone. That can't be, though."

"Why not?" His voice reminded me of Alaric's when he asked me to check my assumptions at the door. I was unsure if he understood the significance of the question.

"It's not the way this gem forms. Any pressure or heating would be on the outer layer of the stone, the one the miners pry through. The center has had the most time to compress and harden. The stone is hardest in the center."

"But the center wasn't always the center, right?"

I guessed that was correct. At one point, the center was the edge, but that would have been ages ago. Years of pressure should have smoothed out this internal mark, and I told him as much.

"What do we know about how adamas is formed, though?"

He was right about that. Everything I knew was about quartz. I only assumed adamas was the same because they looked identical. They weren't, and I knew that better than most.

I was sick of his questions and wanted to turn them on him for a while. "What do you know about adamas?"

He arched his brow, indicating that he was fully aware of what I was doing, and chose to allow it. "Everything I know comes from stories of the Sibling Goddesses."

Out of habit, I glanced at the mirror above the workbench, angled into the front shop to ensure no one was listening. The shop was empty. I could see passersby on the street, but none slowed to enter. It was unlikely anyone else would today. I worked for the Glanmores. Now that I'd taken the Selecteds' measurements, I had everything I needed until tomorrow.

"How are they related?" I asked.

His smile reached his eyes. It was one of the more genuine smiles I'd seen on him. My curiosity made him happy.

He gestured toward the circular blade, his foot resuming the pace. It was clear he wanted me to keep working while he spoke. "I'm so glad you asked."

I sighed and stepped back into place.

"Do you have any siblings?"

I shook my head.

"Ah, well, I'll use this example anyway. Eris was said to

have a little sibling complex. She hated that her older sister, Themis, always thought she was right. Hated having to do things a certain way because that's how Themis had always done them."

"You sound like you know this complex."

His voice sobered. "I have a younger brother. I'm sure he would say I'm a classic Themis."

I glanced over my shoulder to see his gaze held the middle distance like he was lost in thought. He took a moment, but the sound of the adamas, as I let it slide against the blade, seemed to pull him back.

"Themis wouldn't change. So, Eris decided she would create her own chaos. She called the first champion to challenge the Order Themis had imposed on Linia."

"Why?" I asked.

He shrugged. "Who knows the whims of goddesses? It's clear they won't fight each other directly, but they seem happy to do so through those they rule. A descendant of Chaos's Champion still rules Linia."

It was one of the reasons the Library of Linia had appealed to me. Yes, it was widely considered the best source of information on magic, but it was also a kingdom that was said to be different from Kavios in every way.

"Have you ever been to Linia?" I asked.

I'd never met someone who'd left Kavios, but maybe there was more than one reason why Alaric had chosen Hart to escort me through the Oldwood.

His nod sent a chill up my spine. It was possible. I knew it had to be. The obvious next question drew down my elation. Why had he wanted to leave? Why hadn't King Rodric's calm kept him complacent?

He continued before I could voice them. "When Themis realized what Eris had done, she summoned her own champion to fight for the throne—to reimpose her order. The Sisters continue to let their champions determine the fate of each of the continent's three kingdoms."

I thought of the copy of *Champions of Kavios* in the storage closet. That book didn't speak to the origin of the goddesses' champions—only that neither champion in Kavios had yet been victorious.

Even that I questioned, since King Rodric publicly worshiped Themis, but I didn't know when *Champions of Kavios* was written. Regardless, everything Hart said was precisely what Alaric believed.

"So, when Eris and Themis's Champions finally meet in Kavios, one will have to kill the other for the throne?" I asked.

He sighed. "That is certainly what some believe. And definitely what Themis desires, but I'm not sure that was Eris's original intent."

As I asked my question, I pulled the gem back, not wanting to ruin my progress. "What ..." What was I even going to ask? How did he claim to know a goddess's intent? That was ridiculous. "How do you know so much of the Sibling Goddesses?"

The low rumble of his chuckle was back. "I know of many things, Chaos. Where do you think your uncle got all his books?"

My every muscle wanted to turn to the storage room, but I held firm. Some part of me still didn't want to go through them with Hart, no matter how familiar he was with them. I returned the stone to the blade, smoothing the imperfection that had started this conversation. "What does this have to do with the odd patch in the stone?"

He paused. "Eris's champions wield magic based on emotion."

"Her champions are Blessed?" I cut in and immediately winced, thinking of my last conversation with Alaric. The day before his disappearance, Alaric had pointed out that *Champions of Kavios* never said the Cursed King was Blessed, at least not how this city understood the term. It made sense Eris's Champion wouldn't be either.

"Never mind that question. How does the magic based on emotion work?" I asked.

He paused dramatically. "If you stop interrupting, I'll tell you."

I didn't give him the satisfaction of telling him I was waiting with bated breath. I feared he already knew.

"Eris's Champion doesn't steal emotions to fuel her magic. She wields her own emotions—"

"What about Themis's?"

He glared at me, and I pressed my lips together, feigning patience I didn't have.

"We're talking about Eris's Champion now, specifically, her champion in Kavios. The Cursed King is a story for another time." The steady beat of his foot wavered almost imperceptibly. "Now, you want to know how she wields her own emotions?"

I nodded, not willing to trust my mouth to open. There was no telling how many questions would spill forth.

"The way power is taken in Kavios ... It's a bastardization of what it could be. Power, at least how Eris imagined it, is granted by what the champion feels. Her Champion's feelings inspire her magic."

"So, if she feels fear, she wields nightmares like the Cursed King?" I challenged.

No wonder he and Alaric were friends. I hadn't heard this story about Chaos's Champion before, but Alaric studied Eris and Themis more than anything else. He believed, as it sounded like Hart did, that there was more to Chaos than we gave credit.

"She could."

"You're so sure Chaos's Champion is a she; I thought no one knew their identity."

He raised a brow that said I'd get nothing more on that subject.

I returned to his first point. "If Eris didn't create a champion to fight Themis's, then why summon one?"

"I have a few comments," he said.

I pressed the stone harder against the blade, huffing out my frustration. "Of course you do."

My focus on the blade meant I didn't have to see the smirk curl his lip before he spoke.

"Eris doesn't summon. She calls. Those she calls don't have to accept."

I spent so much time reading about the Cursed King and his rebellion against being summoned that I forgot Eris wasn't the same as Themis.

Another piece of the stone fell away, revealing a perfect facet of the adamas. "What's your other correction?"

"More of a response to your question. As I said, I think that Eris's purpose in calling a champion was less nefarious."

"Which is?" I asked.

"She didn't want Themis making every decision unchecked. Eris's Champion would challenge what is known."

I stopped my work and turned to face him. "What does that mean?"

His eyes danced with mirth. "Whatever you want it to."

Scoffing, I turned back to the gem. It was almost hot to the touch. The piece was shaping perfectly. I could only hope the rest of the stones went so well. The imperfection fell off with the next facet line.

"I don't have all the answers, Chaos. There is plenty that only the champions themselves can answer."

"So, your original point—the champions don't need adamas to wield magic. What the Blessed do is a bastardization of the champions' power—what does this have to do with the imperfection in this stone?" I picked up the piece before it fell to the blade. I held it up to the light again. It was definitely melted.

"Just that the goddesses didn't create adamas stone to wield the magic of emotion. They created champions with magic. So, maybe we don't know anything about where the adamas originates."

20

He promised to take care of your tonic. I trust him with that.

— ALARIC SARE'S LETTERS TO ISABELLE ARKOVA

Hart's question stuck with me. I certainly didn't have an answer. What did we know of the origin of adamas? It ruled my life as a citizen of Kavios. I could identify it when others could not, but it was an innate knowing—unexplainable—maybe like how the gem held magic. The discussion with Hart made me miss Alaric. I could see so clearly in my mind Hart and Alaric arguing over the information Hart shared.

Maybe this was what I'd been looking for. Maybe Hart was like Alaric. Maybe he truly worshiped Eris in a kingdom where it was treason to do so. He could have learned about it after the

Blessing. It would explain why he helped the Feared but didn't want me dead.

With Hart's help, I finished cutting and shaping the stones over the course of the afternoon. We had three stones from our first trip to the mines. As I finished each one, I felt a more concentrated warmth within. I was confident these gems would hold magic, but that only brought forth my other dilemma: whether to give the finished gems to the Glanmores.

My back ached from leaning over the blade for hours. Hart, for his part, did whatever I asked. His presence was as overpowering as it was steady and familiar. I wasn't sure what to make of it. It wasn't as if I grew ... *used* ... to his presence. I was always painfully aware of it. But I could admit I trusted him in my space.

I stopped flinching every time he moved closer. To his credit, he did it as infrequently as he could. I turned my thoughts to the Cornucopia tonight, another celebration on the path to the Blessing Ceremony.

Prince Elias would name the Selected since he had been interrupted at the festival. But traditionally, the Cornucopia represented the royal family's generosity to the city. Tables were set through the center of Cross Street, and chairs were pulled from taverns, homes, and shops. It was a special event, bringing everyone together for a feast.

The foods served were similar to those at the Selection. Vendors from the festival were awarded contracts for both nights, but at the Cornucopia, the royal family paid the bill.

"Do you think the Feared will make another display tonight?" I asked.

Hart indicated they weren't on great terms, but maybe he knew their plans. I may believe he would keep me safe, but that didn't mean I wanted to walk carelessly into another event like the festival.

I wasn't sure Kavios could handle another nightmare like that.

Although, the city did what it did best: forgot anything terrible had happened and moved on. The magicless citizens did this daily when we witnessed the *accidental* takings by the Blessed. We were used to it, but the Blessed had no such familiarity with trauma.

The Feared appeared to be on a mission to provide that education, no matter who else it impacted. It seemed unlikely the Cursed King would make a statement like he had at the festival and disappear.

Hart parted the curtain that led to the storefront and ushered me through. "It's impossible to know."

I didn't like the answer but understood the truth in it.

"I'll protect you either way."

This morning had proved that—again. Hart's story during our work today further proved his friendship with Alaric. It had to be one rooted in lore, history, and the divine. Hart claimed to be Alaric's banned book supplier. I didn't see a reason why he'd lie about that. My hesitations from this morning fell away, and finally, I decided to open Alaric's storage closet with him present. In all likelihood, he already knew it was there.

"I have to do something before we go."

Before the Selected had arrived, I'd found a note from Alaric, but I'd stuffed it back into the book in my haste. I needed to read it, and I didn't want to wait until I could devise another way to be here alone to do so.

Hart shrugged as I padded to the bookshelf. His lip curved into a surprised smile when I reached for the hidden latch. Warmth bloomed in my chest as he held my gaze. There was no doubt in my mind he knew it was there. His surprise was ... for me.

Was he surprised that I'd shown it to him? Maybe I was a little surprised at myself. I hadn't wanted to open it with him earlier, but talking to him this afternoon had felt as familiar as my debates with Alaric.

The book was where I'd left it, the paper stuffed inside. I knew it was from Alaric—knew it was for me. Hart didn't follow me in. He couldn't see me from where he stood. I skimmed the note. Water rimmed my eyes and a tear fell on the paper before I finished. I hadn't even realized I was crying.

Alaric had planned to go.

The paper had been rolled, like maybe it was the next riddle he intended to hand me. No. I shook my head. He'd meant for me to find it—because he intended not to be here.

I hope your trip brings you the answers you seek.
Your mother is taken care of. If I'm not here, don't stay.
No matter what you choose, I love you, Ember.

He was gone. What was worse: He had planned to leave. Father's words rang in my head. I was just a project. When I planned to leave, Alaric left to find a new one.

And he hadn't told me. He hadn't wanted to say goodbye.

I let the anger seep in at the second sentence.

If I'm not here, don't stay.

I hadn't even considered continuing with my trip when he was missing. Not that I'd had an option with Vaddon's arrival. Would things have been different if I'd found this note instead of Vaddon finding me in his shop that morning?

Your mother is taken care of.

Fire curled in my chest. That is not the story I'd received from his seller, and it was also one of the reasons I didn't think leaving was an option. I should not be surprised that Hart would lie to me about this, but it felt like another kick in the ribs.

Hart had extracted a promise from me for the youngleaf delivery. He'd exerted power over me, knowing what it was for. Was this all a game to him? This note said he'd already made a deal with Alaric to care for Mother.

My fist closed around the paper, crumbling it.

I needed someone I could trust. Nothing Hart could say would make me believe him. Not when he'd leveraged his position.

Ava would have answers. The bartender at Forest's Edge was one of only a few who'd been straight with me since Alaric went missing. I could tell she cared about Alaric. If I couldn't trust Hart, I wanted to hear about the delivery from her. I believed she would be honest with me.

"Alright, Chaos?" Hart called.

Swiping the tears from my eyes, I pushed my shoulders back. Maybe Ava would be at the Cornucopia tonight. I could speak to her then. I walked out of the storage room and secured it.

"Not bringing anything with you?"

"Just checking something."

His lip twitched like he might smile again, but it fell before it fully curled. His gaze searched mine. I was afraid of what he found there. He said nothing as he parted the curtain again, holding it open for me to leave.

His silence behind me was unnerving. Pretending it didn't bother me, I walked toward the window to tend to the plants. Outside the shop's front window, the tables were set in the middle of the street. I didn't hate the sentiment this event represented. The idea of the city coming together to celebrate its citizens. A feast in honor of those who made the city better by living, contributing, and enjoying their lives here. It wasn't about the Glanmores, and it wasn't actually about the Blessed. It was one time the entire city came together.

The problem was that the sentiment was just that—a feeling, not reality. I pressed my fingers into the dirt of the plant I tended. It was like my false sense of control over the Oldwood—a feeling only, not my reality. Tomorrow, I'd have to face the Oldwood again.

It was a presence impossible to deny.

Just like, during the Cornucopia, it was impossible not to notice that the Blessed ate on the western side of the street and the rest ate on the eastern. The groups only mingled after dinner when residents proceeded to establishments like Forest's Edge.

Finished with the plants, I turned to Hart, meeting his gaze. He'd been waiting for me to do so. It was only then, with eyes locked, that he spoke.

"I'll keep you safe. You have nothing to fear."

Nothing to fear. I highly doubted that.

Alaric wasn't coming back. He'd left of his own volition, thinking I'd also be gone. Clearly, he hadn't intended for me to take his position, but there was nothing he could do about that now. As much as his actions stung, I had to believe he was doing what was right for him.

I'd ignored the thoughts earlier today but knew I had to confront them eventually. It was time to decide what to do about my role and what I could live with. Now that the royal family knew of my skills, they might not accept my disappearance as easily as they'd accepted Alaric's. But if Alaric didn't want to be found and Mother didn't need me to make the tonic, what were my options?

Maybe it was time to find out.

With the setting sun, Cross Street filled. Hart was never more than a few steps behind me, though he let me roam freely. I kept my eyes peeled for Ava but hadn't seen her yet. A smile bloomed when I heard Jasmine's voice across the street.

She dragged Matthew by the hand through a break in the uneven table. "Happy Cornucopia."

"Happy Cornucopia," Serena added, sauntering after them.

Her voice was deeper than I was used to, sultrier. I turned to wish her the same and realized she wasn't looking at me. Her gaze was fixed on Hart. I glanced at Jasmine, whose hand had gone to her mouth to cover a laugh.

My brow furrowed before I focused on Jasmine and Matthew. "Hello, and congratulations to you both."

Hart stood stoically behind me and didn't appear to realize Serena's address was to him.

"Your father is doing well," Jasmine said.

That caught my attention. "Is he getting around alright?"

She tilted her head from side to side. "He's getting by. Mom wants him to stay off it for a few weeks. He says that's not possible."

Maybe I should set up food deliveries for them. If I could take care of any reason he had to leave the apartment, maybe he'd let it heal correctly. "I'll talk to him."

Something like a stone plummeted in my gut as soon as I said it. Even if Mother's medicine was taken care of, which I still needed to verify, Father's shop was light on orders, and he had to stay off his feet. Could he provide the basics for them?

I shook my head—nothing had gone according to whatever plan Alaric thought he had. I'd need to figure this all out for myself based on my current situation. At least now I knew not to search for Alaric.

"Are you going to visit soon?" Jasmine asked.

I glanced over my shoulder. "I'm not sure."

Hart was staring straight ahead. He hadn't conversed with Serena, so I was sure he was listening. Since I'd read Alaric's note, in addition to talking to Ava, I also wanted to check on Mother's delivery. If Alaric had kept to our schedule, she would have received a new batch today. I wasn't sure how I'd get away. My experience this morning only proved how dangerous it was.

Serena interrupted my thoughts, grabbing my sleeved arm.

Hart's stony exterior cracked, and he surged forward at the violation. Serena shrieked at the aggressive movement.

"Relax," I said to Hart. "She just wants to speak privately."

I could guess precisely what she wanted to discuss. I wrapped her hand around my arm to steady her. She seemed to regain confidence with the action and pulled me a few steps away. Jasmine tugged Matthew into the circle.

"What is he doing with you?" Serena asked.

Her gaze flashed to Hart again, making what we discussed all too obvious. He gave us space, though. This gave me hope that I wouldn't have to sneak away to talk to Ava. If I found her, he'd let me have a private conversation.

"Hart is my guard."

"Hart?!" she squeaked. "You call him Hart?"

"What do you call him?" I asked.

"Someone I'd like to fu—"

"That's about enough of that, Serena," Jasmine cut her off as Hart approached.

"Excuse me." He nodded to the others. "Emberline, you're needed for the festivities."

I glanced behind him. He had a helmet in his hand, and another guard strode toward where Vaddon and the prince gathered at the steps. They had intended to present me at the Selection as the new jeweler. Maybe they would include me in tonight's announcement.

"Give me one moment," I said.

He stepped back and slid the helmet over his head.

"How did you end up with him for a guard? I'll do whatever you did," Serena's words were rushed.

"Is he the guard you've been chasing?"

She looked affronted. Jasmine laughed again. "I wouldn't call it chasing. That requires the one being chased to have knowledge that you exist."

"I thought you were getting close?" I asked.

She'd been so excited by the progress she'd made. Something cold and icy slithered in my chest at the thought it was Hart she was after, but I refused to acknowledge it.

"I said I greeted him. That was progress! I heard Soren complaining the other night that he hasn't been around." Her eyes widened. "He said he's been too obsessed with his new charge!" Her hands covered her mouth in a mix of excitement and outrage. She poked me in the chest. "That's you!"

I stepped back, a little surprised myself. Soren wanted me dead. Of course he'd be upset that Hart was protecting me. At least, if Soren hadn't seen him, that lined up with Hart's explanation that he wasn't aligned with the Feared's recent activities.

I swallowed. "I have to go."

"You lucky bit—" Serena didn't even sound mad anymore.

"We'll see you later!" Jasmine waved, pulling Serena and Matthew away.

I wasn't sure what to make of that conversation, but Hart was ushering me toward Centre Street before I could decide. The closer I got to the castle steps, the more I could hear. Realizing the ceremony had already begun, I picked up my pace.

"Welcome!" Vaddon was speaking into something resembling a cone. It amplified his voice, and those down Cross Street heard his words and stopped their conversations. A hush fell across the event, like wings flapping in each direction.

"Welcome to the Cornucopia! I want to present, His Majesty, Prince Elias!"

A roar of clapping broke out, and the clinking of glasses lifted in cheers. The prince accepted the applause with a bashful smile and waves. It only seemed to make the thunderous claps louder. He waited patiently, working the crowd with small gestures. His clothing was more formal than I had seen in his study. Fitted pants and a loose tunic in deep blue showed off his trim frame. A rich blue and gold cape was drawn around his shoulders. The flecks of gold drew attention to the golden crown atop his head. A gem sat in the center of the point of the crown. I didn't have to wonder if it was adamas.

Finally, as the noise dimmed, he began to speak. "This is a Cornucopia, unlike the rest. Usually, you would have been introduced to your Selected by now."

The crowd began to murmur. Hushed whispers of *the Cursed King* filled the space. Prince Elias had to have heard them too, but he didn't stop. Blue glowed from the adamas jewel in the crown, and he continued.

I sucked in a breath. Glowing blue meant he wielded calm. It was a power I associated with King Rodric. I'd yet to see the prince use it.

"The events of this Selection cycle have made that impossible," the prince continued.

I wasn't sure his words were heard as the crowd whispered rumors of the Cursed King and his magic. The press of magic at my neck was feather-light. It didn't seem like Elias was as adept at wielding it as his father. The crowd didn't quiet.

So much for the prince pretending the Cursed King didn't exist.

My gaze roamed the street, snagging on another blue glow from the castle balcony. The one I feared. This one was vibrant, a cerulean blue, like cool, deep waters. I wanted to dive in. As I stared at the gem in the distance, I felt a deeper prick at the back of my neck. The gem's power had reached Cross Street.

The crowd quieted—calming.

The prince glanced momentarily over his shoulder as his audience fell into line. His face pinched at the realization of a second blue glow, but he continued. "So, I'd like to introduce you to them tonight."

Hart's head turned, following the prince's. His lips pressed together beneath his helmet as his gaze returned to the street. He appeared to make the same connection I did.

Was he unaffected like me?

"Wil Stone, Caitlyn Starn, Arthur Pinth, and Deidre Antone." Prince Elias gestured to the group, filing onto the steps behind him. "These are your Selected."

The crowd was too calm from the overwhelming blast of blue light still emanating from the balcony. I wasn't sure they were capable of cheering. The audience didn't even seem to realize the prince had stopped speaking.

The blue glow finally blinked out. The prince sighed and let the adamas in his crown shift to green.

He stretched both arms in feigned exuberance. "Aren't you excited to celebrate your Selected?"

His persuasion pulled the desired cheers from the crowd.

Satisfied with the reaction, he dipped his chin, lifting his hands in applause to the newly Selected.

I glanced again at the balcony where the figure remained. The power he wielded made me think everyone had it wrong; maybe the Cursed King wasn't Themis's Champion but Rodric was. His calm was so strong as to overtake the citizens' emotions completely—so completely it required persuasion magic to pry a reaction from them.

King Rodric was the only Blessed with enough power to make the city forget their fear of the Cursed King.

21

Order will not go quietly.

— FROM CHAMPIONS OF KAVIOS

I didn't have to pretend to be affected by what I'd seen at the Cornucopia. The magic may not calm me, but the reality of the power stunned me into a stupor like the rest of those gathered. I was listless as I waited for an appropriate excuse to slip back into the crowd or leave. The prince hadn't announced a new jeweler, which was probably for the best. He disappeared quickly after his speech. Vaddon descended the steps to greet me.

He nodded. "Emberline."

Vaddon was the last person I wanted to speak to. Now that I saw his face again, I couldn't help but remember his too-convenient appearance at my door this morning and the following attack on the street. I didn't believe in that kind of coincidence. Why would Vaddon set me up? He couldn't be one of the Feared.

I wished I had spoken to Hart about it, but I was also unsure of him again after reading Alaric's note.

No one was making this easy.

A long breath slid from my lips. At this moment, I was supposed to be infused with the king's calming magic and the prince's persuasion. It was not the time to confront Vaddon about trying to kill me. I could sense Hart standing at attention behind me. Vaddon spared him a glance as he addressed me.

He gestured to the street. "It looks like you enjoyed the festivities."

The Selected had merged with their waiting families. Only Deidre stood alone, to the east of the steps. At a different Cornucopia, she'd be the most celebrated Selected. Her story would be the one that motivated magicless families for another year. Tonight, emotions were still mixed from the magic wielded by the Glanmores.

The only good news was that Deidre seemed too lost in her thoughts to notice.

"Did you need me for something?" I asked. Hart had said we'd been summoned.

"Oh, no. We just wanted to ensure you were close for the speech."

I didn't like that. The prince alluding to the Cursed King was not a mistake. It was an intentional provocation of the city's stirring unrest. My eyes widened slightly as I put the pieces together. To soothe the fear, it first needed to be expressed. Prince Elias had baited his audience, and they'd eaten poison berries from his hand.

Vaddon appeared to watch me closely. It was best to let

him lead the conversation. I'd be left pliable if genuinely infused by calm and persuasion magic.

"It's too bad about the trouble at the workshop this morning," he said.

Hart stiffened behind me.

"I was lucky Hart arrived when he did."

Vaddon nodded, glancing again at Hart. The corner of his lip curled down in disappointment. "Indeed. You will return to the mines in the morning. And we'll need to see all the pieces the night before the Presentation. That's two nights from now."

"That won't be a problem."

I'd started slowly today, getting my bearings with the adamas, but now that I understood it, I expected to move faster tomorrow.

Vaddon turned on his heel without so much as a goodbye.

Hart was in front of me when he was out of earshot. "He let you out of the castle this morning?"

"Yes."

As unsure as I was about Hart after reading Alaric's note, I couldn't help but notice he wasn't pretending to be affected by the magic with me. We'd shared a glance as the king's calm was in effect. I wanted to believe it was his own show of trust. He'd told me he'd been to kingdoms outside Kavios. If my suspicion was correct, King Rodric used this magic to calm his citizens into remaining in the city. Hart, having left, only further proved he was unaffected. Now the question was how?

Was he like me? I'd never met anyone else immune to the Blessed before. Even other Blessed were impacted by the magic.

"Chaos, are you listening to me?"

If he'd said something, I hadn't heard it.

He pulled off his helmet and rubbed his forehead. I swear

he growled as he did it. "That group? I told you. I didn't recognize any of them as Feared."

Hart certainly took my safety seriously, if nothing else. He was still stuck on why Vaddon wanted me dead.

I put my hand on my hip. "And let me guess, everyone got away."

Hart arched a brow in question. "Why don't you ask what you want to ask, Chaos?"

"Why do the Feared keep getting away on your watch?"

Even as I said it, I knew it wasn't fair. Yes, some got away, but just as many were dead at my feet.

He sighed. "I'm telling you. Those were not the Feared. Vaddon is not the Feared. There is another threat to you in this city."

It felt too convenient, and I needed to get out of here. I hadn't found Ava, and I needed to talk to her. No matter how ill-advised, I knew I'd have to sneak out and see her at Forest's Edge—this time, without Vaddon's help. If what Hart said was true, as long as no one helped me leave without him, no one could set me up to be ambushed. It was the best I could reassure myself.

"I'm going to my room," I said.

He turned to storm after me up the steps. "You need to take your safety more seriously. I can't protect you if you don't protect yourself."

He was not going to be happy with my next decision.

It's not that he was wrong. I knew there was a real risk to me in the city. But finding Alaric's note taught me that I couldn't let the situation dictate my actions anymore.

Alaric was gone. He wasn't returning, and I needed to find a way out of the mess I'd landed in. I'd learn if Alaric had set up a delivery for Mother with Ava. If there was any chance Mother would be fine without me, I could take more considerable risks. If I no longer needed to search for Alaric, then my current cage would be built only of my responsibility to Mother. It was time to test the strength of the bars.

Hart must have kept on talking as we scaled the staircase. I wasn't listening. He grabbed my sleeve, turning me toward him. I didn't flinch at the reach—only glared.

"The only reason I didn't arrest that little prick was because I thought he meant something to you."

My mind spun, trying to catch up with his words. *Little prick*—was he talking about Macen?

"If you want him gone, all you have to do is say the word."

I tilted my head in question. "And what? You'll have Macen arrested?"

"Sure," he said.

His anger at Macen was genuine. I'd seen it in the Oldwood. This answer left something out. I squinted, reading between his statements.

"You'd have him killed?"

He waved his hand in dismissal. "He wouldn't bother you again. Is that what you want?"

That was so not an answer.

"I don't want you to kill him." I turned and continued my hike up the staircase. "I told you I could take care of it myself."

"I believe you. Like, I hope you believe me when I say I sent other guards after those who attacked you this morning. I haven't heard if any were found."

"Fine."

I took a few more steps. Something he said still rankled, and I couldn't stop from pausing our ascent. I turned to where Hart stopped behind me.

The words slipped out before I knew what I'd say. "He doesn't mean anything to me. Macen. I thought he did once. I've learned from my mistakes."

"Glad to hear it." That smirk curled his lip.

Without another word, I turned and scaled the rest of the staircase into the castle.

Two sentries guarded my door.

"I'll be back early tomorrow, so we can get to the mines," Hart said.

I nodded, not trusting myself to say anything else.

He looked like he wanted to say more but decided against it. Instead, he turned to the guards. "I don't care if the king himself comes for her. Don't let her out without me."

The guards glanced at each other. I couldn't see their expressions beneath the helmets, but I assumed they were unimpressed with the command.

Not wanting to watch a fight, I closed the door.

My only way out tonight would be through the windows on the other side of the room. They were high, but I could climb through one if I stood on the desk. This was a perk of being considered a servant of the Blessed. My bedroom was on the ground floor. I listened at the door for Hart's argument to cease and his steps to fade.

It was now or never.

Quickly, I clambered atop the desk and unlatched the window. I glanced out. No patrols were coming or going. The wall around the city continued around the north side of the castle. I wouldn't expect the garden paths here to be heavily guarded, but I stayed vigilant. Hart would be a living nightmare if he caught me.

I stood on my toes and levered one leg through the open window. Finding purchase on the external windowsill, I pushed off the other. I gripped the window behind me and crouched, looking down at the gardens. It would be a bit of a jump, but ... I looked left and right ... I had no other options.

Hoping it wasn't as far as it looked, I closed my eyes and leaped.

The garden bushes ungracefully broke my fall. Unable to stand in the dense branches, I rolled over, landing on a grassy garden path. I assessed myself as I stared at the sky, wondering how it had come to this. The sting of a few scrapes seemed to be the extent of my injuries. I got to my feet and followed the path to the exit.

Once out of my room, getting around the castle was easier than I thought. Dirt-packed trails led down the hill toward the Eastern Gate. Ostensibly, these trails were for guards on patrol, but I saw none. They must have still been at the Cornucopia.

I didn't second guess myself as I crossed the street and pulled open the door to Forest's Edge. A quick glance had my target in sight. Ava was behind the bar. She must have been there all night. Her gaze locked on mine when I walked in, and she did not look happy to see me. A tip of her head gestured me toward one of the sheer curtain-covered alcoves. As I was here to ask her something, I followed her lead. Parting the curtain, I sat on the edge of the plush couch.

Ava entered and pulled the curtains closed behind her. "You shouldn't be here."

"I need to talk to you."

"To me?" She looked genuinely confused. "I told you the seller would contact you. He did."

I wondered when Hart had found time to return but decided it was irrelevant. "I have new information I want to discuss with you."

She put her hands on her hips and let her head fall back, looking to the ceiling for patience I was sure she was out of. Raising a hand, she gestured for me to proceed.

"Alaric told me the youngleaf was taken care of."

Ava's head tilted to the side. "You spoke with him? You know where he is?" She slid down on the couch next to me, her interest showing as she leaned forward in anticipation.

I shook my head. "No, but ..."

"What? He left a note?"

I sighed. I'd need to tell someone. If I wanted her help, I had to trust her with something. Reasonably, I knew she worked with Soren. She was probably as tangled with the Feared as Hart was, but I couldn't ignore how she peppered me with questions about Alaric. She was eager for a scrap of information about him, as if she cared about him. And whatever else, she didn't seem the type to stab me in the back—she'd have no problem driving the blade through my heart.

"Yes. I found a note."

"What did it say?" Her voice was a whisper.

"Wherever he went, he left on purpose. But he also thought Mother's tonic would be handled. Now, I did talk to the *seller*, as you insist on referring to him, and he drove a different bargain for the herb." I held her gaze as I asked the heart of my question. "I just want to know if I have any options."

She laughed, leaning back and stretching her arms out over the top of the couch. Ava may tend bar here, but her position held power. I was sure of it. "Well, it sounds like the seller has overplayed, hasn't he?"

My brow furrowed, unsure what this meant. She clapped her hands in front of her chest as she rocked toward me. "He thought he held all the cards. Turns out you might have a better hand than he realized. The question is ..." She brought her hands together in her lap and looked at me with a devious smile. "What are you going to do about it?"

I still wasn't sure I understood. "So, Mother's tonic ... It's taken care of?"

She arched a brow at me. "Has Alaric ever lied to you?"

I hesitated before conceding. "No, but apparently, he's seen fit to leave out a lot of information."

"As he did with all of us, Gem. But I choose to believe I knew him. Which meant he had his reasons."

I wished for her confidence, even as her words had me on the edge of my seat. Alaric wouldn't have wanted me stuck in this position with the royal family. It was the only part of him leaving on purpose that didn't make sense. In his perfect world, what? I found the note, knew he was alright, and that Mother didn't need me, and I just ... left Kavios?

Even if Vaddon hadn't found me, I wasn't sure it would have worked that way. Something still didn't make sense.

Ava's information soothed me even as uncertainty raged within. "Do you trust the seller?" I asked.

She'd been so honest about Alaric. I hoped it would continue.

She nodded without hesitation. "I do. But I'm not sure it matters. I don't think trust is transferable like that."

I sighed, conceding her point.

"What did he want in exchange for the herb?" she asked.

My hands balled into fists at my side, thinking of the unspecified favor he'd extracted. Then, I replayed our conversation. First, he'd asked me to trust him.

Maybe Ava was more correct than I realized. I'd told Hart that was unreasonable. He couldn't demand trust that way. Similarly, I knew Alaric had trusted Hart, and I kept latching on to that to convince myself I could trust him too. Neither of those scenarios were how trust works.

I didn't trust easily. Especially not a Blessed. But something in my gut that I'd been working hard to ignore kept telling me to trust Hart.

He'd been as unreasonable as I had been, trying to barter

trust. Talking to him seemed like the best choice. I never got the answers I wanted, but he always seemed to have an answer I needed to hear.

Ava's catlike smile said she knew her question had struck a nerve. She waved me off, wishing me luck with the seller. My thoughts were scattered as I left the tavern. I didn't need a run-in with Soren. It was getting late, but since I snuck out, I still wanted to check on my parents before returning to the castle. I pushed open the door, stepping onto the street, when a hand wrapped around my wrist, lifting and pulling me around the corner to the eastern alley.

I reached for my knife, but my attacker was faster, slamming my hand above my head against the wall before I could stab.

My mouth opened to scream for Ava. Then, the attacker's hood fell back, and eyes the color of the Oldwood's canopy stared back at me. Anger raged in them even as his lip curled into that smirk. His hand around my gloved wrist flexed, pressing it back against the wall again. I was at his mercy, and he knew it. And boy, did he look unhappy I had snuck out.

Hart glanced at the building behind us. "If you wanted a willing partner, Chaos, you need only have asked."

22

I fear this city has forced her to apathy.

— ALARIC SARE'S LETTERS TO
ISABELLE ARKOVA

I fought his hold. "Let me go, Hart."

The panic of an unknown attacker left as quickly as it had arrived. A different feeling pulsed through me as I pushed against my guard. His hand was firmly clasped around my arm—his body inches from mine against the stone wall of the alley.

Even as he manhandled me, he'd been careful only to grab my covered wrists. Now, he leaned into my space. "Not until you listen to me."

I thrashed again. He only reaffirmed his grip. An image, unbidden, flooded my mind. Those rough hands on my bare skin—demanding and unyielding in their conquest.

I shook away the thought and shoved against him again. "Let go."

I raised my knee in my only other defensive move. He saw it coming and sidestepped while his hand clamped harder on my wrist.

"Dammit, Chaos," he said. "What are you doing here?"

I couldn't take it. Heat built inside me at his proximity. It clouded my senses and stripped my tongue of the reason I held so dear. "Why are you blackmailing me when Alaric said the tonic was already taken care of?"

This time, when I pushed against his arm, he let go. Stepping back, he stretched his neck in consideration. "You spoke with Alaric?"

"I just want to know if the tonic has been taken care of. Answer me. Don't wield whatever leverage you think you have."

He pinched the bridge of his nose. "It's taken care of."

"So, you lied to me?"

"I had an agreement with Alaric, not with you."

I leaned into his space. "They were for the same thing!"

His lip curled. The appearance of his smirk told me I was not going to like what came out of his mouth next. "They were not. He asked for a tonic to be delivered to an address. You asked for an herb. Very different."

My hands curled into fists, the nails piercing the inside of my palm in my frustration. "You—"

He folded his arms across his chest. "What, Chaos? I knew what they were for? You see, I didn't. I knew what Alaric's was for. He trusted me with that information. You did not."

"But you ... My mother ... the Oldwood."

I was so mad I couldn't string a complete sentence together. I didn't need to. Hart knew what he did and seemed to have no problem acknowledging it.

“I made a gamble that, as with everything else, Alaric left a lot of information out for all of us. But your mother wasn’t in danger, whether you took my deal or not.”

I hoped my glare expressed how full of shit I thought he was. “You’re an asshole.”

He shrugged, unwilling to deny it. “It could have been for you.”

It was my turn to glare. “Look at me. Why would I need it?”

He arched a brow. I knew from the look that I’d asked the wrong question. And as much as I wanted to blame Alaric again for leaving me so unprepared, I knew my emotions were getting the best of me with Hart.

“The herb has ... other uses. I thought you were aware of that.”

It was too late now to pretend I knew otherwise. “What other uses?”

“It is a powerful stimulant, enhancing emotions, feelings, abilities ...”

“Why would I want to feel more in this Siblings-cursed city?”

His piercing gaze held mine for another beat, debating something. He ran a hand through his hair as he shared a fact that quenched my need for information like water in the desert did thirst. “Your uncle used it to avoid the king’s calming influence. He drank it with his tea.”

My mouth hung open in disbelief.

“So you could imagine”—he gave me a significant look—“why I thought you might do the same.”

Of course. This was why he was unsurprised that the king’s calm didn’t affect me at the Cornucopia. This misstep, I laid squarely at Alaric’s feet. Again, he chose not to tell me. He knew I didn’t need it, but why not explain what he knew?

I turned to walk away. This was too much. Had it only been

hours ago that I wondered if Hart was like me? I thought maybe I'd found someone who could explain why I was the way I was.

The man in question slid into my path. "Absolutely not, Chaos. We are not done."

"Come with me, or don't; I don't care. I'm going to see my parents."

He lifted a hand to gesture me forward. "Fine."

"You're going with me?"

Anger still surged in the depths of his gaze. He let out a breath. "I'm not letting you continue to traipse through a city trying to kill you on your own. I can't begin to tell you how stupid it was for you to walk into Forest's Edge. Now, let's get going, shall we? Before anyone notices your absence."

"How did you notice my absence?"

His hand pressed against the wall on my left side, and he leaned in. "I like the shortened version of your name. Ember. Does only Alaric use it?"

My brow furrowed. Only family did. It added another layer of confusion to hear it from his lips. "What does that—"

"Just answer the question."

His proximity was distracting. "My mother does ..."

He let the silence hang between us, thick and heavy. "You are a single ember, lighting the darkest night, a beacon calling me across kingdoms. I'd find you anywhere, Chaos."

His words shot chills up my spine and gooseflesh across my skin. His gaze was too intimate, too knowing. I was too lost in it.

Finally, he stepped back. His lingering smirk told me he knew his words had landed. Determined not to let them affect me, I straightened my spine and left the alley.

Hart let me lead, though he was never far behind. Every time I snuck a glance at him, his jaw was flexed, hands gripped into fists at his sides. He was fighting some internal battle as we walked through Kavios.

I still couldn't figure out what to think of him. He'd come clean, but as Ava had pointed out, only because Alaric had outmaneuvered him. What I really hated was that his reasons for thinking I might use the youngleaf separately from Mother, unfortunately, made sense.

When I turned to look at him as I rounded the first-floor staircase of my parents' apartment building, he held my gaze like he'd been waiting for it. He hadn't asked anything about what we were doing here, and I didn't share.

"I understand doing anything to care for your mother." His words were a whisper.

Unsure what this was, I waited. Hart had mentioned he had a younger brother, but it was one of the few personal details he'd shared. I was desperate to know more about this man who seemed to know more about my uncle than I did.

His voice remained quiet. "My mother died because of my actions."

I questioned whether I'd heard him correctly. The pain etched into his features when he stopped speaking told me I had.

My heart cracked a little at the words. Cracked in a way that only someone who carried the same weight could. I opened my mouth to say something. What? I wasn't sure. Offer my condolences? I knew it didn't help.

"There was one part of our property I wasn't supposed to go to. I knew as much from a young age, and my mother ensured I had plenty of other entertainment. I had more than I needed. Avoiding the area in question shouldn't have been a problem. But I was young and reckless, and"—he shook his head at his younger self's stupidity—"I went anyway."

Something changed in his face. The pain remained, but a fierce resolve slipped in with it. Telling this story was costing him something.

I wanted to hear the story as much as I wanted to know why he was sharing it.

"My mother, of course, came after me. But there was a reason I wasn't supposed to be there. It was dangerous. She died helping me return."

By his stops and starts, I could tell he'd left out much of the story. His pain was real, though. He believed he was responsible for his mother's death. I couldn't blame him. For a while, I'd believed I was responsible for Mother's condition.

His fists were still clenched at his side when our gazes met.

"I'm sorry," I said.

The words seemed inadequate, but they were all I had.

"Me too."

He offered me this part of him. I wanted to give a piece of myself in return. He knew the king's calm didn't affect me, and thanks to Alaric's need to keep information from me, he knew it wasn't because of youngleaf. If nothing else, this would help him understand.

"I don't know what Alaric told you, but a Blessed—they took too much from my mother. They were trying to take from me, and she knocked me away."

I couldn't bring myself to fill in the gap, to say why they pulled too hard, that their first attempt to take from me had failed.

His eyes widened slightly. I didn't think it was because of my story. It was, unfortunately, a common one in Kavios. More likely, he was surprised that I was saying anything at all. As much as he hadn't shared his history with me, I hadn't shared with him either.

"I'm sorry that happened."

I swallowed, realizing I had much to say now that I'd started. "When I was young, she was nearly comatose, unable to get out of bed. She'd only speak vague words or half-sentences ... for years. Father spent all his time caring for her. Which left me to run the shop."

I'd never told this to anyone. Others in the neighborhood knew, of course, but that was different.

"How old were you?" he asked.

I laughed, but it was hollow. "Eight when it happened. I was ten when Father stopped joining me at the shop."

I chanced a glance at him. Something like horror flooded his features. It wasn't pity, though, and that was the most important thing to me. I didn't want Hart's pity.

"Alaric helped me," I rushed to continue. "He worked both in his position and helped me with mine. I owe him everything."

Something contorted on Hart's face. It was a mix of anger and maybe sadness. "It sounds like he did what he was able to. But you should never have been asked to do that so young."

I shrugged. "We don't always get to make those choices. My family needed the income. Mother and Father were no longer capable of providing it. Someone had to."

"And no one had an issue placing jewelry orders with a child?"

"Father came in when necessary, usually to deal with customers. He wasn't ignorant of the appearances, though it often seemed like it."

Hart scoffed. He opened his mouth to say something else, likely a scathing assessment of my father's character.

I stopped him. "I always thought it was a beautiful story of a love I didn't understand. My father and mother were always so happy. They had their own language in gazes and smiles and laughs."

"It sounds nice," he said.

I sighed. "Maybe. They were a unit. But then she was gone, her mind and body somewhere he couldn't follow. They were so connected. Her pain was his. He couldn't continue his life when hers was on hold."

"It sounds like the lesson is not to let your partner go somewhere you can't follow."

My lip fought curling into a smile at Hart's attempt to lighten the mood. Of course that would be his answer. "Once Alaric created the tonic and Mother's condition stopped deteriorating, Father worked with me again."

Hart nodded.

"I've learned not to take all the guilt myself. I was not responsible for the Blessed's actions." I hesitated, and then the secret part slipped out. The part I repeated often in my head but rarely gave life to in words. "Even if it should have been me."

My gaze locked with Hart's. Something passed between us, an understanding I didn't expect. I saw my pain reflected in his features.

"I can't say I understand your Father's, or even Alaric's, actions ... but that ... I understand."

I believed him. We had a bone-deep understanding—he, too, knew what it was to wonder how things could have gone differently, what might have changed for your loved ones if they had.

Suddenly, I felt too raw. I wrapped my arms around myself. The open hallway was too exposed. So many emotions flooded me. I didn't know what to do with them—where to put them. My sadness at our mother's stories mixed with something close to contentment at knowing someone saw my pain and understood.

I shook them off.

This hardly fixed my and Hart's problems. He was still Blessed—still had some connection with the Feared. Under duress, he may have admitted Alaric had taken care of the tonic, but he hadn't exactly let me out of my end of the blackmail.

We couldn't be ... whatever this was.

I was unsure how to break the strange intimacy. "We should go."

He nodded and followed as I led him up the rest of the stairs.

At some point, as I entered the apartment, Hart stopped following me. He must have decided to stand sentry in the hallway, which was probably for the best. I was unsure what I would find inside.

Father was sitting by the fire, watching a pot of water near boiling, likely for Mother's tea. He startled. "Emberline. What are you doing here?"

Although I had seen him only a few days before, the distance between us felt like it stretched years.

"I came to check on Mother's tonic delivery. Did we get it?"

He looked confused. "Yes, someone dropped it off maybe an hour ago."

The relief that flooded me was more than I could bear. My knees felt weak. Even as Hart leveraged his side of our deal, he'd held true to the one he had made with Alaric. Did this make a difference? I didn't know, but a weight lifted to think I could make decisions without worrying they would cost Mother her tonic.

I swallowed the surfacing emotion. "Alright, I have to go."

He stood to pour the water over the tea leaves. "Say hello to your mother first."

I didn't want to argue. Quick steps led me down the hallway to her room. It was late, but Mother's eyes were open, and she smiled like she'd seen the stars light up the night sky for the first time.

"I've missed you, Ember."

I bit my lip to stop the tears from welling in my eyes. Hart's comment about my name echoed through my head. I didn't know what to make of it. Everything Hart did confused me. Words like those begged me to trust him. But his actions told me to be wary.

"Will you come give me a hug before you go?"

I didn't ask how she knew I was leaving so soon, but I didn't hesitate, stooping to wrap my arms around her. I lost the battle against the brimming tears, and one slipped down my cheek.

"The Cursed King is coming."

Her eyes were cloudy, but I knew she'd recently had tonic. The nightmare magic hadn't been seen again since the festival. I wasn't naive enough to think he'd left Kavios, but I'd hoped to avoid a confrontation.

Her voice was still airy when she continued. "Chaos knew what she was doing."

I shook my head, unsure what to make of the statements. They sounded like a refrain from *Champions of Kavios,* but I couldn't place them.

Her tonic may be taken care of, but standing there with Mother reminded me that it didn't provide the certainty I hoped for about my next move. Leaving still felt out of reach. The prince had threatened Father once already. They wouldn't leave him alone if I disappeared. They'd come for him, even if he couldn't source the adamas.

Mother couldn't travel. She needed to stay close to the youngleaf source. I still didn't know where it came from. It seemed, with every step I took toward freedom, a new obstacle blocked my path.

"We'll be alright, love." She answered my unspoken fears.

"What do you mean?"

She squeezed tight and whispered into my hair. "Be careful and stick close to your guard."

I collected myself while she refused to expand on her comments. We separated, and I departed. Hart paced the hallway like a caged animal. He was close to the door as I opened it, like he'd contemplated following me. It wasn't until he turned and I met Hart's gaze that I realized I hadn't told Mother I had a guard.

23

They both would have to feel deeply. It's no small feat in a city like ours.

— FROM CHAMPIONS OF KAVIOS

As Hart and I held each other's gaze in the hallway, a million questions fought to fall from my lips. He'd delivered Mother's tonic before I knew about it. He proved he would hold up to a deal with Alaric that Alaric was in no position to enforce.

He said he'd keep me safe—and my damned gut wanted to believe him.

I needed more than that. Would Hart continue to take care of Mother's tonic if I were gone? Would it matter if the Glanmores came for Father anyway?

Then there were Mother's words. She rambled, yes, but I'd learned to listen. What did she want me to do about the

Cursed King? I still assumed he wanted me gone, like the Feared. It was best to stay out of his line of sight.

Knowing King Rodric's power over this city, I couldn't stand by and help grow it. I couldn't create more Blessed for him. I didn't know where that left me, and I needed someone with whom I could talk about all this.

My gut wanted it to be Hart, and while I hated it, it didn't tend to be wrong. The rest of me would feel better if I could find some logical reason to back it up.

Hart didn't speak, though some of my burning questions must have been evident on my face. Hart helped the Feared. Maybe he could tell me more about the Cursed King. Finally, I opened my mouth to speak.

"Not here," he said.

I gestured to the staircase. "Lead the way."

He raised a brow. "Your place or mine?"

I sucked in a breath.

"To talk," he clarified.

I knew that, obviously. "Someone posted sentries outside my door. So if we go to mine, we have to be quiet."

"I have no illusion that you'd be quiet." The low rumble of his voice made the double entendre even more suggestive. It had my toes curling in my boots.

"I guess that leaves yours."

I spoke with more confidence than I felt. I was in over my head, but if I was going to seriously consider not handing over the adamas, I'd need an ally.

He led us to the stairs. I glanced over my shoulder before we descended. I didn't know the next time I'd get to see my parents. If I left the city because of whatever plans I concocted, I may never see them again. The feeling was as freeing as it was suffocating.

I was starting to take more of a liking to the Cursed King's story. His defiance in the face of a goddess's summons at times seemed petulant. Now, with the trappings of the Glanmores dictating my actions, I understood it.

Whatever I did next would be my choice, and I needed to live with myself once I made it.

My chest tightened as I thought of all that could go wrong. Hart must have seen something in my face, putting himself in my line of vision.

His eyes were so green they felt like they held their own power of persuasion. "Hey. You'll be back."

I let out a shaky breath. He had no idea what I was thinking —no idea what I might do. I knew all that but still chose to believe his words. His voice held that conviction that consistently made me believe he prioritized my safety, even when everything else begged me to question him. I wanted to believe him on this too.

I couldn't help the nervous laugh that bubbled in my chest when Hart led us to the door of Forest's Edge. The heavy wooden handle was one I was becoming too familiar with.

"Your room is in the tavern?" I asked. "What a revelation."

His glare said he was unamused. "There is nowhere better for a conversation you don't want to be overheard."

Given the number of conversations Serena had shared with me in the last few days, I wasn't sure about that. I said as much to Hart.

The way his lip curled told me I was in for something I wasn't sure I'd like.

"The conversations in the curtained alcoves are as private as they come."

My heart raced of its own accord. Ava must agree with him

since she'd taken me to one a few hours ago. I'd been anxious enough with Ava, and she'd kept her distance. What exactly would this entail?

I'd be damned if I asked.

Hart's smirk was smackable, but to his credit, he waited before opening the door and ushering us in. Our gazes locked, tempting me to suggest an alternative. The flutter in my abdomen said this was a bad idea.

I swallowed and pulled the door open.

He whispered in my ear as we crossed the room, searching for an open alcove. "We'll be able to keep our distance unless someone comes by, wanting to take the space. They are ... prioritized for taking."

This was the fullest I'd seen the tavern. Every seat at the bar was occupied. Guests sprawled through the central dining space. Many sat at packed tables, and some stood, moving between groups. The room was alive, even more so than the city at this hour.

Orange flashed through each curtained alcove we passed. Most were occupied, but Hart must have spotted one that was open as he turned and led us to the back corner.

The alcove he led us to was well shielded from prying eyes. A staircase to the second floor partially blocked its view of the room, but there was a door beside it that few slipped through. I took a position on the plush seat.

"The gambling rooms," he said, noticing my attention. "Most going in won't give us a second glance."

I was at a loss for words. This alcove was different than the one Ava and I had spoken in earlier. The plush seat was more of a daybed. Large enough for two, maybe three people, but didn't provide the luxury of distance. Scooting back on the seat, my shoulders hit the cushion, and my legs curled beneath me.

Hart tracked my movements. His eyes finally met mine. "Ready?"

Ready as I was going to be. I dipped my chin.

He crawled the length of the daybed. My heartbeat spiked with each movement. As he rolled to a seated position, his arm sprawled across the cushion behind me.

"This alright?"

Words escaped me. No matter what we discussed, this felt like a choice of its own. Had I ever let a Blessed so casually close to me? I swallowed.

"You know you'll have to speak for this to work, right?" His smirk was back.

The deep desire to wipe it from his face helped balance my nerves. In practice, I knew he was correct. I'd obviously need to say something, but I could feel the heat of his hand behind my neck. These alcoves didn't seem like they were meant for talking.

I sat up straighter, desperate to maintain some control.

"Do you know the Cursed King?" I asked.

He knew the Feared, even if his opinion on them seemed to be shifting. How long had the famed figure been with them? What were his goals? The story of Themis's Champion was hundreds of years old. He hadn't shown himself in the city in all that time. What could he want now?

He chuckled. "Why do you ask?"

At that moment, the curtain parted, and Ava walked in. She had a tray full of drinks balanced atop her hand. "I saw you two sneak back here and figured I'd better be your server."

She set down two glasses with heavy pours of warm brown liquid.

"Thanks, Ava," Hart said.

"I was already covering the alcoves tonight, so no one else

should stop in." She held Hart's gaze like she was trying to tell him something else. Something I wasn't privy to.

He waved away her concern. "It'll be fine."

She shook her head and closed the sheer curtains behind her as she left.

Hart's intense focus returned to me. "Now, what was your question?"

"Do you know what he wants?"

Hart sipped his drink before setting it on the table beside the daybed. "What any man summoned by a goddess and cursed by another wants—freedom to choose."

I clutched the glass of my own drink for reassurance. "Does he lead the Feared?"

"More or less." He picked up his drink as if the words caused his need for another sip. "The Feared are a rebel group united around an idea. They follow his lead, so long as they see the mission they believe in accomplished."

"But they're magicless ... He's not. How can they have the same mission?"

Hart raised his brow. "Surely, you don't have to experience a wrongdoing to know the behavior is wrong?"

I hummed softly, considering. He was correct, but wasn't that a little too convenient for Themis's Champion? Shouldn't he simply take the throne and be done with it?

"So, Themis's Champion is interested in taking power from the Blessed?"

He nodded.

I set aside the complexities of that for a moment, needing to be a little selfish. Mother's words had me on edge. "Then I'm a problem to him, just like I'm a problem for the Feared."

He shook his head. "The fastest way to stop the Blessed's number from growing may be to remove you. But to take the city from them? No. To hold power in this city, it must be taken from King Rodric."

"Easier said than done. The Cursed King may have nightmare magic, but King Rodric can wipe away the memory of it," I said.

Hart's jaw clenched. Then, the alcove curtain parted. A man and woman stumbled in. The man's hand caressed the woman's neck, moving south, and the adamas gem on his finger flashed orange.

"This one is occupied," Hart grumbled.

"Doesn't look like it." The man's gaze lingered on the space between Hart and me—the space that proved he wasn't currently taking.

I hoped never to be on the receiving end of the glare Hart gave in return.

"I don't expect everyone to understand that there is a finesse to the process," he said pointedly. "Rushing only disappoints your partner."

He glanced at the woman, whose eyes widened as his words registered. She turned and stormed out of the alcove, the man chasing after her.

"Is that true?" The words were out of my mouth before I could stop them.

Hart rounded on me, and a smile curled his lip. "I'd be happy to help you find out."

He leaned forward, and my heart was in my throat. I hoped he couldn't hear the erratic beats it made as the distance closed between us.

"Blessed take emotion. When collecting lust, to continue to make it...enjoyable for one's partner, you have to stoke more lust than you take." He glanced over his shoulder at the retreating Blessed. "His focus should be entirely on his partner's satisfaction."

My throat was dry at his words.

His focus returned to me, his body caged mine on the seat now, and he whispered in my ear, "I do need to be a bit closer now. He'll complain to Ava. We need to make this more convincing."

I tried to swallow and ended up clearing my throat instead.

He lifted his hand, reaching for a strand of my hair that had fallen into my face. "You alright with that? I won't touch your skin."

Disappointment curled in my stomach. "Alright."

He studied the hair as he wrapped it around his fingers. "What's your next question?"

Forming a complete sentence was a challenge. He knew the Feared and didn't make it sound like the Cursed King was a real threat to me. I wasn't sure I believed it, but maybe Mother's line was really from *Champions of Kavios*. I could check in the morning.

For now, I needed more truths from Hart. "You saw the king's magic at the Cornucopia."

He tucked the hair behind my ear, careful not to touch me. "That's not a question, Chaos."

"What was he doing?" I breathed.

Hart's hand moved to my hip. His other hand was hidden beneath me, so those around us could not tell where it lingered. "You know what he was doing."

Even with the layer of clothing between us, his touch was like a brand, burning through to the skin beneath. The stories of siren songs luring unsuspecting sailors to their doom flashed through my thoughts. I grasped for a composure that was steadily slipping through my fingers.

I pushed Hart's shoulder back, and he rolled with my guidance. He ended up seated in the chair, and I crawled onto his lap, hovering just above him. The flex and grip of his fingers at my waist said he wasn't as unaffected as he appeared.

He reached again for a blond strand that had freed itself with my movement. "Careful, Chaos. We don't need to make this *that* good of a show." He closed his eyes momentarily as if reminding himself of the question. "The king used his magic to calm the populace, to lull them into a sense of safety."

His thumb stroked my hip. I tentatively placed my hands on his chest, bracing against the strength of him.

This was a terrible idea. "It's not the only time he's done such a thing." That was another statement. Quickly, I added, "Is it?"

Hart's chuckle was low and dark as his thumb slid across my hip again. "It's not."

I leaned forward, my mouth hovering just above his ear. My knees spread wider of their own accord, sinking me lower over his lap. His length was hard beneath me. I closed my eyes, savoring the moment for the seconds I had before I unleashed my treasonous suspicion. "He uses it on the populace regularly. He makes them complacent in Kavios, so they won't want to leave."

Hart's piercing gaze held mine as I pulled away. He didn't correct me this time, even though there was no question in my words. His throat bobbed as he swallowed, and then he nodded.

Unable to determine if his struggle was lust or treason, I eased back.

His hand tightened on my hip, a slight pressure on my back leading me forward. We were partners in crime tonight. It was a reminder of why we were here. I needed an ally in all of this, and for some reason, I wanted it to be Hart.

The next words that fought to free themselves would tip

the scales. They would mean I trusted Hart myself, and not because my uncle or Ava did first.

I reasoned that he already suspected. We'd made eye contact during the king's calm at the Cornucopia. Thanks to Alaric's secrets, Hart knew I didn't take youngleaf to prevent its impacts. He hadn't asked me for another justification.

I wanted to give it to him anyway.

Still, I wasn't sure I'd ever spoken the words aloud. Tentatively, I tasted them on my lips. "His power doesn't work on me."

Hart's smile was sinful, as his hand gripped tighter on my hip.

In for a penny, in for a pound. "None of the Blessed's magic works on me," I continued. "The day Alaric disappeared, the day you were supposed to walk me through the Oldwood—I was planning to go to the Library of Linia to try to find out why."

"Why are you telling me this?"

I wasn't sure he was breathing.

"Because I can't give Rodric the adamas. And now that the Glanmores know others in Alaric's family can source it, I can't leave. It's too dangerous for my father."

His hand slid up my side. "The real question, Chaos, is what will you do about it?"

I sat back, his challenge clearing my head. What was *I* going to do about it? I wanted to run but couldn't, not with my family in the crosshairs. "What about you?"

His fingers twitched at my side. "I've chosen my path."

"Working with the Feared?"

He ignored my jab. "Using my position to get resources for those working against Rodric. You could ... help." His words were hesitant, and his grip loosened.

It was as if he hadn't realized what he would say, as if

maybe he had surprised himself. He was quiet for a moment. Contemplative. I got the sense he wasn't waiting for me to answer.

His hand lay loose at my hip now. Sanity returned to my lust-addled brain. "The youngleaf. It wasn't only Alaric you gave it to. You must distribute it to the Feared if it provides resistance against the king's calm."

Something like an idea sparked in his eyes. Its intensity would be alarming if I weren't already spilling secrets that could see me killed.

He cleared his throat. "Yes. You could come with me tomorrow to pick it up."

I wasn't sure how that would help, but something in his gaze begged, once again, for trust. "Is this you calling in the bargain for Mother's allotment?"

My words were a test, and we both knew it. He'd delivered on his deal with Alaric tonight. He had to have known I would eventually learn Mother was receiving the tonic.

He sighed. "You know the answer, Chaos. Do it or don't—your Mother will receive her tonic."

"Then why—"

He shrugged and reached for his drink again. "This city had done nothing but take from you. Then, you were thrust into this position. With Alaric gone, you have no one to trust and a big decision to make."

I laughed. "Blackmailing me was a funny way to earn my trust."

His hand curled around my hip again. The slight pressure reinforced his point. "You were never going to trust me. Not with who I am and who you are. But I was happy enough to see your anger—to see you feel something."

Stunned, I rolled off him and curled back in my original position to his right. "Why do you care what I feel?"

He laughed, but it was hollow. “What did Alaric’s note say, Ember?”

I swallowed thickly. He was changing the subject, but whether it was the use of the name or the new topic, I found myself responding. “The note told me Alaric intended to leave. Clearly, he expected me to find it before the royals found me.”

Hart set his drink down and leaned over me again. His brow arched, reminding me our show wasn’t over. “And just like that, Alaric left you trapped in the position he hated.”

Tears pricked behind my eyes. His words were harsh, but they weren’t incorrect.

He leaned in, his breath warm against my neck. “I want to help you.”

The scent of the liquor on his breath reached my nose. It was more intoxicating than the drink itself. “Why?”

His chuckle shot jolts of pleasure through my body. I was holding on by a thread. “Maybe because none of this is fair. Or maybe because you don’t deserve this fate. Maybe I just think you need it.”

That was rude but accurate.

He paused again. “You’re supposed to have a choice. A real one.”

“What does that mean?”

He shook his head before he started speaking. “I was so mad at Alaric when he left. So mad when I found you—realized you were—”

His words cut off, but I could remember his anger that afternoon in the alley. Then the way it had shifted as he seemed to recognize my fear of being in close quarters with a Blessed.

“It doesn’t matter. I wish he’d trusted me with more, but—”

“I know that feeling,” I said. “Although a wise woman told

me trust isn't transferable. I don't think loyalty or friendship are either. Please don't help me because you think it's what Alaric would want. I only want your help if it's because you want to give it."

His mouth was at my ear. "Alaric is the farthest thing from my mind."

I couldn't stop my lips from tilting into a smile. We'd covered so much ground tonight. This discussion might have been needed, but things felt too heavy, too serious. I wanted something lighter to break the tension. "Tell me something true."

He didn't hesitate. "I do live here at Forest's Edge. There are stairs to my apartment in the alley."

I laughed. Then pushed him back to look at his face. He was serious. "What?"

"I know you'll find this hard to believe since I'm so good at it, but I'm not *just* a guard. I own this place. Originally, I became a city guard to help the Feared. Then, when your uncle went missing, I decided it was worth getting assigned to you."

My heart beat rapidly again as his thumb at my waist slid back and forth in a gentle caress. "Why did you want to get assigned to me?"

He leaned back farther and picked up his drink to take a sip. "At first. It was to see what Alaric was hiding."

I needed the momentary distance to clear my head. My attempt at light conversation brought us back to all of this. At least he was giving me the honesty I craved. I just wasn't sure how much more I could take tonight. I swallowed. "And now?"

He arched an eyebrow, set down his drink, and rolled back over me. His hand moved to the strand of hair falling from my braid again. He wrapped it around his finger. "Now, I think you feel trapped. But I want to show you your options. Seeing how I collect the youngleaf will be good for you."

This was what I wanted: an ally who knew what was happening in this city—someone to help me decide my next move when so much seemed unstable.

"I'll go with you tomorrow. But now, I need to return to my room."

He gave me space, letting me scoot out from beneath him. As I stood and straightened my clothes, he parted the curtain, gesturing for me to go.

Tonight had been a huge gamble, but I thought it paid off. I wanted to know what he knew. There was more outside the city he was trying to show me, and I wasn't one to turn down information. I'd take all I could before the Blessing Ceremony.

24

They are more alike than either of them would ever believe.

— ALARIC SARE'S LETTERS TO ISABELLE ARKOVA

True to his word, Hart was at the door to my room before the sun rose. Something passed between us when our eyes met. With the night guards standing sentry just behind him, I couldn't comment. Mostly, I wanted to believe something had changed for us last night. Eager to learn more about the youngleaf and his role in its distribution, we walked in companionable silence to Alaric's shop.

If the youngleaf's properties were as varied as Hart said, it was a critical resource for the city's residents. Where was it grown? How was it distributed? I had many questions, and the answers might help me think of a future for Mother outside of

Kavios. If I could get her and Father out of the city with a steady youngleaf supply, maybe I'd be free to run.

We didn't have unlimited time. The Selection events continued, leading up to the King's Blessing. Today, we collected more adamas—the four gems needed to be ready for the Presentation. I could finish the settings and rings the day after. Technically, that was the day of the Masquerade, but it wasn't an event that required the jeweler. It was more of a debauched celebration of the Blessed, welcoming new members into their circle of opulence.

I unlocked the door to the workshop with cautious optimism. Maybe a plan would take shape with more information on both of these topics. One that didn't risk my family. I was almost too excited to worry about the walk through the Oldwood this trip required.

Or maybe I didn't worry because Hart would be with me.

I grabbed my bag from the back of Alaric's workshop. "Do we need anything else today?"

Tamara, the mine foreman, had said I'd do more than sort gems this time. I couldn't help but expect to go through the locked door. I desperately wanted to know what was inside.

"They should let you into the adamas cavern. But I don't think you need any tools besides your hands."

I turned to face him as I leaned against the workbench. "And what is the order of operations for our journey?"

His brows raised. "You really want to go?"

The hesitation in his voice made me realize I wasn't the only one unsure of our alliance. I nodded.

He looked conflicted. "You don't owe me anything—"

"Can you give me a hint about where we're going?"

His lip tilted into a smile as I ignored his objections. "It's ... well, it's a settlement in the foothills."

"A settlement?" I couldn't imagine how that was possible.

Someone should know, shouldn't they? I guessed if the king made everyone so calm that they didn't care about the outside world, maybe this was proof that it was working exactly as intended.

Hart's excitement was growing. "We should be able to get there and then over to the mines this morning if you're sure. It's not too far out of the way."

He looked almost boyish. Except anyone looking into his eyes wouldn't mistake him for a youth. His gaze held knowledge, sadness, and desperation that only came with age.

A question formed on my lips. It slipped out before I could stop myself. "How old are you?"

I'd had my hands on his chest last night, and in the heat of the moment, I hadn't checked for an adamas pendant. My cheeks flushed. That uniform hadn't hidden anything.

Was there any chance he wasn't Blessed?

Hart laughed. "No need to be that honest with each other, Chaos." He turned to leave.

"Hart, I'm serious."

I took pride when his head dropped back, looking at the ceiling. When he asked a goddess for patience in dealing with me, I knew I was on the right track. "I'm old."

"Older than Alaric?"

"Yes," he grumbled.

Alaric wasn't so old, just over fifty, but older and looking the way Hart did proved he was Blessed.

"One hundred?" Now, I wouldn't be satisfied until I had the answer.

He pinched the bridge of his nose. "Older."

Even if I couldn't see the ring, it was there somewhere. I wasn't sure why I was trying to prove to myself that maybe ... he wasn't.

I sighed. "A hundred and fifty?"

He turned and gave me a knowing glance. "Two hundred and twenty."

My gaze darted to the storage closet and the history books that Alaric had made me study. "This city is only officially two hundred years old."

"Alaric taught you everything, didn't he?"

"Not everything." The sting of his voluntary abandonment lingered. I wished he'd taught me about whatever drove him to leave Kavios.

Hart stepped toward me, reading too much on my face. "I know the feeling. Come on, Chaos. I need to stop by the tavern before we go."

The memories from last night came rushing back in. Even the ones I'd tried to repress as I thought about my hands exploring his chest. That was one mistake that would haunt me for years to come.

As much as his body tempted me—our conversation had given me hope. Not the misguided hope the Blessed foist upon the citizens of Kavios, but something real. There was something in this settlement he wanted me to see. I wanted to understand what it was and decide if it could help change my course—give me an alternate path besides giving more adamas to the Blessed.

Hart and I walked to the Eastern Gate less than an hour later. A smell unlike anything I'd experienced made my nostrils flare. The measly breakfast I'd eaten that morning roiled in my gut as my other senses caught up with what my nose already knew.

Bodies hung on both sides of the gate.

The smell of the rotting corpses was too much for me to

take in. My knees weakened.

"What—"

Hart stepped closer, cursing under his breath. "I didn't think he'd—"

"Who are th—" I was going to vomit. The pieces fitting together. "Those aren't ..."

Hart nodded. "The group I killed yesterday trying to ambush you? They are."

There were six of them hanging. Three on each side of the gate. Throats slit, knife wounds to the chest, each body was more brutally executed than the last.

"Did you ..." I wasn't sure what I was asking.

Hart's face contorted. He held himself rigid, like he wanted to step closer, to keep me from falling. I settled a gloved hand on his arm to put him out of his misery. That it steadied me as we passed through the Eastern Gate was a bonus.

"Close your eyes, Chaos. I'll guide you."

I shook my head, putting more pressure on his arm as we walked.

Hart cursed again. "I didn't think he'd dispose of them this way."

My breathing was steadier now that they were no longer in view. "I didn't even think of what happened on the street after we left."

"I don't disagree with the message Elias is sending. They weren't going to stop."

I waved my hand callously behind us, toward the vicious display. "They appear to be stopped."

He chuckled. Actually laughed.

I swatted at him. "What is wrong with you?"

His face held no remorse. "They were going to kill you. They deserve worse."

Did I regret their deaths? I wasn't sure. Mostly, I was glad it wasn't me. Seeing the bodies of those who meant to kill me wasn't something I'd considered my position on. "You said it wasn't the Feared?"

"It wasn't anyone I recognized," Hart said. "But what does that matter? After the display at the festival and the half-assed attempt to reassure the city at the Cornucopia, Elias needs a good story. And that"—he gestured—"is a great story."

"Those are dead men and women," I said dryly.

"Who were going to kill you, Chaos. Has that still not sunk in?"

I hmphed, unable to determine where I fell on the matter. My brain said they were trying to improve Kavios, removing the Blessed's ability to source adamas. My gut said they were trying to kill me, and maybe Hart was a little too easy on them.

I hated my gut.

But it also reminded me that whether they were Feared or not, I had little question that Vaddon was behind the attack.

"Does Vaddon work with the Feared? Like you ... do ... did?"

Hart tilted his head. "Not that I know of. I'm still determining his motives in all of this. He hasn't escaped my notice, either. It's clear he wanted you to be alone on the street that morning. I just can't prove it."

Leaving the scent of death with the city, we entered the Oldwood. I eyed the bag slung over Hart's shoulder. He had slipped into the alley next to the tavern and returned with it. I wanted to know what was inside. Or, possibly, I wanted to distract myself for as long as possible, hoping the Oldwood wouldn't overtake me.

"We'll go to the pickup first. Then the mines. They wouldn't expect us this early anyway."

That would also ensure we missed the miner's shift change. I glanced up to evaluate the sun's light, but the stubborn tangle of branches and the thick layer of leaves refused it access.

I didn't know how I ever thought I could make it through the woods alone in my original plan. The trappings of this place never stopped reaching for me. With only a few steps, it felt like something called me—without words. I didn't know where to look—didn't know what it wanted.

Hart's gaze was heavy on the back of my neck. He saw too much, but this was not something I could explain. His presence reassured me. If I strayed from the path again, he would be there. The Oldwood could try, but in a battle of wills to take me, it would lose against Hart.

I attempted to distract myself. "What's in the bag?"

"Supplies."

Could he be any more unhelpful? Something may have changed between us, but at least this was familiar.

"Do I need to know anything else about this ... settlement?" I was unreasonably nervous. Whether it was due to the Oldwood or the illicit side trip before we ventured to the mines, I didn't know.

"Just be yourself."

He was giving me nothing to work with. "Will they know who that is?"

"Some will. Some won't. For them, it's more about others knowing of their existence and caring about their choice to live ... outside. Who or what you are won't be the focus."

All too quickly, the Oldwood distracted me from my questions. I fought for each step I took as the forest's magic threatened to pull me under.

The sound of Mother's cries, searching for me through the trees, rang in my ears.

"No."

I spoke the word aloud, hoping that giving voice to it would push back whatever hold the forest had on me.

Hart was beside me now. His presence an anchor. “What do you ... see in the Oldwood?”

His words were hesitant, which, at this moment, I appreciated.

There wasn’t any point in keeping this from him. He had already seen the impacts. “Not see. Hear.”

He cleared his throat. “What do you hear?”

I shook my head. “A voice calls to me. It has since I was a girl. I’m unsure if it’s even there or just some phantom magic of this place.”

Hart arched a brow.

“What?”

He chuckled. “Phantom magic?”

“Great, now you’re laughing at me too.”

“I’m just curious. You know, they say sometimes the Oldwood tells us what we need to hear.”

I glared at him. “Who says that?”

He shrugged. His teasing distracted me, but the Oldwood’s magic was still very much present. I hoped this settlement wasn’t too much farther.

25

He might not right his wrongs if she leaves, but maybe he'll avoid new ones.

— FROM CHAMPIONS OF KAVIOS

Hart took the lead when we turned east at the Oldwood Trail fork. The path was there, but it was overgrown and wild, making it appear rarely used.

I blamed King Rodric. While traders still brought goods in and took ours out, few, if any, other visitors came to our city. Kavios was nestled near the mountains. It wasn't an easy trip from the continent's other kingdoms, but it must be even less appealing with the influence of Rodric's magic. Did the other kingdoms know of his influence?

It always came back to adamas. What was Hart's question? What did we know of its origins? Not much, but we knew the Oldwood Mine was the only source. The other kingdoms may have champions, but what was one or two magic wielders versus hundreds of Blessed?

"Where are we going?" I asked as Hart led us from the path.

"Don't get scared now, Chaos. We're just getting to the good part."

I could do without his taunt, although the low tug in my belly at his voice said otherwise. Fear of where Hart would lead hadn't crossed my mind. Maybe fear of the Oldwood, but I was managing its pull. Last night, I'd told Hart the secret that defined my life. After I had trusted him with that, there wasn't much more to give.

"The settlement is only a few more miles this way."

He was lucky I was a fast walker. Trekking from Woodside to Lower Hill regularly was no small feat. I'd learned to do so quickly to avoid notice. In his uniform, Hart looked like he exercised every hour of the day. Realistically, I knew it was from magic. Stolen joy honed the Blessed's bodies into the standard of beauty. Yet, a niggling reminder in the back of my mind told me I'd still never seen Hart take. Even Serena said he ignored all willing partners, not just her. I wasn't sure why that made me smile.

A raven cawed overhead. It landed on a low branch and screeched again. It was directed at Hart if I didn't know better.

"We're coming," Hart said.

"Are you talking to that bird?"

"Would you believe me if I said yes?"

I would, but I questioned my sanity.

"We're almost there." He picked up the pace, and the bird flapped its wings, taking flight. We had veered slightly north in the off-path trek, and now boulders, twice my height, came into view. These must be fallen pieces of the Pinnacle Range. Our journey had taken us into the foothills.

Hart led me through a maze of massive stones. I hoped no

one had been around when they'd fallen. Finally, we turned again, revealing a settlement of tents I hadn't seen until staring at them straight on.

A woman stood before us. "About time you showed up."

Her dark brown hair was almost black and braided down her back. She stood with her hands on her hips, and a sword was strapped to her back. The raven in question landed on her shoulder. This woman had the beauty of a Blessed. Her white skin was flawless from my vantage point, even as her clothing told another story. The trousers and tunic she wore looked like they'd seen better days. A tear in her cloak snagged my attention—probably from the bird's talons. She was a contrast in every way, and nothing showed it more clearly than when a man walked up beside her and handed her an adamas pendant.

"You might need this," he whispered.

Hart leveled a glare at him. "We're invited guests, Reid."

The man—Reid—was dressed similarly to the woman. He shrugged at Hart. "Can never be too careful."

His arm draped protectively around the woman's shoulders as he slid the pendant over her head. The bird flapped at the disturbance, and the woman laughed, meeting my gaze.

"Overprotective men, am I right?"

I laughed as she brushed off both Reid and the bird.

She gestured toward the tents. "I'm Alysa. Welcome to The Storm."

"The Storm?" I asked.

"That's what we call our settlement. Let me show you around."

The Storm was small, but I was surprised by how many people it contained—at least fifty, by my count. There were men, women, and even children. Alysa knew everyone. I couldn't explain it, but it was clear she held some position of power with them.

She waved to a family amid morning chores. "The Trellis family joined us a few months ago. They feared their daughter would be Selected and didn't want to be separated. Most families here had some reason to leave. They felt they had no options."

At the tent next to the Trellis family, a man slowly pushed back his tent flap, also starting his day. He moved like he was eighty—he looked it too.

"A Blessed over-took from Patrick," Alysa said. "I wasn't sure he'd survive. They just left him there, in the alley." She gestured at Hart. "Lucky that one found him, got him some of your uncle's tonic, and got him to us."

Is this what Hart wanted me to see? A community outside the walls of Kavios, not subject to Rodric's influence? That thought gave me pause.

"The Storm," I said aloud. "As in the opposite of King Rodric's calm?"

Alysa nodded. "We're not rebels like the Feared. We've chosen to live outside the system, but we'd rather face the storms of life outside Kavios than exist within it in such a state."

It was almost fantastical to think about. Immediately, I knew it could solve so many of my problems. Mother and Father could live here. The community knew Alaric's remedy and had access to the necessary herb.

As much as it had the potential to help, it also hurt. I shouldn't be surprised by now, but this was another secret Alaric had kept. He hadn't told me about a community outside the city walls. He hadn't shared that he helped get those who wanted to leave out of Kavios.

I couldn't believe I'd thought I was the first one planning to leave. Alysa was already moving on, talking about another family or resident.

Hart met and held my gaze before I followed. His face was impassive, and I had no idea what he read from mine. This place seemed unreal. As disappointed as I was that Alaric didn't tell me about it, I was just as astounded that Hart had.

Did he know I contemplated leaving? Did he think I should? I guessed he knew my mother's condition, meaning it wasn't a big leap to recognize that she would need a place like this.

Although he'd brought me here and must see it as a solution to some of my problems, he was still on edge. His fingers twitched near his sword, though he didn't draw it. How many times must he have been through this encampment, yet he was still on guard?

Maybe that was just his way. Not trusting anyone seemed lonely, but I couldn't exactly cast stones. I was much the same. Perhaps Hart and I were more alike than I had considered.

"Come on, you two. Keep up!" Alysa called.

I hurried to catch her, falling into step at her side. "So, the bird is your ... pet?"

She laughed. "I guess that's the best way to explain it."

"And Reid ..." I was prying now.

"Not my pet. He's my husband."

I looked at the gem hanging from her neck. "Are you Blessed?"

She gestured to the tent before us, pulling back the flap. "You should come in. We can talk." Hart moved to follow. She held up a hand to stop him. "Ladies only."

"Abso—" Hart started.

"That's it. We do this privately or not at all. I don't know what you're up to, but I know it's part of why you brought her here." She folded her arms across her chest. "Take it or leave it."

A string of curses left Hart's mouth. He glanced at me. "I'll be right outside."

Alysa giggled, another contradiction to the fierce woman who had just put Hart in his place. I wondered what I'd gotten myself into.

The tent felt more at home than anywhere I could remember—except maybe Alaric's workshop. Although, that hadn't felt the same without him in it.

Alysa fit here. The inside of the tent had the same contrasts as her person. Two bedrolls were pushed together, with a large heaping of heavy blankets atop. The scene looked like a cozy cottage. A makeshift bedside table was erected, holding a book and a mug with something that smelled like mint. The other side of the tent looked like a blacksmith's workshop. Blades, bows, and axes were laid out on a trunk acting as a display table.

I didn't know Alysa, but I thought I liked her.

Alysa turned. She leaned against the trunk and gestured for me to sit on the bed. "So ... am I Blessed?" She tapped her chin. "The short answer is no."

"And the long answer?" I asked.

"Well, it's a different story."

"I'd like to hear it if you're willing to share it."

She considered me. "Before I do, can I ask you something?"

I nodded. It seemed only fair.

"What's Hart to you?"

My answer was mechanical. I didn't allow myself to think. "He's my guard."

"But why? You're the Jeweler to the Blessed. The key to breaking the Blessed's hold on Kavios, if rumors are correct. No jeweler, no adamas. No adamas, no Blessed." She shrugged, like discussing my death was nothing more than an inconvenience.

My gaze darted toward the tent entrance. I wondered if Hart should have fought harder to be allowed entry.

"You misunderstand," she said, sensing my rising panic. "I don't want to hurt you. My path is set. I don't fight Rodric's system. I live outside of it."

That, I understood. It was a path I'd considered myself. One I would consider again if I could ensure my parents' safety.

Alysa continued, "I don't care what the Feared do, but don't you find it odd that Hart guards you? Defends you from them? He's worked with them for years."

I couldn't fault her question. I struggled with it too. Ultimately, I'd accepted that he would defend me—he'd proved it time and time again. This question didn't feel like mine to answer. It felt like something she should ask Hart.

"I don't think he had a choice," I said. "He was assigned."

It was hedging. Given our conversation last night, I was sure it was true, but technically, it was his job.

She furrowed her brow, deciding if I knew better. "Do you think that man has ever done anything he doesn't want to do?" She pointed to where Hart stood, then smiled. "Except maybe standing outside for this discussion?"

I laughed. I'd thought the same the first time I'd heard him and Alaric talk. Their conversation had shown their familiarity, their friendship, but Hart also hadn't hesitated to issue commands.

She tapped her lip. "So, you do know. You're just not sure what to trust me with. That's fair."

"You'll have to ask him for the answer." I shrugged. "He works with you, though you claim no allegiance to the Feared. What are you getting at with your question?"

"I'm not sure," she said slowly. "Hart has never brought someone to our settlement who didn't desperately need to be here. I guess I'm only trying to assess your role. You're right. Hart has worked with me. He's worked with the Feared. And he's Blessed—though no one has ever seen that damn adamas."

My ears perked up, vindicated that I wasn't the only one bothered by that.

"He's driven by something, a purpose none of us can pin down. So long as my people continue to benefit from it, I have no quarrel with him." She pushed off her perch and began to pace. "But I've seen others like him. Whatever drives him, he'll stop at nothing to get it. He's been teetering on the edge for months, close to whatever he seeks."

She stopped pacing and turned to me. "This is nothing more than a warning to be cautious. If you're in his way, between him and his prize, he'll turn on you quicker than the Blessed taking on the street."

I didn't know what to say. She had shared much but asked for nothing. "What if I did need to be here? Would you offer me a different path?"

She smiled in a way that showed all her teeth. It was as ferocious as it was disconcerting. "I would. But before I do that, let me tell you my story. My parents were Blessed."

My eyes widened, and immediately, I thought of Alaric's history books. There was a story of a young woman who rejected her life as a daughter of the Blessed. I'd always hoped this was true, but had never imagined I'd meet the woman herself.

"I was soon to be Selected when I learned the truth."

I was hanging on the edge of my seat now. "What truth?"

"That Rodric's blessing means nothing. Only his power over the adamas distribution allows him to call it such." She tilted her head. "But I would wager you already know that."

I didn't respond.

She looked into the distance. "That, and learning the king used that influence to calm everyone into a stupor of complacency, was too much for me."

Her hands balled into fists at her side as she spoke. I wondered what sent her over the edge. She would have had a good life growing up in a Blessed household. Not many would search for trouble.

"I was to be Selected. There was no question, given my lineage. I had to decide who I wanted to be and what I could live with. I don't judge Hart's choices." She shook her head. "Actually, I don't know his choices. I considered what I believe to be his choice: accept the stone and not use it. Even that didn't sit right with me, though. So, I did this instead."

"What is *this*?"

"Like I said, we'd rather weather the storm outside Kavios than live within its walls. We collect those who feel they have no choice, like I did, and we give them one. The Storm is a community of shelter and survival."

"How is it no one knows you're here?"

She shrugged. "Rodric's magic helps. As does the magic of the Oldwood, I think. We move from time to time as well. It's a nomadic existence, but it keeps everyone safe."

"Why stay by Kavios at all?"

She laughed, but it rang hollow. "I ask myself that all the time. The truth is, I want to be here for others who seek our sanctuary. I also want to provide the youngleaf, found only in the foothills, to help people improve their lives in Kavios, should they choose to stay."

I sucked in a breath. Hart had given me more than I could imagine today, and I thought he knew it. This knowledge about the youngleaf would let me make decisions for my family I'd only dreamed of.

"We could use you here," she said. "If you're looking to leave."

Was Hart so sure Alysa would offer me a place? Would she take my family with me? It seemed too perfect to be coincidental.

I wouldn't exchange one cage for another. Alysa had been open with me, but so far, it all suited her story. Her questions about Hart sounded genuine, but they could just as easily be an attempt to indicate Hart had his own agenda and that maybe I should trust her instead.

"What would you have me do?"

She smiled again. "Nothing you aren't already doing. I'd still ask you to collect adamas, but we distribute it amongst ourselves. All use is consensual … truly consensual, not what passes for such in Lower Hill."

It sounded too good to be true. "You have access to the mines?"

She nodded. "We do. There's a defunct entrance in the foothills. The paths are treacherous, but it does the trick. We've been unable to get into the locked door where the adamas is mined, though."

"I haven't been allowed in there myself yet," I confessed.

"I'm sure you will be soon. They have little choice but to send you."

Entering the locked door would be part of my duty on this trip, which reminded me: We needed to get going. "Could my parents come with me?"

She nodded. "We take all who seek freedom from Rodric's magic."

I stood, still not sure what to make of the offer. "I'll consider it. But for now, we have to go. Do you have the youngleaf?"

Her stare was hard. A final appraisal. A final nod. "Hart will already have it. I hope to see you again, Emberline."

I followed her out of the tent. Hart bounced a small pouch in his hand, and his bag was gone. The new packet was small enough to fit in his pocket. It wasn't even midday, and I didn't know what to make of our trip.

Hart had shared a refuge for me and my family, should I choose to run.

As soon as I had an escape that kept my parents safe, part of me assumed I'd take it. Now, I hesitated. I wanted to talk to Hart. This conversation made me consider what role I could play for the city. Could I be like Hart and disrupt Rodric's rule from my position in the kingdom? I wasn't sure how that would work, but either way, Alysa's Storm was the safety net I needed.

I shook my head, unable to believe things were finally going my way. As we turned to leave, I waved goodbye to another of Alaric's histories, leaping off the page and coming to life.

26

I fear the connection you predicted. But I also fear they'll need it. It's the only way to unleash them both.

— ALARIC SARE'S LETTERS TO ISABELLE ARKOVA

Hart and I left The Storm and walked in silence to the path. As we returned to the Oldwood, its presence made itself known.

"Well?"

It probably wasn't the first time he'd asked me something. I turned toward him as he towered over me. "I don't know."

I tried to focus. He was asking about the settlement. What had happened with Alysa. Her offer was ... perfect. The fact that Hart knew it would be confused me. How long had he planned to take me there? Why had Alaric never done the same?

Hart arched a brow. “Did she ask you to join them?”

I rubbed my temples as if to ward off the delirium sinking in. “If you know, why are you asking? Why did we even pretend to leave you out of the conversation?”

I wanted to return to not trusting Hart so that I could think the whole thing was a setup. But I knew it for the lie it was.

“Are you upset?” he asked. “I thought you’d be happy to know such a place existed.”

I didn’t know how to explain. I was out of practice at explaining the complexities of emotions. “I am. It’s exactly what I needed. I just ...”

He stepped closer. “What is it, Chaos?”

I shook free of the magic’s hold. “How did you know I wanted that option?”

Hart’s lip tilted into a smile. “I’m not sure it’s that option you do want. My job is to make sure you know you have many.”

That might be worse. I compared Hart and Alysa’s choices. They both had the same gruff exterior but had taken opposite paths to deal with the mess that was Kavios. She worked outside the system. Hart had chosen to work against it from the inside.

“Why do you work against the Blessed?” I asked.

He canted his head. “You think it impossible to work against my own supposed interest?”

“Your words. Not mine,” I said. “I’m just trying to understand.”

“Is it so hard to imagine that I don’t believe a third of the population’s comfort should come at the cost of the rest?”

Well, when he put it that way ...

“As I said yesterday, it doesn’t take an impeccable moral

compass to know what Rodric does is wrong. The use of his calm like a drug for the masses is bad enough. Everyone deserves to make the choice about where they want to live and why."

He sounded so rational when he said it like it was the easiest decision he'd ever made. Not the most dangerous.

On the walk out here, I thought I'd already put all my trust in Hart, but with the Oldwood's magic pressing down on me, I knew there was something more I must do. I hadn't truly let it overtake me since that day with my Mother. The experience had scared her, scared Alaric, and I hadn't thought to try it again.

I fought to free another question from my lips as the Oldwood's magic surrounded me. "What you said about the magic here. Was it true?"

He didn't hesitate with my meandering topics. It's like he was aware of my current internal struggle.

"I don't know. Some say the forest is sentient. I don't think *that's* true."

His voice centered me and would keep me from venturing where he could not follow.

Leaves rustled, and his pace quickened as he closed the distance between us—his mouth now inches from my ear. "I like to think what I told you is true. It's magic balances what Rodric has done. It tells us what we need to hear, away from the calming influence."

I could *feel* the smirk curl his lip as he said his next words. My senses were alive not to the Oldwood but to him.

"What is it telling you, Chaos?" A pause. "Are you ready to hear it?"

That couldn't be true, could it? I had no reason for my reaction to the Oldwood, the same way I had no reason for my immunity to the Blessed's magic. Hart baited me like Alaric did. Like he knew I'd have to test what he offered. If I wanted to ... explore his taunt, I acknowledged there was no safer time than with Hart at my side.

I could trust Hart with this too.

As if seeing the set of a decision in my features, Hart held my gaze and nodded.

I closed my eyes and listened. What was it trying to tell me? Or what did I need to hear?

My thoughts spun as I stopped fighting the Oldwood's magic. Memories of Mother's cries as she searched for me mixed with the desperate need to sink my fingers into the soil —to unearth what was below.

Letting myself succumb to the forest's hold, it was different than the press of the Blessed's magic against my neck. This was a bone-deep desire to be below. Clawing, digging, searching, endlessly searching. Something was here, and it was mine.

"*Emberline.*"

Whatever it was, it called to me. Scenes blurred in my mind. Stories of magical beasts and magnificent terror.

The voice called again. "*Only you can free me.*"

It was ancient. It was magnificent. It was ... trapped.

My eyes shot open. I was unsurprised to find myself off the path, hands covered in soil, as I'd reached deep into the dirt. I searched the brush and bushes. The forest growth was so dense that I couldn't see the path.

Hart leaned against a tree. His gaze was so intense, I wondered if he'd experienced everything I just had. I knew he hadn't. That smirk curled his lip as he pushed off the trunk, realizing I was ... back from wherever I'd been.

Someone needed me to free them.

Hart stepped forward cautiously, leaning down to return my gloves. I must have torn them off in my attempt to feel the ground. Wiping my hands together, I brushed what dirt I could from them.

What did this mean? I slipped the gloves on, covering the evidence of my undoing. Hart reached for me, and I stared at his open palm. There was little risk. My hand was gloved again. He knew my secret. The action seemed so small, but to me, it represented how everything between us had shifted.

This trust between us grew, and I craved more. I was sick of denying my gut reaction. It was too late anyway. There was no taking back the information I'd shared or what he'd shown me today with The Storm.

I knew I stared too long at his outstretched hand, but Hart didn't rush me.

He had decided he could do the most for this city from his position of power, no matter how he'd come about it. Could I do the same? Could I use my position as Jeweler to the Blessed to help this ... captive?

I couldn't say why, but I knew this was important. I had a list of other things to worry about: the Blessing Ceremony, my parents, and my future.

What had Hart said? This was what I needed to hear.

My gloved hand slipped into his.

The flimsy barrier between us wasn't enough. His touch scalded. A stark contrast to the Oldwood's chilled depths. It burned past my hesitations as he pulled me up.

"What's the verdict, Chaos?"

I couldn't begin to determine the layers of his question. "Someone needs me. I just have to find out who."

He gave me a brief once-over. "Determination suits you."

It should worry me how right his words felt. A man I had met only days ago saw whatever spark this brief sojourn had ignited.

I had a plan before all this started—a plan to protect my

family and to learn about myself. Only an hour ago, I thought I'd found a safe place to run. My plan continued to evolve. I'd fit everything I could into the time before the Blessing Ceremony. That was days away. I still had time to fix things—time to figure out who was trapped, who called to me.

Alysa's offer was still a safety net.

That smirk crept into place on Hart's stupidly handsome face, and he quickly turned us toward the Oldwood Trail, leaving me to wonder if this, too, was what he had wanted me to learn on today's journey.

Tamara greeted us at the entrance and led us into the mines. As we descended, I let my hand drift along the tunnel wall again, curious if I could still feel the Oldwood's magic. The way I dug into the ground when the magic overpowered me, I was beginning to believe the magic came from somewhere in the mines. Maybe whoever I searched for—dug for—was here. Maybe the adamas itself called to me.

The voice was absent as we trekked down to the locked door. No pile of gems to sort sat outside the door today. We were going in.

Tamara held a cloth long enough to wrap around my eyes. "King Rodric requires anyone but Gregory and me to wear this when they enter. Use it as a blindfold. Gregory will also be with you. He'll report if you take it off."

The threat was clear, but she only had one piece of cloth.

Hart noticed too. "I'm going with her."

"Absolutely not," Tamara said.

"I'm sorry you thought that was a question," he said. "It wasn't."

Tamara straightened her spine. "Prince Elias—"

"Has tasked me with keeping her safe. I cannot do so when she's blindfolded and behind a locked door."

The foreman appeared to consider her options: further delay while she dealt with this or let him through. He had a point about the prince's expectations. Tamara must have agreed because she gritted her teeth and pulled another cloth from her pocket.

My feet were already moving of their own accord. Similar to the pull of the Oldwood, something beyond that door called to me. I was sure it was the adamas—or whatever made the adamas. My ability to identify it when cut must mean the pull to the raw, unmined material was strong. I nearly bounced in excitement. No matter the rest of the day's learnings and decisions yet to be made, one of the mysteries that most fascinated me might be unveiled shortly.

I handed the blindfold to Hart to secure. "What do I do?"

He didn't secure it yet, while Tamara provided instructions.

"Behind the door is a cavern. You'll be identifying the new workspace. Move around the outside wall until you feel the presence of adamas. Point it out to Gregory, and he'll note it for the next crew."

Gregory looked white as a sheet. Was he trembling? He did not look happy with his assignment.

"What's wrong with you?" Hart asked Gregory.

"Don't mind him," Tamara said. "It's just nerves. He will know if you disregard an order, and the consequences from the royal family will be more than severe."

Her threat was once again noted, but I wasn't sure that explained Gregory's ... condition. Sweat dripped from his brow, even though we were deep underground where the air was cool against my skin. Gregory opened his mouth, but a bright blue glow stole over Tamara's ring before he could speak. "You'll be alright, Gregory. I have full faith in you."

His shoulders fell, relaxing instantly under the influence of the adamas.

Tamara patted Gregory on the shoulder before returning up the path. "I'll see you all in a few hours."

Hart and I shared a look. The need for calming magic was beyond suspicious, but I wasn't sure anything could prevent me from going through that door. When I shrugged, he secured my blindfold and his own.

Gregory unlocked the door. It sounded difficult to move. Gregory's panic returned in the form of heavy breaths as he pulled the door open just enough for us to enter.

"Turn left," he said. "The cavern is a circle. Stay on the outside."

My immediate question was, what's in the middle? But I knew better than to ask.

Hart followed closely. I don't know how he tracked me, but I could feel his presence in my space even without sight and touch.

I'd just been thinking about how cold the depths of the mines were, but as the door clanged shut, the temperature skyrocketed. This room was an inferno comparatively. I guessed I shouldn't be surprised—the adamas stone was always warm to me.

Without delay, I removed my gloves and set my hands against the wall. It was warmer than the tunnels leading down here, but it didn't hold the heat of adamas. I took slow steps, spreading my hands to feel as much of the wall as possible.

I reached higher, not meeting a ceiling of any kind.

"Hart, can you reach up? How tall is the room?"

He must have done what I asked. "It must be taller than me."

The low rumble of his voice echoed through the room, making me wonder how big the space was. We had hours before we had to return, but I was fascinated by what this room held. It felt like the key to what made me different. What was in here that only I could handle?

I kept searching up and down the wall, as I walked in the circle Gregory had set me. His whimpers were getting farther away with every step. He must not be following. I probably should be more worried. The foreman had to calm him to send him with us. She must be a powerful Blessed to wield the magic. Whatever he could see, and I couldn't, was not for the faint of heart.

But I was not afraid.

Wind blew hot against my neck. It made me wonder at how close Hart was. I swatted behind me, halting when I felt the seams of his uniform.

His laugh was low. "Not that I'm upset, but this hardly seems the time or place, Chaos."

When he finished the sentence, his breath was hot against my ear. The movement told me he hadn't been close enough to breathe on my neck before. There must be an air current unique to this room.

I swatted him again. "I was just checking something."

"Check away," he replied.

I was sure that smirk was firmly in place on the uncovered part of his face. As I pulled my hand back to return it to the wall, it bumped into something.

Gregory whimpered loudly.

Whatever I hit was toward the middle of the room. Were there stalagmites in here? It was jagged like the slowly piling rock formations. But something about it was ... slippery. It reminded me of the snakes I used to chase on the edge of the Oldwood before we started waiting at the gate. And it was hot ... like the adamas—but different.

The heat flooded me, and something deep within flared to

life. Whatever it was, this heat fanned that single ember buried deep in my chest.

I wanted more.

Even as wonder overcame me, an equal part of anger bubbled alongside it. Something—someone—was trapped in here, making the adamas. I needed to find them.

"Hart," I said. "Feel this."

I reached for him again, grabbing his hand. Heat bloomed, reminding me I didn't have my glove on—I'd touched his bare skin. He knew he couldn't take from me, but his hand ... spasmed when we made contact. I loosened my grip, wondering if I made him uncomfortable. He intertwined our fingers with a sigh, letting me do what I originally wanted. I brought his hand to where mine had been.

Whatever moment our touch drew from him was forgotten.

"Fucking Chaos," he hissed.

That one was definitely a curse.

He pushed me behind him. "Get back against the wall."

Gregory whined again. It sounded even more like a cry than the previous sounds.

My hand hit the wall. Hart knocked me into a new section in his attempt to shield me. A familiar warmth flooded me.

This was the newest adamas deposit. I was sure of it. "I found it."

"*You found me, too, Emberline.*"

The voice was in my head. The same voice from the Oldwood. The one who needed me.

"Hart," I hissed.

He still pressed me against the wall. His body shielded me from whatever threat he deemed to be in the center of the room. I didn't know what to say or how to communicate the voice I heard. Gregory was still somewhere, so I couldn't speak plainly.

"I'm busy right now, Chaos."

What did that mean?

"Diiidd yyou ffffind it?" Gregory stammered.

I pointed. "Yes. It's here."

"Could you move aside?" He'd done something to calm himself. Or maybe Hart had taken care of whatever threat they both seemed to believe existed.

Hart allowed us a shuffle to the right. His body was still firmly between me and whatever lurked within the cavern.

Steel clashed against stone. Gregory must have brought a pickaxe. He struck again. I did need more of the gem, but I heard more than enough rubble fall to the ground. He repeated the motion.

"Gregory, I think you have enough."

He took another swing, and more debris fell to the cavern floor. "The prince said to send you back with twice what you need. He has another project for you."

I swallowed, uncomfortable with that information. What more could the prince want? He should be entirely focused on the Selection.

Gregory stooped to pick up the pieces. I'm sure he dropped them into the cloth bag he'd carried over his shoulder.

"Let's get out of here," he said.

Hart didn't need to be told twice. "Put your gloves on."

I did, and before I could protest, he grabbed my hand and pulled me behind him, returning to the cavern entrance. His breaths didn't slow until we were on the other side of the locked door with our blindfolds off.

27

He thought the price of his curse had already been paid. It will cost him more before the end.

— FROM CHAMPIONS OF KAVIOS

I wanted a minute to think about what just happened—about what I'd heard. The voice was gone as quickly as it had come. It was in the cavern, though. I knew it. I needed to get back.

What could be in there that had Gregory, and even Hart, so nervous? The heat in the room made me think about Hart's words in the workshop. I had said the adamas couldn't be melted. The imperfection we'd found had to have been something else. I no longer thought that was true as I wiped sweat from my brow.

Something, someone, was in there, who could make the room that hot. Childhood memories flooded my mind: games with Mother, a friend I knew existed but couldn't get to, and the urge to dig beneath the Oldwood.

I stared at the door. Whoever was in there needed me. How did I get them out?

Gregory was already halfway up the path. He'd put as much distance between himself and the door as possible. "Let's go."

"You can't get to him," Hart's voice was a whisper next to me.

Him. He knew someone was in there—someone who needed me to free him. Somehow, I wasn't surprised that Hart knew it too.

I lifted my chin, staring up into his face. "He's trapped."

Hart didn't shrink away from my defiance. "I'm well aware, Chaos. We'll get him. Just not now."

We'll. Hart stayed true to his word even with my shifting priorities. Or maybe he had heard the voice, too, and felt his own calling to save him. I acknowledged that trying to rip the door from its hinges in front of the mine's second-in-command wasn't a great plan, but the voice left me desperate to save it.

"You heard him too?" I asked.

Hart shook his head.

"How do you know?"

He opened and closed his mouth. A hesitation I wasn't used to from Hart. He always seemed so sure of himself. Whatever he wanted to say, he was struggling to find the words. Which meant I desperately wanted to hear them.

The ground started to shake before he spoke.

My gaze locked with Hart's. Over his shoulder, Gregory scurried farther up the path.

A crack sounded, and panic struck Hart's features before I understood its meaning. He was just out of arm's reach.

The ground shook harder.

Hart was moving, lunging for me. A wall of stone and debris crumbled where I'd stood moments ago.

The tunnel path connecting us to Gregory—and the exit—collapsed.

I was on the cold ground, blinking, as I assessed my surroundings. The tunnel was dark. The only light on our side of the cave-in, a torch beside the locked door, had gone out with the movement. Dim light from the other side of the path streamed through the giant rock pieces now in our way.

An intriguing weight pressed against me as I heaved in deep breaths.

The back of my head hurt, even though it was cradled in something soft. Fingers flexed against my hair. I knew the rigid lines of his body better than I cared to admit. As I fully opened my eyes, Hart's forest green gaze was boring into mine.

"Dammit, Charon," he said.

The name was unfamiliar. Knowing Hart, it was another forgotten god he cursed.

"Are you alright?" he asked.

My body shook as my panic set in. An earthshake, a cave-in. We were trapped in the mine. My head throbbed, but Hart had saved me—once again.

"I'm good. You?"

While our chests were awkwardly pressed together, the rapid beat of my heart must have given me away because he laughed outright at my response.

"How's your head?" His fingers moved carefully around my crown, likely checking for the thick dampness of blood.

"It's alright. I think you stopped most of the damage."

My senses were alive, cataloging every place our bodies connected. His arms were braced on either side of me, trying to hold himself apart. Our legs entwined, his knee separating mine. What was wrong with me? Now was not the time for this.

“Are you hurt?” I asked again.

His voice was low. “I’m fine.”

I wasn’t sure it was the cave-in affecting him.

With trouble, I tore my gaze from his and looked at the blockage over his shoulder. It must have broken whatever spell also held him in position. He rolled away and was silent as his breathing evened. Mine followed suit.

“I’m sorry,” he mumbled.

At the same time, I said, “Thank you.”

He turned his head so he could look at me in the dim light.

“I’m sorry I tackled you. I didn’t see another choice.”

I laughed, and something in Hart’s expression shifted at the sound.

“I much prefer you lunging at me to being crushed under a pile of rocks.”

He grunted as he sat up.

“What do we do now?” I asked.

Standing, he offered a hand to help me up. It was almost second nature to accept. He pulled me toward him, and I went like a moth to flame.

He assessed the pile of rocks blocking our path. “We have to get out.”

Moving closer, he lifted one and tossed it aside. A few others shifted with the motion. It wasn’t an insurmountable task. Although the more he revealed, the larger some of the chunks of stone proved to be. Some would be too big to lift.

Hart didn’t seem deterred. He kept tossing rocks in an attempt to clear the path.

I stared at him, watching the activity until the obvious answer struck me. Hart...was Blessed. He could use magic-enhanced strength to break through the rocks quickly.

He glanced at me. His head tilted in question. "What?"

"You," I said. "You can get us out, can't you?"

I still didn't know where he kept his adamas. My curiosity didn't matter, though. It was hidden somewhere, even if the reason why he did so eluded me.

The line of his lips flattened. He looked toward the tunnel ceiling like he was ready to curse another set of gods. When his gaze returned to mine, he nodded slowly, like this was the last topic he'd expected.

I gestured toward the rocks. "Do you have enough anger stored to get us out of here?"

I'd never seen him take. Who knew what emotions he had stored for magic? I hoped he had some because I couldn't offer to help him replenish. My stomach knotted as I considered the implications of my thoughts.

Hart had to have stolen anger. That's what would fuel his magic to get us out of here. Stolen emotion. Like any other Blessed.

He surveyed me again, and I wondered if he saw what my mind had only just unlocked.

"You don't like the Blessed," he said. It was almost like he spoke to himself as he continued. "I knew it conceptually, but I didn't understand it viscerally until that look you gave me in the alley. When you realized you'd be within my grasp when you passed."

I distinctly remembered the way he had flinched then—like he'd been slapped with understanding.

My brow furrowed. Of course I didn't like the Blessed. They took without remorse, thinking only of themselves, their vanity, and their power. Did Hart do that? I was sure I hadn't looked at him like that in a long time. And I didn't know how that made me feel.

I had always known Hart was Blessed—all guards were.

Just because I hadn't seen him take didn't mean it didn't happen.

I thought of Alysa and her people—their stolen adamas and how she said they used it. Maybe Hart had similar rules? His looks guaranteed he wouldn't have difficulty finding willing partners.

But that wasn't right either. Serena had said at the Cornucopia that he didn't take from any of those who offered themselves. Her words had given me a perverse pleasure at the time. Now, I needed to understand: How did he take if it wasn't from those willing at Forest's Edge?

"Do you have the magic?" I asked again.

He let the hesitation show on his face. "I have the magic, Chaos."

Alaric had taught me never to shy away from tough questions. I voiced the one I didn't want to ask. "Where did you get it? Was the participant willing?"

His lips pressed together. The hesitation wasn't ideal.

"Talk to me."

I'd say it was guilt that lined his features, but I couldn't tell if I was only seeing what I wanted to see. Alysa had thought he'd accepted the gem but didn't use it. His response indicated he did, and I might not want to know the details.

Hart's brow furrowed. "I'm not a good man, Chaos. I've done plenty I regret and even more that I don't."

I wasn't sure how we'd ended up having this conversation trapped in the mines, but there we were. "That's not an answer. You could only take from those willing."

"I can't provide the reassurance you seek. If you're in danger, I won't care. I'll take anything to protect you. The only comfort I can offer is, you're safe with me."

It sounded like a vow, one I wasn't sure I understood.

He'd made the choice and accepted the power of the Blessed. Once he had it, it made sense he'd use it.

"If it's to protect me, you should take from me—"

I shook my head. My words were foolish—I asked for the impossible. My immunity meant someone else was paying the price of my protection. Scarier still, I wasn't sure this changed how I felt about Hart.

How I felt about Hart wasn't something I wanted to examine at this precise moment. I shoved that thought down and focused on something more tactical. "Use the magic."

He nodded and turned to the pile of rubble that blocked us from the way out.

Many of the rocks were too large for me to lift, but I tossed aside a few to feel like I was doing something productive. Hart didn't need it. He moved the rest like they were nothing more than pebbles.

The largest ones, he hit. His powerful swings broke through them in moments. I couldn't help but search for the glow of red somewhere, anywhere, on his person—a needed distraction from the sour taste of confusion.

Instead, I found myself sketching the outline of his well-muscled body in my mind. I bit my lip as he effortlessly lifted a boulder almost my size. Was I so distracted by a pretty face?

He wasn't just a pretty face. Hart was a culmination of unimaginable choices. If Alysa worked outside the system, Hart worked within it. There were costs to doing so. Watching Hart break us free of the cave-in brought those choices to the forefront.

Gregory was gone when we broke through enough to see the path—probably to find Tamara to free us.

A few more swings and Hart finished. He turned to look at me, and a wary caution crossed his face. The space he cleared was large enough for us to escape. He gestured for me to crawl through the opening and took a few steps back, allowing the distance between himself and the opening to span.

He was giving me space again, like the first time he'd found me in an alley. That small knot in my stomach twisted like a dagger, already inserted and turned for additional pain.

He was Blessed. He'd made choices I didn't understand. But he used his position in Kavios to do what he could for others. How many people at Alysa's settlement were there because of him? Would Alaric have known of youngleaf without Hart?

I couldn't tell him it was alright. Our gazes locked as I approached, stepping into his space. I took his hand, gently squeezing it. I hoped the action said what I couldn't—that I might not like the Blessed, but I knew he was not the same as them.

28

I have an idea to test. It will buy them more time.

— ALARIC SARE'S LETTERS TO ISABELLE ARKOVA

The next day, when we entered the workshop, Hart was quiet. I still didn't have the words to adequately describe how I felt, so I focused on planning instead. Someone was trapped in the mines, and they needed me to free them.

Whether she meant to or not, Alysa had given me hope with her transparency. There was another entrance to the mines—old and defunct, maybe, but it existed. Which meant I could get into the mines during the limited hours when no one was on shift.

The real problem would be getting into the adamas cavern. Hart had pulled at the door the first time we were left alone outside it. It hadn't budged. Since I still didn't know where his adamas was, I had no idea if he used magic to fuel his strength when he did.

I'd have to ask him. It would be my only chance of getting in. I opened my mouth to ask about the somewhat sensitive subject.

He beat me to it with his own question. "Can I see the note Alaric left you?"

"Go ahead." I gestured toward the hidden room.

Hart parted the gold curtain, walking to where the shelf opened with the hidden latch. He'd seen me do it a few days ago, but the way he reached the exact right location behind the books told me he'd done it before.

"Did you study with Alaric too?" I asked.

"In a manner of speaking."

"Was this part of the project he researched for you?"

Hart ignored my question and walked into the storage space.

I sighed. "It was in his copy of *Champions of Kavios*."

Silence followed my words. I walked toward the door and saw his fingers running along the edges of the text.

"He never let me read this one. He always claimed he didn't have it. I knew, of course."

"But you—"

"What? Procured his collection for him? Yes—but this one couldn't be purchased."

"Why?"

I wasn't sure what he was getting at, but I could tell he wanted to share something with me.

Hart chuckled. "It's the only copy in existence."

"What?"

He pushed back the strands of hair that had fallen from his knot. "You don't strike me as someone who believes in prophecy, even as it unfolds before you. But I believe, as Alaric does, that some of what's written here is history, and the rest is foretold about the Cursed King and Eris's Champion."

He did sound like Alaric. But still, the way he glanced at me, it made me want to ask questions I'd never bothered to ask my uncle. "Foretold by whom?"

It was unclear why that was important, but the slight smoothing of his brow as he leveled his gaze to meet mine told me I was on the right track with my question.

"A talented seer."

That didn't really answer my question. I also wasn't sure his assessment of me was right anymore. Previously, I was on the fence about the book holding true prophecy, but I had to admit that seeing the Cursed King's nightmare magic in action had certainly been convincing.

I knew his collection was rare, but this seemed extreme. "Why would Alaric have the only copy in existence?" I asked.

"I wondered the same thing, but over time, I was sure he had it." He tilted his head. "When I first met you, I wondered if that's why he protected you. Maybe you were the author."

I shook my head.

Another face popped into place. The same blond hair that made mine and Alaric's familial bond all but obvious, though hers was now gray. Mother's ramblings that somehow made perfect sense. Her comment about my guard. The things she couldn't know. Before her accident, had she been this seer? It was a leap, but knowing everything Alaric had kept from me, it no longer seemed like a big one.

Hart didn't question any evidence of the revelation on my face. I wondered if he'd made the same assessment once he'd decided it wasn't me. Alaric's note slipped into his fingers as he opened the front cover.

His gaze skimmed the short note. "Do you still want to leave?"

He hadn't asked so directly yesterday. After our trip to Alysa's, he'd spoken of options, making sure I was aware of them, but he hadn't asked what I'd pick.

"I'm not sure."

"Alaric spent years collecting stories that showed what Kavios could be. He never accepted its current state. Never stopped fighting from the inside," Hart said.

"But he still left," I whispered.

"So he did."

Hart set the book down and closed the storage room door. With long strides, he crossed the room to where I leaned against Alaric's workbench. My fingers gripped the wood as he neared.

"He didn't leave because he gave up. You know that, don't you?" He held my gaze. "He left because he had hope. He wanted to show you how things could be."

I tilted my head. That was oddly specific. "You said you didn't know where he went."

"I don't know where he is, but that note also says '*if* I'm not here.' It doesn't sound like he intended to be gone for so long."

I was shaking now. "Then why is he not here? Why did he leave me to become the one thing he kept me from? Why didn't he tell me anything about you?"

He lifted a hand like he'd reach for me, but at the last second, he instead ran it through his hair like he wanted to rip out every strand. "He'd want you to focus on what you wanted to ask as soon as we entered the shop."

"You know who is in the adamas cavern?"

Hart's gaze was piercing, but he gave a brief nod.

"Who is it?"

The shift of his gaze told me I wouldn't get a straight

answer before his mouth opened. "That's not really the most important question."

I hated that I agreed with him. The fact that I would free them was all that seemed to matter to me.

"Did you try using magic to open the door to the adamas cavern the first time we were there?"

He shook his head.

As much as I wanted to ask why, it also wasn't the important part. "Will you help me free the captive?"

"There's nowhere you can go that I won't follow, Chaos."

The comment was too raw. And echoed too strongly of what I'd told him of my parents' relationship. I shook my head, loosing another question I'd turned over last night. "Would you do this if you were me? Or would you run?"

He tilted his head. "That's not something I can answer for you. It's for you to choose."

I sighed, somehow knowing that would be his answer.

"Did something else happen?" he continued. "Did Alysa pressure you yesterday?"

Admittedly, our conversation about the settlement had been overshadowed by the Oldwood's magic and my relinquishing control to it.

I shook my head. "She just gave me a lot to consider."

He arched a brow. "Such as?"

I laughed as I recalled Alysa's warning. While I couldn't put my finger on what Hart wanted, it no longer worried me as much as it probably should. He'd proved he was on my side, even when it was clear he wasn't sharing everything he knew about the captive. I trusted there was a reason.

Still, I shared Alysa's question. "Inquiring minds want to know what drives you, Hart? What are you after?"

His chuckle was low and rumbling. He waved his hand

dismissively. "She knows how to hold a grudge. Alysa and I have disagreed on priorities in the past."

That was the crux of things, wasn't it?

I gestured between us. "What happens when our priorities are no longer aligned?"

His brow furrowed as he searched my face. There was more consideration for the question than I expected.

"I'll support whatever path you choose." He swallowed like the statement held more meaning than I realized. "I'd hoped that was clear."

The only thing that was clear was that my choices were growing by the minute, and Hart stood beside me at the crossroads. This was what I'd wanted, the reason I'd shared my secrets with him. Now that we were here, though, I couldn't help but want more. Maybe I didn't just want information—I wanted his opinion too. Opinions he seemed reluctant to share. I needed to know his reluctance didn't have to do with our conversation about his magic.

"I don't know why you hesitated yesterday when we talked about taking, but I see the man you strive to be."

I wasn't sure he was breathing. I'd started this, so I guessed I had to continue.

"I didn't say anything yesterday, and it bothered me all night. It wasn't the fact that you are Blessed that concerned me; It was that I was so ready to use your power. Seeing what you do in the city, I acknowledge the value you provide by leveraging your position. I don't know what made you choose the blessing, I don't know when you decided to start choosing differently, but I see that you're making choices every day that stand against what Rodric is doing. And that means something ... to me."

He held my gaze, and I felt a thousand things flash between us.

"You heard me yesterday? You're not hiding from it?" He leaned into my space, his arms caging me against the workbench.

"I heard you. You take."

He shook his head, stepping back. "You don't know what you're saying."

"I'm saying that I need your help and your perspectives. I might want to leave now that I know there's somewhere safe for my parents, but I *need* to free the captive. Both require your assistance."

He held my gaze as if weighing the sincerity of my words.

"I have a plan to free the captive—the night of the Masquerade," I said. "We'll need your magic to get in. But, if it doesn't work, or I can't have both, I want your opinions. I'll want the information I know you're not sharing."

He dipped his chin and pulled out the stool, readying to work the foot pedal that powered the shaping blade.

"I also reserve the right to change my mind," I added.

He smiled a real grin instead of his usual smirk. "As is your wont."

Before long, the constant beat of his foot brought the tool to a steady spin. I worked on the new gems, or, at least, those for which I had commissions. They were due tonight. The prince wanted to inspect them before the Presentation. That took away any ideas I had of switching them for quartz. Part of me hated that I was excited to see him test the adamas—to know I cut and shaped the gem with the necessary skill to secure the stone's magic. I shook my head. The adamas would be ready for his inspection, and I'd still have days to decide what to do for the Blessing.

Hart led me through the trappings of Cross Street as the sun set. It was startling to think that only days ago, this would have been my worst nightmare. A street packed with Blessed—bumping into passersby and taking on a whim.

Even as we walked, a man's laugh was stolen from his lips. A Blessed passing by latched onto his exposed hand and pulled until the man's smile faded. He stumbled forward as if nothing had happened. Hart spied it too, stepping closer to me as he did.

I clung to the satchel that hung across my body. Inside were the cut and polished adamas stones for the Blessed and the replacement. I still had to finish the settings, but this was all the prince requested before tomorrow's Presentation.

Hart grabbed a helmet from the guard post at the castle entrance, and we walked silently to the prince's study. There was only one guard outside the door today instead of his usual two. The guard held up his hand as I approached.

"She has a meeting," Hart said.

The guard glared at Hart. "I'm aware. It's just not here."

"Where is it then? I was told to bring her here."

"Change of plans. It's in the throne room," the guard replied.

Hart's hands balled into fists at his side. He looked ready to break something.

I looked around. The castle was still a maze of hallways to me. "It's fine. Do you know how to get to the throne room?"

Hart flared his nostrils, freeing himself from this new spiral. I wished I could see his face. The square lines of his jaw shifted as if he were gritting his teeth. This wasn't that big a deal.

"Hart?"

He cursed under his breath. "Let's go."

With one final glare at the guard, he ushered me toward the throne room.

I whispered to him as he walked. "What is it?"

"I don't like this."

Didn't like going to the throne room? I had yet to see the room at the heart of the castle. The room that would host the Masquerade in two days and the Blessing shortly after. It was said to be grand—the only place King Rodric had been seen in years.

King Rodric.

Hart's anger, his ... fear suddenly made sense. If I were meeting with Prince Elias and Vaddon, we would have done so in Elias's study. There was only one reason we'd been redirected to the throne room.

Before I'd completed the thought, we were before a larger, ornate set of doors. Gold and blue swirls trimmed the edges. My head tilted back to take in the details. Two guards stood before the door, with another four waiting in the wings.

I was meeting with King Rodric.

"Are you coming with me?" I asked under my breath, without looking at Hart.

I knew the answer. He never attended my meetings with the prince. He certainly wasn't invited to this.

"I can't," he whispered.

That was desperation in his voice—barely leashed.

My fingers itched to reach for his arm, to reassure him I'd be fine. My left hand twitched and stretched toward him before I let it fall back to the space between us. His eyes must have followed the motion, and amusement curled his lip, breaking his stoic determination.

"I'll be right here." He pointed to the line of guards. "And I'll break through that door if you call my name."

His words were whispered beneath his helmet—meant

only for my ears. They didn't reassure me about what I faced, but I believed them for the genuine threat they were. I nodded and steeled my spine as I walked toward the guards. A green glow shone on the guard's left hand. His questions differed slightly from what they'd asked outside the prince's study, confirming my suspicions.

"Do you intend the royal family any harm?"

It was no longer just the prince.

I responded as they expected, my heart rate spiking. "I do not."

As much as I knew the prince was not to be underestimated, at least he played at being the genial royal.

When the doors opened, I knew that version of the prince was nowhere to be found. The room was massive. White marble floors with the same blue and gold swirled pattern of the doors spread out before me. Alcoves similar to those at Forest's Edge lined the room. The curtains, a material thicker than the sheer ones I was used to, alternated between the same gold and blue of the floor. A chasm for me to cross—the room was empty save for more guards.

My gaze was drawn to Prince Elias. He was in a traditional uniform, the same one he'd worn at the Cornucopia, more finely made than Hart's and of the same bright blue as the hall. For the first time since I'd met him, he didn't greet me with a grin. He stood at the bottom of the steps leading to a raised dais. When he turned his head toward where his father sat, mine followed.

The throne was gold and covered in gems. Even from the entryway, I could tell they were quartz. The sheer volume of adamas necessary to complete the design would have been untenable to demand. A golden throne wasn't the threat in this room, though.

King Rodric Glanmore sat in it—waiting to greet me.

29

Her breaking point will be the city. His will be her.

— FROM CHAMPIONS OF KAVIOS

The doors clanged loudly behind me as they closed. The echo cascaded across the length of the marble floor. I had nowhere to go but forward, even though the face that stared back at me was anything but welcoming.

I assumed the Blessed saw King Rodric regularly in situations much like this. I imagined rows of chairs covering the floor. Blessed in attendance to show their gratitude and hear their king's words. Monthly sessions for the Blessed to mingle with royalty. Those without magic invited would have found themselves behind the curtains with a Blessed needing to take. Not even Serena attempted to garner an invitation to these events. She said she was quite happy with the pleasure brought from Forest's Edge. There was no need to add impressing royalty into the mix.

King Rodric did not look impressed at my approach.

I should have assumed this was coming. Alaric had missed a meeting with the king on the day he disappeared. It was the reason Vaddon had found me. The thought inserted itself into my mind like a rude guest.

Vaddon drew my gaze as I crossed the chasm of a room with slow steps. I pressed my hands against my side to stop myself from twitching. I need not show how nervous I was. Even if they needed me—even if the prince had forbidden anyone from taking from me—all bets were off with the king.

Better not to give him a reason to try.

The king's advisor was with the guards. Even farther removed from the dais than Prince Elias. He apparently couldn't stop his arms from folding over his chest at my approach.

I swallowed and continued my strides across the marble floor. My focus was on the only question worth answering. What did the king want with me? Was this truly to test my skills with the adamas?

He sat stalwart on his throne, cutting an imposing figure. One hand scratched at the silver-flecked beard on his face, and the other draped lazily over the armrest. The magic of the Blessed was at Rodric's disposal, but still, he let his hair gray. It was an interesting move. One I assumed was intended to further impress his power. The salt and pepper color didn't make him look old but refined. Where the prince inspired love and joy from the citizens of Kavios, the king used his legend. He'd built this city with his father two hundred years ago. He let his age show to inspire confidence, fear, and loyalty for all he'd done since then.

Too bad the rest of the city didn't know what he really did to them.

Finally, my gaze moved to the crown atop King Rodric's head. Eight triangle points topped the gold circlet. What stole my focus was the gem fixed to the center triangle ... it was glowing.

Green light filled the room. He hadn't yet spoken and already wasted the adamas's stored magic. If nothing else, the king was confident in his ability to harvest more.

The king studied me just as intently as I did him. I took care not to let my gaze linger on the gem's color. They knew I could find the adamas. I didn't know what else they knew about my abilities. Giving them more information to lord over me was not my goal.

"You're right, Elias." King Rodric didn't bother to glance at his son. "She does appear to have Alaric's spark."

I didn't know what that meant, but the king's voice exuded confidence.

My steps slowed, and I attempted a curtsy. It wasn't much better than the one I'd tried in the prince's study.

"Rise, child," he said. "Do you know why you're here?"

The green glow of the adamas didn't falter.

I glanced at the prince and gripped the satchel still slung across my body. "I understood I needed to provide the adamas to Prince Elias before the Presentation."

I didn't want to leave anything out lest he think his magic wasn't working.

A smile briefly crossed his face. It felt as fake as it was fleeting. "I hear you're quite good with adamas. The Presentation must go well. Even with our reassurance at the Cornucopia, rumors of the Cursed King still spread."

I wouldn't precisely call lulling the populace into a magic-drenched calm the same as *reassurance*. But that was just me.

"The people need more hope—more happiness to latch on to during the Selection." He stroked his chin. "Do you know why your uncle lied to us about your talents?"

The shift in topic was unexpected. I couldn't follow how one connected with the other in his mind. No matter how much I wanted to glance at the prince to glean his expression, I didn't dare. The adamas in the crown still glowed green. It required a response.

"I didn't know, Your Majesty. Many knew I apprenticed with him regularly."

The king rolled his eyes. "Being a jeweler and being a jeweler who can find adamas are very different skill sets. He hid the more important of the two."

I wasn't sure how to respond to that. Thankfully, King Rodric hadn't asked another question.

He stroked his beard again. His gaze finally left mine and fell to his son. "Elias speaks highly of your capabilities."

I dipped my chin in acknowledgment. Until this moment, I'd been feeling very confident about the stones, but now I wiped my sweaty palms briefly against my skirt.

He held out his hand. "Let me see the gems."

I didn't dare approach. The prince stepped toward me. His lip tipped up into a forced smile. Interesting that he appeared as intimidated by his father as I was. I pulled the gems from my bag and placed them in his cupped hands. He scaled the dais, holding them out for his father's review.

"Send the girl in," Rodric said.

Vaddon opened another large door near the front of the room. A young woman hesitantly stepped in. She curtsied immediately. My stomach churned, putting together what my mind hadn't yet.

Her long brown hair fell in soft curls down her back as Vaddon led her to the dais. She looked older than me, but only just. Rodric removed his crown, handing it to Vaddon, and plucked a single gem from the prince's palm as she neared.

I couldn't watch this. My confidence in my skill collided with the horror at what I'd done. I wanted to vomit.

The woman approached carefully as Vaddon gestured her forward.

She curtsied again the closer she got to the king. "It's an honor to be used, Your Highness."

The breath I'd been holding let loose. At least she wasn't fooling herself about what she was getting into. No matter my morbid curiosity at my own skill with the gems, I still didn't want to watch as the king's hand snaked out and grabbed her wrist.

I found I couldn't look away.

Her words weren't false. The gem Rodric held shifted to yellow flashes as he stole joy from the woman. He held firm as he reached for another stone, swapping them out in his palm. Each gem he tested continued to pull emotion from the woman. Her joy turned to pleasure the longer he took. The last two gems flashed orange instead of yellow.

Satisfied, the king waved the woman away. Vaddon looked murderous as she took his arm, needing support to retrace her steps down the dais.

They'd all worked.

Not only could I source the adamas, I had shaped it into the powerful stone. While a part of me had known I'd done it based on the feel of the stones as I worked them, the horrifying reality of seeing my stones hold magic sent a shiver through me. I needed to get out of here. My legs felt like they could buckle at any moment.

"Very good," the king said. "We have another request for you."

My stomach still roiled. I hoped desperately that Hart and I could free the captive tomorrow night. If even a sliver of me had been considering Hart's path, working against Rodric from the inside, everything within me raged against it now. I couldn't turn the gems over for the Blessing, even in service of a larger goal. Not when they were used for this.

The woman may have known what she was there for and even enjoyed it, but the power imbalance still stood. There was no freedom of choice when the king controlled our fates as he did.

He continued speaking, oblivious to my thoughts. Rodric returned his circlet to his head, ensuring the adamas gem faced me. "My crown requires more jeweling."

The gem was already one of the largest I'd seen. The crown was much larger and sturdier than a ring. It was similar to the pendants, holding a more substantial gem.

How much more magic did he need?

As soon as I asked myself the question, I knew what he wanted. The crown's design made it obvious. My head tilted as I considered how each of the points of the crown could hold its own gem. I was already calculating in my mind...there were eight points. The extra raw material Gregory had mined made sense even as understanding sent a chill up my spine.

"I require a gem for each point on the crown."

It wasn't as if I could refuse him, but he proceeded to try to convince me.

"This piece will be the ultimate test of your skill. So many gems in so small a space for one bearer. Do you know what that does?"

I couldn't imagine what so much power would do. How many would he take from to fill them all? How many emotions? How many years from their lives would it be? I shook my head slowly in response.

He seemed happy enough to tell me. "You will be personally ensuring the protection of Kavios. The defense of the Kingdom will no longer be a worry."

His smile showed too many teeth for me to believe the response.

Was it a worry to begin with? I weighed what I was supposed to think versus what I knew of the other kingdoms on the continent. We controlled adamas production, but as I'd recently learned, champions didn't need adamas to wield magic.

I'd thought Kavios was protected because of the magic—and I was sure that was true, to some extent. Magic and the natural landscape of mountains and the Oldwood didn't make it an easy target. But what if another champion wanted the stones in their city?

Hart had said Chaos's Champion ruled Linia, but I had no idea about Aven. Maybe they considered Rodric's idea to impose order to be a good one. My hand grew unsteady at the thought.

There was also the more obvious answer: Rodric feared the Cursed King and the rebels. In his mind the city may need protection from internal threats as much as external.

As if on cue, a blue glow overtook the gem. "All will be well. Kavios will be safe. You will assure it."

I nodded slowly, allowing my body to mimic one of the citizens impacted by the calming drug of his magic. This was too much power. I'd already seen what the king could do to Kavios. The way he wrapped a soft blanket of calm over the city at the Cornucopia.

His magic was too strong. It removed the citizens' ability to think, the ability to consider their fears and their joys. It wasn't enough that he took their emotions. He also took away their ability to feel.

The irony was not lost on me. I'd started hiding my feelings long ago, but that didn't mean they weren't there. They were becoming increasingly insistent in recent days—demanding to be felt. There was my anger the night of the Selection Festival, my fear of Vaddon's attackers, my anger at the captive's fate in the mines. And then there was every emotion Hart provoked that I still refused to acknowledge. Just because I didn't wear them on my sleeve didn't mean all citizens of Kavios didn't have a right to. I envied those who laughed as easily as they cried and those who weren't afraid to show their heart or mind to everyone they deemed worthy.

I'd created this wall around myself that was taller than the castle towers. It was formed of harder stone than the gems we painstakingly carved from the mine. It meant that nothing was visible to tempt the Blessed, but it also meant not much got in.

It worked for me—or at least, it had been working.

It had been too long since I'd replied. The king had said I was contributing to the defense of Kavios. There was only one response to that. I dipped my chin and slipped into another curtsy. The less I said at this moment, the better. I could hide things, but I was no actor. If I tried to speak disingenuously, it would be to the detriment of whatever plan I devised not to do this.

And I wouldn't do this—my decision had solidified.

Prince Elias stepped down from the dais, returning the gems to my hand. My nostrils flared. I felt dirty reclaiming them, disgusted by what I'd done—what they'd been used for.

"We're glad you agree, Emberline. I know you have much to do with setting the stones, but we'd like this piece as soon as the Blessing is complete."

I nodded again. There was no other response. The prince's words were gentle, but they weren't a question.

"You'll be well rewarded for this, Emberline." The king looked down over the prince and me at the foot of the dais.

I didn't contemplate what it meant. It was the dismissal I needed. Turning on my heel, I walked more briskly across the floor than I had upon entering.

"We're excited to see what you can do." The king spoke to my back as the guards opened one of the doors and let me slip into the hallway.

30

He's fading fast. Adamas she's touched helps sustain him. Getting it to him is a problem.

— ALARIC SARE'S LETTERS TO ISABELLE ARKOVA

Hart followed me into my room after my audience with the king. It was early enough that the sentries weren't present yet. He stood by the door while I paced before the fireplace.

"What did he want?" Hart asked.

The king wanted seven adamas gems added to his crown.

I couldn't do it. I'd have to leave. My parents could leave with me—go to Alysa's settlement. I wasn't sure that was even good enough.

Lost in thought for too long, Hart pressed again.

He looked like he wanted to step toward me, his body lurching, but remained in place. "Are you alright?"

There was something ... different about me. Something different about the way I connected with the adamas. Not only could I find and shape it, but I was also immune to its power. And whatever made this so, it was dangerous for others to know—especially the royal family. They already knew too much. Because here the king was, with what little he did know, asking me to make an eight-pointed adamas crown for him.

My stomach churned as I considered that kind of power sitting atop the king's head.

"What happened in the throne room, Ember?" Hart's voice had softened again. And something warm encircled me at the use of my name.

"He wants me to enhance his crown," I said.

Hart waited patiently for me to continue.

"He wants each of the eight points on the circlet to house an adamas gem."

With that news, he froze. His nostrils flared before he took a slow step forward. "You can't. We'll get you and your family out of the city. It can be The Storm, or it can be another kingdom. I don't care. I'll get you where you need to go."

Something inside me warmed, and I wanted to stretch toward him like a plant for the sun. He was still halfway across the room.

Slow, careful steps brought him closer. "Do you hear me, Ember?"

He wasn't calling me Chaos. This had to be serious. He invaded my space, and I let him. His broad shoulders overtook my view. I tilted my head back to see the harsh lines of his face softening, signaling I'd be safe, even with his proximity. Little did he know, this wasn't something he needed to show me—it was something I already knew instinctively.

"I know you'll keep me safe, Hart."

He held my gaze.

I was still unsure of my decision regarding the city. Rodric couldn't be allowed that much magic, but that didn't mean I had to leave. I searched for the third option, not Hart's or Alysa's paths, but one uniquely mine. I didn't know what it would look like, but even without the additions to the crown, King Rodric's power over Kavios made me sick.

At least I knew one thing: "We have to free the captive first. He is the source of the adamas. I'm sure of it."

Hart had nodded, accepting my decision.

The Oldwood didn't scare me anymore.

I couldn't say the same for the rest of those who made the hike to the mines alongside us. The Blessed who did so looked ... nervous. The insistent press of something against my senses was still present as we walked, but I knew what I had to do. Hart and I had a plan. The night of the Masquerade, I wouldn't be needed. Hart had said he could open the door to the adamas cavern with magic. We'd trek to the old mine entrance Alysa mentioned and free the captive.

Having a goal calmed me. It was something I'd been sorely lacking lately. Never was it more apparent than in my discussion with Hart last night.

I glanced at him over my shoulder as we walked the Oldwood Trail. I couldn't believe he'd simply ... accepted it. He was letting me lead whatever this was.

The cut and polished stones bounced against my thigh in my cross-body bag. They would be shown to the Selected before the mine entrance today, then returned safely to me. I still had time to determine what to do with them. Maybe I'd give them to Alysa and her people.

Our pace slowed as we arrived at the mine entrance. The Oldwood seemed to thicken here as if hiding entry to a long-protected secret. Hart slipped on a helmet I assumed was actually his own, and we cut through the amassed crowd toward the staircase.

Prince Elias looked in better spirits today. He smiled and waved to those who made the trip into the Oldwood. His presence was once again reassuring, starkly contrasting with how he hid his fear behind formalities with his father. He nodded at my approach, and I climbed the remainder of the steps toward him. Hart followed without invitation.

The prince chuckled. "I see you take your duty as a guard very seriously. I think she's safe here."

"All the same, I'd prefer to be within arm's reach."

Beneath his mask, I could tell Hart searched the crowd. The energy was anxious. Like with the Cornucopia, those attending must be wary of actions from the Feared.

The prince followed Hart's gaze, though he directed his question at me. "Good turnout, don't you think?"

He deigned to allow Hart his imposition, but that didn't require further discussion.

I glanced around. "Yes."

There were more in the crowd than I expected. How many had Prince Elias used his persuasion magic on to influence their arrival? With the threat of the Cursed King looming and the gruesome display at the Eastern Gate only days ago—it didn't feel like a celebration.

"I'm glad you accepted Father's commission," the prince said quietly.

I hadn't realized I had a choice. I gave him a practiced smile, unsure how to respond.

He leaned in—closer than I expected. "I think you'll enjoy your reward."

The hair at the back of my neck stood on end. I didn't have to look at Hart to know he stiffened at the prince's proximity. I did not think I'd enjoy my reward, but that was a problem I didn't have time to worry about yet.

Prince Elias held out his hand. "The gems?"

I opened my bag to show him. Each was wrapped in a black cloth and tied with a tag that named the Selected. I handed him the first one. "Where do you want them?"

The prince was determined to let no detail go unchecked. He pulled the tie, keeping the cloth in place, letting it fall to the sides, exposing the gem. Even though King Rodric had checked them only yesterday, Elias still wanted eyes on the gems before the ceremony started.

Did he know something about the Feared's plans that we didn't?

He lifted the stone, squinting at it. "Very good."

I must have imagined the slight shake of the prince's hand as he held the gem. He dropped it back into the bag before I could confirm. His lips pressed into a firm line as he glanced at the others.

I was starting to think the prince was ... scared.

Suddenly, I was grateful for the broad-shouldered guard at my back. As Vaddon approached, Hart's hand was on the handle of his sword, fingers twitching as he surveyed the crowd.

"Are we ready, Your Highness?" Vaddon asked.

His smile was unsettling, showing all his teeth and arms spread wide as if this were the most joyous occasion of the year. Maybe to him, it was.

I lifted the strap over my head to hand the satchel to Vaddon. "I'll leave you to it."

“No, Emberline, why don’t you stand here and hand me the gems.” Elias pointed to a position just behind him before the mine entrance.

Vaddon’s smile quickly turned into a frown, though the prince didn’t notice. This must have been Vaddon’s responsibility, and though the prince had phrased it as a question—it was anything but.

I shrugged at the advisor, and his returning glare was filled with daggers. He couldn’t hate me more than he already did. I took his position behind the prince, and Hart flanked me.

“Welcome!” Elias’s voice raised well above the muffled din of the crowd.

They silenced immediately as the show they’d gathered for began.

“Thank you for joining us for the Presentation!”

My gaze wandered as the prince spoke. The other guards had spread out at the foot of the steps. Any attackers would have to break their line before reaching me and the prince.

Unfortunately, I found Macen in the gathered group. He must have been required to attend as part of his shift at the mines. He spoke to someone beside him, his mouth moving rapidly and his chin tucked.

I sidestepped slightly to see if I could glimpse the person next to him from a different angle. I couldn’t, but that didn’t matter when Macen’s finger raised, pointing at me on the platform. My heartbeat raced.

“We gather in this location to acknowledge the natural beauty representing the King’s Blessing,” Elias said.

The Selected, just below him on the steps, stared up at him with wide-eyed wonder. For most, I was sure it was the first time they’d seen the majesty of the mine entrance.

“The King’s Blessing grants you power, but the adamas gem is the physical reminder of that Blessing. These mines,”—

he gestured behind himself to the towering stone entrance—"are a critical resource for our city. We wouldn't be who we are without them."

The words struck a nerve. What would this city be like if adamas didn't exist? I hoped to find out if my suspicions about the captive were true.

"The mines supply our precious resources, but they couldn't become the beautiful symbol we know them to be without our jeweler."

My head snapped up at the prince's words. Macen shrugged in indifference to whoever stood beside him. His identification of me was no longer relevant. The prince had done it for him.

Elias had decided not to introduce me at the Cornucopia. I assumed it was because making my name more widely known would risk my life.

The Feared were already after me. We didn't need to make me a more visible target. After having strung up the supposed Feared on the Eastern Gate, the prince must have felt more confident.

The feeling was not mutual.

The prince turned to smile at me, his body bent slightly at the waist, an acknowledgment of who I was, and the crowd applauded.

Elias continued like nothing out of the ordinary had happened. I worked to slow my rapidly beating heart as he called the Selected to hold their adamas for the first time. He was scared, yet he still introduced me. It didn't matter, I guessed, since Macen was in the crowd pointing me out to anyone who asked.

As Elias called each of the Selected, I handed them their wrapped stone. After receiving their gem, each Selected stood in line at the bottom of the steps. I let myself be distracted by the sheer joy on Deidre's face as she received her adamas.

The Selected were instructed only to touch the gem through the cloth. They had yet to be Blessed by the king. Deidre, in her excitement, stumbled as she turned, catching the stone in her palm as she fell toward me. Hart stepped forward to steady her. The red flash was instant though brief. She looked down, seeing the color, her brow pinched.

I sucked in a breath. She must have touched him. How hard would she consider what she'd seen? I hoped for her sake she didn't second-guess it. I'd never realized the distinction, but I'd bet simply wearing the stone meant you could see the color of its magic. If Deidre realized the stone could sense emotion before the Blessing Ceremony, she might wonder what value the king actually provided.

She was still smiling from ear to ear at being on stage—being Selected. Quickly, she dropped the stone back into the cloth and righted herself, turning to face the crowd as the prince finished.

As the last Selected held out their gem, my spine tingled—something pressed against my skull. I knew it for what it was: the magic of the Oldwood. The mine entrance where we stood was just beyond the Oldwood's reach, but the magic was the same. It was here.

My part in the Presentation was done. With Hart behind me, I didn't fear the magic fully taking me. We had plans to rescue the captive tomorrow, which meant I needed to hear whatever else it would tell me. So, I let it in.

"This ... Presentation ...."

The ground shook beneath us.

Prince Elias paused his speech. He glanced at Tamara. A crowd, already on edge, began to murmur.

"Is a mockery of what you are."

The prince continued his speech.

I couldn't let myself be pulled under again. My fingers twitched as I longed to sink them into the soil. I felt Hart's glare. If I succumbed to the magic, everyone here would know. I didn't need anyone to notice my oddities more than they already did. Balling my hands into fists at my side, I dug my nails into my flesh to stay present.

My knees buckled.

A press of heat at my lower back grounded me. Hart's hand rested there—strong, steady.

The crowd erupted in cheers with Elias's closing remarks. I stood straighter, just in time, as the prince raised his lightly clapping hands in my direction, offering me and my work a round of applause.

I nodded in acknowledgment as the Selected returned their gems before filing back into the crowd to celebrate. It was the middle of the day, but food and drink were set at a long table beside the mine entrance. The prince must have said something, releasing the crowd's attention. They shifted toward the refreshments.

"Everything alright, Emberline?" Prince Elias asked.

I could only nod as I glanced back at the mines. The captive and the earthshakes were connected. I could feel his anger, his rage with his words. He thought the Presentation a mockery of ... what *I* was. *That* had implications I wasn't ready to consider.

My neck craned back to look up at the colossal stone entrance to the mine. How big was the captive to cause such a disturbance? I shook my head. It didn't matter. I knew I had to get him out.

31

He will make her acknowledge what she is.

— FROM CHAMPIONS OF KAVIOS

Prince Elias proved how he'd earned his reputation after the ceremony. No matter his nerves, he worked the crowd. Chatting, smiling, even laughing with those who had attended. As much time as he spent with the Blessed, he also spent with the other citizens. Everyone he spoke with left the conversation looking like they floated on a cloud.

I stood at the foot of the stairs, not straying into the group. Hart's steady glower drove away any brave enough to approach.

"You shouldn't have done that," he said when we were finally alone.

I didn't question what he referred to. His touch pulled me back. For all he knew, I could have been digging my fingers into the dirt before the gathered crowd. I'd already known he could anchor me. His voice usually did, but his hand on my back also did the trick. I would have thanked him ... if he hadn't sounded so condescending.

"I knew you could handle it."

The heat of Hart's glare warmed the back of my neck.

Then, the prince approached Deidre near the refreshment table, and I stretched my fingers at my side. I was still worried about whether she had processed what she'd done during the Presentation. Luckily, she'd been angled, so I hoped only Hart and I had noticed.

Now, she was standing on her own, staring at the mine entrance. With the prince's approach, she rushed to swipe something from her face.

A tear. She must be thinking of her partner. Anger flooded through my veins as the prince took her hand. To many, it would look like a genuine offer of condolences, but the blue flash of his adamas pendant told me another story.

He took her sadness. Now the anger I fought to hide wanted to show itself. Deidre smiled as her sorrow left her, though I was sure whatever remembrance of her partner she experienced had also disappeared as her mood shifted. The prince's other conversations started to make more sense. He had been approaching those alone, those pensive. I thought he'd been trying to unite the city, but I should have known better. He only required sadness to power the numbing calm he laid upon his citizens.

"Macen pointed me out to someone in the crowd," I murmured. "It didn't matter after the prince announced me. But ..."

"Elias is nervous," Hart finished. "And you're worried he knows something?"

"I'm not sure. It was unexpected of him to announce me like that. It was almost like he was … daring them to come for me."

Hart stiffened and his hand went to the sword handle at his belt. "We'll be ready for them."

Across the crowd, Vaddon approached the prince. Elias nodded and clapped his hands, commanding the crowd's attention with a simple gesture.

"I'm being told the miners must continue their shift. Thank you for joining us. Those returning to the city, we should leave now to avoid travel after dark."

His smile was captivating even as he told people to return to work. His head swiveled as if he were meeting the gaze of every person in attendance. They were all his personal guests, and he appreciated them.

I wasn't buying it.

"We should be in the middle of the crowd," Hart whispered.

I nodded and found a place as citizens began trekking to the Eastern Gate. The urge to go below the ground pulled taut with each step I took away from the mines. I hadn't yet learned how to communicate back to the voice—the captive—but I hoped he knew we were coming for him. We wouldn't leave him as a prisoner of the Glanmores.

As we reached the midpoint between the mines and Kavios, the Oldwood claimed its toll.

The first shot was an arrow striking the shoulder of the woman walking next to me.

Hart had me behind him before her scream registered. Steel sang as he pulled his sword from its sheath.

With one arrow loosed, a full volley followed. Screams erupted from the Blessed as they scattered. Some sprinted down the path, seeking the safety of the Eastern Gate. Others forgot their fear of the Oldwood and fled into the trees for protection. I wanted to laugh as the Blessed ran like livestock from a predator. Maybe the problem with having their power was that it made them feel unassailable. They fed on those who didn't fight back. Now, rebels attacked the Blessed, and the Blessed fled without thinking to use their magic. For the first time, I saw merit in the Feared's idea. The Blessed might not be ready when the rebels decided to fight back.

Unfortunately, today, I was as good as one of the Blessed to the attackers. I wanted to cry out to those fleeing and tell them to stand and fight. They should use the magic they'd stolen from the citizens of Kavios to defend us.

Reluctantly, I acknowledged the sharp shake of Hart's head as he pulled me to him. "Don't give away your location."

A line of men and women with swords drawn sprinted from the trees after the volley of arrows. They cut down any that stood in their path. Not many did. Their target was clear: me.

Hart pulled me into the trees. "I'll kill Elias myself."

He grabbed my gloved hand, but the warmth between us pushed away the chill of the Oldwood as we plunged into its harsh protection.

The attackers followed.

The first two to reach us were quickly dispatched. I grabbed my dagger. Not an ideal weapon with so many swords, but I'd defend myself any way I could.

"Not our primary concern," I hissed.

Hart still gripped my hand, unwilling to let me out of sight. He grunted in acknowledgment as his sword slid into another attacker. He pulled again, leading me deeper into the Oldwood.

Hiding me behind the tree, he stabbed the next man who came barreling through the bushes.

"You can't stop us all," the next man said as their weapons clashed.

Hart kicked the man back, his sword following, thrusting through the man's heart before he hit the ground. "I assure you, I can."

"Do we have a plan?" I asked.

Hart spun me into his arm as another attacker rounded the tree. His blade greeted the woman where she thought to sneak up on me.

"More than killing them?" he asked.

I'd admit he was doing fine, but the attackers weren't stopping. The longer he tried to keep me safe while fighting them all off, the greater chance he'd take too significant a risk. He, like the other Blessed, hadn't reached for his magic. I trusted him to know what he was doing. He said he'd use it if my safety was on the line.

Clearly, he didn't think it was.

I bit my lip as another attacker came around the next tree. I stabbed him in the neck before Hart pulled me away. He tucked me behind a different tree, and steel met steel as another attacker found us.

But what about Hart's safety?

His moves never slowed, but I knew they would eventually. We needed a plan. As if proving my point, the next swing from his attacker tore a groan from Hart's lips.

Something unfurled within me at the sound.

Hart still wore his helmet, but his head turned, and he glared at the cut across his arm through his shirtsleeve. His sword met the man's again, pushing it back with a brutal strike.

More were coming. Hart would take this one down, but then there would be another. My thoughts scattered.

I couldn't lose Hart. I'd finally found someone to trust—someone to plan with, someone who wanted things to change in this city as much as I did. They couldn't take him from me.

Hart was mine.

There was no time to examine the feelings swirling within. I unleashed them on the attacker, and he screamed.

The man who'd sliced Hart's skin was on his knees, words falling from his lips that made little sense. "Jessikah! No!"

It reminded me of the horrendous sounds of the Selection Festival. He screamed in agony. "I can't lose you!"

Then he crumpled to his side in a fetal position on the Oldwood's forest floor. Hart only hesitated for a moment. With a brief glance at me, his blade slid home to end the man's nightmare.

And I was confident that's what it was: a nightmare.

Ice-cold fear coated my chest. The Cursed King must be here.

Hart pulled me toward him, his sword lowering. "Come here, Chaos."

My body shook.

"It's alright." His tone was gentle now, though moments before it had boasted only death.

The attackers stopped. Hart let his sword hang limp at his side. As I stepped out from behind the tree, I saw why. Blue glowed from Prince Elias's pendant. Any remaining enemies were frozen in place. The guards around the prince dispatched those who hadn't approached me.

"What about the ... Cursed King?" I whispered.

I couldn't see Hart's face beneath his helmet, but I was sure his brow arched. "That wasn't him."

"But ... the nightmare."

His hand pressed lightly to my lower back as he ushered me back to the road. As he did, he leaned in close to whisper in my ear: "That was you, Chaos."

I couldn't process that statement as the prince approached. No enemies remained alive. Any scattered Blessed slowly returned to the path. One limped, another sobbed, and with so many having sprinted for the gates, it was impossible to tell how many died in the ambush. The limping man's ring glowed orange. With each step, the prominence of his limp depleted. He was healing himself with stored energy from lust.

Now that the fear was gone, the Blessed thought to heal themselves. Orange glows spread through the slowly darkening forest. Minor scrapes and bruises alongside stab wounds closed before their eyes.

The prince reached for my gloved hands. "Are you alright, Emberline?"

I nodded as he took one, squeezing.

He gestured at Hart. "I see your guard is as good as he claims."

Hart wiped his blade on a body sprawled at our feet. "Only doing my duty."

"The Feared will stop at nothing," Vaddon said.

He looked strangely unrumpled comparatively. The prince nodded.

"If that was the Feared, where was their king?" I asked.

I could already tell by the way Hart searched the bodies that he didn't recognize any of them. In the same way, he hadn't recognized those who lay in wait outside Alaric's workshop. I couldn't precisely tell Elias and Vaddon that Hart was known to work with the Feared and didn't recognize these men and women, but I'd at least make them think twice about their assumptions.

The prince tilted his head. "What are you saying, Emberline? We know the Feared want to take you—to stop the sourcing of adamas."

Hart kicked over a body with his foot. "The Cursed King would have made this attack a lot easier. If he's proven to work with the Feared, why wouldn't he be here?"

Vaddon sneered. "Who else would they be?"

"I'm not sure. But it seems like something to look into. I'd bet a lot of coin that whoever they were, they were the same group that attacked Emberline outside Alaric's workshop."

I shivered at the use of my full name. I knew the words showed distance between us before Vaddon and the prince, but I didn't care for it. Maybe Chaos was growing on me.

"We'll look into it," the prince said. "Good work ... Hart, was it?" Hart nodded, and the prince returned his attention to me. "You're sure you're alright?"

"Yes. Thank you."

It was mostly a lie, but what else could I say? Hart had just called me the Cursed King. We needed to discuss that more than I needed to reassure the prince after his stupidity.

The captive's statement flared to life in my head. He'd said, *"This Presentation is a mockery of what you are."*

Who was I? Was Hart right?

Prince Elias was still speaking, not noticing my world collapsing behind a face void of emotions. "Good. I wouldn't want anything to stand in the way of you enjoying the Masquerade."

His comment brought me up short. "The ... Masquerade?" My question was inappropriate, given the bodies littering the ground around us. But I didn't understand. "I didn't think I was needed for the ..."

The prince waved his hand. "Nonsense, Emberline. Of course you'll join me at the Masquerade. I wouldn't hear otherwise."

I dipped my chin.

"We should get you back to the city," Hart murmured. "The sun sets."

"Of course," the prince said. "I'm sure we should follow."

He glanced at the guards over his shoulder. "Go ahead. We'll be right behind you."

I swallowed down my objections about the Masquerade. There was nothing I could do about it now. We'd revise our plan accordingly. Hart guided us to the trickle of folk returning to the city. The Presentation had extracted a heavy price. I shuddered to think what King Rodric would do about it.

I wasn't sure where it was safe to talk. Hart kept close until we were in the city, and as we passed Alaric's workshop, I shoved Hart toward it. He grunted and changed course, watching my back while I unlocked the door, ushered him in, and locked it securely behind us.

"What do you mean that was me?" I hissed.

He removed his helmet, set it on the counter, and folded his arms over his chest. "Exactly what I said."

My head was shaking in denial before he finished the sentence.

"Ember." The name absent the flirtatious tone of the nickname he usually preferred. "Think about it. What did you feel?"

I felt too much. I didn't want to think about it. "It was nothing."

He dipped his head, forcing me to meet his gaze, even as I tried to look away. "Do you ever think that maybe you avoid too much?"

I snapped. "Have you ever considered what it's like to walk this city's streets without magic?"

He raised his hands in surrender. "I'm not saying you did anything wrong, Chaos." The honeyed warmth in his tone soothed my anger. "It's worth considering the repercussions of actions this city made necessary. When you express emotions, they take. Understandably, you learned to hide them, but that doesn't mean you don't feel them." The workshop door was locked. No one could get in, but Hart didn't seem to be taking any chances with his following words. He leaned in so close I could feel his breath on my ear as he spoke. "You said the gem's magic doesn't affect you."

I shivered at his proximity even as I nodded.

I wanted to flee, to be anywhere but here, talking about the way I dealt with emotions. At the same time, I didn't want to move as his warm breath promised a safety I wasn't guaranteed elsewhere.

He continued. "Now, why would that be? I only know of two people in this city that would create magic as you do—that would not succumb to what's clearly a bastardization of the real thing."

"I'm not the Cursed King," I said with a lot of conviction I didn't truly have.

Hart glared at me, unamused. He had told me a story another time we were in this same room together. A story not about Themis's Champion, but about Eris's: a champion chosen not to spite her sister but to defy the order she imposed. Hart had said she would *challenge what's known*.

I shook my head, unable to voice the question. I thought he saw it in my face anyway.

That smirk curled his lip. "I told you that story could mean whatever you wanted it to."

"I don't have magic."

Maybe if I said it enough times, it would hold.

His green eyes danced with something merciless, and I knew I'd hate his following words. "Your magic is fueled by emotion, Chaos. Emotion you rarely allow yourself to express. Tell me there haven't been times other than today when you've done something that didn't make sense. Something impossible. What did you feel?"

The bastard. He had an event in mind. He was goading me toward it. The night of the Selection Festival, I'd raged at my circumstance. I'd been so angry that I hadn't stopped to consider how I'd pushed Mother's chair, with Father in it, for fifteen blocks. It shouldn't have been possible—and he'd known it.

I glared. It had happened again when the group attacked me outside of Alaric's workshop. He'd been there for that as well. The man then fell before me as fear built within me, so similar to what happened today—except this time, my fear wasn't for me.

His smirk crept impossibly higher, dimpling his cheek.

"And what? My fear of the attackers granted me the power of nightmare magic?" I asked, playing into his theory.

His smirk broke into a full-on grin, and I knew I'd misstepped. "No, Chaos. If I'm not mistaken, the emotion slipped out today when you were scared for me, not yourself."

I glanced at the bleeding cut on his arm. The screams had unleashed right after it occurred. Still, he couldn't know that. I didn't grant him the satisfaction of asking about his assumption. He tracked my gaze, looking more than confident in his assessment.

I met his outrageous implication with a rational question. "Why wouldn't Alaric have said something?"

No one studied Eris more than Alaric. He would have known.

Maybe he had known. And he didn't tell me.

Alaric doesn't have friends. He has projects. I hated that Father's words were there, waiting to be weaponized. The ones I wielded against myself were always the most dangerous.

Hart pinched the bridge of his nose. "I don't know what Alaric was doing. He didn't trust me with the information."

"Why?"

"Ah, Chaos, that's what I've been asking myself every day since he's been gone."

"You haven't come up with any answers?" I asked.

He held my gaze. "I have my suspicions. But I've been striving to prove them wrong."

The words sank below my skin in a way that felt familiar.

"If you think I'm ... *that* ... what's your role in all of this?"

His gaze held a little disappointment as he spoke. He stepped toward me again. "I thought I'd made that clear, Chaos. I'm here for you."

Something in my chest fluttered, and I pushed it down. It occurred to me that I was doing exactly what he accused me of, but this was too much.

I couldn't feel this. I couldn't be this.

"We should get back to the castle."

Hart gave me a final assessing gaze before following me from the workshop.

32

I worry she closed off too much and buried everything too deep. She needs safety and security to feel freely.

— ALARIC SARE'S LETTERS TO ISABELLE ARKOVA

Unsettled was the best way I could describe myself that night. Hart didn't say another word about magic or our plans. It was better that he didn't. I needed time to think.

I was supposed to be immune to their magic—that was all. That was my … condition. Well, that and my connection to the stones. And … I guess the connection to the captive in the mines. I sighed as the evidence, even in my own mind, stacked against me. I wasn't supposed to *have* magic.

Arguing further with Hart would be nowhere near as

convincing as arguing with myself, which I did—the entire evening.

The sun rose too quickly. I was no closer to certainty, but I couldn't disregard the points that he'd made. I'd done things when I felt strongly that didn't make sense.

Could I really be Chaos's Champion?

Hart looked me up and down when he greeted me the following day and ushered me to the workshop to finish the rings. He was a quiet presence while I worked, settling into one of the wingback chairs, a book open in his lap. The chair remained between me and the front door.

I gave up on my internal argument and focused on the Masquerade that evening. "We'll stick with the original plan. We'll just have to start later than anticipated."

Hart looked up, setting down Alaric's copy of *Champions of Kavios*.

I glared daggers at the book. It had always bothered me that so much was said about the Cursed King, and there was next to no clear information about Chaos's Champion. If what he'd said the other day was true—if this was the only copy in existence, and the seer was someone close to Alaric—I needed to talk to Mother. She would have to know. Whether she could access the information when I asked for it was another question.

If Hart's assumptions about me were true—if I was Chaos's Champion—it changed nothing about tonight. I couldn't begin to untangle the implications for my future, but that was another matter. We would stick to our plan to save the captive. Then, I would try to talk to Mother after that.

"Is it everything you thought it would be?" I pointed at the book he'd waited so long to get his hands on.

It hadn't crossed my mind until now that I might wonder

why Alaric didn't let him read it. Alaric had always shared his books so freely with me.

He set the book on the table. "It's infuriating and devastating."

"Hence its appeal." I stared at the book a beat longer.

How could Alaric have kept so much from me? It was no easy task to re-read everything in a book I'd studied almost daily, to study it through a new lens, one that I thought I should have had from the start.

"Did Alaric ever talk about me?" I wasn't sure what answer I wanted, but Hart and Alaric were friends.

It looked like it pained Hart to respond. "No, he didn't talk about you or your abilities. I knew his sister was sick. He mentioned his niece trained with him to take over the quartz shop in Woodside, but—"

"He talked about me like I was normal." Hart had said as much before. I didn't know why that bothered me. It was to protect me, after all.

Hart's fist clenched. "You are magnificent. He knew that. It's why he did everything he did to protect you. To give you the best chance."

I swallowed. "The best chance against the Cursed King?"

He laughed. "The Cursed King has had over two hundred years to take the throne. I assure you, he is not a threat."

Hart had said he knew him. He said the Cursed King wasn't dangerous to me as Jeweler to the Blessed. Now, he reinforced it when he called me Eris's Champion. I wanted desperately to believe him. We'd need to discuss it more if I sought to change things before the Blessing. I was getting ahead of myself. First, we needed to get through tonight.

Hart's face sobered as if sensing where my thoughts had turned. "You want to venture into the Oldwood after the Masquerade?"

I nodded. "We need to free him before the Blessing. This is our best chance."

I had considered going last night, but with the attack on myself and the prince, the Oldwood would have been filled with soldiers until sunrise.

Hart stood. "You lead, I'll follow."

Something in me warmed. If I believed, as he did, that I was Eris's Champion, it might be the third option I had been looking for. If I could harness the magic of a goddess, maybe I wouldn't have to deliver the adamas, and also, I wouldn't have to run.

Maybe I could free the city from King Rodric Glanmore's adamas-fueled grip.

Hart returned me to my room to wash and dress. He sent one of the sentries to find him a mask for the ball, taking their place outside my door while I readied.

Penelope was waiting for me. She had a box with a familiar stamp on it, one that only took me moments to place.

"You got me a dress from the modiste?"

"Prince Elias did. He insisted you required a proper garment."

This whole thing made me uncomfortable. I couldn't remember if Alaric had ever been required to attend the Masquerade. It was irrelevant, I was sure, but why did the prince want me there? If what Hart and I had discussed was true, I was in even more danger with the Glanmores.

One of the clearest pieces of information from *Champions of Kavios* was that Themis's Champion was a Glanmore. Three generations of the family had founded the city—and its mines

—together. With the power of the adamas, and its eternal youth, it wasn't entirely clear which generation the Cursed King was a part of. As far as I knew, neither Rodric nor Elias had nightmare magic. The most agreed-upon theory was that Elias had a brother.

Whoever he was, we all knew he was cursed. Although, no one agreed upon the details of that curse. Why hadn't he taken the throne and ended any potential fight between Chaos and Order's champions for Kavios?

If I were Chaos's Champion, and the Cursed King was at the founding of Kavios, then Hart was right. The Cursed King would have had two hundred years to take the throne uncontested.

What kind of curse would stop him?

Penelope pulled the dress from its box, and I held my breath. All thoughts about the Cursed King paused as I worried about whether the prince's tastes would match mine. The women in the castle appeared to enjoy lower cuts and more exposed skin than I cared to display.

There'd be no time to fight whatever had been chosen. Penelope held it proudly for my review. The dark green reminded me of the exact shade of Hart's eyes. I shook the thought away, examining the long, flowing sleeves. At least my arms would be covered.

The upper back of the dress was made of sheer material with a high lace collar. It protected my neck, and while the gossamer showed off my skin, it didn't expose it to touch. If I looked at it only from behind, it would be perfect.

Then Penelope turned the dress.

The front dipped low. It would show a daring amount of skin between my breasts.

I sighed. At least this was the front of the dress. I had a

chance to defend myself if someone reached for my chest. It was the best I could hope for. There was no point in arguing. Penelope couldn't change it anyway.

She brought in hot water to wash and, after I was clean, helped me into the dress. I was uncomfortable with how well it fit, clinging to every curve.

With the dress in place, Penelope braided my golden hair into a crown around my head. Then, she came at me with a stick of kohl.

I stepped back. "What are you doing?"

She glanced down at the stick, which looked like a thick writing instrument. "Lining your eyes."

"Do you mind wearing ... gloves?" I asked.

Rationally, I knew she wasn't Blessed, but I still didn't like a stranger's exposed skin so close to my own. The thought alerted me to how quickly I'd stopped worrying about it with Hart once I'd finally told him the truth.

Penelope smiled sadly like she understood—she probably did. I gestured to a pair of mine lying on the table. Once she pulled them on, she was right back in my face with the dark crayon. I blinked rapidly as she pressed forward. I'd never had such attention.

"It'll go faster if you don't flinch as much," she said gently.

Oh, how I wished that was within my control. "Sorry."

There was no fixing this behavior. As Hart had said, the necessary actions I'd taken to protect myself had made me who I was. It wouldn't change overnight.

When her work was finished, Penelope stepped back and smiled. "There. You look lovely."

She picked up a matching mask from the box. It tied with a black satin ribbon around my head.

I stood. "Thank you."

A looking glass was propped in the corner of the room by the wardrobe. Hesitantly, I stepped before it. As I did, Penelope offered matching slippers for my feet. They were much thinner than my usual leather boots, but the delicate material matched the elegance of the evening. And I did look elegant.

With a final nod to me in the mirror, Penelope left. The hairstyle she'd chosen highlighted my slim neck. The dress's dip guided my eye to more skin than I had ever shown in public. Those arriving to seek the raptures of a Blessed's touch would wear much less, but still, I hesitated.

Nothing about this made me comfortable—but tonight wasn't about being comfortable. It was about getting through the evening and getting to the mines. The sooner I arrived at the Masquerade, the sooner we could leave.

Hart entered, a dark gray mask covering his face like his helmet usually did for formal occasions. He held himself apart as he glimpsed the front of the dress in the mirror's reflection. His pupils dilated, making his hooded gaze darker, demanding.

"Do you want to wear that?" It seemed to take some effort for him to get the words out.

I'd be offended by the question if I didn't know why he was asking. He knew my preferences better than most. Our proximity over the last few days had made him more than aware.

My silence must have made him realize how his words sounded. "You're perfect," he continued, nervous energy seemed to fuel his words. "Absolutely beautiful. I just ..."

"I know," I said. "It's fine."

He looked like he'd argue further, but we had more pressing matters to take care of tonight.

I slipped on black gloves to match the mask and dress's lacing. "We might as well get this over with."

He offered me his arm. "I'll never get over this."

I couldn't help how my chest fluttered. I told myself it was just nerves. We had a big night. We'd make an appearance at the Masquerade, ensure the prince saw me, and then we'd trek to the mines. If everything went according to plan, we'd free the captive tonight.

33

More than the fate of the Kingdom will hang in the balance between them.

— FROM CHAMPIONS OF KAVIOS

My mind was already elsewhere as we entered the throne room. The double doors were open wide—inviting—so different from my meeting days ago. Candelabras on gold metal stands lined the room, and a chandelier of the same hung above us. Many of the alcoves already had the drapes pulled. At first glance across the room, I couldn't begin to guess how many magicless citizens danced with the Blessed.

Flashes of orange on the dancefloor indicated at least a few couples. A flash of green envy being collected for persuasion also caught my eye. The throne was empty. Prince Elias wore a mask, but his pristine hair and dark blue dress uniform were easy to find in the center of the dancefloor.

Holding tight to Hart's arm and still unclear about what part I played here, I pushed my shoulders back and glided into the room. We circled the perimeter, and I could not keep my attention from the alcoves. Soft noises of pleasure emanated from most that we passed. The curtains were too thick to see color, but it was all too easy to assume lust and joy were collected.

I wanted so desperately to ask what I was doing here. A jeweler wasn't needed at the ball. Was this the reward the prince kept referring to? All things considered, maybe it wasn't so bad. I could think of worse things they could offer under the guise of a prize.

My stomach fluttered uncomfortably. Something about Prince Elias was unsettling. He was too smooth, too sure of himself. He didn't seem to have his father's unassailable ability to calm, though he could wield the magic when prepared, as he'd proved on the Oldwood Trail.

His charm made him dangerous. The king had given up on people deciding to do what he wanted. Instead, he went straight for his magic and required their compliance. Unfortunately, it seemed Elias understood that the illusion of decision is more important than the actual decision-making. He took a little extra time if it meant those he influenced felt it was their idea to do what he wanted. It did seem to make a difference. Citizens flocked to him at the mines, and they'd cheered him at the Cornucopia. The same citizens shuddered in fear of his father so much that the king stopped attending events except those exclusively for the Blessed.

We drew past where the Selected would be seated at the bottom of the dais. Five chairs sat empty. The Selected must be occupied throughout the room.

"A dance?" Hart asked.

I turned to face him. "You dance?"

"Depends on your answer."

He didn't need to ask twice. My gloved hand slipped into his open palm. Warmth flared, even with the layer of silk between us. He pulled me to him, slipping us seamlessly into the couples moving about the room. His brow arched as my eyes widened. I was unfamiliar with the movements, but he knew every step.

With our bodies pressed close, I focused on the flame building between us, a heat, it seemed, only his touch could stoke. Our proximity returned my thoughts to our night in the alcove at Forest's Edge. My hands pressed against his chest, his thumb stroking my hip, so many possibilities left unexplored. The rest of the dancers disappeared around us.

That night at Forest's Edge had been the first time I put *my* trust in Hart, not my uncles. He hadn't disappointed me. As I studied him now, I knew Hart would watch each perceived threat in the room. I took advantage of his protection and dared to dream of different circumstances for us. What if I wasn't Jeweler to the Blessed? And he wasn't my Blessed guard, protecting me from a rebel group that wanted me dead?

Maybe I could forget I was Chaos's Champion, chosen to free the city from the Glanmore's abuse of power. What would it be like if we'd found each other in a happier place? This moment, in the safety of his arms, was one of the few places I could consider such things.

I shivered. In that imaginary world, our connection would surely spark an uncontrollable flame.

In our reality, I wasn't sure we had that luxury.

"What are you thinking about?" he asked.

There were so many ways I could have answered. I could tell him I was thinking about the captive. Or that I wasn't sure what I'd decide to do if my parents verified everything he'd claimed about me.

But he knew all that.

How he tracked each reaction of my body led me to believe he would know if I lied. I knew, too, that would disappoint him.

I glanced down at my chest. "How much exposed skin the prince's dress selection features."

He appeared to fight hard not to follow the direction of my gaze.

"And if we'll see each other after this is over," I added.

His lips parted, and he held my gaze as he seemed to consider his response. He'd been clear after I met with the king that he'd get me out. Anywhere I wanted to go, he'd take me. But he didn't say he was staying. If I was Chaos's Champion, I wasn't sure running was still an option. We'd need to know whatever my parents did before deciding, but something about our circumstances made me think our time together was ending.

I hadn't intended to ask but was very invested in his answer.

"There is no over for us, Chaos. I told you I'm here for you. I follow you."

His green eyes held mine, though his expression was indecipherable. Before I could respond, the dance steps changed, and he spun me away and reeled me back in. Every couple in the ballroom did the same.

It was so easy to forget he was Blessed. He'd probably been to many such balls in his lifetime. His hold was a little tighter when I returned to his side. Desire flared hot like the flame in that different world I imagined.

"Why?" The question slipped from my lips.

I cursed my need to understand.

His gaze was half-wild, half-hooded, that of a man at odds with his own thoughts. He opened his mouth to speak as a cough sounded behind him.

"Mind if I cut in?" The voice was smooth, firm, and unused to being denied.

Prince Elias stood behind Hart, and he'd asked me to dance.

Hart's fingers flexed along my side like he was deciding whether to let go. His brow furrowed, and I squeezed his hand gently before sliding from his grasp. My smile securely in place, I dipped into another awkward curtsey.

"It would be my pleasure."

The scowl on Hart's face would have been a treat if Elias were anyone but the prince. He gave me a slight bow before stalking from the dancefloor, not bothering to acknowledge the royal he'd walked away from. My gaze followed him as he left the ballroom.

Prince Elias stepped into his place confidently, secure in his position. "Who was that?"

I saw no harm in the truth. "My guard."

At my words, something flashed in Elias's gaze. He paused in thought, as if he wasn't sure my answer was the one he was searching for. "I knew his voice sounded familiar." He shook his head. "He does like to stay close, doesn't he?"

I let the comment pass. Surely, the prince wasn't interested in discussing his jeweler's guard. The music swelled as the new dance started, and we were off. Elias held me formally, a good few inches of distance between us. I tried to keep myself loose in his arms instead of stiffening at the contact.

His gaze lingered a moment too long. "You look stunning."

I attempted a dip of my chin as we moved between the other couples. "Thank you for the dress."

Elias wasn't as graceful as Hart, but I found it didn't matter. The other couples on the dancefloor parted, giving way to the prince. Did he even notice?

He waved away my comment. "I wish I could give you more. You've been such an asset to us—Jeweler to the Blessed."

I didn't like his enthusiasm, but I thanked him for his compliments.

He held my gaze. "Your work is impeccable. Your talents are unmatched. I'm not sure you realize the prize you are."

"You're too kind."

Had Alaric done things differently with the Glanmores? Had I made a mistake by fulfilling their requests? I wished I could ask Alaric any of these questions because I certainly didn't care for the prince's attachment to my talents.

Elias didn't realize the effect his words had on me. "I'm not kind enough. I know you must have questions, especially about your uncle ..."

He let the sentence trail off, and I stiffened. He couldn't possibly know what I'd been thinking. Lost in thought, I hadn't tracked the flow of our dance. Our movements had taken us toward the same set of doors through which the woman had entered during my last audience with King Rodric.

As if taking advantage of my surprise at his mention of Alaric, we exited the dancefloor. The awaiting guards opened the door, and the prince slid his hand into my own, pulling me behind him.

I didn't see Hart anywhere in the room. He must have gone outside to the courtyard. The idea of leaving with Elias had me uneasy. "Where are we—"

"I need to show you something, Emberline. Don't be upset. I want to be honest with you."

My stomach dropped. I had yet to understand why, but wherever he led me, I knew I'd rather not go. His long strides took us down a hallway and through another set of doors.

The room was very much like the prince's study. Shelves of books lined the walls, and a portrait of Themis holding a golden scale hung behind a large wooden desk.

I knew whose study we were in. My gaze snapped to the corner where King Rodric sat in one of the plush chairs. All breath left my lungs as I realized who was beside him.

On his knees, bloody, bruised, and bound—was Alaric.

I was across the floor and kneeling beside him before the prince could catch me.

"Uncle."

Alaric's mouth was covered with a dirty cloth. His gaze met mine in one of resignation. So many unspoken words passed between us.

Questions flooded my mind, but I dared not voice them: What happened? Why didn't you tell me ... any of this? Why did you leave?

I couldn't believe he was here.

My gaze lingered again on his appearance. He was definitely not a welcome guest. Not dressed in finery and turned about the dancefloor like I had just been. Rope tied his wrists like those of a prisoner. Ice shot down my spine, and I masked my fear. Alaric was most definitely in trouble. I just didn't know why.

"Why is he bound?" I asked with all the authority I could muster. "Free him. Let him retake his place if he's been found."

King Rodric sipped a light brown liquid from a fine glass. "I don't think I will."

My gaze turned to the king. "What has he done?"

The king set down his glass. "As if you don't know."

I had plenty of suspicions but I'd be damned if I voiced any of them. He had left to chase after something, some history. That's what Father had thought. I wondered how much of that had to do with me—what I was. I couldn't think about that now. My anger at all he kept from me could wait. The only thing that mattered was getting Alaric out of this.

I turned to the prince. "Please. What has he done?"

The king snorted at my supplication of his son, but I didn't regret it. Prince Elias couldn't help himself. He wanted to be liked, even when he stood no chance.

"Your uncle was found in the mines. He was trying to destroy the adamas source."

Now, it was Alaric's turn to snort. He flexed his jaw until the tie slipped enough for him to speak. "He is not a source!"

So much for claiming Alaric wasn't guilty of what they accused.

I took a breath. This was bad. Part of me wished Hart was here, his steady presence would calm my racing heart. As quickly as I thought it, another piece of me was glad he wasn't. I didn't want him caught up in whatever this was with the Glanmores.

Then Uncle's words clicked. *He. The mines.* Alaric was trying to free the captive. The captive … created the adamas deposits. I knew I'd been right.

"That's enough from you," the prince said. His gaze returned to mine. "Your uncle was arrested for treason."

"How long?" The words were out before I could stop them. I knew it was irrelevant in the grand scheme of … everything, but I couldn't help but feel I'd been played.

Elias attempted confusion, but it was too late. I'd already seen the flash of understanding cross his face. I held Alaric's wrist and squeezed in a way I hoped was reassuring. This was bad. I had no idea what to do, but I would get him out.

"How long?" I pressed again, latching on to something that

Elias appeared to want to hide. If nothing else, it would give me a moment to think.

"Days. We found him before we found you." Elias's head hung with the confession.

I knew Alaric would never miss a meeting with the king. It made more sense that Alaric thought I would have had time to find his note before being discovered by the Glanmores. It made even more sense if that note was only a precaution—if there had been a chance he wouldn't be caught at all.

I knew that calculation of risk too well. It was the same one Hart and I had done about tonight's task.

My rage-filled glare met Elias's. He'd let me believe Alaric was dead. Only Alaric's note gave me hope he was chasing down something useful—that he had a purpose in his departure.

When I thought things couldn't get any worse, Vaddon stormed in. "Why did you bring her here, Elias? She's a traitor, just like him."

I wouldn't leave Alaric's side, but for the first time it occurred to me that not only Alaric was in trouble here. King Rodric's words echoed in my mind: *As if you don't know.*

Alaric worked around his loosed gag. "She didn't kn—"

"Silence." Vaddon's glare turned from Elias to Alaric.

My hand ran down Alaric's back in as soothing a gesture as I could muster. My gaze bored into his as the royals and the advisor argued. I didn't care what they thought I knew. He was my priority. How was I going to get him out of here?

"We don't have proof she was a part of her uncle's scheme. She deserved to know—deserved the chance to prove her loyalty," Elias said.

"And does this look like loyalty?" Vaddon spat.

I didn't have to look to know he gestured to my place on the floor at my uncle's side.

"Enough about Alaric," the prince said. "He is a traitor to Kavios. We're here to speak about Emberline."

I tensed.

"Her talents and her beauty."

Vaddon groaned.

"She is wasted without magic," Elias continued.

"You can't be serious." It was Vaddon's turn to be surprised. "Rodric. She's as much a traitor as Alaric."

Rodric waved a hand dismissively.

The prince came to my other side, and gooseflesh covered every inch of my skin. He glanced at the king as if to ensure his mind was unchanged by Vaddon's outburst. Whatever he was about to say, I was positive I wouldn't like it.

"I told you I had a surprise for you," Elias said. "Father has decided to include a fifth Blessed with this year's celebration. Someone who has served Kavios and this family beyond the call of duty."

No. My body tensed as if I'd been slapped. I had seen *five* chairs at the foot of the dais in the ballroom. There were only four Selected. I hadn't even considered what the extra one was for.

Alaric's words echoed my internal thoughts. "No, Ember. You can't."

His words were like a knife in my gut. Like a wound I knew was there but couldn't yet identify.

Elias rested a hand on my shoulder, drawing my attention from Alaric. "You, Emberline. You are to be Blessed."

My vision tunneled. Elias kept speaking flowery words, but they sounded like a soft hum in my head. This couldn't be right. I couldn't be Blessed. My gaze met Uncle's. The horror in his eyes reflected my inner thoughts. I only hoped I wasn't as transparent.

Elias took my hand, lifting me from the floor. "I knew you'd be excited. I'll announce it now. We should return."

"I'm so sorry, Ember." Alaric's words pulled me back. "I never meant for any of this ..."

Vaddon seemed unable to take more. In two quick strides, he crossed the room and kicked Alaric to the floor.

Alaric's gasp as the breath left him had me ready to vomit. Saliva coated my tongue. None of this could be real.

I looked to the king. It was his Blessing, after all. "What will happen to him?"

"That's entirely up to you, Emberline. My son is convinced your value outweighs your uncle's crimes."

"Highn—" Vaddon started to protest.

The king held up his hand. "If the scales are balanced, Order is preserved."

Prince Elias pressed his hand to my lower back. "He would remain a prisoner, Emberline. He couldn't return to life in the city, but you could see him."

I hated the entitlement of his touch as much as I needed it —needed him to value me the way he did to save Alaric.

Much like when I'd decided to become Jeweler to the Blessed, my choice was no choice at all. I would do anything to keep Alaric safe.

"It would be an honor," I said.

A moan slipped from Alaric's lips. "No."

Vaddon kicked him again, and I winced, feeling the pain as if it were my own.

Alaric's blood splattered my dress. Prince Elias looked me up and down as I stood. "Maybe we shouldn't announce it tonight. It will be all the more of a surprise when you arrive tomorrow with the gems, and the audience realizes there is one for you as well."

He didn't even acknowledge that he'd given me less than a

day to make another ring. It wasn't the kind of detail the prince would care about.

I nodded, unable to find words.

The prince guided me from the room. "Let's go find that guard of yours."

In a daze, I followed. My heart broke as the door shut with Alaric behind it. I told myself he'd be alright. So long as I became Blessed and did what they asked, Alaric would live.

Fury built within me. I'd been so close to doing something for myself—making a decision I could live with for how my future played out. That went out the window now that the Glanmores had Alaric. I wouldn't even consider what they'd do to him if I ran. It was no longer an option.

Even as the fight left me, rebellion raged inside me. At least I would accomplish what Alaric could not. I'd remain with the Glanmores. Stay Jeweler to the Blessed. Become Blessed myself. But they couldn't blame me if the source of adamas disappeared.

Then, at least in this new cage I willingly entered, I wouldn't endlessly funnel power to the Blessed.

34

I wish I'd prepared her more. I'm sorry. I didn't think I could do it without clouding her judgment. So I taught her all I could, hoping she could judge for herself.

— ALARIC SARE'S LETTERS TO ISABELLE ARKOVA

As we returned to the Masquerade, I took slow, deep breaths. They did little to stop my heart from beating through my chest. We were lucky the candle lighting was so dim. I'd tried to set myself to rights on the walk, but I was a mess. Unfortunately, the blood splatter on my gown was the least of my worries.

The prince wasn't so invested that he wanted to search the grounds for Hart. He handed me off to the first guard he saw.

"Don't leave her until she's with the other one," he said.

Once the prince's back was turned, Hart found me, dismissing the temporary guard.

"Ready?" he asked.

Chaos save me. I couldn't believe they had Alaric. The price to save him, accepting the King's Blessing, and becoming one of them—becoming everything I hated. Doing everything I didn't want to do. It wouldn't just be turning over the gems for the Blessing. I would be making the crown the king commissioned.

I glanced at Hart through my partially clumped lashes. My tears from the king's study had barely dried. I didn't hate *Hart,* and he was Blessed. He fought the Blessed from inside their walls. Maybe I could do this.

My thoughts returned to our first trip to the mines. He'd asked me offhandedly if I cared about what happened to a Blessed. At the time, I'd considered it the Blessed's choice to become what they were—to accept the adamas.

What did I know? How many Blessed were coerced the same way the Glanmores were doing to me?

The thoughts ricocheted in my mind, giving me whiplash. I couldn't accept adamas. I couldn't become Blessed.

I *could* and *would* for Alaric.

Alaric. The task that had him caught was the same as mine. To make my fate worthwhile, I would do what he couldn't. He strove to free the captive and failed. He wasn't Blessed. I could only guess he knew about the secret entrance. I hoped its presence hadn't been revealed in his capture.

Hart would help me complete what Alaric could not. Then, I'd resign myself to life within a cage. I could do what Alysa said: I could accept the adamas and never take. It wasn't like the king tracked it. It wasn't like I needed to take to use the magic.

Fleeing had been a beautiful idea, but I wasn't made for

pretty things. I was made to suffer at the pleasure of the Blessed.

I'd do it gladly for Alaric. The man who raised me. The man who ensured I had the support I needed for my livelihood and the love I needed to exist outside it. There was nothing I wouldn't do for that man.

"Everything alright, Chaos?" His brow furrowed now as he reassessed my appearance. He stepped closer.

I couldn't tell him here. My skin itched just standing inside the castle walls. I needed to get out of here—away from all of this. If this was my last night of freedom, I would use it well.

Hart said he'd follow me anywhere—I might put that to the test with this. Would he follow if I chose to become what I claimed to hate? Yes, he had chosen to fight from within, but he also knew how I felt about the Blessed. I could tell him he'd opened my eyes to shades of gray with the Blessed. In my mind, they could no longer all be painted with a single stroke.

My spine straightened. We didn't have time to have this argument here. The captive was waiting.

"Let's get out of here."

He searched my gaze. I knew he saw more than I wanted, but he didn't press.

Though the castle was more than distracted by the delights and debauchery in the ballroom, we decided walking down the front steps wasn't a great idea. It was better if everyone thought I'd returned to my room.

Hart left me with the night guards, giving me time to change before he waited below my window. My dress was a bit much for our journey through the Oldwood.

Outfitted in trousers, a long-sleeved tunic, and sturdy leather boots, I grabbed my gloves from the table before climbing on the desk and levering myself onto the window's ledge again.

“What kind of chaos are we unleashing here?” The voice I was only too familiar with said quietly from below.

With everything closing in around me, this felt normal. It felt right. “A wise man told me Eris inspires chaos. She doesn’t cause.” I paused. “Feeling inspired?”

The heat in his gaze set my skin aflame again. I wanted to let it consume me. There was so much to do on my last night of freedom, but the look in his eyes had me wondering if we should add another item to the list.

“A wise man, you say? You should probably listen to him more often.”

I sighed. “Ready?”

He’d insisted on this part. Last time, I’d fallen clumsily into the bushes below. This time, he would catch me. He knew my secret, knew of my immunity. He’d proved time and time again that I was safe with him. This trust between us, it was like a barrier removed—a layer of clothing peeled away by a new lover.

That thought was too on the nose.

Free the captive. That was my focus. I had planned to do it before everything began to unravel around me. The same part of me that knew which gems were adamas and which were quartz had known the captive was the true source of the adamas. If I removed them from the equation, I’d accomplish what the Feared desired—I’d remove their adamas source. It was convenient that my approach didn’t come at the cost of my life.

It reassured me as much as it worried me that Alaric had the same plan. He’d been caught trying to free the captive. I had to believe Hart and I could be successful where Uncle failed.

With a final glance at Hart, I jumped from my perch on the windowsill.

His touch was another problem altogether. I may no longer fear it, but I could feel *something* between us every time, even through a layer of clothing.

Goddess, save me. His touch would be my undoing.

I shook away the scalding images of his hands freely roaming my skin. We didn't have time for whatever obscene fantasies my mind conjured. Searching the path, there was no sign of guards in either direction. We made our escape toward the mines.

Hart tugged me close behind him, our hands linked, as we hiked through the Oldwood. He was unwilling to risk that I slip under its spell in the darkness. I found comfort in the solidity of his grasp, a comfort that had been sorely lacking this evening. So I didn't tell him the magic of the forest wasn't pressing against me.

I had a feeling its message had already been delivered.

I contemplated how to get the words out that I needed to as we hiked by what little light spilled from our stolen torch. The darkness beneath the canopy of the Oldwood dimmed any help from the moon.

"What did the prince want?" Hart asked as we left the city.

The command of his voice soothed as much as the question granted me a way to broach the topic I'd been struggling with. Words I'd been searching for slipped from my lips with little further encouragement.

"The Glanmores have Alaric."

Hart stopped walking and turned slowly to face me. Something in the stern set of his features urged me to continue.

"They've had him the whole time. They caught him trying to free the captive."

Hart's fingers massaged his temples. "You didn't think that was relevant to tell me before *we* went to free the captive ourselves?"

My hands were on my hips. "I'm telling you now."

Somehow Hart was smirking. He knew I'd been wrestling with something since returning with the prince. The shape of the problem may not have been known, but he'd known there was a problem nonetheless.

He'd followed me anyway. That fact was more reassuring than it should be.

"Is he alright?"

I shook my head, remembering the state of him, the tattered garment, the blood, the way Vaddon kicked him as I left.

A muscle in his jaw twitched with his next question. "What do they want from you?"

I tore the bandage from the open wound. "I'm to be the fifth Blessed tomorrow."

His arresting green eyes held mine. Even in the dark, I could feel the fire burning behind them.

"We can get you and your family out. Tonight. Alysa will take you all. Alaric wouldn't want this."

My intensity matched his. "It's not his choice. I won't leave him to die."

"They won't kill him if you're gone. They will need him."

I sighed. Hart may have a point, but it still didn't change my mind. "I won't leave him with them."

"This is not a choice, Chaos. It's the illusion of such, something Rodric is far too good at."

I knew he was right, I did. It just didn't matter. I tried to explain. "You've shown me that Blessed don't have to be mindless servants, forever grateful for the power Rodric grants. I can accept the adamas and never use it. That keeps

Alaric safe and me close enough to find a way to eventually free him."

Hart looked like he would argue.

"We need to keep going."

Silently, Hart recaptured my hand and continued our hike. The strength of his grip told me we weren't finished with that conversation. As we neared the foothills, the slope increased, and every step, every crunch of dirt and leaves beneath our feet, had me wondering what we were walking into.

I focused on our mission for tonight: to free the captive. If we could succeed at that, it would ease the pressure on everything else.

"We're headed toward the original mine entrance," Hart said. "If Alaric was captured days ago, I can confirm Rodric and Elias still don't know about it. It hasn't been guarded since you took the position of jeweler."

I wondered how he knew that. Is this where he went at night while he left other guards at my door? He didn't give me time to ask.

"When the Glanmores first found the quartz deposits and dug to see how much was here, they used the path in the foothills to haul it out."

"That must have been ... hundreds of years ago. That was Rodric's father, right?"

Hart nodded. "Phillip Glanmore was a simple explorer once. Sometimes, I wonder if he knew what his actions would eventually bring."

I turned to face him. "Before his grandson became Themis's Champion and the Cursed King?"

"Exactly."

"When you first told me about the goddesses and their champions, I asked if you knew the Cursed King's story. You said we'd save it for another time."

He nodded slowly.

"Will you tell it to me while we walk?"

The Cursed King's part in this still didn't make sense. He was a Glanmore. He was Themis's Champion, but he hadn't directly attacked me. I guessed he might not know I was Eris's Champion, but being Jeweler to the Blessed had been enough for the Feared. They supposedly acted in his name.

We hadn't seen his power unleashed since the night of the Selection Festival. No matter what power I had, I knew that night hadn't been me. It was too big, too bold, and too connected with the Feared's escape. Why do it then? Why not use it again since?

While Hart might not have those answers, I'd take anything I could learn about the figure of legend that sat opposite me in this game of goddesses.

Hart tipped back his neck, offering his face to goddesses I wasn't sure he worshiped. "I'm not sure I could deny you anything."

His words sent a shiver up my spine that had nothing to do with the forest.

"Phillip discovered the mine and built the city. Rodric inherited the Kingdom. The mines continued to produce, and new settlers joined. Some say Rodric was content with his power. It was his firstborn who pushed further. His firstborn who unearthed mysteries that weren't meant to be found."

My heart skipped a beat. "What did he do?"

"He took Order to a new level. Introduced schedules for the mines and grand plans to dig deeper and find more quartz for export. He wanted to inherit a city twice the size his father did."

"That sounds like what Themis would want in her champion."

"Ah, but the firstborn wasn't yet summoned. He pursued

what *he* wanted. The firstborn's plans were what unearthed the adamas. He is responsible for all of this." Hart gestured back toward the city.

"How so?" I asked. If this was what the firstborn wanted, why didn't he sit on the throne now?

"Themis summoned him with his discovery."

"Still, the firstborn worshipped Themis, right? Wouldn't it have been an honor?"

"Isn't it an honor for those in Kavios to become Blessed? Think of how you feel about the mandate Rodric is forcing on you. I know it's not the same, but ... much can lose its luster when required to do it," Hart said.

"So we're back to the point—what the Cursed King is known for—Themis's Champion had no choice in his summoning, which he rejected. What did he do?"

Hart was silent for a beat. "He searched for any way to change his fate. One such path included discovering how to harness magic with the adamas."

"You're saying the Cursed King, the firstborn, is responsible for trapping the captive we're trying to free? And for ... creating the Blessed?"

This didn't make sense. The Cursed King worked with the Feared now, literally on the opposite side of the Blessed. But Hart nodded slowly in answer to my question.

"How did they source the gems? Was there a jeweler before Alaric?"

Something like disgust crossed Hart's features. "The first-born could feel the difference in the stone, much like you. He wasn't a jeweler, but could work with one to ensure the integrity of the gem." Hart shook his head. "At one point, he thought if others could wield Themis's magic, maybe they could be her champion. Maybe it would mean he didn't have to be."

It felt like an animal was burrowing into my gut. I was nauseous thinking about the Cursed King's choices and what they had led to. Some part of me understood wanting to escape the mandated fate ... but at what cost? I wanted to ask if there was more to that part of the story, but Hart was already continuing.

"The Kingdom of Linia had already seen Chaos's Champion challenge Order's. When the other ideas failed, the firstborn knew the only way out of the summoning was to let Chaos's Champion take the throne or die. He didn't want to die, and he didn't want to wait."

What hubris of this man to challenge the timing of a goddess? He shouldn't have survived. Even as I thought it, I knew there was more to the story. The Cursed King wasn't destroyed. Chaos cursed him, but no one knew how.

"He sought Chaos," Hart said. "An altar that shouldn't have existed. A place he was not supposed to be, the firstborn raged against Eris. He wanted to face her or her champion right away. That was his choice."

I wasn't sure I was breathing. This was the part of the story I'd never heard.

"Chaos was not forgiving of his actions. He almost died then and there on the altar."

He really should have died. It didn't make sense that he was only cursed. "Why didn't she kill him?" I asked.

"The queen intervened."

The words held a sadness to them that the rest of the story had not. I waited through the silence until Hart continued.

"The queen was a loyal follower of Eris, though she'd married into the Glanmore family. She was the one who had made the altar upon which the firstborn stood. The queen begged for his life even as she offered her own. Eris wasn't so cold to dismiss the request of her devoted. She would allow the intercession for the firstborn, but there would have to be a cost."

The Cursed King was responsible for a lot of things I hated. For the fate of magicless citizens in this city, for the captive's fate ... Whether he intended so or not, whether he now worked against those offenses or not, those sins lay at his feet. Still, my heart clenched in my chest as I understood the cost of this action.

I knew the weight of a loved one bearing the burden of my calling. It was what my mother had done for me, after all.

"The queen gave her life," he said. "The firstborn was cursed."

"What was his curse?"

"I told you the champions don't need adamas to wield. They wield magic based on their own emotions. Since the firstborn was responsible for discovering adamas, for creating the Blessed, Chaos wanted his fate to match what he'd brought upon others, but with a twist only she could appreciate."

My heart pounded in my chest as I waited for his next words.

"The firstborn can only use his magic by taking from Chaos's—"

I turned to ask why he stopped. Hart was already racing toward me. But a rustle in the trees behind me told me he would be too late.

35

He's a force to be reckoned with. If he chooses her, she'll be safe.

— FROM CHAMPIONS OF KAVIOS

I knew a blade would strike with my step, but I couldn't stop it. The noise of shifting feet alerted me too late that someone lurked in the shadows, waiting for our passage. I may have been unprepared, but Hart wasn't. Swift movements allowed him to slide between me and the blade.

He grunted in pain.

I shouted in protest, finding my footing as he shoved me back. Prepared for another attack, I pulled my dagger from my waist.

"Run," Hart gasped.

His sword was out as he faced his attacker. Even in the

dark, I recognized the short blond hair and the scar on the right side of his face.

I didn't run.

"Dammit, Hart. Don't do this," Soren hissed.

As angry as his words were, they still held a plea. He didn't want to fight Hart. He only wanted me. Something soured in my stomach. I didn't want to die, and I didn't want the Feared to take me.

"I told you I would," Hart said. "You want her. You go through me."

Soren's face held regret as he pulled the blade back. It was coated in Hart's blood. I couldn't see from my angle where he'd struck. Soren's lips pressed in sheer determination as he readied another swing.

As if remembering something, he glanced down. I was unsurprised to see R. Lourd's ring on his finger.

The adamas glowed green. "You don't want to do this."

Hart laughed. "That won't work on me."

With effort, he swung his blade at Soren. Steel clashed, the sound echoing through the Oldwood.

"I wasn't sure I believed that," Soren replied.

The ring glowed red as he changed tactics, using strength.

I didn't know what to do. Hart winced. He was clearly in pain. How deep had the blade gone? Why didn't he heal himself? Surely, he knew healing himself was necessary to protect me in this moment. I didn't think I could fight Soren.

Another terrifying thought crossed my mind. Hart might not have more anger stored. What if he'd used it all at the mine cave-in?

"I thought you understood." Hart sounded genuinely disappointed, but he didn't lower his blade.

Soren laughed, but it was hollow. "I did. Until that advisor came in with a better proposition."

Hart paused momentarily.

Vaddon? He had finally made his way into the Feared. Soren charged Hart again. Their blades connected with a clang. Hart kicked Soren back and swung. The red of Soren's adamas cast an eerie glow in the Oldwood. His power surged as he fought with a ferocity that had likely earned him his scar.

I could tell Hart was fading as he took a step back.

There was no clear path for me to help. I'd only be in the way if I tried to intercede with my dagger. Any skill I had lay in one-on-one defense. So, I stood helplessly on the sidelines as a magicless Hart fought a rage-fueled Feared.

The blade meant for me must have cut deep. His moves were slower than I'd become used to. Feigning left, he must have known Soren's anger would drive him to overcommit. Hart withdrew another dagger from the sheath at his lower back. A groan tore from Soren as the dagger slid into his exposed right side.

Soren fell to his knees.

Instead of attempting another swing, a dagger I hadn't seen soared across the distance of trees—heading directly for my chest.

Hart, again, was there before I could think.

The careening blade pierced Hart's chest instead of mine. Horror flooded me, icy and pointed, as he pulled it out and threw it back.

He fell to his knees. "Dammit, Soren."

Soren was too slow to avoid Hart's return throw. The dagger lodged in the side of Soren's neck, and he fell back with a final grunt.

Somehow, Hart stood. He crossed the distance to Soren to check that he was actually dead. Whispered words fell from Hart's lips, and he closed our attacker's eyes with a soft touch.

I wanted to say something—apologize—or yell at him for not letting me take the daggers aimed at me.

None of the words would do.

Again and again, Hart had put me first. Before I could process that in its entirety, his knees buckled. I ran to his side, attempting to shoulder his weight as we fell together to the forest floor.

"Hart." My words were garbled, my eyes rimmed with tears.

He grunted.

"Can you heal yourself?" I asked.

He shook his head. "Go get Ava. Tell her where I am."

His breathing was ragged. My gaze shot to his wounds. Blood soaked his right side from the first strike. Each beat of his heart appeared to bring forth more blood from the second chest wound.

Even if I could leave him to get Ava, he wouldn't be alive when we returned. His eyes fluttered closed. He was fading too quickly. The answer was so simple; I mentally lashed myself as I realized what my hesitation had cost.

Hart's words from the other day's attack rang in my head: *That was you, Chaos.*

"I can heal you."

He laughed, but it sounded pained. "Don't—"

A gurgled cough sounded, and more blood pooled in the wounds.

I had to try, but there had been no instruction manual. I didn't know what to do. Champions didn't need adamas to wield magic, but did we need touch? I couldn't remember—didn't have time to think too hard about whether I'd learned.

Quickly, I removed my gloves and searched for accessible skin. My hand hovered over his cheek. I cupped it. Warmth flooded between us at the contact.

"You didn't have to take both blades, Hart."

He grinned at that. "Yes, I did."

"I'm going to heal you."

Another cough. "Don't, Chaos."

I ignored him as I considered what came next. "I just need to feel …" My mouth caught up with my brain as I completed the sentence: "Lust."

A half-laugh, half-gurgle sounded beneath me, drawing my gaze back to Hart.

He'd managed to put that stupid smirk on his face, even as he coughed again, pushing more blood from his wounds.

"I'm not sure I'm much of an inspiration at present."

I clenched my teeth. If he survived, I'd worry about the appropriateness of my actions. Now, I sifted through every lustful thought I'd had of Hart since I'd met him.

There were more than I remembered.

The thrill of Hart's voice the first time I'd heard it.

His piercing gaze finding mine in Alaric's workshop.

In his guard's uniform, Hart pushed me against the wall as he defended me from attackers.

The curl of his lip as he held me against the alley wall at Forest's Edge.

Hart and I in the tavern, his body above mine. Mine above his. His length thickening beneath me … His hand inches from my skin as I told him my secret.

He groaned. This one didn't sound like the same kind of pain. "I'm fine."

"Liar," I said, sitting back on my heels, assessing what, if anything, had happened. Was the wound smaller? I couldn't tell. His breathing was still labored. I leaned over him again. My hand returned to his cheek. I let it slide down his neck, extending the contact.

"Ember—"

I was sure he was about to tell me to stop again, but he choked on what must have been blood pooling in his air passage. My hand rested above his heart.

"That's enough, Hart." I crawled closer.

My legs found their way to either side of his. I hovered over his lap in a move that reminded me too much of Forest's Edge. Tonight, his life hung in the balance. His breath hitched with every shift of my body. It'd be more satisfying if each breath he attempted weren't interrupted by his choked-off cough as air fought to reach his lungs.

I tilted my head, focusing solely on his face. He was dirty and bloodied from the fight, but it only made him more appealing. He'd used no magic himself and took down the power of a Blessed—even if Soren wielded stolen adamas.

And he'd done it for me.

The shadow of stubble accented the sharp lines of his jaw. I ran my hand along it again. He really was the most handsome man I'd ever seen.

Our eyes locked as my left hand reached for his right and pulled it toward me. Maybe it was better if he touched me too. I didn't know what else to try.

"Chaos," he whispered.

I placed his large, calloused hand on the soft skin of my neck. It was such an odd sensation. I didn't have time to consider it. Rationally, I knew Hart couldn't take from me. I hoped his touch would help strengthen our connection, so that I could heal him.

But I didn't know how to use my magic. The times I'd done so had been without thought.

Now, I very much wanted to use it.

His hand lay where I placed it, at the junction of my neck and shoulders. Heat flooded through me again where it rested.

This was so far past inappropriate, but I didn't need to

reimagine any of my lustful thoughts. This connection, his touch, was bringing new ones forward.

I leaned into it.

Fear shot down my spine. If there were an adamas gem between us, it would have flared purple. My eyes flicked down again to the bleeding wounds just below my eyesight. Worry mixed with the inferno created by his hand on my skin. I pushed down my fear. That wouldn't help Hart. I focused on his hand, on his touch, letting the fire of our connection burn through me. I sank lower over his lap.

The feeling of his touch consumed me. I held his hand in place, unwilling to give up. But was anything changing? This heat between us was a building inferno, but I didn't know if it was healing him. My hand slid to his chest. I wasn't sure what led me, but I was sure I needed my hand on the wound.

My hair fell forward, creating a golden curtain around us. For a moment, I could imagine that it was just me and Hart. And maybe we would close the distance because we wanted to, not because his life depended on it.

His fingers twitched, featherlight against me. "You don't have to."

I wanted to.

Everything I knew about being Chaos's Champion said she had a choice. I hadn't made a decision. Hart had told me I had magic, but if I were honest, I wasn't sure I'd accepted it.

His hand sliding across my skin drew me to the present. It turned the heating fire not to light but to the absence of it—if my body were adamas, the deepest black overtook my senses.

It was darkness, the unknown, and it felt like anything could happen there. Any choice could be made, and all outcomes had potential.

I made my choice—picked my outcome.

I chose this. Chose to be Chaos's Champion.

I chose him, and with that decision, something incandescent shot through me, reigniting all the colors of magic I was familiar with.

I sucked in a breath, my head falling back, as my hand pressed against his wound. It knit together beneath my touch. His grip on my waist was exquisite as he held me close, and I knew I would never be the same. Moving on instinct, I rolled forward into it.

A hiss that sounded nothing like the pain he'd been in loosed from his throat. Another hint of hesitation fell away as his fingers caressed the length of my neck and danced along my collarbone.

His eyes met mine—ravenous—in a way that meant I didn't have to search for memories of lust to heal him.

He knew what I was doing. He was helping.

Or, at least, that's what I told myself.

My emotions surged, coating my senses as he pulled me to him. Our lips connected in a featherlight press. Tentative, but I wanted more. Every part of me waited for his next move. My gaze met his. There was a question there, one I needed to answer. I brought my lips back to his, my tongue searching to deepen the connection.

He didn't make me wait. His fingertips curled into my hip as our kiss intensified. I rolled forward against him, and his other palm pressed against my chest, slid beneath the neckline of my tunic.

I wished his hand would drop lower—would explore the curve of my breasts, would do anything to prolong this feeling ...

A distant memory told me I was doing this for a reason. In the ecstasy of his touch, his kiss, I almost forgot his wounds.

Regretfully, I pulled back and dared to look down,

wondering if this had worked or if I was causing Hart more pain in his final moments.

The wound had closed.

Every heartbeat we touched, every bit of lust he awakened in me that he couldn't take, I gave to him. I slid my hand down his side to where the first blade had struck, that wound had closed too.

His breath evened out, and his other hand was at my waist, clasping as if his life depended on it. My heart stuttered to realize: It no longer did.

He was clear of danger. I'd done it.

"Chaos," he whispered the name like a prayer, but I knew it was directed at me.

His hand at my hip slid up my back and he pulled me closer, past the point of no return.

We shared breaths, my lips hovering above his. The hum of magic between us had cooled, but a connection still tugged from somewhere deep in my chest.

My magic had worked. My emotions healed him.

As I shook off the haze, I couldn't fight the slight smile curling my lip. This city made it dangerous to feel. Showing emotion was a weakness to be exploited by the Blessed. But I'd proved to be more powerful by taking that risk. I didn't want to stop feeling. With Hart's touch, with his kiss, I had felt *more*.

"Are you alright?" My voice was breathier than intended.

He cleared his throat. His hand left my chest as he disconnected everywhere we'd blurred together. "You didn't have to do that."

His hand still lingered on my hip, like it was loathe to separate from me fully.

I smiled and looked down again at his healed wounds to hide it. "But it worked?"

"It worked." He stared at me with a reverence I wasn't sure I deserved.

He appeared to come back to his senses then. He gripped both of my hips and lifted me off his lap, placing me beside him. Slowly, he stood to ensure his body believed what his mind did—that he was completely healed.

He walked over to Soren's body again. Kneeling, he pulled the ring from Soren's finger and shoved it into his pocket.

My thought spun, and I started to shake. I couldn't be sure if it was the absence of Hart's touch or the adrenaline crash. I'd saved Hart with Chaos's magic. Tonight, I'd accepted my calling. How had I not known I was Eris's Champion? How had no one told me? What would I do now?

"Chaos," he said in a way that made me think he'd said my name multiple times already.

I turned to look at him. So many emotions I couldn't decipher flitted across his face. There and gone before they ever had a chance. Hart may be the only person in Kavios better at hiding his feelings than me.

Hart held out his hand as if sensing my impending breakdown. I took it. He pulled me to my feet, and I stumbled into his solid frame. I steadied myself on the hand I still held. My gaze rested on the connection. It was so easy with him. A wave of heat rushed through me. Hart defended me with a severity that bordered on religious devotion. The way his questing fingers had slid across my skin—I wanted more.

"We should get back." Hart's words were an icy douse over the flame raging within me. "With Soren's attack, we missed our window. We won't make it to the mines and back without being seen now. Miners will be heading out for the shift change soon."

My hands balled to fists at my sides. I hadn't even been able to accomplish this one thing for Alaric. First, I'd lost the chance to run. Now, I couldn't free the captive before submitting to everything I hated.

Did my choice tonight change anything? I'd still need to go through the ceremony. The unpredictability of my magic proved I couldn't directly challenge the king tomorrow.

But it gave me hope. Maybe I could still try to free the captive once I was Blessed.

"I'm sorry about Soren," I said. I didn't know the extent of their relationship, but it was clear there had been one. Hart had taken no joy from what he'd had to do—for me.

Hart stared at the unmoving body. "He made his choice. I need to get you back to the castle, then I'll deal with this."

His brow pinched as he searched me. Following his gaze, I confirmed my suspicions. I was covered in Hart's blood.

"I can't go back like this. Even if I returned through the window, Penelope would have questions when I called for a bath."

He nodded. "You can clean up at my place."

We had failed at my objective for the evening. I would still go through with the Blessing tomorrow, and without freeing the captive, I'd have to confront granting King Rodric additional adamas. My mood wasn't as dark as I thought it would be, though, with all of that being true. I'd made a choice tonight. I'd accepted a calling the full extent of which I still didn't understand. As Hart's hand gripped mine again for the return trip, I couldn't help but *feel*—and I didn't want to stop.

How can you be so sure she'll choose him? He appears to represent everything she hates about Kavios.

— ALARIC SARE'S LETTERS TO ISABELLE ARKOVA

Hart led me to the alley where he'd caught me when I snuck out. Farther down the path, an external staircase led to a door on the second floor of Forest's Edge.

While part of me was glad we didn't have to traipse through the tavern as we were, another part wondered about Hart's life outside of guarding me. Did he sleep here at night instead of in the barracks? I was overwhelmed by an intense desire to know more about this Blessed.

I tried to tell myself it was curiosity. Tomorrow, I'd be like him—a Blessed one who didn't entirely desire the title I was granted. But I was also past fooling myself.

Whatever was between Hart and me had a life of its own. I'd struggled to think of anything but his kiss since I'd had it. The heat that flared between us was something I'd never experienced.

He stopped to fill a bucket with water before we scaled the stairs. His gaze darted to my bloody clothes again before he opened the door. "You can heat it if you want. I have to ask Ava for something for you to change into."

"You don't look much better than I do." The room was small—efficient—but with odds and ends like Alaric's workshop. It seemed like a kitchen and living space blended together, and a hallway farther west must lead to the bedroom.

His smirk returned as he pulled off his tunic. "I can fix that for myself."

He disappeared into the other room and reappeared wearing another dark tunic.

"So ... what? You don't have any lady's garments hanging around from ... overnight guests?"

My cheeks heated as I finished the sentence. What was I saying? I absolutely did not want to hear the answer.

Something fluttered almost uncomfortably in my stomach as his piercing green gaze held mine. "I think I've been very clear on that front."

Had he? I let out a shaky breath as he walked past me.

"Make yourself comfortable. I'll be back in a minute."

The door closing behind me was my only confirmation that he had left. Yes, he'd protected me. He'd said he was here for me, that he would follow me. But part of me couldn't help but wonder if that was truly for me, or my magic. My fingers strayed to my lips, where he'd kissed me. I'd convinced myself it was to inspire my lust to drive my magic.

Had it been for me, just because he'd wanted to?

It wasn't something I could answer without him, so washing off with cold water seemed to be the best option. I found a rag and wiped the blood from my face and hands. Too curious by half, I wandered the room as I scrubbed. I didn't want to think too hard about the blood staining my skin. That I'd accepted my calling as Chaos's Champion tonight felt big, but so did the fact that I'd almost lost Hart. What if my magic hadn't worked?

I shook my head, unable to consider it. Too much was left unsaid between us.

Even though my tunic had a high neckline, Hart's bloody hand had slipped beneath it to draw forth my feelings. My cheeks flamed again as I remembered how well that had worked. Before thinking too hard, I pulled the tunic off, using a rag to wipe the blood from my sternum. I still wore a band around my breasts, but it hadn't occurred to me how quickly Hart would return until the doorknob twisted, and he was standing directly before me, another tunic in his hand.

He cleared his throat, his gaze once more locking with mine. This time, it felt like he used the connection to stop his focus from drifting lower. My bloody tunic was steps away. Something flared hot in his green gaze, that ravenous hunger I'd only glimpsed in the Oldwood. It made me want to step into his reach.

He kicked the door shut behind him, his eyes not leaving mine. "This should work."

I took it and turned, pulling it on as I headed toward the kitchen. "Thank you."

I felt him on my heels when I dropped the rag back in the bucket.

"Hart." I turned again, looking up at him through long lashes.

I wasn't sure what I wanted to say. I just wanted his name on my lips. I'd felt so much when I'd chosen him tonight. I wanted to choose him again. We weren't guaranteed infinite time.

"We kissed," I finally said.

His smirk was back, but the smolder in his gaze changed its meaning. "I'm aware."

"Was it to help my magic?"

His hand lifted, like he'd touch me. He let it fall again, unsure. "No."

It was what I wanted to hear. I believed it; I just didn't know where that left us. Something of my intent must have crossed my face.

"It's a bad idea."

I thought I'd known that once. At some point, I'd thought no Blessed could be trusted. I'd thought they all took indiscriminately—but not Hart. Hart gave. Hart protected. Hart cherished.

He was still in my space, standing much closer than necessary.

Something in my gut—something deeper—said I needed to reach for him. That I'd regret it if I didn't. And as much as I didn't want to trust my gut, it'd proven itself on more than one occasion. Some things couldn't be reasoned.

This *felt* like one of them.

My hand quested the length of his arm, following the curve of his shoulder to his neck, his cheek—just as I'd cupped it in the forest. Conflicting emotions flitted across his face, but I didn't miss the nearly imperceptible tilt of his head into my palm. His eyes widened when heat flared again with our contact. Whatever I felt every time we touched—he felt it too.

"I want you."

If possible, he went even more still. I wasn't sure he was breathing. "Chaos—"

"Please don't. I don't care about the reasons we shouldn't. I don't want to think about being Blessed, being Eris's Champion, Vaddon, or the Cursed King."

My hand slid down to his beating heart as I took a deep breath. "I just want to feel this."

He raised a brow at me, assessing the honesty of my words.

I let him read the truth on my face. "Tell me no if you don't want me, but please don't say no out of some thought that I don't know my own mind."

He growled—a primal battle warring within him. I didn't know the stakes. But that smirk was back, and I felt the scales tip in my direction. "No part of me doesn't desire you, Chaos."

"Then what's the problem?" My hand slid to the back of his neck, exploring the feeling of our connection.

I opened my mouth to question this strange heat coursing between us, and then all thoughts scattered as he took my invitation, his lips closing over mine.

If his kiss in the woods had set me aflame, this was obliteration. I wanted more, demanded more, and he was a man unleashed.

His breathing was uneven as his hands tangled in my hair. He cradled my head, and his tongue swept into my mouth. I moaned in delight and my eyes widened in surprise at the sound. Our gazes locked, and satisfaction danced in his. Then he captured my lips again, savoring the sound like a fine wine.

"Tell me, is this the chaos you meant to loose?" his words whispered across my skin as he kissed my jaw, my neck.

I wasn't sure, but I knew I wanted more. My back arched, my body pressing farther into him. Understanding the command, his hand dropped from my neck to my chest, cupping my breast over my tunic. I wanted him closer. The next whine that slipped from my lips encouraged a low chuckle.

His fingers found my pebbled peak through my tunic. The pinch was exquisite, shooting heat straight to my core. And he was there, catching my gasp with another scorching kiss. His tongue swept in again, leaving me breathless.

More. I wanted to remove the barriers between us and chase this feeling from which I knew I'd never recover. "That was a good start."

He growled again at my goading. My legs wrapped around his hips as he hoisted me from the ground. He carried me to the back room with his lips never ceasing their exploration.

I was sprawled on the bed before him in moments. Immediately, I was cold, bereft of his touch, even while his heated gaze slid down my body.

"Take the tunic off."

The command had me moving before I could consider another option. That smirk was back at my efficiency.

"Come here." I crooked my finger at him. "I need to touch you."

He moved slowly, as if savoring the sight of me, savoring these moments before desire overtook our senses. I was sure he felt the same heat of our connection. Every part of me wanted it back. He pulled his own tunic over his head, and I inadvertently licked my lips. Honed muscle covered every inch of him.

"See something you like, Chaos?"

It wasn't worth lying. I nodded.

"I've wanted you since I caught you about to start the street brawl to save that man." He crawled toward me on the bed. "So defiant. So creative. So utterly destructive. So careless with your own well-being in the face of others' suffering."

My heartbeat raced as he hovered above me. I'd never thought of myself in such a manner. Through his eyes, I appeared a fearsome creature. Mostly, I tried to survive in a kingdom not made for me.

I raised my hand to touch his chest.

He caught it and placed my palm over his heart. "I was yours the moment I heard you call me *my guard*."

My cheeks heated as I remembered my description of the man who'd saved me multiple times.

"And I will be—your guard—no matter what happens."

The heat surged between us where my hand rested on his chest. I brought my other hand to his neck and pulled him to me. "I know. Take me. I'm yours too."

His kiss consumed me—tongue searching, heat building as his weight settled over me. Each place we touched brought a new flare to life. I chased the feeling, my hands roaming over his shoulders and back. My legs wrapped around him, chasing more connection, more friction—all desire.

He pressed me into the bed, giving me what I so obviously craved. In this, he wouldn't deny me. My legs uncurled as he tugged at my leggings, granting him access to remove them. His heated gaze traced each new inch of exposed skin as he peeled them away. The final stitches of clothing between us removed, his hands mapped my curves as they traveled toward my throbbing center. With the slide of his first finger into my heat, my head tipped back, and a heady groan escaped my lips.

"That's a good start," he echoed the challenge, and I knew I was done for.

Another finger. The heat between us shot straight to my core. My hips bucked as he stoked my pleasure.

"You're going to come for me, Ember."

The command in his voice was back, and I didn't want to resist. He worked me as he slid down my body. Teeth scraping, lips nipping, tongue tasting, he explored me while his mouth moved to meet his fingers.

Another whine slipped free with the first languorous lick against my center. The next thrust of his fingers had my body arching into him.

He smiled against me. "Ready?"

Ready? Probably not. This man protected me with a dedication that bordered on religious devotion. The first stroke of his tongue had been enough to tell me I was ill-prepared for what came next.

But that wasn't going to stop me.

I didn't know what tomorrow would bring. There were too many unknowns and so many things we had yet to discuss, but they wouldn't change this feeling. I wanted to capture it, for it to be ours before we were forced into another situation over which we had little control.

He must have seen my nod. Another moan escaped while the pleasure built from his touch. I wouldn't need much more. The way he feasted with ravenous attention made me think he didn't care. Tongue and fingers moved together, building our connection to a fiery inferno.

My back bowed, my thoughts scattered, and heat flared inside me as I shattered.

That didn't stop him. He continued with a single-minded focus, wringing every drop of pleasure as I rode my release.

My legs turned to jelly, my hips fell to the bed, and he crawled the length of me to catch my lips in another scorching kiss. Our gazes met and held. He searched for something there, though I wasn't sure what.

"Hart." My breathing was still ragged.

"Tapping out, Chaos?" He lifted his weight as if seriously readying to leave the bed.

Immediately, I missed it. I reached for him, my fingers wrapping around the silk and steel of him. "Not even a little bit."

A low sound escaped his throat, and part of me couldn't believe I'd drawn it from him. I stroked the length of him again, his hips bucking forward to follow the motion. His reaction to me was a heady thing, but I was too impatient to explore it further. I lined him up with my entrance, and as if in tune with my thoughts, his mouth captured mine, and he brought us together.

The heat of our connection transformed again as we joined. I didn't know what to make of it, but my every limb was alight, alive, and attuned to his touch. His hands roved my skin as if he knew it. With each steady stroke, I careened toward a new cliff. I wasn't sure what tomorrow would bring, but I wanted us to meet it together.

"Hart." I just wanted to say his name—wanted the grounding his voice brought—wanted to know he was here, that we were together.

He pressed his forehead to mine as we moved. "I'm with you."

I didn't know what he responded to, and I didn't care. Desire coursed through me as I fell into that absence of light again, just as I had in the forest. With every stroke, every touch, I chose Hart—again and again.

We came together in searing pleasure.

"Ember." My name on his lips was like a light in the dark—a flare at the crescendo calling me home. I returned, my body descending from molten to languid.

The penetrating green of his gaze held mine, the hint of a challenge in them alongside the raw emotion that lingered there. Before I could speak, he pressed a kiss to my lips. "If you tell me that was a good start, you won't be able to walk tomorrow."

My lip tilted into a wicked smile. "That's not the deterrent you think it is."

He brought his forehead to mine. “You are Chaos incarnate.”

I found I no longer minded the use of the name. It was still astounding that I inspired so much from this man. I wanted to capture the feelings written across his features and store them away to remember always. Maybe I wanted to do the same with my own feelings swirling within me. Desire, maybe more, joy, at being so desired in return. Fear and anger over what tomorrow would bring.

I let the reassuring warmth of his touch seep into me as our breathing evened. Tomorrow’s problems would come soon enough.

37

Choice—real choice—is its own magic.

— FROM CHAMPIONS OF KAVIOS

Even though my mind was made up, we still had much to do before today's ceremony. I barely had time to lounge in the satisfaction of last night's activities. I'd returned to my room late. Most in the castle were still celebrating at the Masquerade, even as the sun rose.

I had no such luxury. Today was the Blessing Ceremony.

Prince Elias had added me to the list of those Selected, which meant I had another ring to make before this afternoon. It was doable, though it would be rushed. It wasn't like I cared about the state of the gem.

At least it would give me an excuse to ignore the king's crown commission for another day.

Despite all we had to accomplish, all we had to discuss, Hart didn't say a word as I veered off course from Alaric's workshop. I wasn't sure where my feet were taking me until it became clear. We entered Woodside, and I knew what my gut had already decided. My parents' building loomed ahead.

With everything that happened yesterday—what I'd chosen—the inescapable truth solidified: I needed answers. The modest building felt like a bastion of secrets at that moment.

Someone in my family must have known I was called to be Chaos's Champion. I couldn't speak with Alaric about it. My parents were next on the list.

Today, I would submit to King Rodric's whims to keep Alaric safe. I didn't yet know how to use my magic to fight. Any hope I had of fleeing Kavios was gone. I clutched hope tight in my chest that I'd eventually find a way to free us both, but I had other concerns too.

Vaddon wanted to kill me. The Cursed King needed something from Chaos to use his magic—Hart and I had yet to return to those conversations.

We hadn't even been able to free the captive last night. I told myself that just because we failed once didn't mean we couldn't try again.

We.

I let out a breath. Hart was with me. It didn't fix anything, but it was a welcome positive when everything else seemed stacked against me.

The taste of him was still on my lips. All I had to do was close my eyes, and I could feel his hands on me—his touch—and the heat flaring between us.

"Do you want me to come in with you?" Hart asked.

He hadn't said much on our walk, but maybe he was cycling through as many questions about what happened next as I was. We'd have time to discuss it while working on my ring.

"Yes." I didn't know what I'd learn, but I knew I wanted him with me.

I let us in through the unlocked door. Father was in the living room, reading. He looked up at my approach. His questioning gaze turned to a glare as it moved over my shoulder to Hart.

"Emberline, what are you doing here?"

"I need to talk to Mother. Is she awake?"

He stood, crossing his arms over his chest. "What's this about, Emberline?"

My tone must have given me away. I studied him, wondering what he knew. Did he know what I was? Did he know fate would come for me?

"It's about my choices." I wondered if that was enough. "About the information that's been kept from me."

His jaw set, and I knew he knew of what I spoke. "You'll only upset her."

I shook my head in disappointment. "I need to talk to her. You can join, or you can stay out here. I don't care."

The hallway to Mother's room was just as bare as usual, but my every step felt like it took me toward something complex, a tapestry woven with infinite colors. Hart's familiar footsteps trailed behind me.

Mother lay in bed ... staring at the ceiling. She blinked a few times at my approach and tilted her head slightly to capture me in her sight. Hart stayed at the door. Father followed me into the room, but Mother's gaze never left mine.

"Ember," she whispered. "I hoped you'd come."

"Mother." I knelt next to her and took her hand. "I need to ask you something."

"Of course you do, dear." Her voice was distant.

"Did the latest tonic arrive?" I asked.

Father nodded, a look of confusion on his face. "She's been quite strong recently. We went for a walk around the block yesterday." His brow furrowed, and he looked at me with blame. "Ask your question, Emberline. You're upsetting her."

I released a deep breath. I needed to know what she did. "Did you know I was Chaos's Champion?"

Father sucked in a breath behind me. From the corner of my eye, I saw his hands ball into fists. Mother's lips curled into a smile.

I focused on her. "Why didn't you tell me?"

"It's your choice, baby," she said dreamily.

I had made it, but it didn't explain why they'd told me nothing. "What does it mean, Mother?"

"You are her champion. You can challenge what is known."

Those were the exact words Hart had used in a time that felt so long ago. I glanced at him over my shoulder. Mother's gaze seemed to follow.

"You trust him. I knew you would."

My head spun back toward her. "Who?"

"She told me you would inspire chaos just like her—that your connection would change the tides of Kavios."

Mother's words were a jumble in my head. My connection with Hart? Again, I glanced at him over my shoulder, unsure what I was searching for in his features. His brow was furrowed.

I focused on the information I could retrieve from Mother. "You spoke with Eris?"

She giggled—actually giggled. "Oh, yes. It was quite terrifying. I was there when she granted Alaric his boon to protect you."

"What?" I asked.

Mother was still giggling about Eris.

I turned to Father. "What did she grant Alaric?"

Father sighed. "Alaric said Rodric had too much power. You'd be noticed and found before you had a chance to choose. He asked to have the ability to source the adamas in the hope of buying you time."

My heart clenched in my chest.

"Why didn't any of you tell me?" I once again looked to Father. Mother wasn't really answering my questions.

"We couldn't," he said, like this entire thing was my fault. "Chaos's Champion chooses their fate. None of us could interfere. It was more than she cared for that Alaric would protect you, but she allowed it because of how adamas was being used in Kavios." He rubbed his forehead. "Isabelle, tell her."

Mother's eyes fluttered closed. "You will know her as Eris's Champion because Chaos will be the language of her heart."

The hair on the back of my neck stood on end. Those words were from *Champions of Kavios*. The other suspicion I had yet to verify flooded to the forefront.

"How do you know those lines?" I asked Father.

"They're in that damn book!" he said.

"The book Mother wrote?"

He glared at me like he couldn't believe I'd make him say it. I shook my head. I didn't know what he was so upset about. This was my life—written into the lines of a book—by my mother, and she hadn't bothered to tell me.

"The Glanmores have Alaric."

Mother closed her eyes, her lips turning down. "The cost to save him is your freedom?"

I didn't even know how to answer that.

Father clenched his fist at his side. "Alaric was in over his head. He deserves his fate."

I turned to him. "How can you say that? After all he did for us?"

"He tried to control the uncontrollable. He thought you would save Kavios. He refused to acknowledge that what you are is inherently intractable!"

I stood, gesturing for him to continue. The way his voice shook, I knew something was there, and I needed to know what it was.

"Chaos's Champion isn't a savior. What did your Mother say? She'll challenge what is known. That means her champion will destroy, devastate, and raze. Only when it's burned to ash does something new grow." He spoke with a resignation I was all too familiar with.

"I see."

And I was starting to. I was a danger to him. My path wasn't set in stone. It didn't guarantee a happy ending for those in Kavios.

Maybe I'd built a cage around my emotions, lived without feeling too deeply, without trusting myself for years. But Father had done the same. His cage was a city that took from his kind, a wife whose light was dampened by their excess, but he was content to move within the world he knew, not risk a new world I could create.

He opened and closed his mouth. Like maybe he realized he'd said too much. But I could tell part of him thought he hadn't said enough.

Mother reached for his hand, pulling him to her side. "You have a choice to make, baby."

I'd already made it. Or, at least, I knew the immediate next steps. I'd need time to figure out how to challenge what was known without risking Alaric.

It all came roaring in. The King's Blessing. His commission that he would demand days later and the power it would grant him. I wouldn't have as much time as I hoped.

"I don't know when I'll see you," I said.

Mother held my gaze as if seeing my resolve. "We love you. You'll do great things in her name."

My gaze turned to Hart, who stood with his arms folded at the doorway. It was time to leave. I wouldn't find any other answers here. He nodded in some unspoken understanding, and we slipped out my parents' front door.

I searched the hallway. There were so many magicless families and so many more like them in Kavios. Could I really make their lives any better?

It wasn't about wresting control of the city from Themis's Champion, the Cursed King—it was about doing so from King Rodric. As I'd proved while trying to save Hart yesterday, my control over my magic was unpredictable. I'd spent too long burying my emotions. Feeling them deeply and freely enough to wield wasn't something I could turn on by simply snapping my fingers.

I shook my head. Today, Alaric was my priority. If I could survive accepting the King's Blessing, I could find a way to free the city.

Hart let me get situated with the gem preforming before the questions started. I was surprised it took him that long.

"Is this really what you want to do?"

My back was to him. He worked the foot pedal while I shaped the stone on the spinning blade. "Yes. I'm going to be Blessed. It's the only way to save Alaric."

Silence. I desperately wanted to know what emotions flitted across his face.

"What about ... everything else?"

I'm glad he, like myself, couldn't seem to decide what other aspects of this situation to focus on.

I huffed a laugh. “I don’t know. The best I can say is that I’ll figure it out later. I’m choosing to be Blessed.” I stopped working the stone and turned to face him. “I still want to free the captive. I’m not hiding from the fact that I’m Chaos’s Champion. I just can’t do anything today. You saw how hard it was to use my magic last night. And in the meantime, I must do this to keep Alaric safe.”

Hart nodded. “I respect your decision, but let’s not call it a choice. You’re taking a path you’ve been coerced into.”

I shrugged.

He stopped pushing the pedal and reached for my hips. It was the first time he’d initiated contact since last night. I let him draw me toward him. He positioned me between his legs as he sat on the stool.

“Mostly, I’m angry you’ll become everything you hate. Even if it’s in name only.”

I pushed back a lock of his hair that had fallen free from the knot. “It doesn’t matter. It will be a meaningless gesture to wear the adamas. I won’t take. I’m honestly not even sure I could. And it will buy me time to figure out everything else.”

“Buy us time.”

My lip curved into a smile. “I was supposed to be fleeing. Maybe joining Alysa and The Storm. You were supposed to be rid of me.”

Hart glared, unamused. “You were never going to be rid of me.”

Something inside me warmed, and his fingers weren’t even touching my skin. This—this was a choice I was glad to have made. The ground was moving around me, but Hart was my stabilizing force.

“What about the crown?” Hart asked.

“I’ll put it off another few days with this.” I held up my ring. “There is only so much they can expect me to do.”

I swallowed. It wouldn't be much more time. I doubt it would be enough to learn about my magic.

"Rodric already proved he'd test the stones, so I can't put quartz in."

Hart's fingers pressed into my hips, returning my attention to his intense gaze. "We'll figure something out, Chaos. I just want to make sure we think everything through."

Everything was a mess, but Hart's dedication to systematically solving our problems was reassuring. "The best we can do is try to free the captive again. Maybe tonight? The Blessed celebrate the Blessing Ceremony the same as they do the Masquerade, right? Everyone should be distracted."

He nodded.

"Alright. Well, let's finish my ring and get back to the castle."

Hart looked like he'd say more. His mouth opened and closed around words that wouldn't seem to slip out. "I'm with you, Ember."

And that was good enough for me.

38

I may not have protected her from much, but at least I saved her from Rodric.

— ALARIC SARE'S LETTERS TO ISABELLE ARKOVA

The dress Prince Elias had made was even more beautiful than the last. It was white, as was traditional for those to be Blessed. Penelope helped me into the gown. This one was much more conservative, and I couldn't help but be thankful for the coverage. The flowing silk was artfully decorated with lace. It had a high neckline and long sleeves. It was beautiful, but I wished it was for literally any other event.

I knew this Blessing was in name only. It was a performance for the Glanmores. I didn't have to take, I didn't have to act like any other Blessed once it was done, but I had to let

Rodric think he'd won.

I could do this.

Hart was in a formal uniform, with a helmet covering his features as he guided me to the ceremony. The throne room looked even more beautiful than it had for the Masquerade. Stained glass windows framed the throne on the dais, the sun's setting rays lighting up their colors. The white marble floor was set with chairs. They were grouped into two sets on the left and right, creating an aisle in the center.

Before we separated, I sought Hart's gaze, but his helmet deprived me. My jaw clenched in frustration. My fingers stretched to reach for him. I shook my head. This was how it had to be right now. He was my guard, and I was Jeweler to the Blessed, about to join him as one of them.

He went to the right side of the aisle where he would have the best view of any approaching the dais. I took my position on the stage.

The other Selected were already there. Their finery was pristine. Like mine, the jackets and dresses were even more extravagant than what they had worn to the ball. I watched Deidre fidget, last in line in the row of Selected. I hadn't spoken to her since the Presentation, but she looked like she might be having second thoughts.

Elias greeted me with a familiarity I despised. He took my gloved hand and pressed a kiss to my knuckles. Vaddon hovered just beyond his shoulder, looking disappointed by my every breath. Soren's words last night returned to my mind. *I did. Until that advisor came in with a better proposition.* Given that, I guessed he probably was.

I needed to find out why he wanted me dead so badly.

Then, King Rodric entered, and all rose. My worries about Vaddon could wait. The gem around Rodric's neck was glowing blue before he even started speaking. I wondered why he bothered. Were people still scared of the Cursed King? They hadn't seen his power since the Selection.

Hart and I still needed to finish our conversation about him. It, too, had fallen aside in the wake of his injuries and my decisions.

Mostly, the Cursed King confused me. What had Hart said? He needed Chaos to use his magic? I don't think he'd finished explaining the curse before Soren attacked. If he were a Glanmore, did he need magic to take the throne? Even if he were upset about his summoning, it had been hundreds of years. Why not claim the city for Themis and render me, Chaos's Champion, useless?

"Blessed, Selected." King Rodric's booming voice pulled my attention. "Welcome to this year's Blessing ceremony. I need not impress on you the importance of today or others like it. This Selection cycle has been trying on all of us. There are those within the city who would push for chaos within its walls."

Hairs on the back of my neck stood up. Goosebumps pebbled my flesh. He was coming dangerously close to referencing the goddess *he* had banned.

"But we stand firm—we stand for Order."

My glance slid to Elias, who stood with shoulders back and arms folded behind his back like nothing could bother him. What worried me the most was the curve of Vaddon's lip—a cat with a canary already in its mouth.

"I don't think I have to tell you my Blessing isn't just a boon. It's a necessity. The people of Kavios need us. They need our magic to keep the city running smoothly. Some would see that interrupted, as we saw at the Selection Festival."

Someone in the crowd gasped. I expected the king's calming at the Cornucopia had worked too well—the Blessed had forgotten the prince's remarks about the Cursed King.

They treated today as if a dirty little secret were being dragged forth in polite company.

"Today, we celebrate another jab at the so-called Feared. We celebrate elevating more of our own. Those to whom we give the sacred responsibility of keeping order in Kavios."

The crowd, once riled to the point of snapping, now seemed serene. It didn't take long to realize that the king pressed harder with his magic. The blue glow on the amulet shone brighter as his calming power filled the room.

It took every ounce of control not to look at Hart. What was Rodric saying? Why mention the Feared?

"We thank you for what you do for us, and today is about you—your reward for caring for the city we so love."

The blue of his adamas faltered, fading to the clear stone I was so familiar with. Was he actually ... out of stored sadness? Given the amount of calm he wielded, I assumed he had dozens of citizens to take from. I didn't want to dwell on what he did to draw out the sadness.

Rodric gestured to someone at the back door. "We will begin the ceremony with the Selected showing their dedication to Kavios."

Ice shot down my spine. I couldn't claim to be all that familiar with the Blessing Ceremony, so I was unaware of how we'd be made to show our dedication to the city.

The double doors opened on creaking joints, and city guards escorted a parade of men and women up the aisle. Amidst the half-dozen who came toward the dais, one face stood out: Macen. None of them had visible adamas, and given Macen's presence, I had to assume they must be rebels.

"These Feared were found preparing to ambush the Blessing Ceremony. We are tired of their attempts to bring chaos to our city. We'll show them what we do to traitors."

I stared straight ahead, though I could feel Hart's gaze on

my skin like it was his touch. It seared. I knew he'd already put together what I was only now realizing. I swallowed thickly, saliva pooling on my tongue.

They couldn't be asking me to do this.

This wasn't what I'd signed up for.

"The Selected will take from these rebels as a testament to the city they love. They will fill themselves and their adamas to the point of bursting."

My heart was beating so hard I thought it would break free of my chest. *Fill to the point of bursting.* He wanted us to kill them. To drain them to the point of death to fill the stores of our gems.

There were just enough rebels, one for each of us.

"I know this will be hard. It's not our way to drain to excess," the king continued, confirming my horrifying realization. "I ask you, the Selected, to bear the weight of this burden, to push the city forward."

The Blessed were monsters, but most weren't ruthless killers. There was a difference between taking without seeing the impact of your selfishness and taking to the point of murder. The king asked for the latter. He knew what this would do to these people. I suspected he did it for a reason. It was unclear to me what it was.

The Selected would do this. No one among them would want to lose the chance to become Blessed, but it was clear from their shifting glances that they would feel deeply about murder.

I was going to vomit.

This wasn't what I'd signed up for. This path had been viable because it was in name only. I counted again: five rebels. One of the Feared ... was for me to kill.

There was a faltered step from the line of guards on the right. I couldn't look. I knew it was Hart—knew he would struggle to hold his place with this revelation. There was nothing he could do without interrupting the ceremony.

What would I do?

They still had Alaric.

"Wil," the king called the first Selected. My body moved on instinct as I handed him his adamas gem.

Rodric gestured to the foot of the dais. "Go, with my Blessing, to bring Order to this city."

The guards pushed one of the Feared forward. The young man fell to his knees. He looked the same age as Macen. His light brown hair fell over his eyes as he peeked at the newly Blessed.

Wil, for his part, didn't hesitate. He required no instruction on how to use the adamas. He needed no urging to take the man's life. Without prompting, his hand reached for the man's neck. He pressed his hand down hard and took.

If Wil were a different Blessed, I was sure the ring would have glowed purple. Fear was plain on the rebel's face, but so was his rage. Wil's adamas flashed red as he collected from the man. And the anger didn't abate quickly. It ran deep. The man looked young but must have known significant loss to have joined the Feared carrying so much hate. The fire in his eyes didn't dim until they closed. His lifeless form fell onto the dais steps.

The other children of the Blessed were much the same. Caitlyn may not have looked at the woman she took from, but she did it all the same—the bodies stacked at the bottom of the dais. Of the original Selected, only Deidre remained.

Her moves were stilted as she collected her adamas from me and received a Blessing from the king. Whatever her decision, it was clearly not made.

"Is complete draining necessary?" Her words were soft. I

wasn't sure I'd heard them correctly. The king's answering smile said I had.

"It's necessary."

She looked at the man on his knees.

"This is not a negotiation. These are traitors to the crown. We must unite and show strength."

Deidre nodded, I thought to herself more than to the rest of us. She knelt, the tips of her fingers grazing the man's wrist. Her ring started to flash blue. Sadness? This one must be a gentler soul. The other Feared had shown only anger—the Blessed in the room, who could see the gem's light, started murmuring.

Her body shifted as the process continued, and I could glimpse the game she was playing. The ring was not yet over her knuckle. She placed it on the tip of her finger so that when she touched the Feared, he could just as easily wield it as she could.

He was draining her.

Her knees buckled before anyone else realized what she'd done.

"Stop him," Vaddon said, but I knew it was too late.

Deidre entirely collapsed, rolling to the foot of the dais. The man stood, focused on King Rodric, and the gem's flashing blue turned to an aquamarine glow.

The king's eyes went glassy as the man stormed up the dais, escaping the guards at the base. He wouldn't be able to control them all like Rodric. He focused his energy on the king, his mouth moving, but I couldn't hear the words. I was sure he tried to calm the king into stopping the ceremony. He didn't stand a chance.

As the Feared scaled the steps, one of the guards threw a dagger, its blade pierced the man's back. He fell forward against the stairs without so much as lifting his hands to protect his face. The point must have pierced his heart. The guard collected the body, dragging it back toward the rest.

"What a waste," Rodric said as he freed himself from the tentative hold of the gem's magic. He looked at the Feared and Deidre with distaste.

The crowd didn't seem to know what to think. They were restless and unsure. Deidre was meant to be the celebration of the magicless citizens. The story of hope that kept them happy and complacent until the next Selection—the story that anyone could be Blessed.

Instead, she lay at the foot of the dais, cold and forgotten by the king.

"We have one more surprise. You've been so patient." Rodric spoke to the crowd. "One who has distinguished herself with service to the crown. She has stepped into a critical position to keep our celebration on track. Emberline Arkova, Jeweler to the Blessed, and the final Selected."

39

She may be his curse, but she will have his heart.

— FROM CHAMPIONS OF KAVIOS

I failed to steady my hands as I stepped into place on the dais. My gaze roamed the crowd, taking a moment to linger on the line of guards. There was a tension in Hart's shoulders that made me want to speed things up. He looked like a taut bowstring prepared to let an arrow fly. An anger radiated from him that reminded me of that first meeting with the Feared at the Selection Festival.

Then, he'd brought the brawl to a standstill with only his glare. I didn't think he'd be able to accomplish the same here. If he interrupted, Alaric's life would be forfeit. I took another step, pulling the final ring from my bag and sliding it onto my finger.

Hart's helmet still masked the green of his irises. I was confident they'd attempt to persuade me not to do this, to let him save me instead. But I couldn't, not with Alaric's life on the line.

A low growl emanated from his general direction. No one else seemed to notice. Where he previously stood erect, arms behind his back, like any of the other guards at the ceremony, now his hand twitched, and his foot slid forward. Every part of him seemed at war with himself, determining what to do.

I needed to see this through. He'd have more time to think of a plan the longer I hesitated.

Of course Macen was the remaining rebel. I'd known in the pit of my stomach he would be. This wouldn't just be murder. It would be the murder of someone I knew—even if they had recently tried to kill me themselves.

"Just so that we don't have any further surprises." Vaddon's voice was low, likely only for me to hear. He must have slipped out while the other Selected took. He returned now with Alaric in tow, meeting me at the foot of the dais.

Alaric looked like death. The beatings must have continued wherever they held him. His face was covered in bruises. They'd given him a clean tunic and trousers, but even from here, I could see the stains on them—like he had wounds beneath the fabric that weren't adequately bandaged.

I wanted to run to him but held my ground. This was how I would help him. I might have questioned that when his look froze me in place. Disappointment creased his brow, and devastation turned his lips. I knew he wouldn't be happy with my choice to accept Rodric's Blessing, but this was worse.

It was one thing to convince myself Alaric needed this. It was another to watch his heart break while I did the unspeakable.

"Ember, don't—"

Alaric fell forward before he finished, as if Vaddon had elbowed him in the back while they walked.

Catching himself on his hands and knees, his gaze met mine. "Don't do this."

My face must have held a resolve I wasn't sure I had. It sent Alaric on a frantic search of the room like a mouse realizing he was trapped with snakes. I didn't know what or who he sought.

None of the Blessed would help him.

"Nah-ah-ah." Vaddon roughly lifted Alaric and pushed him forward. "We're here to watch, not to speak. We just wanted Emberline to remember the cost of her actions."

"Bring Alaric here," the king said. "Proceed, Emberline. We don't have all day."

I was out of time. They wanted me to drain Macen. I didn't think I could do it. Even as I lifted my foot to step toward him, my body shook in revulsion. I wasn't sure that Macen deserved to live—but I knew I wasn't meant to kill him.

They would kill Alaric if I didn't.

Alaric, the man who'd taught me everything I knew.

Alaric, who wanted me to trust my gut more. I shook my head. My gut—my heart—knew this was wrong.

I couldn't just leave him to die, though. A shaky step forward took me closer to Macen.

"You don't have to do this—"

Vaddon elbowed Alaric again, cutting off his words. This time, when Alaric stood, he smiled. I didn't know what could make him do that. Following his gaze, my eyes locked on a familiar ring. A ring Hart had used to tap against the glass of Alaric's workshop. The duplicate of the commission for R. Lourd. The ring Soren wore last night when he attacked. The one Hart had pocketed. Did it hold any magic, or did he only use it to signal to Alaric that he was there?

Alaric's grin broadened. He'd been looking for Hart.

How he thought Hart would get us all out of this mess, I wasn't sure. Even with magic, Hart couldn't get us all out of the throne room unscathed.

I took another step toward Macen.

Macen held both hands up in an attempt to halt my forward progress. "Emberline, your uncle is right. You don't want to do this."

I didn't, but I didn't have a choice. What was that line from *Champions of Kavios*? *He had no good choices, only the best, worst ones.* I found myself identifying with the Cursed King as I took another step down the dais.

Alaric would forgive me for this. Of course he would.

Will you forgive yourself? My conscience gnawed at the back of my mind. It didn't matter. Alaric would be alive, and that was what mattered.

I tilted my head from side to side, weighing the thought, as I took another step.

My plan had seemed so simple when I'd walked into the ceremony.

Become what I hate, in name only. Save Alaric.

Figure everything out after.

The plan fell apart when King Rodric announced the taking, and any remaining scraps blew away in the wind. I had refused to see it, but I needed a new plan—something that got us all out of here alive.

I was at the bottom of the dais now. Macen's hands were still outstretched in a plea not to proceed. My jeweled hand reached for his. I knew I didn't have to take from him to make this work. I just wasn't sure how long the ruse would last. Hopefully long enough for me to get to Alaric.

"Ember—don't!" Alaric threw himself forward as I took Macen's hand.

My gaze bored into Macen's, urging him, begging him to go along with this. The ring glowed red as I let my fury rise. I didn't have to reach deep for the anger. It was brimming at the surface at the position I'd been put in. At the inevitability of it all.

Macen's brow furrowed, his eyes focused on the red glow. His fear was as apparent as his confusion. I tilted my head slightly, my back to the king, Vaddon, and Alaric. I let my eyes drift closed as Macen stared into them. I hoped against hope he could figure out what I wanted of him.

His eyelids started to flutter, and my heart skipped a beat.

This might work.

He swayed back and forth as the red flash on my ring continued to draw the eyes of the crowd.

"Ember—" Alaric yelled again. "Stop! Before it's too late."

I couldn't stop.

Finally, I chanced a glance toward Hart. It was unbearable to look at him, given what I knew he felt about the situation—but I hoped he understood my actions for what they were. His helmet was still in place, but the way his hand flexed, his head twisted slightly to the side—I knew he waited for the moment he was needed.

Not yet.

Macen fell to the ground, his body collapsing atop the other Feared at the foot of the dais. The crowd cheered.

Exhaustion plagued me. I'd put so much of my anger into the ring. I hoped they wouldn't look too closely at Macen.

"Very good," the king said behind me. "Now, Selected, to me."

The grin spreading across his face said this couldn't be

good. He'd already given us the Blessed stones, what more did he need us for?

"You have each proven your dedication to this city. Now, I need you to prove it to me. I will take from each of you, making you part of us, part of those keeping Order in Kavios."

He raised his hands and gestured for us to join him at the throne. I was going to be ill. This was everything I feared. Every part of my life had been designed to prevent this. What good was the ploy with Macen if everything fell apart at this step.

The task now made sense. Each of the newly Blessed were irrevocably altered by what they'd done. King Rodric expected to take sadness from each of us.

He wouldn't be able to take from me.

The thing I'd avoided since childhood. The event Mother gave her life to prevent. I was now walking into it with open arms, and not with just any Blessed. Not with someone who cared for me, who would kill to protect me, like Hart, but someone who sought only to control.

What would King Rodric do when he realized I was immune?

He'll kill you.

Thankfully, the other Selected were all too eager. My panic went unnoticed by most. Of course, I felt Hart's gaze on me. But what could he do?

Wil got to King Rodric first and took a knee. Rodric didn't even wait for the rest of us to arrive. He reached for Wil like an addict reaching for his next hit. The blue flashes shot forth from the adamas around his neck before I blinked.

The king needed sadness. How much of the sadness Elias collected at the Presentation had been for himself versus his father? I wasn't sure it mattered. Everything I'd done would be for nothing if I didn't act soon.

Rodric took from the others. My steps slowed to ensure I

was last in line. Then he reached for me, and I was out of time. The dagger at my hip was heavy against me. I could reach for it. I could stab the king. Would that accomplish anything? It would buy me precious seconds.

"Sebastien! You promised!" Alaric yelled.

I turned from the king—to where Alaric's shout was directed. Hart's hand flexed a final time. The ring he wore glowed purple, and then the nightmares unleashed.

40

He has the potential to be a good man. I almost wish I could tell him more. He promised to protect her, no questions asked. Whether he keeps the promise if he learns all I kept from him is another story.

— ALARIC SARE'S LETTERS TO ISABELLE ARKOVA

I wasn't sure I was breathing. Something heavy plummeted in my chest, descending rapidly, sinking deeply into a place with no room for this information. This couldn't be right. Hart strode toward me, and steel screeched in my ears as he drew his sword. His face was still covered, but I knew him. The shape of him, the way he moved —they were permanently painted in my mind. I couldn't convince myself it was someone else, but if it was him, it meant ...

Without hesitation, he climbed the dais, purple glowing brightly from the familiar ring he wore.

Everything fell into place.

The way the Feared in the alley deferred to him.

His conversations with Soren.

How he knew so much about the firstborn's curse.

The fact that I'd never seen him wear adamas to wield.

The purple glowing on the first adamas we worked together. It matched the purple of the stolen ring he wore now. He may use it, but I *knew* he didn't need it.

The entire room fell to their nightmares.

Sebastien—that's what Alaric had called him. That was the name of Rodric's firstborn from the history books.

Hart was the Cursed King.

Unlike the night of the festival, he no longer *pretended* to be affected by the magic. I felt so stupid that I hadn't recognized his act for what it was.

Shrieks filled the room. Even Alaric, who had called to Hart, lay crumpled on the ground, screaming from the tortures of his own mind.

"Hart." The word broke free of my lips.

He pulled off his helmet. His gaze lifted to mine before he finished scaling the steps.

"You're him."

With all I knew about the Cursed King, the words I'd read a hundred times, I couldn't believe I hadn't put it together.

Maybe I hadn't wanted to.

If this was true, Hart wasn't Blessed—he was cursed. He wore adamas now but didn't need it to summon this magic. He only needed to find Chaos's ...

Hart hadn't finished the story in the woods. My stomach

churned. I didn't need him to finish it now. He'd said Chaos wanted his fate to match what he'd brought upon others, but with a twist only she could appreciate. He'd been so impatient. In his desire to avoid his fate, he'd created the Blessed. When that hadn't worked, he decided to face Chaos herself rather than wait for her champion. The poetry of the missing end to the sentence was too perfect to ignore.

His curse was to take. And he could only take from Chaos's ... Champion.

He could only take *from me.*

I swallowed, my lips pressing into a thin line as I held his stare.

He had grabbed my wrist in the crowd the night of the festival, before he unleashed nightmares. I had even touched him in the adamas room, grabbing his hand before asking him to wield strength.

I flushed. He had all of me only last night. And I'd experienced every emotion. Happy to have found the safety to feel freely. Scared of what came next. I'd felt it all. He must be bursting at the seams with magic.

A hollow laugh escaped my throat.

A thunderous clap erupted before I could string a sentence together, and a woman stood beside Vaddon. A curtain of long blond hair fell to her waist, and she wore a white gown much like my own. I couldn't look at her directly. A glow emanated from her body and seemed to assert what my mind already suspected: She was the Goddess Themis.

She shook her head in disappointment while the rest of the room's occupants still screamed from the fear that took over their minds. "That was a little unfair, don't you think?"

Her touch pulled Alaric from his nightmare. His gaze refocused on the room as Themis held him by the throat.

She glared at Hart with steely gray eyes. "You're not

supposed to wield the powers I gave you to save her champion. I knew you were rebelling, dear, but this is a little much."

The words sank below my skin. My current thoughts were working to keep up with what I already knew. Hart was the Cursed King—Themis's Champion—and she was here to watch him claim his prize?

That didn't make sense.

"Themis?" Hart dropped his helmet to the floor as he stared at the goddess.

"You've been avoiding me, but surely you recognize your goddess after all these years?"

Hart looked unsure, as if he hadn't expected this. In this particular situation, it was a wholly unsatisfying expression to see.

"Get her out of here, Seb!" Alaric yelled.

Hart pulled his gaze back to me. The purple glow faltered. The room's other occupants regained consciousness. They were slow to sit up, slow to move. The guards didn't seem to understand what was going on. Hart still appeared to be one of them.

"I tried over and over to help you." The goddess kicked Vaddon. "He was so willing to help kill her. Unfortunately, his methods proved insufficient."

I swallowed. Themis wanted to kill me? She used Vaddon to do so, instead of Hart?

"I didn't want your help. I didn't want any of this," Hart said through gritted teeth.

"So you've said." She clapped her hands together. "Let's finish this."

King Rodric woke from his nightmare as Hart lost control of the power. He glared at his son. "You should have never come back."

Rodric looked disappointed as he pointed at Hart. "Seize the Cursed King!"

"Sebastien?" Elias asked the name like a question as he, too, awoke. "What are you doing here?"

Hart rolled his eyes. "Nice to see you too, brother."

Elias's gaze darted to me. "I knew it was her."

I didn't like the look that crossed his face as he made whatever connections he thought he understood.

This had gone so far past sideways. Hart was the Cursed King. I couldn't begin to process that. How did I get Alaric and myself out of this battle between goddesses and kings? That was what I needed to focus on.

The guards had risen from their stupor. They struggled to connect King Rodric's words with the man before them—the man in guard's uniform, whom they knew to be one of them. A few at the bottom of the dais glanced between Hart and Rodric. They moved slowly, as if waiting for reassurance.

"He's the Cursed King, you fools! Seize him before he accesses more of his power!"

Something about that should have worried me, but the guards began to move at the king's words. They flooded the dais. Hart regripped his sword and pushed me behind him as he prepared to fight us free.

Shadows filled the room, swelling to the same all-encompassing darkness I'd seen when I made my choice. When light finally parted the inky black that could only be magic, a woman stood next to Themis.

Her gown was black silk, slinking elegantly against her skin. Her hair was the color of a bonfire blazing in an autumn sunset. With lips painted the color of blood, the smile that crossed her face was anything but welcoming.

"Sister, dear, I don't think you're playing fair either." Her words were directed at Themis.

"It's over, Eris."

The woman's otherworldly beauty was apparent. I knew her for what she was the moment she graced the stage—Eris, Goddess of Chaos. Her power thrummed through the room, freezing the occupants outside the dais in place.

She tilted her head slowly from side to side. "I don't think so, and you interfering like this isn't very sporting. Didn't we agree to let the champions decide?"

"You cursing my champion wasn't very sporting!" Themis said.

Eris giggled. The sound was so at odds with the power that radiated from her; I wanted to laugh, but not more than I wanted to remain unseen in this room. Hart repositioned himself between me and the goddesses, deeming the frozen soldiers a lesser threat.

I wasn't sure what to think of the action. He was the Cursed King. His use of magic proved he'd taken all he needed from me last night.

Tears pricked my eyelids as I held them shut, wishing this mess away. He hadn't trusted me with this, even though I'd trusted him with everything. I didn't know what to do. Anger bubbled beneath my skin at the thought.

Hart couldn't be worse for this city than Rodric. How easy would it be for him to claim the throne in Order's name?

But he didn't.

The sharp smile that curved Eris's lips was even more confusing than her giggle. "He's lucky he isn't dead."

"I summoned him. He was mine. You aren't allowed to kill him," Themis shouted, lifting Alaric's feet from the ground as she shook him by the neck.

"Unlike you, Sister"—Eris's gaze drifted to Vaddon at Themis's feet as a reminder of the claims Themis had made upon arrival—"I didn't skirt the spirit of our rules. Your champion challenged me. I had every right to kill him."

Themis glared at Hart like she was seeing him for the first time. "You didn't."

I needed to get myself and Alaric out of here. Any hopes I had of keeping him safe by submitting to the royals was gone. But I had no idea how to get Alaric away from the angry goddess.

"That's the problem with summoning your champions instead of letting them choose, dear. Especially such a proud one like him." Eris's glance at Hart was almost leering.

That raw, gurgling anger twisted in my gut, even as I told myself he wasn't mine.

As if she knew my thoughts, Eris winked at me. "Oh, but he is, Champion."

Was she talking to me?

"Why didn't you just kill him?" Themis hissed. "I could have summoned another."

I wondered the same thing. A man summoned by one goddess, cursed by another—but a man determined to write his own destiny. It would have been easier to start fresh.

Then I remembered the end of the firstborn's story. I thought of what Hart had told me in the hallway of my parents' building—the guilt he carried for his mother. I realized the cost of his choice. He had confronted a goddess. His life was forfeit, but it wasn't his life that had paid the debt.

For the first time, Eris looked a little sad. "His mother paid it for him."

"So, his summons still stands," Themis said.

Eris pointed to me. "The summons didn't stand a chance once he met her."

Hart's gaze was finally drawn to mine as the goddess

pointed. He looked resigned to his fate. Something the hero of *Champions of Kavios* should never be.

"What did you do?" Themis asked.

"I didn't do anything. He did." Eris twirled, the silk of her dress flowing with the movement of her body as she all but danced at the chaos unfolding around her. "My curse made him find her, should he wish to use his magic."

"You didn't even need your magic to take the throne," Themis raged at Hart.

Eris ignored her sister's outburst. "He fell for her all on his own."

This time, I definitely wasn't breathing.

Hart's gaze held mine. His lack of denial, his unwillingness to even look at Themis while Eris made these revelations, was too much.

Themis erupted. Alaric's shout was in my ears, and then something snapped. His body was flung across the room, cracking against the opposite wall.

I screamed and lunged for Alaric. Hart grabbed my arm and held me in place. I scratched, I clawed, I kicked with everything I had in me as I tried to reach Alaric's unmoving body.

Eris's smile faded. Oblivious to my struggle, she turned to her sister. "That wasn't very nice."

"I don't care." Themis held her sister's gaze. "Your champion needs the curse too. There is Order in an even playing field."

Her words didn't register. Alaric wasn't Blessed. No mortal could survive the snap and crash I'd just heard. I screamed again, and with tooth and nail, I fought to get free of Hart. His hold was unrelenting. He was impervious to my pain and my attempts to break free.

Eris gave me a hard stare as I fought Hart's hold to get to Alaric. Her gaze flicked to him behind me, holding me in place.

"Done," Eris said.

With a final wink at me, Eris disappeared.

Themis folded her arms across her chest. "I won't wait forever."

Then, giving Hart a hard stare, she disappeared like her sister.

Hart stooped to lift me. He must have found a slip of skin because the flame of our connection raged through my body. I recognized the heat for what it was. It must be him *taking*.

He threw me over his shoulder, his arm wrapping over my legs at the front of his chest. "We have to go, Chaos."

I wiggled around him enough to see the ring turn purple again—the room fell again to nightmares. With me thrown over his shoulder like a sack of potatoes, he carried me down the aisle. His hand encircled my ankle. The sizzle of our connection didn't drain me, though, like when I'd saved him.

It made me feel alive.

"What are you doing?" I scratched and clawed at the parts of his uniform I could reach.

"What I have to."

My fists banged on Hart's back. "I don't want to go. Leave me here with Alaric."

His steps didn't slow. "He wouldn't want that, and you know it."

I squirmed and kicked, but Hart's grip was like an iron vice.

"Let. Me. Go." I banged my fist on his back again, but with his hand on my skin, whatever emotion I was feeling, he felt it too.

He could feel my anger, my fear, and my growing sorrow as he dragged me from Alaric's unmoving body.

"I can't do that, Chaos."

The power flowed between us, and his command of it was

clear. It was useless. He whisked me away, leaving the king's Blessed to languish in their nightmares.

41

His heart will change the tide of Kavios.

— FROM CHAMPIONS OF KAVIOS

Hart carried me from the throne room. When I next looked up from the work of clawing free from him, we were on the path headed east around the back of the castle—the one I'd used to escape to Forest's Edge.

"Put. Me. Down!" I pounded against his back again. I had no idea if he was still using magic. There was an awareness of the place where his hand gripped my ankle, but I blocked out all else associated with it. It reminded me too much of when we'd touched for other reasons.

He dropped me.

I clambered to my feet, readying to run back to Alaric.

"He's gone."

I froze. A new pain struck my heart, icy and direct, like a dagger piercing flesh. It was like reliving the scene, the crack of Alaric's head against the wall. Every part of me was taut like a bow. I needed a direction to aim toward. Then I thought of Alaric calling Sebastien's name.

"Alaric knew who you were? What you were?"

Hart nodded.

Another piece clicked into place about Hart and Alaric's relationship. "The thing he was helping you research, supposedly helping you find. It was Chaos's Champion." I clenched my teeth briefly in frustration. "It was me."

He didn't deny it. "We need to keep moving."

I tried to bury my feelings. I'd been practicing this for years, but I found with this—with Hart—it wasn't so easy anymore.

"You expect me to go with you? You're the Cursed King. You lied to me—"

"I left information out."

It might have been worse, but at the moment, my anger was pushing down the pain of Alaric's loss. I needed it.

"Only because you didn't know what to do with me yet. That's your curse, right? The one you never finished explaining. Your curse is that you can only take from me."

I'd already convinced myself this was true. The way he touched me as we left the throne room was proof enough. For some goddess-forsaken reason, I just needed him to say it.

Those piercing green eyes held my glare. "I don't have time to explain. We have to go."

He would have known as soon as he'd touched me what I was. That was back on the night of the festival when he tried to stop me from following Macen.

"I'll go on my own."

He sighed. "You can." The fight fled from him, and his broad shoulders fell like he'd been carrying the weight of this city for too long. "But if you want to free the captive while they're still distracted, you'll need me. Themis made sure of it."

"What does that mean?" Themis's words echoed in my head. *She needs the curse. There is Order in an even playing field.*

"Your curse matches mine. If you want to use your magic, your emotions will no longer do. You'll need mine."

Fucking goddesses.

Something churned in my stomach. I didn't know where to look, what to do, how to think.

Alaric was gone.

He'd known what Hart was. Why hadn't he told me? Why hadn't Alaric told me anything?

Now, I'd never know. I couldn't think of that.

Hart had used me—shamelessly. My cheeks heated at the thought. I didn't care if he followed. He was right, but I needed to get out of here. I'd do what Alaric wanted to, what had gotten him captured in the first place. What we'd failed to do last night. I'd free the captive.

Tears sprang to my eyes. It was a moot point now. Rodric had lost his leverage over me. He no longer had a jeweler. I wouldn't risk it though. Alaric had thought it was important enough to risk. The captive needed to be freed.

I shook my head and started walking. "Do what you want."

He followed, and for whatever reason, I still didn't fear him at my back. When I was first deciding whether to trust him, I knew he'd had too many opportunities to kill me and hadn't taken them. That was still true. He was honest when he said he didn't want me dead.

"What do you want, Hart?" I paused. "Or should I say Sebastien?"

"Hart was my mother's surname before she married. Sebastien Hart—the name I gave you wasn't a lie."

"It wasn't the truth either." I wiped away the past eight

days of not even knowing his real name. It was low on the list of information he'd hidden.

Hart briefly slipped into the tavern before we left through the Eastern Gate. No one stopped us. I had a feeling his nightmare magic had strayed farther than the throne room. The guards seemed too busy putting themselves back together to care about our business.

I tried to swallow my sadness with each step, but tears stung the back of my eyes. Every time I tried to close them, even just for a second, I heard the crack and saw the flail of Alaric's body as Themis tossed it like a ragdoll across the throne room.

It was a long hike to the foothills.

As we neared The Storm, Hart took the lead, guiding us around the settlement's edges. The climb steepened, and my thighs burned as we pushed toward our goal.

The hardest part of the hike was knowing we'd be on a steep decline as soon as we entered the mines. I was not looking forward to that or the return trip.

A thick copse of trees covered the overgrown entrance. Hart gave me a sidelong look, and I thought maybe he was waiting for me to change my mind. I wouldn't.

Everything had changed, but this remained. Alaric wanted the captive free. With Alaric gone, I had no reason to submit to the Glanmores. I'd take their adamas supply and run.

Pushing through the leaves and branches, we finally entered the mines. My thighs shook as I learned the descent was steeper than the main entrance and just as slippery.

The mines were closed today, the one day of the year that the workers were given off. Instead, they would gather on Cross Street in a few hours to celebrate the newly Selected.

We made our way to the door to the adamas chamber. Two guards remained at attention there. I was sure the royal family had increased the protections on the room after Alaric's attempted liberation.

Hart's blade was in his hand, and the guards were dispatched in moments. The only sounds were their bodies hitting the ground as Hart dropped them. I exited the tunnel we'd descended, waiting for Hart to break the lock.

"You have to open this," he said, pointing to the chamber door.

"Can't you? You've taken more than enough."

He shook his head.

He had to be lying, but I could see an unwavering resolution in his gaze. His answers after using his power in the mine cave-in made so much more sense. He said he'd take without consent to keep me safe—to protect the source of his power.

We'd spent a night in each other's arms. I was sure he had plenty stored. But he'd also held my ankle as we'd left the throne room. That feeling, when he took my fear to unleash nightmares, was different from our other connections.

I shook my head. There was no time to deal with this.

I couldn't believe where we'd ended up—hated that I could read it all on his face. Maybe I had been free to choose my place as Eris's Champion, but it seemed those around me were doing all they could to manipulate that choice. Hart, Mother, Alaric—even thinking his name was like a dagger twisting in my chest.

Hart held his hand out to me. "You can do it ..."

I was sure he was about to tack on the nickname "Chaos" but stopped himself.

"Take some of my anger. I have plenty to share. Use it to open the door."

What did he have to be upset about? He'd used me. All of this was his fault.

My blood boiled even as my heart twisted. This was a mess.

I took his hand and let his anger flood me. I didn't calm my own either, even if it made no difference. I was angry at him, at Alaric, at Mother, at the goddesses, and most of all, at myself.

I ripped the door from its hinges with a strength that shouldn't have existed. I tossed it to the side and glared at Hart.

He raised his hands in surrender even though his gaze was reverent, something I noted was lacking with his goddesses in the throne room. I shook my head and stepped into the adamas cavern.

"Be careful," Hart started, trying to angle before me as we entered.

After what he'd made me do, I gave him the glare that comment deserved. I couldn't ignore the pulse of magic alive within me.

"*Champion*," the voice called.

It was still in my head like it had been in the Oldwood. I couldn't tell if Hart could also hear it. The words were soft in my head, but something rumbled loudly in the cavern.

"He'll be weak," Hart whispered. "He's pure Chaos, and he's been caged by Order for too long."

"*Chaos curse him again. I'm not too weak to burn him alive.*"

I paused at that, even though the threat wasn't directed at me. Something shifted in the darkness, and hot air blew toward my face. Hart raised the torch from outside the cavern entrance. I stepped back as I glimpsed my first sight of the captive.

As long as I lived, I'd never forget the wonder and devastation of the sight.

I hadn't been far off when I'd likened the thing I'd touched to a snake. The light spilling from Hart's torch showed scales black as night. The captive's tail curved around the length of the cavern, and as we entered, Hart looked up. I followed his gaze to see the captive's wings spreading out and filling my vision.

A dragon. The captive was a dragon.

"Charon," Hart said as if soothing a wild beast. "We're here to free you."

"*Champion. Your uncle was here.*"

The dragon's words to me were soft, or as soft as I deemed the creature capable of as he bared his teeth at Hart.

I nodded stupidly, unsure how to respond to the dragon's words in my head. Hart raised his hands in a gesture of peace. I should have been better prepared for this, the heat and magic birthed from the captive.

"Your fire—it makes the adamas?" I asked, unable to help myself.

Hart glared at me, hands still raised in peace at the dragon's obvious displeasure. A claw swiped toward Hart, and he lunged away. "Not the time."

"*Yes, Champion, it's my fire. I try not to expend it since I've been held prisoner, but I've been here a long time.*"

An earthshattering roar was loosed in Hart's direction.

More dots connected in my mind. "Hart—Sebastien—he's why you're here." I was suddenly surprised the dragon hadn't eaten Hart already.

"It'd be best to put your hand on him," Hart said, ignoring my revelation.

"*Don't rush her,*" Charon growled. "*And yes. The Cursed is the reason I'm here, though Alaric tells me he's not wholly unredeemable, hence his ability to still draw breath.*"

He glared at Hart, and that time, I knew he spoke to Hart as well.

"You look like shit, Charon. Whatever Alaric tried didn't work."

I glared at Hart. He knew this was where Alaric was headed.

"Why did he need to do anything? What's wrong?" I asked.

"He needs Chaos's magic," Hart said.

The dragon—Charon, Hart had called him—growled again, flashing teeth at Hart. "*If there is anything you want to say to me you'd rather not say before the Cursed, just think it.*"

It was another reminder that everyone had known who Hart was but me. Charon must be able to control when he spoke only to me versus when he spoke to both of us.

"*Think of what you want me to know, and I'll hear it,*" he said.

I didn't need to hide things from Hart. He already knew everything, and if Alaric had been here, trying to save Charon, he deserved to know.

My head hung as I spoke the words. "Alaric is gone."

Charon's head hung with mine, even as he flashed his teeth at Hart.

"*Where do we stand with the Cursed?*"

Hart snorted, so I assumed that went to both of us.

I felt Hart's gaze on me, though I couldn't bring myself to meet it. "I don't know."

To cut off the conversation, I let quick steps take me across the cavern. Charon lowered his snout as I moved. It wasn't the pull of moth to flame, like what I experienced with Hart. But something drew me closer, a string taut between us. It was the same feeling I had when I entered the Oldwood before I submitted to its call.

"It's your magic, not the Oldwood's," I said.

The rigid scales of his snout were within reach. It dipped in assent to my question. His nostrils flared at my approach, his lip curling, exposing teeth the length of my arm.

I pulled my glove from my hand and pressed it against him before fear overtook me.

"You've been calling to me for years."

It was more of a statement, not a question. Charon seemed to understand. I thought of Mother's replies when I spoke of my friend in the forest. It was just another way everyone in my life had kept things from me.

Under the guise of giving me a choice.

Heat consumed me when I made contact with Charon.

It was the heat of the adamas stone, the heat I'd dug for in the cold, hard ground of the Oldwood. It connected us even as it burned through us. I fell to my knees as emotion rushed through me. His, mine, I couldn't tell one from the other. I gave him everything I had—everything I'd taken from Hart when we'd opened the door.

A scene from this cavern filled my vision. Alaric here, with Charon. A vial, very similar but much larger than what he prepared for Mother.

"*He tested the youngleaf on you?*" I asked through the connection.

"*He tested a great many things.*" Charon's words were silenced as the image of Alaric being hauled away by guards sketched out between us.

Tears filled my eyes as the image moved to the one playing in my mind on repeat, even as I worked to suppress it: Alaric's body crashing against the wall, Themis's arms outstretched ...

"*What are we doing about it, Champion?*" Charon's voice was gravelly and filled with disgust at the sight of Themis.

"Ember, we need to get Charon out of here. We won't have another chance."

Shock must have shown in my wide eyes as I looked at Hart and then back at the entrance.

"He will fit. But he'll need you to heal him afterward."

I shook my head again, trying to clear my thoughts. I

couldn't focus on multiple conversations. "Where will we take him? He's not exactly inconspicuous."

"He won't be so out of place in Linia."

I turned to stare at Hart. "What?"

"There are other dragons in Linia. We just have to get him away from Kavios. You'll need to use me to heal him as he comes through," Hart said.

My heart constricted in my chest for Charon. He'd been trapped here for, what? Hundreds of years? And the first thing I did would cause him pain.

A completely different kind of panic set in as I realized the emotion I'd need from Hart to heal him: lust.

Hart's usually taunting green eyes were dull as he watched the realization dawn on me. "He needs this."

I shivered inadvertently, thinking about our night together —about the inconceivable pleasure of his touch. I hated myself as lust pooled low in my stomach. I wasn't sure if it was worse to take lust from Hart or use my own.

"Why don't you do it? Use what you already have from me."

He shook his head. "He needs the magic to come from you."

It was all so stupid. The magic might flow from my hand, but due to Themis's curse, it would be Hart's emotions that fueled it.

"*You will need to explain your relationship with the Cursed at some point. I don't know if you want to fuck him or kill him.*"

"*I'll let you know when I figure it out,*" I thought back.

Charon snorted.

Hart still moved carefully around Charon but after his declaration seemed relatively confident he wouldn't be attacked. He followed me into position on the other side of the door.

"*We will be talking about this later.*"

I had known him for mere minutes, and already, I rolled my eyes at him.

Charon huffed and then started moving.

I could hear his scales scraping against the tunnel edges. My shoulders tightened like I shared his pain. He didn't cry out, though his large teeth clenched, a muscle ticking in what had to be his jaw. I tried not to look at Hart as I took his hand. With my other, I reached for Charon as he stepped into the too-small opening.

Hart's gaze said too much I refused to think about. The flare of our touch was incandescent. Charon's wings pressed against the tunnel walls, and rocks fell around him as he worked to widen the parts he wouldn't fit through.

"Almost there," Hart said.

Something rumbled in the cave, and I realized it was Charon. He must be fitting through the tightest spot. I pushed more of the healing magic into him, hoping that every scrape and tear of his wings as they clenched to his sides would be immediately healed.

"Thank you, Champion."

Finally, he pushed through. His wings spread as we made it through the tunnel and into the open path, although even the path we'd descended would be difficult for him to scale. It was not wide enough to fit the breadth of his legs.

"I'll manage."

His magic shook the earth, leaving no question where the earthshakes had originated. It shook until the fork that took us to the hidden passage collapsed. I dropped Hart's hand but let mine rest on Charon's scales as we climbed. The warmth I'd come to associate with the adamas was a comfort as it flowed between us until I'd emptied everything Hart had given.

I hadn't even had a chance to get used to how I accessed my magic before it changed. Only yesterday I could have used my own emotions to heal Charon as we walked. Now, thanks to the goddess's game and Themis's idea of balance, I was wholly dependent on Hart's emotions for magic. I could only take from him.

I didn't want to think of it, but I couldn't help comparing the connection with Charon to the one that flared when Hart and I touched.

When Hart touched me, there was heat, yes, but it was consuming, not comforting. And it was different with Hart when we'd left the throne room, different than what I'd felt last night.

Hart didn't spare me a glance as we hiked up to the entrance. My mind returned to the words of *Champions of Kavios*—another line that seemed so straightforward: *Her Champion will take until the point of breaking.* As I considered it now, I wondered if Mother meant it for him or me.

42

Tell Ember I love her. I don't think I told her enough.

— ALARIC SARE'S LETTERS TO ISABELLE ARKOVA

Charon's wings snapped open as we reached the surface. I knew I should have tried to take more from Hart to continue to heal him as we climbed, but I couldn't summon the energy to ask. I wondered what else Alaric had tried to sustain Charon—another item on the list of things kept from me.

My heart clenched just thinking of Alaric. He couldn't be gone. There was too much left to say—too much left to unravel.

Instead of telling me who waited in the mines, he'd tried to solve the problem himself. A problem that inherently only I—with Chaos's magic—could solve.

So much would have been simpler if Alaric had told me what he knew. Like Mother, I guessed he'd been trying to preserve my choice. It felt like no matter his intentions, he'd done the opposite.

"We have to keep moving." Hart pushed through the trees guarding the mine's entrance.

He turned to face me, and I knew I wouldn't like what he would say.

"I'll help heal him once more, then you two should go."

Anger flooded me, and I was too tired to hide it. "What?" I balled my hands into fists at my side. "Where are you going?"

He shrugged. "Does it matter?"

This was what I'd planned myself as I'd stormed through the Oldwood, but for some reason, I hated hearing him say it.

"I can't leave my parents," I said.

Finally, some rational thought was returning. They would be targets for the Glanmores. New leverage to control me now that Alaric was gone.

"Ava is getting them to The Storm. They'll be fine with Alysa."

My shoulders sagged. That must have been his stop at Forest's Edge before we left. Even as my anger pulsed, I didn't want to slot this kindness into place. I didn't want to examine why he would do something like that. Maybe he just wanted control over where they were.

He didn't control The Storm, though. That much was clear. I shook my head.

I probably should let him leave. Whatever was between us was broken. He'd kept so much from me. While some day I might understand the secrets Alaric and Mother kept, I couldn't understand it from him. We were supposed to be partners. I swallowed thickly, even as I thought it.

We were supposed to be more.

A consuming heat flared inside me as I considered us parting ways. Something else shifted uncomfortably within me, demanding his touch.

"*You can't, Cursed,*" Charon said. "*I don't know what happened, but she's like you now—she'll weaken if you're separated.*"

Hart glared at Charon. I closed my eyes and let my head tip back, wondering why the goddess hated me so much. "What do you mean, like him—"

"We don't know if that's true. It might not be the same; Themis didn't know all the impacts of Chaos's curse," Hart said.

I didn't need to look at him to know he was lying. Words from the first time I saw Hart fell into place. His one moment of vulnerability with Alaric. *You know what this means to me. I'm running out of time.* That's what he'd said to Uncle.

Anger roared again at more information withheld. "There was more to the curse than being unable to use your magic without me?"

He rubbed his forehead, exhausted. "Chaos ensured I'd have to find you. Not just for magic. She was clever enough to know that might not be a motivating factor for me."

I wanted to scream. There was a lot he wasn't saying again, but it was clear from what both he and Charon had said that he'd be in physical pain at separation. I rubbed at my chest, at the unfamiliar ache the thought of him leaving brought. Maybe I would be, too, now that my curse mirrored his.

"I still have no idea what you want, Hart—Sebastien—whatever, but I know the goddesses didn't give up on their game for Kavios."

"*You* don't have to do anything," he said.

I heard what he wasn't saying again. "But you will. Themis said she won't wait forever. I'm surprised she waited this long. Why don't you just take the throne and be done with it?"

Charon growled. "*The only reason he's still standing is because Alaric insisted the Cursed has tried to change what he started.*"

I considered that. What had Hart said? The firstborn found the source of the adamas. He must have done so as he expanded the mine's production.

"You tried to stop it, didn't you? That's what you glossed over after talking about the creation of the Blessed."

He raised an eyebrow at me. The first sign of life I'd seen in his expression in hours.

"You hated the adamas. I've seen the way you glare at those who wield it. You found Charon and were summoned. You were stupid, impulsive, and shortsighted in your methods to escape your fate. But then you left. Your Father must have concocted the plan of Order, the Selection, and Blessing all on his own."

Charon growled again, and I knew I was on the right track.

"It's a nice story, Chaos. What does it matter? You're free to leave. You have nothing binding you to the Glanmores."

Oh, how I wished that was true. It disregarded the fact that Sebastien Hart was, in fact, a Glanmore, and I found myself inextricably connected to him.

"What did you say to me that first night at Forest's Edge? *Surely, you don't have to experience a wrongdoing to know the behavior is wrong.* I can't pretend what's happening in Kavios doesn't exist when I have the power to stop it." I held his gaze. It was no longer just my power. I cleared my throat. "When *we* have the power to stop it."

My body thrummed at the rightness of the sentence as much as I hated myself for having to say it aloud.

"You don't mean that," he said.

"His curse was that he needed her. What he'd do when he found her was far from certain." It was a line from *Champions of Kavios*. I now realized that even in a book of prophecy, this line was evidence that the future was unknown.

And now that I knew who it was about, I knew we had the power to shape it.

Hart's gaze met mine.

My fingers stretched at my side, desperate to reach for him, to cross the growing chasm between us. Then I considered all that entailed, the lies, the truths he kept from me, and I crossed my arms over my chest. "Just come with us. Chaos got us here, and Chaos will finish this. We can go our separate ways after that."

Still, he hesitated.

"*Cursed*," Charon growled.

I hated that that was what it took. Hart's shoulders sagged as he finally responded. "Fine."

Tears stung behind my eyes, and my cheeks heated in embarrassment. His response was like a knife to the chest. Not only was I unsure if I wanted him here, but he also didn't want to be here. Thanks to the goddesses, we didn't have much of a choice. I swallowed the hurt, the shame, the rage, and a million other emotions I wouldn't dare name. "To Linia?"

Hart conceded. "Charon will be free to do what he will there. And we can see if the queen knows anything about this curse." He gestured between us.

I hadn't even thought of that. The Library of Linia was known for its texts on magic. I'd wanted to journey there originally because it might have had information on my immunity to the Blessed. Knowing what I did now, I was sure it would have records, at least, of Linia's Champions.

We'd return, though. This was just for Charon. This was just to regroup. I wouldn't leave Kavios to Rodric.

"If you two are finished ... I will take us. Get on."

I tilted my head back to look at him. He set his body lower, so his stomach touched the ground. Even with that help, I'd have to climb on his ... elbow to get to his back.

"Are you ... sure?" I asked.

His hiss was anything but reassuring. "*Champion. Get on. Now.*"

I wanted to laugh but couldn't even force the sound out. "Fine."

Hart crawled up behind me. We were both positioned at the base of Charon's neck. I felt the distance between us as Hart ensured no part of us touched. I knew we'd need to change that eventually. Charon still needed to heal, and I'd have to take from Hart to do it. But it could wait.

A somber thought crossed my mind. Everything had changed from the intent of my original quest, but it felt ... full circle that it was now our destination.

Charon's wings snapped open.

"We'll return," I mumbled to myself as Charon's powerful wings flapped and lifted us. There was nothing but uncertainty in our plan, but it was all I could muster at present. I was cursed, and I'd have to come to terms with that—have to come to terms with what it meant for me and for Kavios.

I glanced behind me at Hart—the Cursed King. My gaze narrowed even as I swallowed thickly. I wished again for emotions that were easier to repress. Too many uncomfortable feelings fought for dominance within me. I shook my head. We'd have to determine what our connected curses meant in freeing Kavios from the Blessed.

The story continues in Trials of the Cursed.

Dying for a little more? Hart has a lot to answer for. Grab Hart's Bonus Epilogue for a little taste.

If you enjoyed Jeweler to the Blessed, please consider leaving a review on your preferred platform(s).

ABOUT THE AUTHOR

Jillian Witt reads more romantic fantasy than is strictly necessary and writes books she would love to read. Her stories unleash powerful women into fantasy worlds, usually turn enemies into lovers, and always offer an escape from reality.

When not reading or writing, she's enjoying all four seasons in Michigan with her partner and their dog, Loki.

instagram.com/author.jillianwitt
tiktok.com/@author.jillianwitt

ALSO BY JILLIAN WITT

For a full list of Jillian's books, please go to www.jillianwitt.com/books, or use the QR code below:

www.ingramcontent.com/pod-product-compliance
Lightning Source LLC
Chambersburg PA
CBHW020911310726
48980CB00011B/839/J

* 9 7 9 8 9 9 2 3 3 6 1 5 3 *